Doug

The world is an unfair place. Blow up just one multi-billion-dollar research facility, and suddenly nobody wants to be your friend.

Except me, and I'm dead. You, on the other hand, are going to have a really amazingly good life, thanks to the bottle. Enjoy it, that's the main thing. At times it may get scary, dangerous, harrowing, agonisingly painful, even life-threatening. It may quite possibly kill you, who knows? But whatever happens, always remember. It's supposed to be fun.

BY TOM HOLT

Expecting Someone Taller
Who's Afraid of Beowulf?
Flying Dutch
Ye Gods!
Overtime
Here Comes the Sun
Grailblazers
Faust Among Equals
Odds and Gods
Djinn Rummy
My Hero
Paint Your Dragon
Open Sesame
Wish You Were Here
Only Human
Snow White and the Seven Samurai
Valhalla
Nothing But Blue Skies
Falling Sideways
Little People
The Portable Door
In Your Dreams
Earth, Air, Fire and Custard
You Don't Have to be Evil to Work Here, But It Helps
Someone Like Me
Barking
The Better Mousetrap
May Contain Traces of Magic
Blonde Bombshell
Life, Liberty and the Pursuit of Sausages
Doughnut
When It's A Jar
The Outsorcerer's Apprentice

Dead Funny: Omnibus 1
Mightier Than the Sword: Omnibus 2
The Divine Comedies: Omnibus 3
For Two Nights Only: Omnibus 4
Tall Stories: Omnibus 5
Saints and Sinners: Omnibus 6
Fishy Wishes: Omnibus 7

The Walled Orchard
Alexander at the World's End
Olympiad
A Song for Nero
Meadowland

I, Margaret

Lucia Triumphant
Lucia in Wartime

Doughnut

Tom Holt

orbit

www.orbitbooks.net

ORBIT

First published in Great Britain in 2012 by Orbit
Reprinted 2013 (three times), 2014 (twice)

A CIP catalogue record for this book
is available from the British Library.

ISBN 978-1-84149-780-8

Typeset in Plantin by M Rules
Printed and bound in Great Britain by
Clays Ltd, St Ives plc

Papers used by Orbit are from well-managed forests
and other responsible sources.

FSC
www.fsc.org
MIX
Paper from
responsible sources
FSC® C104740

Orbit
An imprint of
Little, Brown Book Group
100 Victoria Embankment
London EC4Y 0DY

An Hachette UK Company
www.hachette.co.uk

www.orbitbooks.net

To the nice young lady behind the counter at NatWest, Chard, whose name I didn't catch, but she says she reads my books, the following is gratefully and respectfully dedicated.

PART ONE

In The Beginning Was The Misprint

"One mistake," Theo said sadly, "one silly little mistake, and now look at me."

The Human Resources manager stared at him with fascination. "Not that little," she said breathlessly. "You blew up—"

"A mountain, yes." He shrugged. "And the Very Very Large Hadron Collider, and very nearly Switzerland. Like I said, one mistake. I moved the decimal point one place left instead of one place right. Could've happened to anyone."

The Human Resources manager wasn't so sure about that, but she didn't want to spoil the flow. She brushed the hair out of her eyes and smiled encouragingly. "Go on," she said.

"Well," Theo replied, leaning back a little in his chair, "that was just the beginning. After that, things really started to get ugly."

"Um."

"First," Theo said, "my wife left me. You can't blame her, of course. People nudging each other and looking at her wherever she went, there goes the woman whose husband blew up the VVLHC, that sort of thing—"

"Excuse me," the Human Resources manager interrupted. "This would be your third wife?"

"Fourth. Oh, sorry, forgot. Pauline dumped me for her

personal fitness trainer while I was still at CalTech. It was Amanda who left me after the explosion."

"Ah, right. Go on."

"Anyway," Theo said, "there I was, alone, no job, no chance of anyone ever wanting to hire me ever again, but at least I still had the twenty million dollars my father left me. I mean, money isn't everything—"

"Um."

"But at least I knew I wasn't going to starve, not so long as I had Dad's money. And it was invested really safely."

"Yes?"

"In Schliemann Brothers," Theo said mournfully, "the world's biggest private equity fund. No way it could ever go bust, they said." He smiled. "Ah well."

"You lost—"

"The lot, yes. Of course, the blow was cushioned slightly by the fact that Amanda would've had most of it, when the divorce went through. But instead, all she got was the house, the ranch, the ski resort and the Caribbean island. She was mad as hell about that," Theo added with a faint grin, "but what can you do?"

The Human Resources manager was twisting a strand of her hair round her finger. "And?"

"Anyhow," Theo went on, "it's been pretty much downhill all the way since then. After I lost the house, I stayed with friends for a while, only it turned out they weren't friends after all, not after all the money had gone. Actually, to be fair, it wasn't just that, it was the blowing-up-the-VVLHC thing. You see, most of my friends were physicists working on the project, so they were all suddenly out of work too, and they tried not to blame me, but it's quite hard not blaming someone when it actually is their fault." He grinned sadly, then shrugged. "So I moved into this sort of hostel place, where they're supposed to help you get back on your feet."

The pressure of the coiled hair around her finger was stopping her blood from flowing. She let go. "Yes? And?"

"I got asked to leave," Theo said sadly. "Apparently, technically I counted as an arsonist, and the rules said no arsonists, because of the insurance. They told me, if I'd killed a bunch of people in the explosion it'd have been OK, because their project mission statement specifically includes murderers. But, since nobody got hurt in the blast, I had to go. So I've been sort of camping out in the subway, places like that. Which is why," he added, sitting up straight and looking her in the eye, "I really need this job. I mean, it'll help me put my life back together, get me on my feet again. Well? How about it?"

The Human Resources manager looked away. "If it was up to me—"

"Oh, come on." Theo gave her his best dying spaniel look. "You can't say I haven't got qualifications. Two doctorates in quantum physics—"

"Not relevant qualifications," the Human Resources manager said. "Not relevant to the field of flipping burgers. I'm sorry." She did look genuinely sad, he had to give her that. "You're overqualified. With a résumé like that, you're bound to get a better offer almost immediately, so where's the point in us hiring you?"

"Oh, come on," Theo said again. "After what I've done? Nobody's going to want me. I'm unemployable."

"Yes." She smiled sympathetically. "You are. Also, you're a bit old—"

"I'm thirty-one."

"Most of our entry-level staff are considerably younger than that," she said. "I'm not sure we could find a uniform to fit you." He could see she was struggling with something, and it wasn't his inside-leg measurement. He betted he could guess what it would be. "And there's the hand."

Won his bet. He gave her a cold stare. "You do know it's

against the law to discriminate on grounds of physical disability."

"Yes, but—" She gave him a helpless look. "Frankly, I think the company would be prepared to take a stand on this one. We've got our customers to think about, and—"

He nodded slowly. He could see her point. Last thing you want when you're buying your burger, fries and shake is to see them floating towards you through the air. It was an attitude he'd learned to live with, ever since the accident had left his right arm invisible up to the elbow. He wished now he'd lied about it, but the man at the outreach centre had told him to be absolutely honest. "Fine," he said. "Well, thanks for listening, anyhow."

"I really am sorry."

"Of course you are."

"And anyway," she added brightly, "a guy like you, with all those degrees and doctorates. You wouldn't be happy flipping burgers in a fast-food joint."

"Wouldn't I?" He gave her a gentle smile. "It'd have been nice to find out. Goodbye."

Outside, the sun was shining; a trifle brighter than it would otherwise have done, thanks to him, but he preferred not to dwell on that. He had enough guilt to lug around without contemplating the effect his mishap had had on the ozone layer. Cheer up, he ordered himself; one more interview to go to, and who knows? This time –

"Worked in a slaughterhouse before, have you?" the man asked.

"Um, no."

"Doesn't matter. What you got to do is," he said, pointing down the dark corridor, "wheel that trolley full of guts from that hatch there to that skip there, empty the guts into the skip, go back, fill another trolley, wheel it to the skip, empty it, go back and fill it again. And so on. Reckon you can do that?"

"I think so."

The man nodded. "Most of 'em stick it out three weeks," he said. "You, I'm guessing, maybe two. Still, if you want the job—"

"Oh yes," Theo said. "Please."

The man shrugged. "Suit yourself. Couldn't do it myself, and I've been in the slaughtering forty years, but—" He paused and frowned. "What's the matter with your arm?"

Theo sensed that the man probably didn't need to hear about the quantum slipstream effect of the implosion of the VVLHC. "Lost it. Bitten off by a shark."

"Too bad. Won't that make it awkward, loading the guts?"

"Oh, I'll have a stab at it, see how I get on."

"That's the spirit," the man said absently. "OK, you start tomorrow."

In the beginning was the Word.

Not, perhaps, the most auspicious start for a cosmos; because once you have a Word, sooner or later you find you've also got an annoying Paperclip, and little wriggly red lines like tapeworms under all the proper nouns, and then everything freezes solid and dies. This last stage is known to geologists as the Ice Age, and one can't help thinking that it could've been avoided if only the multiverse had been thoroughly debugged before it was released.

But things change; that's how it works. You can see Time as a coral reef of seconds and minutes, growing into a chalk island sitting on top of an infinite coal seam studded with diamonds the size of oil tankers; and each second is a cell dividing, two, three or a million roads-not-travelled-by every time your heart beats and the silicone pulses; and every division is a new start, the beginning of another version of the story – versions in which the Red Sea didn't part or Lee Harvey Oswald missed or Hamlet stayed in Wittenberg and got a job.

So; in the beginning was the Word, but ten nanoseconds later there was a twelve-volume dictionary, and ten nanoseconds after that a Library of Congress, with 90 per cent of the books in foreign languages. It's probably not possible after such a lapse of time to find out what the original Word was. Given the consequences, however, it could well have been oops.

The first week wasn't so bad. Well, it was; but at least he found the work so shatteringly exhausting that all he could do at the end of his shift was stagger home, stuff a pie or a sandwich in his face (for some reason, since he'd been working at the slaughterhouse he seemed to have lost his appetite), roll into bed and sleep like a corpse until it was time to get up and go to work. This suited him fine.

By the second week, however, he found he was coping with the exertion of gut-hauling rather better, which meant that he had enough stamina to allow him to sit staring aimlessly at the walls of his room for an hour before falling asleep. By the end of the fourth week, he could manage three hours of aimless staring with no bother at all. This wasn't good. Staring at the walls proved to be a primitive form of meditation, in the course of which he analysed his life so far, and ended up reaching the conclusion that it hadn't been going so well lately. Alone, all the money gone, living in a ghastly little shoebox and spending all day loading still-warm intestines into a galvanised box on wheels; it wasn't, he couldn't help thinking, the sort of life he'd quite reasonably anticipated five years before, when he was appointed as the youngest ever Kawaguchiya Integrated Circuits professor of multiphasic quantum dynamics at the University of Leiden.

Still, he told himself, it could be worse; at least he had a job, and somewhere to live.

The week after that, he was consoling himself that at least he had a job; furthermore, he had kind, understanding employers who didn't mind him turning up to work looking like he'd slept in a cardboard box in the supermarket car park. This was just as well, since the landlord of the horrible little room had thrown him out for smelling overpoweringly of entrails. The cardboard box had been a lucky find. It was big. If he curled up in it like a hibernating dormouse, he could close the flaps and imagine they were the roof of a tiny, tiny little house. Generally speaking it was peaceful in the car park after 2 a.m., when the last of the local kids had gone home. Count your blessings, he told himself, it could be worse.

But then it rained, reducing his beautiful cosy box to brown porridge, and Theo started to feel despondent. His boss, a man with a heart of gold and absolutely no sense of smell, took pity on him and let him sleep beside the guts skip, but only short-term, until he could get himself fixed up with a proper home. He couldn't, he pointed out as kindly as he could, have employees sleeping rough on the premises indefinitely. It lowered the tone.

Still, Theo told himself, as he wandered the streets one night, waiting for it to be time to go to sleep, think of all the money I'm saving not paying rent. He sat down in a shop doorway and fished out the crumpled brown envelope in which he kept his money. He counted it. Not quite enough for the man he'd once been to buy half a pair of his customary brand of socks, but, to someone lulled to sleep each night by the placid drip-drip-drip of stale blood from the hole in the guts skip floor, a tidy sum. You could buy all manner of things with that much money. Some of them in bottles.

There was a late-night off-licence just down the road. He

stood up, folded the notes round his right hand and stuffed it in his overall pocket. Booze had never been one of his problems; but, given his present circumstances, he could see no reason why he shouldn't go for the complete set. In the distance, the liquor-store window glowed a sort of golden amber, like a lighthouse guiding him home.

Inside the store it was bright and warm. A tired-looking woman stared at him, and her expression changed just a little bit. Just a little bit can mean so much – the length of a nose, the gap between lower lip and chin. Scientific studies of the human face have established that the difference between heart-stopping loveliness and look-the-other-way ugly can sometimes be as little as a quarter of an inch. On this occasion, just a little bit was plenty.

"Small bottle of lemonade, please," Theo said. "The cheapest you've got."

Later, with his back snuggled against the sharp edge of the skip and his invisible hand loosely holding a half-empty bottle of something that tasted like neat citric acid but wasn't, he reflected on rope theory. It was a hypothesis of his own: a bit like string theory, except that it was more robust and slightly less prone to tangling itself into knots. In particular, he contemplated the notion that reality is made up of an infinite number of universes, all occupying the same place and time. In which case, somewhere nearby (so close he ought to be able to reach out and touch it) was a universe in which he'd moved that pesky decimal point right instead of left. In that universe, where would he be, right now? Switzerland, probably; in his palatial, air-freshened, carpeted office, working hard on Phase 9 before going home to his comfortable house and his loving wife. He lifted the bottle and stared through it; first through the glass, then through the clear liquid that wasn't neat acid. The distorting effect of the bottle and the opacity of its contents blurred his focus just nicely. He tapped the bottle with the fingernails of his visible left hand, and admired the gentle, clipped ting. It looked nice and snug inside there, he decided, probably a great place to live, almost certainly better than where he was living now. He could climb inside, pull the cork in after himself, and be peaceful for a while. He'd like that. Then, maybe, after he'd been – what did wine do? – maturing in the bottle for a thousand years or so, perhaps he'd mutate or evolve into something rather better; a genie, obviously, a powerful, magical entity trapped in a bottle but capable of being released, to do good deeds and grant wishes. Maybe. Or maybe he could turn into a message, bobbing through an endless sea, bearing an awful warning.

He glanced at the label, which told him nothing he could understand.

Drowning your sorrows won't help, said a voice in his head. It sounded a bit like his mother, a woman who'd lied to him about the existence of Santa Claus and was therefore not to be trusted on matters of any importance. Rope theory. End-of-rope theory. At the very end of your rope, you can either hang on or let go, but in most cases it makes very little difference in the long run. Besides, he wasn't drowning his sorrows, he was dissolving them in acid. There's a difference.

Here endeth the lesson. He drank a bit more, altering the optical qualities of the bottle, whose value as an instrument of scientific observation he was beginning to question. People reckoned the world looked better seen through the bottom of a bottle, but it didn't. Just a bit rounder, and sort of an orange colour.

If only the heartburn wasn't fuzzing his powers of concentration, maybe he could combine string theory and rope theory to make macramé theory; whereby it should be possible to take all those flailing strings and weave them into what you wanted them to be – a lifeline, perhaps, that'd be nice, or a halter, or a noose. Or even – how about this for a really neat idea – one of those South American rope bridges that sway alarmingly above a mind-numbing abyss, seconds before some clown with a machete cuts through the rope, as always happens in the movies, and the whole lot goes twisting and crashing back down into the –

Um. Not the sort of image you want in your mind when you've just drunk two-thirds of a bottle of saturated solution of saccharine on top of an end-of-date meat pie. He sat up, which made the world stop swirling. Excellent. Cause for a celebration. He celebrated with three gulping mouthfuls, dropped the bottle, closed his eyes and flopped against the side of the skip.

The bottle didn't break when it hit the ground. Instead, it rolled a little way, bumped against the toe of Theo's boot, and stopped. Theo was well away by then, asleep and dreaming the one where he was being chased by giant cucumbers across the shuttle bay of the Enterprise. Accordingly, he wasn't watching the bottle as the last inch or so of acid drained out of it, revealing a small object.

To identify the object he'd have had to lean forwards and peer closely through the glass. This would've had a bad effect, probably culminating in the return of the meat pie, so it's just as well he didn't. But if he had, he'd have seen inside the bottle a tiny model of a ship, barely an inch long but perfect in every detail, right down to its gossamer rigging. The ship floated on the outgoing tide until its draught was too great for the meniscus to support it; then it flopped sideways, touched the glass wall and vanished as though it had never been.

The guts next morning were mostly sheep: grey, tubular and pungent. He tried not to look at them, with the result that he missed the trolley with a heaped armful and dumped them on his feet instead. Stooping to pick them up was no fun whatsoever. Something broke loose inside his stomach as he bent over, and he could feel his intestines being eaten from the inside out. A year ago, he told himself, just over a year ago, I was running the simulations for the quantum phase feedback inversion trials. Maybe at some point I swallowed the reactor pile, and I'm only just starting to feel the effects.

One year; how time flies. How would it be, he thought, as he slopped the last few yards of sheep gut into the skip, if I took this remarkably fine trolley and pushed it down this well-tiled corridor as fast as it can go; really fast, until it's travelling at the speed of light? Then all I'd have to do is jump in, and – no, no point. I'd go forward in time, not back, and forward in time would probably find me still here, and that'd be too depressing for words. Oh well.

Eleven trolley-loads later, he looked up and saw his boss waddling towards him down the corridor, his nose buried in the filthiest handkerchief he'd ever seen in his life. The smell, presumably. Odd. Theo hadn't noticed the smell for weeks.

"Got something for you," his boss said.

"Me?"

His boss nodded. "Came in this morning's post, addressed to you."

What? A refrigerator? A camel? "A letter?"

The boss nodded. "Here." He took an envelope from his pocket. It was white, apart from a big brown thumbprint. "Who's writing to you, then?"

The address was printed, not handwritten. "No idea. Thanks," he added.

"You going to open it, then?"

Theo nodded. "Later," he said. "In my own time."

His boss shrugged and walked away. Theo waited till he was gone, then looked down at the letter. He didn't get mail any more. For one thing, who knew where to reach him? The writer of this letter, obviously. He frowned at it, then stuffed it into his overall pocket. The only place the letter could possibly have come from was the past, and he wasn't sure he wanted to have anything to do with all that, thanks all the same. The past had been nice to him for thirty-odd years, but they hadn't parted on the best of terms. If the letter was from his wife's lawyers, he wasn't in the mood.

His iron resolution lasted three minutes. Then he perched on the edge of the guts trolley, wiped his hands on his overalls and carefully prised back the flap of the letter, like an engineer defusing his thousandth unexploded bomb.

Dear Mr Bernstein

He glanced up at the letterhead and saw a bunch of names, huddled together like penned-up cattle. Lawyers. But not the bunch of timber wolves retained by his ex-wife. He frowned.

Dear Mr Bernstein

This firm acts for the executors of the late Professor Pieter van Goyen. In his will, Professor van Goyen –

Time inverted, distance collapsed, and just for a moment he was a brilliant, arrogant, twenty-three-year-old research fellow (the youngest ever in the university's history) unpacking his books in his new rooms in Leiden. A faint knock at the door; vexed at the interruption, he calls out, "Come in, it's open"; suddenly there's a man standing in the doorway.

A tiny man; four feet ten, if that, and almost perfectly circular; two perfect circles, head and body, with no perceptible neck, no hair, and huge, perfectly round spectacles that made his face look like a Venn diagram. An immaculate dark blue suit, with the trousers turned up almost to the knee, tiny fingers poking out of the turned-up cuffs like little pink worms.

Carpet slippers. "Hello," said a soft, impossibly deep voice, "you must be Theo Bernstein." Not a request for information, not even a statement; more like an order, to be obeyed without question. Pieter van Goyen.

Professor Pieter van Goyen, the greatest physicist of his age, triple Nobel laureate, the man whose drive and vision transformed the Very Large Hadron Collider into the Very Very Large Hadron Collider; the man whose life work he'd blown up. On the day Theo left Leiden, at 5 a.m., disguised as a nun to avoid the photographers, Pieter had been there to see him off, a magisterial Michelin man in a bespoke camel coat whose unadjusted hems pooled around his feet, silk pyjamas and flip-flops.

"I'm sorry", Theo had mumbled.

A slight shrug. "Stuff happens. What'll you do now?"

Theo couldn't stop his face cracking into a jagged grin. "That," he'd said, "is a very good question."

"Don't worry. I'll fix everything." And, for a fraction of a second, he'd believed it. Except nobody could fix it for the man who'd just turned an entire Alp into a cloud of fine dust, currently grounding all air traffic from Istanbul to Reykjavik. "It may take a little time, but I'll see to it, don't you worry."

Then the taxi had taken him away, and now Pieter was dead. The world's shortest giant was gone for ever, and that – well, the things that had happened to Theo Bernstein since he left Leiden had been annoying, verging on tiresome, but Pieter's death was bad.

He looked down at the letter;

– left you the sum of five thousand US dollars and the contents of his safe deposit box.

Theo never remembered his dreams, even the ones with cucumbers; so, when he woke up on the train to Leiden with a crick in his neck and a mouth that tasted slightly worse then the guts trolley smelt, he was amazed to find that there were scenes and images in his head. It was like finding a stranger in his bath.

The dream, however, was no big deal; in fact, it had been so dull he could remember yawning, stretching, vainly fighting the unbearable heaviness of his eyelids, and waking up. He'd been in the audience at one of those conferences he'd always found an excuse for not going to. Pieter van Goyen was up on the stage, back turned, writing equations on a huge blackboard. The maths didn't work, but Pieter didn't seem aware of it; he carried on chalking and scribbling until he reached the end, whereupon he scrawled $x = 7$ and triple underlined it with a great flourish, and everybody started to applaud. But x didn't = 7; a ten-year-old could've pointed out the flaws in the algebra. Still, the audience were on their feet, a full-blown standing ovation, and Theo realised he was the only one still sitting down. He shifted uncomfortably, and then he was sitting in the same seat in the same auditorium, next to the same thin woman with glasses and the same tall, bald man, and Pieter was up on the stage writing out more equations, but it was a year later. The equations didn't work this time, either; but everybody seemed so engrossed in the proceedings that he didn't dare say anything. Instead, he covered his face with his hand, and that was when his eyelids started to droop, and the clacking of Pieter's chalk blurred into a raindrops-on-roof soothing lullaby, and he'd yawned and stretched, and –

Woken up on the train, feeling as though he'd been lynched twice by an apprentice hangman. His left foot had gone to sleep, and so had his right hand. He blinked and licked his lips, and noticed that the seat next to him, which had been empty for the last four hours, was now occupied. Furthermore, his right hand (the invisible one) had gone numb because it was wedged between the armrest and the thigh of the new occupant, a pretty girl in her early twenties.

Oh, he thought.

It wasn't easy to think with his head full of sleep, but he had a stab at it. Apologising and explaining – no, probably not. Gently easing his hand away could well cause more problems than it solved. He'd almost decided on standing up as quickly and as sharply as he could and walking very fast to the next compartment, until he realised that he couldn't do that, not with a left foot he couldn't feel any sensation in. That just left staying perfectly still and pretending he was still asleep; an unsatisfying plan, but the best he could think of under the circumstances. Unfortunately, before he could close his eyes and do the deep, regular breathing, the girl looked up from her book and smiled at him.

"Hi," she said.

It's like this, he rehearsed. My right arm's invisible, because of an industrial accident, and you got in after I fell asleep, and my right hand – no, not really. "Hi," he sort of gurgled.

"You were fast asleep," she said. "I hope I didn't disturb you."

"What? Oh, no, not at all." He tried to sit up a bit straighter, but his trapped hand tethered him like an anchor. Any moment now, he thought, she'll go back to reading her book, and then maybe I can sort of wriggle my back up the seat a bit and get straight.

She really was very pretty, which didn't help; straight, shoulder-length black hair, deep brown eyes, and she'd been reading Hawking and Mlodinow on string theory. Under different circumstances this wouldn't be a bad place to be. As it was –

"I couldn't help noticing," she said. "Your book."

"What?" He glanced down. In his lap, where it had fallen, was the copy of Greenidge and Chen's Macrodimensional Field Inversion Dynamics which had sent him to sleep in the first place. Properly speaking, in fact, this whole mess was their fault. "Oh, that."

"You're a physicist."

"Was," he said. "Not any more."

"Wait a minute." She was looking at him, and he was sure he could see the usual signs. Very occasionally, people recognised him (his face had been all over the TV for a short time, while they were shoring up what was left of the mountain) and their reaction was always the same. Fascinated horror, embarrassment, curiosity. You're the guy who blew up the VVLHC.

"You're Theo Bernstein," she said.

Here goes. He sighed. "Yes."

"Oh, this is so amazing."

It was as if he was a boxer, and his opponent, having just belted him in the solar plexus, had leaned forward and kissed him on the nose. "Excuse me?"

"I'm such a fan of your work," she said. "Your paper on the supersymmetry of fermions was just so—" She paused and took a deep breath. "It changed my life," she said.

He frowned. "It did?"

"Oh, yes. It was like I'd been blind since birth, and then suddenly, wham!"

Then suddenly, wham. Not how he remembered it. His abiding memory of that particular paper had been sitting in front of his laptop at 3 a.m. with a violent coffee headache, trying to figure out where the glaring inconsistency he'd just noticed had crept in from, and how he was going to get round it in time to meet a horribly close deadline. Now, after all this time, he couldn't remember what he'd actually said.

"Um, I'm glad you liked it," he said. "So, you're a physicist too."

"Well, kind of." She actually blushed. He'd never met a girl who blushed. Red-faced with fury, yes. "I'm just starting as a postgraduate at MIT, working on Reimann manifolds, though I'm hoping one day I could join the SGBHC project." She paused and looked shyly down at her hands. "If I'm good enough," she added. "Which isn't very likely."

It felt like a cue, and he didn't know his lines. "Well," he said, "they took me, so they can't be too picky. Provided you don't blow anything up, you should be just fine."

"That was so awful, wasn't it?" She gave him a look of deep, sincere compassion, which made him feel like he'd just been hit over the head with a million dollars. "I mean, I can't imagine how you must've felt, all those years of brilliant hard work, and then one little bit of bad luck."

Bad luck, he thought. Not really. His only slice of bad luck was being the older child of parents whose eldest son was an idiot. The sort of thing that could happen to anyone, perhaps, but it had happened to him. "Nice of you to say so," he mumbled.

"And I definitely think they were all so horrible to you afterwards," she went on. "I mean, if it hadn't been for you, there wouldn't have been a VVLHC to blow up."

That's a way of looking at it, he thought. A bit like saying the Allies owed their victory in the Second World War to Hitler, because they could never have won the war if he hadn't started it. Time, he decided, to change the subject. "Reimann manifolds," he said. "That's a pretty interesting field."

Her eyes shone. "Oh yes," she said, and spent the next five minutes telling him a lot of stuff he already knew about Reimann manifolds, time he spent vainly trying to figure out a way of getting her to move her leg without actually pushing her out of her seat. At the end of the interval, the numbness in his right hand had been replaced by the most violent attack of pins and needles he'd ever experienced.

"Excuse me," he said, "but you're sitting on my hand."

"Sorry, what?"

"My hand." Oh well, he thought, and gently pulled it free. For a moment or so, the world was a brilliantly coloured firework display, each scintillating hue a variation on the central theme of pain. "It's invisible," he explained. "That's why you didn't see it."

"Invis—" She stared at him. "Oh my God. I'm so sorry."

"That's quite all right." He spread his fingers out on his knee and took a couple of deep breaths. "It was the accident, you see. I was the only person in the building at the time, thank God, and something really, really weird happened, I honestly don't remember anything about it; and when I came round in the hospital, it was gone. Only it wasn't. I tried to tell the doctors it was still there, but they didn't believe me. They just told me about phantom limb syndrome and arranged counselling." He shrugged. "It can be a real nuisance sometimes, but what the hell?"

She was looking at the end of his sleeve. "Couldn't you, like, paint it or something?"

He grinned. "Anything that touches it disappears too," he said. "There's an invisible shirt sleeve covering it right now. When I take the shirt off, it'll reappear."

"Oh wow." Her eyes were wide. "That's just so amazing. What makes it do that, do you think?"

He shrugged. "Like I said, I was a physicist. These days, I'm just a one-armed unemployable. I just try not to think about it."

"But—" She stopped. "I understand," she said. "It must be so painful for you. But still, it's such a waste, I mean, one of the most brilliant minds of the twenty-first century—" She stopped again. "I'm sorry," she said. "I'll shut up now."

He grinned. "Actually, I've been called worse," he said. "But you're wrong. A brilliant mind doesn't make all that extra work for the cartographers."

She laughed, then immediately resumed her serious face. "If I had a talent like yours, nothing on earth would stop me using it. I'd force them to listen to me, no matter what. I mean, you actually discovered the twelfth dimension. That was so cool."

There's only so much of that kind of thing a man can take. "Tell me more about what you're doing," he said. "It sounds really—"

Fortunately he didn't have to supply a suitable adjective. She launched into another long and detailed account, allowing him time to give himself a stern talking-to. No more self-belief, because look what that got you into the last time. And positively no more falling in love. Absolutely not.

"So I was wondering if . . ." She'd sort of ground to a halt, and was looking hopefully at him, like a dog that can see the biscuit in its owner's hand. "I know, it's, like, so presumptuous of me, and if you say no, no way, I'll quite understand, I really, really will. But if you could see your way to just running your eye over these equations, see if you can find where I've gone wrong—"

Ah. Right. Actually, he was so grateful to her for exhibiting properly normal opportunism that he forgave her completely. It made the whole encounter that bit less surreal. "Sure," he said. "Let me see what you've got."

She dived into her bag like a trained seal and emerged with the latest model LoganBerry. "The truth is," she said, "my maths isn't good enough for me to tackle a set of equations like this. I mean, I can ask the question, but I'm, like, not equipped to answer it, which is so frustrating, because I'm sure I'm nearly there, only—"

"Mphm." He glanced at the complex patterns of numbers

and symbols and blinked twice. Hot stuff. Tuning out her voice, he began to trace his way through the maze.

Halfway down the screen, he stopped. I know this place, he thought.

Or at least, once upon a time I came quite close. So, let's see: if x is the interface, the dividing wall between dimensions, and y is the energy required to convert that interface into matter, and z is – He frowned. He could see quite clearly that z in this context was a whole lot more than just the last letter of the alphabet, but what, exactly? Hell, if he didn't know better, he could almost believe that z was –

He realised he'd stopped breathing. "Are you OK?" she said.

"What? Oh, yes, fine."

"Only you went this funny colour."

"I'm fine. Really."

If z was what he thought it was, and if he followed it through and actually found z, which was more than likely, given the direction the numbers were flowing.

He lifted his head a little and looked at the screen. I know what this is, he thought.

It's a bomb.

"Excuse me," he said, "but what's it for?"

She frowned, just a little. "What?"

"The purpose of the exercise. What you're trying to achieve."

She smiled. It was the sort of smile you might come up with if you'd heard smiles described but never actually seen one. "It's, like, pure research," she said. "It's not actually for anything."

"Ah," he said. "That's a comfort. Because you do realise, if you were actually to solve these equations, you'd be able to punch a hole clean through the fabric of—"

With a hideous, ear-splitting screech she lifted both arms

into the air, as though grabbing hold of something (but there was nothing there.) In that split second, her face seemed to change. Her eyes turned yellow and sank back into her skull, her nose melted like cheese, some sort of fangs or tusks splayed out of the side of her mouth. Then it was as though a small but intensely concentrated tornado formed around her, twisting her head and body into a thin spiral, like a screw-thread. "So long, loser," she screamed, and vanished.

He reached the Leiden branch of the Credit Mayonnais an hour before closing time, and was shown into a huge steel box whose sides were lined with small steel boxes. A sour-faced man spent a hundred years checking through the paperwork, and then they performed the holy ceremony of the twin keys. Then he withdrew, leaving Theo alone with a grey stove-enamelled shoebox.

He didn't open it straight away, even though time was running short and they'd be along any minute to throw him out. Instead, he sat in the wobbly plastic chair and looked at it. A tin box. A container, an enclosure of space. A quotation whose origin escaped him floated into his mind and got stuck there, like sweet corn skin in the gaps between the teeth; one little room an everywhere. Well, quite. The box only seemed small because he was six feet one inch tall. If he was a trifle shorter – say one inch from head to toe – he could live in it quite happily, raise a family there, maybe even rent out the bit he didn't use to bring in some extra cash. Thanks to science and technology, the days when human achievement was limited by what a man could lift or pull were long since gone. A race of one-inch-tall life forms would have no difficulty conquering the galaxy if their technology was sufficiently advanced. And a box could hold an entire world.

Thanks, Pieter, he thought, as he reached out and turned the little key. True, he had no idea what he was going to find in there. Knowing Pieter it could be anything, from a kilo bag of uncut diamonds to a small pile of pencil sharpenings; but how many people would give you an entire world? On the small side, maybe, but one thing was for sure. It had to be an improvement on the one he was living in right now.

He opened the box, and found in it –

A small bottle
A brown manila envelope
A pink powder compact
An apple

Ah, he thought. He picked up the bottle and shook it: empty. The label was starting to peel off. There was a picture of a planet and some stars, and several columns of tiny lettering too small to read. He unscrewed the cap and sniffed; it smelt vaguely of spring flowers, stagnant water and horse dung. He put the cap back on and rested the bottle gently on the table.

There was, of course, the envelope; another container, infinite in its possibilities until he opened it. He ripped open the flap and teased out a folded sheet of paper and a smaller white envelope addressed to someone whose name he didn't recognise. The sheet of paper was a letter, starting off Dear Theo. He leaned back in the chair, reached for the apple, sank his teeth into it and started to read.

Dear Theo,

About the only good thing I can think of about being dead is being able to give you something I was too selfish to share with anybody while I was alive. Enjoy it.

You'll have forgotten, but I clearly remember when you were a second-year undergraduate and I was your tutor, and I set you a pretty routine assignment (I forget what it was about). You handed in your answer, and when you got it back I'd crossed out the whole thing in red and written, 'wrong – do it again' at the bottom in capital letters. You did it again, and I gave you full marks. I can still see the sad expression on your face the first time. You apologised.

Well, now I'm dead, so I can tell you the truth. Yes, the answers were all wrong. According to the rules of mathematics everybody uses, your equations didn't work. I remember marking your paper, putting it down, going into the kitchen to make myself a coffee. Then I stopped dead, turned round, went back and sat down again, and I looked at the figures on the paper, and I thought: yes, but—

Damn, I wish, I really wish I'd asked you, back then, what in God's name you were thinking about. Those calculations of yours couldn't work in our universe. But maybe I was missing the point. I went back and read it through from the start; not looking for what I was expecting to see, but actually reading what you'd written.

What the hell. If Columbus, aged twelve, had been set a geography test – the world is (a) flat (b) round – he'd have got zero marks. But the world is round. It was that sort of a moment for me.

I spent the next seven years trying to figure out what mathematics would be like on a round world. The result is in the bottle you've just looked at. Take very good care of that bottle. It's one of only five in existence. Read the label very carefully, and do exactly what it says. You'll have to work out the maths for getting inside by yourself; I don't want to leave instructions lying around where anyone could get hold of them, even in a safe in the Credit Mayonnais. But you shouldn't have any trouble. You always were a bright boy.

The letter you'll find in this envelope is addressed to a very good friend of mine who runs a small hotel on the edge of town. When he's read the letter, he'll give you a job. I expect you need one. The world is an unfair place. Blow up just one multi-billion-dollar research facility, and suddenly nobody wants to be your friend.

Except me, and I'm dead. You, on the other hand, are going to have a really amazingly good life, thanks to the bottle. Enjoy it, that's the main thing. At times it may get scary, dangerous, harrowing, agonisingly painful, even life-threatening. It may quite possibly kill you, who knows? But whatever happens, always remember. It's supposed to be fun.

Cordially,
Your friend & colleague
Pieter van Goyen.

Crazy, he thought. But, on the other hand, consider the source. If Pieter van Goyen were to give you an enormous grin and tell you he'd just found out he was a teapot, your first reaction would be to look round for a tea cosy to keep him from catching a chill. He finished off the apple, looked round for a bin or something to dump the core in, found none and put it in his pocket. A job in a hotel; well, better than the guts trolley, but he couldn't really see what a hotelier would need a quantum mechanic for, even a disgraced one. Maybe his job would be to prove the hotel still existed each morning, before Pieter's friend went to all the trouble of cooking breakfast. No, properly speaking you'd need a philosopher for that, not a physicist.

He caught sight of the clock on the wall; two minutes to closing time. He stuffed the bottle and the powder compact in his pocket and picked up the papers, just as the door opened and the guard came in. He shifted the papers from his right hand to his left just in time.

There was something about the hotel he found off-putting. He couldn't quite put his finger on it. Maybe it was the burnt-out cars blocking access to the gates, or the thick tangle of brambles that made it so hard to fight his way up the drive. Just possibly it was the faded cardboard sign fixed to the front door with peeling yellow Sellotape: NO ROOMS GO AWAY. Or maybe he was still feeling a bit jumpy after his encounter with the vanishing girl on the train, and it was making him ever so slightly paranoid. Yes, he decided, on balance that's probably it.

He glanced down at the envelope in his hand. It was in Pieter's handwriting, so of course it was practically illegible; he could make out the initials A B, and the last name began with an N. The rest of it looked disturbingly like the last desperate squiggles of a vital-signs monitor in a hospital, just before it flatlines. Ah well.

He hadn't been knocking for much more than a quarter of an hour when the door opened, and a pretty girl smiled at him through the narrow crack between door and frame. "Hello," she said.

"Um."

"Sorry?"

He'd rehearsed a little speech, but for some reason he couldn't remember it. "I'm here about a job," he said.

The girl looked desperately sad. She was, he decided, the most beautiful girl he'd ever seen in his life – perfect oval face, shoulder-length wavy chestnut hair, clear blue eyes and all that – but not in the least attractive, as though she'd been assembled by a computer program, with the net result that, when you examined her closely, she wasn't nearly as pretty as she looked. Nietzsche would've christened her the Uberwench. "I'm so sorry," she said. "But I don't think they're looking for anybody right now."

"I've got a letter."

"And you're not afraid to use it?"

"Sorry?"

She shrugged. "That was what we call a joke," she said. "You'll get used to them in time. What sort of a letter?"

Rather than try and explain, he held the letter out, as if it was a lion tamer's chair. She looked down at it but didn't touch it. "A B – sorry, I can't read that. What does it say?"

"No idea."

"Ah. Still, it's a very nice letter. Cute envelope. Very clean."

He took a deep breath. "It's from a friend of mine. As a matter of fact, he's dead."

"I'm so sorry. What did he die of?"

Actually, Theo realised, I don't know the answer to that. "It's a letter to a friend of his."

"Right. That'd be you, yes?"

"No."

"Oh. I thought you said this dead person was your friend."

"No, a different friend. He had two friends. At least two."

"Ah. Mister Congeniality, in other words."

Theo forced himself onwards, like a swimmer battling upstream through a custard tsunami. "My friend," he said, "wrote this letter to his friend."

"Fine. So why've you got it?"

"He gave it to me," Theo said, "to give to his other friend. That's A B thing. You know, on the envelope."

"Ah," she said sweetly, "I see. You're a postman."

Theo sighed. "The letter," he ground on, like the mills of the gods with a ruptured bearing, "is asking Mr A B to give me a job."

The girl looked at him and blinked. "Really?"

"Really."

"Gosh. Well then, you'd better come in."

"Thank you."

She pushed the door wide, then stepped aside to let him pass. He found himself in a wide, airy hall, standing on a deep, soft carpet. The walls were panelled in a light, honey-coloured wood and there was a handsome walnut desk with phones and a VDU on it.

"So," the girl was saying, "this Mr A B's a guest here, then."

"Um, no." Theo noticed the ceiling; moulded plaster, painted white with gilded highlights. "I sort of thought this was his hotel."

"Oh, you mean Mr Negative." The girl gave him a smile you could've grown aubergines under. "Sorry, I should've guessed. Wait there a second, I'll go and find him."

"Mr Negative?"

She nodded. "I know," she said, "it's an odd kind of name, isn't it? Won't be long. Take a seat."

She walked away through a doorway he hadn't noticed before, and he looked round for a chair. There weren't any. A B Negative, he thought, for crying out loud.

Almost at once a hidden door slid sideways in the panelling and a tall, middle-aged man in a smart blue suit stepped forward, smiling and extending his hand. Theo stuck out his own hand to shake, then remembered and lowered it again. With his left hand, he gave the man the letter.

"Ah," the man said. "Poor, dear Pieter, such a great loss to us all. Now then." He ripped the letter open like a wolf savaging a rabbit, and glanced at it. "You need a job."

"Yes."

"No problem. What can you do?"

"Well." Here we go. "I used to be physicist, specialising in particle dynamics, but then I—"

"So you're good with telephones."

"Excuse me?"

"Telephones." The man pointed at the desk. "I could use someone to man the front desk. When we're busy."

Apart from the two of them (and the girl, presumably, wherever she'd got to) there was no sign of another living creature on the premises. "I could do that."

The man was peering at the end of his right sleeve. "The arm thing not a problem?"

"Um."

"Well, we can work round it. Fine. Great. When can you start?"

Theo caught his breath. "Now?"

"Perfect. Just in the nick of time." He folded the letter neatly four times and tucked it in his top pocket, like a handkerchief. "I'm the owner, by the way. It's my hotel," he explained.

"Mr Negative."

The man laughed. "Call me Bill. Fact is," he added, lowering his voice and grinning, "A B Negative isn't my real name."

"You don't say."

"I mean," Call-me-Bill went on, "what sort of a world would it be if we went around calling ourselves by our real names? I'll get Matasuntha to show you to your room."

Calling it a room was accurate but misleading; like describing the *Titanic* as a boat, or Pol Pot as a bit of a scallywag. Theo had been in rooms like it before, but there'd been lots of other people there at the time, in evening dress, dancing. In the exact centre of it there was a bed, and, far away on the wall opposite the door, a small wardrobe and a plain, straight-backed chair. Apart from that, it was empty. "Staff quarters," the girl told him sympathetically. "Still, it keeps the rain off."

"It'll be fine."

She shrugged. "Staff bathroom's in the basement," she said. They'd just climbed twelve flights of stairs. "Breakfast in the kitchen, seven sharp. Well, seven till ten thirty, this isn't Nazi Germany. Laundry—"

"Excuse me," Theo said.

"Yes?"

"Well." He had no idea how to put this. "This hotel."

"Yes?"

"It doesn't seem terribly busy."

She looked at him as if he'd just commented on the arid dryness of the sea. "We do all right," she said.

"Oh, I wasn't suggesting—"

"In fact," she went on, "this is our busiest year since 1947."

"Ah."

"Even as we speak," she went on, "we've got two guests. Mr Nordstrom and Mrs Duchene-Wilamowicz. Both," she added, "at the same time."

"Ah," he said.

"So really," she went on, "you're a bit of a godsend. What happened to your arm, by the way?"

"Accident." She was waiting for further and better particulars. "I blew up a mountain."

"Oh, right. Well, as I was saying, laundry day is Tuesday, just chuck your stuff in the basket outside the housekeeper's room. There's a uniform goes with the job, but we're bound to have your size in stock, I'll bring it up to you later. That's about it, really, unless there's any questions you'd like to ask."

He looked round at the vast, empty room and the beautiful girl called Matasuntha, his co-worker in the huge, ornate hotel with brambles crowding the drive. "No, no questions."

"Splendid." She gave him a big smile. "Ciao for now, then. Bye."

She closed the door behind her. He stood for a moment like the first man on the Moon, then walked all the way across the room to the bed. He closed his eyes and sat down.

No guts, he told himself; no shiny grey coils of intestine to be shovelled into a trolley with his bare hands. It was something to cling on to. But, that said, a man can get used to hauling guts around. Other stuff can be harder to cope with.

The room, he noticed, had no window; the light came from a gigantic crystal chandelier, hovering way above his head, like a distant galaxy. The bed was quite exceptionally comfortable. He lay back, and, as he did so, something dug into his thigh. The bottle.

He wriggled sideways and fished it out of his pocket. It snagged in the lining, as if it didn't want to come out. He looked at it. A bottle. Great.

Read the label very carefully, Pieter's letter had said, and do exactly what it says. He squinted at it, but the lettering was tiny; he'd need a magnifying glass or maybe a microscope. He looked around for somewhere to put the bottle, but there didn't seem to be anywhere, so he reached down and stowed it under the bed. A slight eddy in his stomach reminded him that he was hungry. He hadn't, in fact, eaten anything all day, not since the apple in the bank –

He sat up straight. Odd, he thought.

He reconstructed the sequence of events. He'd arrived at the bank, gone down to the safe deposit box room, opened the box. Inside it, among other things, a crisp, delicious, perfectly fresh apple, which he'd eaten. He was no expert, but how long exactly will an apple stay fresh? It was quite possible that the safe deposit boxes were airtight, which would make a difference, he supposed; but he'd eaten elderly apples in his time, and they tended to get soft and waxy, which this one hadn't been. So; a week, maybe? Two weeks?

It was over a month since Pieter had died. He cast his mind back. The box had been covered with a fine layer of dust, he remembered brushing it off his hands. Strange, he thought. For a start, why would anyone keep a perfectly ordinary apple in his safe deposit box? By the same token, why would the bank have gone to the trouble of putting an apple in there a day or so before Pieter's heir was due to arrive? No, they couldn't have done that; the box needed two keys to open it. Pieter must've put the apple in the box.

Pieter, now he came to think of it, hated apples.

Beyond all question, there was a perfectly simple, logical explanation for all of it. Bound to be. Just because he couldn't think of one right now didn't mean to say there wasn't one, just as the fact you can't see the Moon doesn't mean it's not still there. If he really applied his mind, no doubt he could come up with a unified theory of everything which would account for the apple, Mr A B not-my-real-name Negative, the beautiful Matasuntha, the empty five-star hotel with the wrecked cars out front, and the empty bottle in Pieter's safe deposit box. But figuring out united theories of everything; that was the sort of stuff scientists do, and Theo was through with science. Other people, laymen, mundanes, don't bother with the deep thinking, they just accept stuff and get on with their lives. They don't ask questions. They don't read the small print.

So he went down to the lobby, which was deserted, and looked in the drawers of the beautiful walnut desk. Rather to his surprise, he found what he'd been looking for: a magnifying glass. He looked round to see if anyone was watching, then quickly slipped the glass in his trouser pocket and dashed back up the stairs to his room.

Matasuntha was waiting for him when he got there, with a jacket and trousers over her arm. "Your uniform," she said.

He'd forgotten all about that. "Thanks," he said. "That's great. I'll, um, try them on in a minute."

She nodded. "What's your name?" she asked.

"Theo Bernstein."

"The Theo Bernstein?"

Oh God, he thought. "Yes," he said. "It was me who—"

"Theo Bernstein who used to do the morning weather on KPXE Kansas City? Oh wow."

"Um." He frowned. "No."

"Oh." She pulled a sad face. "Sorry," she said. "I thought you were him." She laughed. "Stupid of me. I mean, if you were someone famous, what'd you be doing working here?" She leaned past him and looked at the bed. "What's that bottle?"

It was lying on the pillow. When he'd left the room, it had been under the bed. "That? Nothing. Just an empty bottle."

She moved forward. "I'll put it in the trash for you on my way down."

"No, really."

"It's no bother."

"I recycle."

A look of deep suspicion settled on her face, like rooks on a cornfield. "That's really public spirited of you."

"Green to the core, me." He moved slightly, so that she'd have to make a serious detour to get past him to the bed. "Do you have any idea what volume of non-biodegradable material gets dumped in landfill every year? It's enough to keep you awake at night."

"Quite." She was trying to peer round his shoulder. "Well, in that case I'll leave you in peace. Bill will let you know when you're due for your first shift."

"Right. Thanks."

"Meanwhile." One last peek, which he blocked with a slight repositioning of his shoulder. "Settle in, make yourself at home. Welcome to the team."

"It's great to be on board. Do we get baseball caps?"

"What?"

"To help foster a shared-goals mentality and a sense of common purpose, going forward?"

"No."

"Shucks. Well, thanks again. Bye."

There hadn't been many occasions in his life, he reflected as he closed the door behind her, when he'd put so much effort into persuading a beautiful girl to leave his hotel room.

Maybe if he had, he wouldn't be in this particular hotel room right now; no way of telling, of course, because the sea-anemone strands of causality wave and sway in the currents of the timestream, and any damn thing could happen. The main thing was, she'd gone, and he was alone with his bottle. He grabbed it and held it up to the light. Still empty. Well.

He sat down on the bed, took out the magnifying glass and peered at the minuscule letters on the label. It turned out to be the same message translated into a bewildering number of languages, including cuneiform, Klingon, Elvish and one whose alphabet was entirely made up of smiley faces, grouped in strange, cloud-like blocks. Eventually he found English, and read –

INSTRUCTIONS:

1 Obtain access to the bottle

2 Follow the instructions

And that was it. He frowned. Read the label very carefully, and do exactly what it says, Pieter's letter had urged him; also, You'll have to work out the maths for getting inside by yourself. He closed his eyes. Obtain access to the bottle, for crying out loud. What was that supposed to mean? Take off the lid?

He did that. Then he put it back on again. Clues, he thought, I need clues; I'm too old, tired and disillusioned to relish challenges. In desperation, he turned the bottle upside down and peered at the bottom through his glass. And saw . . .

$$(x + a)^n = \sum_{k=0}^{n} \binom{n}{k} x^k a^{n-k} f(x) = a_{0 + \frac{\delta y}{\delta x} \sqrt[2]{a}}$$

Well, of course, he told himself. Everybody knows that. But what, he couldn't help wondering, was it doing embossed on the bottom of a bottle, instead of the more usual 33cl please dispose of bottle tidily? And, anyway, strictly speaking, since the bottle was a cylinder topped by a sort of distorted cone, shouldn't that be . . .?

But that wasn't what it said; and Pieter's letter had been quite categorical, do exactly what it says. In which case –

There was the stub of a pencil in his top pocket. Before he realised it, he had the back of the manila envelope on his knee and was jotting down figures. Of course, it simply didn't work if you had 4-theta instead of 2. But just suppose for a moment that it did. After all, that was what Pieter had done all those years ago, when he'd marked the all-ballsed-up assignment. Yeah. Right. What if . . .?

He came to a dead end, and scowled at the gibberish he'd written on the envelope. For a moment there, a brief, fleeting moment, it had seemed as though he was on to something. But now the way ahead was blocked, as if (to take an example entirely at random) some fool had just blown up a mountain, and the whole lot had come tumbling down on to the freeway.

Just a moment, he thought. Not a cylinder topped by a cone; a cylinder topped by a distorted cone. He groped for the bottle, stared at it and lunged for the pencil. There was a slight but definite curve to the neck of the bottle; concave, just a little bit, and why the hell, when it really mattered, could he only remember pi to seventy-four decimal places?

Ten minutes later, he stopped and stared in horror at what he'd just written. He'd seen it before, not so very long ago; on the screen of a latest-model LoganBerry, on a train.

The bomb.

Oh no, he told himself, not again. Blowing up a mountain had been bad enough. He was three, maybe four calculations away from arming an equation whose effects would make his previous boo-boo look like a trivial mishap, like laughing while drinking coffee. If he made the same mistake again, after Fate had gone to the trouble of dropping so many helpful hints (career trashed, wife gone, lost all his money et cetera), they'd be justified in keeping him in after class and making him write out I MUST NOT BLOW UP THE WORLD a hundred times. And yet –

Pieter had said, follow the instructions. If that included what was on the bottom of the bottle, not just the label, then he couldn't see he had much of a choice. He frowned, trying to remember. Now he came to think of it, it had been Pieter who'd got him the job at the VVLHC. Or at least he'd recommended him highly for it, which was more or less the same thing. Could it possibly be that Pieter wanted him to blow things up? Unlikely. Not unless they needed to be blown up, for some obscure but entirely valid reason.

You are going to have a really amazingly good life, thanks to the bottle. It may quite possibly kill you, who knows? Enjoy it. It's supposed to be fun. He scratched his head, entirely unable to decide what to do. He thought about the girl on the train; so far he'd managed to blot that memory out of his mind, but that wasn't possible any more, not now that he had the same bomb resting on his knee, recreated from scratch by himself. Was it possible, he wondered, that Pieter had more than one favourite student? One of only five in existence. That left four of the things unaccounted for. Oh boy.

The pencil was still in his hand. Anyone walking into the room right now would see it hovering in the air, like a wingless dragonfly. I could finish the maths, he told himself, that wouldn't hurt. Just because I arm the bomb doesn't necessarily mean I've got to set it off. And maybe –

Maybe just one small, teeny-tiny controlled explosion, to get into this stupid bottle and find out just exactly what's going on. Besides, he rationalised, the weird girl on the train suggested that he wasn't the only one facing this dilemma; and the impression he'd got from her was that she wasn't bothered at all about the possible risks to the fabric of the multiverse. So; if he didn't do it, then she, or someone like her, would almost certainly get there first, and then where would we all be? Good question.

It's a lot of bother to go to, though, just to get inside a bottle. Ah, but you don't know what's in there. Fair enough. Let's find out.

There was a knock at the door. Moving faster than he'd have thought possible, he pocketed the pencil and the envelope, stuffed the bottle under his pillow and said, "Yes?"

The door opened and Call-me-Bill's head craned round the side of it. "Hi," he said cheerfully. "Settling in all right?"

"Fine, thanks."

"Room OK?"

"Fantastic."

"Splendid." There was a pause, as if he was searching his mind for more small talk to make. "Got the uniform?"

"Right here." Theo pointed to the jacket and trousers lying on the bed. "I was just about to try them on."

"Ah, fine." Another hiatus. "Well, soon as you're ready, why not wander down to the lobby and I'll show you what to do? No rush," he added quickly. "Take your time."

"No, that's fine, now would suit me perfectly." He got the impression that he hadn't given the response Call-me-Bill had wanted to hear. "If that's all right with you."

"Absolutely. Unless you'd rather have a snack or a shower or something."

"No."

"Right."

"I'll just get changed."

"Sorry?"

"The uniform."

"Ah." Call-me-Bill looked a bit like a chess Grand Master who's just lost in six moves to a nine-year-old. "Of course. See you downstairs in, what, ten minutes?"

"Fine."

The bottle, he was pleased to discover, sat quite happily in the pocket of the uniform jacket without bulging visibly. The pink powder compact (he'd forgotten all about that) went in the inside pocket, along with Pieter's letter and the magnifying glass. That was that. He set off down the stairs, thinking hard.

Call-me-Bill had been Pieter's friend; cling on to that thought, because otherwise he was profoundly creepy. There was no doubt at all in Theo's mind that his room would be meticulously searched while he was downstairs – by Matasuntha, presumably, since she was the only other living creature he'd seen in the place, and she'd definitely been interested in the bottle. But Call-me-Bill had seemed reluctant for him to leave the room, implying that he knew the search would take place and didn't want it to happen, but was powerless to prevent it. Crazy. But no problem. They could search all they liked, since there was nothing to find. He thought about the vanishing girl on the train, and the equations on her LoganBerry that were practically identical to the ones he'd come up with working through from the formula on the bottom of the bottle. More bottles like it out there somewhere. But the bottle contained nothing but stale air.

"Here are the telephones," Call-me-Bill said, and he pointed at them helpfully. "If someone calls up, answer them."

"Right." Theo nodded. "Um, what shall I say?"

A slight pause. "Sorry, but we're fully booked till further notice. And after that, we'll be closed for redecoration."

"Got that." Theo tried not to ask the next question, but failed. "Is that right, though? Matasuntha said we only had two guests."

Call-me-Bill shuddered slightly. "That's right."

"And we're fully booked."

"Oh yes."

And then he was alone again, sitting in a very comfortable chair in the deserted lobby. He moved the phones so that they were exactly square to the corners of the desk. He opened the drawers and found two pencils and a pencil sharpener. He sharpened the pencils. He also found a state-of-the-art Kawaguchiya Integrated Circuits XZP6000 calculator, the kind they'd wished they'd been able to afford for standard issue at the VVLHC, a protractor, an ivory slide rule, two rusty iron keys and a set of log tables. He put them all back where he'd found them and tried playing with the computer, which turned out to consist of a monitor and a CPU but no keyboard. Easy mistake to make, he told himself; maybe they'd got it cheap for that reason.

The envelope, with his unfinished calculations on the back, felt alive inside his jacket, as if he'd got a bird beating its wings in his inside pocket. Absolutely nothing else to do.

Theo was one of those people for whom prolonged inactivity is the worst thing that can possibly happen, with the possible exception of the Earth colliding with a very large asteroid. He knew his limitations. He could stick ten minutes of doing nothing, if he absolutely had to. After twelve minutes, he started scratching his chin or rubbing the palm of his hand with his thumb. Thirteen minutes, and the most luxuriously comfortable chair ever made felt like a medieval torture chamber. Fourteen minutes, and he'd be twitching all over, shuffling his feet, squirming in his chair. Fifteen minutes; unless there was something productive he could do, like count the number of bricks in a wall, he was ready to kill someone.

He held out for twenty minutes. Then he pulled out the envelope, took one of the newly sharpened pencils, and got to work.

He didn't need the slide rule, the log tables or the calculator. The numbers and symbols just seemed to move gracefully to their allotted places, like actors at a dress rehearsal. When the calculation had arrived at its inevitable conclusion, he leaned back in the chair, as though he was trying to put as much distance as he could between himself and the envelope, and stared at it. Here we go, he thought.

Had Pieter, at some point before his death, found himself staring at the same neat, slender line of characters? Presumably he had; the letter implied that he'd known what the bottle did, and had made it do it. The thought made him feel very slightly better. There's a difference, albeit only one contour line on the gradient of the moral high ground, between being the inventor of a weapon of mass destruction and the man in the warehouse who uncrates the fiftieth completed bomb. Also, consider this: Pieter had done the maths and found the answer, used it to get inside the bottle, and the universe was still here, still reasonably intact and not-blown-up. Therefore, if he were to duplicate what Pieter had done, there couldn't be any harm in it. Could there?

It's supposed to be fun.

Slowly, he put the envelope back in his pocket. It occurred to him as he did so that he'd just made a discovery of a Newton–Einstein–Hawking level of magnitude, and if he was back in the university, if he hadn't accidentally pulverised an Alp and with it any chance he'd had of being taken seriously ever again, he'd be minutes away from being worshipped as a god. Instead, here he was with two phones and a keyboardless computer for company, and nobody to share the glory with but himself.

He frowned. No, he thought, not me. Pieter had got there first – and Pieter hadn't blown up any mountains, so there'd have been nothing to stop him publishing his results and clearing a space on his mantelpiece for seventy kilos' weight of awards. But he hadn't, and it occurred to Theo to wonder why the hell not. Because –

Quite, he thought. There are some things you don't share, in the same way that a policeman doesn't drop by the holding cells and ask if anybody fancies having a go with his gun. It may quite possibly kill you, who knows? Enjoy it. It's supposed to be fun. Was that what Pieter had done? Invented the ultimate Doomsday equation and somehow reverse-engineered it into a game? And, while we're asking awkward questions, what exactly had Pieter died of?

"You there." Theo looked up and saw a man standing over him, scowling. "Clerk."

That was the sort of thing you'd expect this man to say; along with we meet again, Mr Bond, or guards, seize him, or I like a girl with spirit or, quite possibly, I smell the blood of an Englishman. Given time and a huge dose of steroids, Arnold Schwarzenegger might've grown into his hand-me-down trousers, and he had a thin black moustache, like a fine line of eyebrow pencil drawn on his upper lip with a steady hand, and a perfectly bald head. He was wearing a light grey suit and one of those bootlace ties you occasionally see on senators from Texas.

"Um," Theo said.

"My key."

It made no sense; until, quite suddenly, Theo remembered that this was a hotel. In which case, Grendel's big brother here was a guest. Which made him –

"Mr Nordstrom."

The monster grunted. "Key," he repeated. "Now."

"I'm sorry, I don't know—" Then he remembered the two rusty iron keys he'd found in the desk drawer. He yanked it open and chose one at random. "There you are, Mr Nordstrom," he said, with a degree of composure he found quite remarkable in the circumstances. "Is there anything else I can do for you?"

Mr Nordstrom nodded. "Get me a bottle of Château d'Yquem 1932. Now."

"Certainly, Mr Nordstrom," Theo said politely, and ran.

Through the door that led to the stairs; instead of up, towards his room, he went down. The down staircase was improbably long, straight and pitch dark; he could feel it getting steadily colder as he descended, and when he put his hand out to steady himself against the wall, the surface he touched was damp and rather sticky. He could smell mould, saltpetre and something else he couldn't quite identify. Eventually, though, the stairs ended in a door, which he discovered by walking into it. He turned the handle, took a step forward and groped until he found a light switch.

He'd found the wine cellar, no doubt about it. He also understood at once why there had been so many stairs. It was like being in an underground cathedral. The ceiling, supported by a forest of fluted marble pillars topped with Corinthian capitals, was so high he hurt his neck looking for it. He didn't want to guess how big the room was. If you were into model railways, you could probably have fitted in a 1:1 scale replica of the Gare du Nord, but you'd have had to move an awful lot of stuff out of the way first. The room was crammed to bursting with wine racks, whose top layers reached almost to the roof. And all the racks were full; not an empty slot to be seen.

His first impression of Mr Nordstrom was that he probably wasn't the most patient man ever to see the light of day. Tough. Unless there was a catalogue of some sort, and there was no sign of one, he was going to have to wait a while – years, possibly – while Theo searched for a 1932 Château d'Yquem in all this lot.

He picked a rack at random and squinted at the labels, but they were thick with dust and illegible. Theo didn't know very much about wine, but he clearly remembered getting yelled at by his father for picking up a bottle and thereby disturbing the sediment; it was something you weren't meant to do, he knew that much. So he leaned as close to the bottles as he could get and gently wiped at the dust with his forefinger. Château d' Yquem, he read. 1931.

Too easy. He tried a few more bottles and found the 1930, the 1933, the 1934, the 1935. Would it matter so terribly much if he was a year out? He pictured Mr Nordstrom in his head and decided that, yes, it probably would. He tried the next row down, which proved to be 1936 to 1941. The three rows above were all 1929. He remembered his mother giving his father an incredibly hard time over a wine merchant's bill, and it occurred to him that the contents of the cellar must represent an absolutely colossal sum of money. Ah well.

At the far left end of the next row, a solitary bottle of the 1932. He sighed with relief and, as tenderly as he could, he picked it up, trying his level best to keep it at the same angle it had been lying on the rack. It felt curiously light.

A thought tore across his mind like a light aircraft making a forced landing in a maize field. The hell with it; he shifted the bottle upright and held it up to the light. The cork and the foil were intact, but the bottle was empty.

He stared at it. What was most surprising, however, was how relatively little he was surprised. He put it carefully down on the floor, then pulled out another bottle at random. Also empty. Likewise the next, and the one after that, and the one after that. It was only after he'd dragged out thirty-odd bottles that he found one that held anything apart from air: a 1968 Margaux contained a very, very small amount of crumbly red dust.

He put the bottles back where he'd found them, shrugged, hefted his 1932 Château d'Yquem and headed for the door. With his hand on the light switch, he paused and turned back. He'd left footprints in the dust, but there was a broom leaning up against a rack not far away. He walked back to where he'd been standing, took Pieter's bottle out of his pocket and put it in the slot, the one empty slot in the entire room, where he'd taken down Mr Nordstrom's bottle. Then, as carefully as he could, he paced out the distance from the door to the exact spot on the rack, and jotted down the number on his envelope. Then he swept about fifteen square metres of floor, to eradicate any helpful tracks. He put the broom back where he'd got it from, and grinned. If you want to hide a needle, get a haystack. He shifted the bottle into his visible left hand and started up the stairs.

By the time he got back to the reception desk he was exhausted; the long, long climb up from the cellar, followed by a frantic search for the kitchen, where he found, in a huge and otherwise empty cupboard, a single dusty wineglass. "Sorry to have kept you," he panted, as Mr Nordstrom looked up from his copy of the *Wall Street Journal*. "One bottle of 1932—"

"Thanks." Mr Nordstrom grabbed the bottle, forced it into his jacket pocket (Theo heard a seam ripping) and waved away the glass. "Put it on my bill."

"Mr Nordstrom."

"Hm?"

Theo took a deep breath. How to put this? "If the wine isn't, you know, exactly perfect—"

"It'll be fine."

He must have noticed, Theo told himself, like I did, by the weight. He'd turned his back and was lumbering away towards the stairs. But then, Theo thought, wine's such a transitory thing. It has no real existence in time. You open the bottle, you drink it, it's gone, and such enduring pleasure as the experience holds lies in the memory, or the anticipation. You can, of course, soak off the label and pin it up on the wall to impress your friends, but that's the only lasting trophy you get, like a stag's head mounted on a board to remind you of the hunt. So; if the wine's not actually there, does it really matter all that much?

Mr Nordstrom stopped and turned round. For a moment, he looked at Theo, as if noticing him for the first time. "You're new," he said.

"Yes, Mr Nordstrom."

"Name."

I mean, Call-me-Bill had said, what sort of a world would it be if we went around calling ourselves by our real names? "Pieter," Theo said. "Pieter van Goyen."

"Mphm." Mr Nordstrom nodded and plunged through the door to the stairs. It took some time for the air to refill the volume he'd displaced. It occurred to Theo to wonder if he'd given him the right key, although somehow he doubted whether any locked door would delay Mr Nordstrom for very long.

Still, he thought, it's a job; on balance, marginally better than the slaughterhouse. And Pieter had arranged it for him, don't forget that; Pieter, his friend and benefactor. Even so; a million empty bottles, and Mr Nordstrom too. If he was still a scientist, if he cared, it'd be enough to drive him crazy. It's supposed to be fun. Right.

"Hello."

Not again, he thought, and looked up.

She really was very beautiful. But nobody's parents would choose a name like Matasuntha. "Hello," he replied.

She perched on the edge of the desk and smiled at him. "So," she said, "how's it going?"

"Oh, fine. I just met Mr Nordstrom."

She grinned. "He's such a lamb."

Maybe, he thought, but where I come from we don't call them lambs, we call them rhinoceroses. "I fetched him a bottle of wine from the cellar," he said. "I suppose I ought to make a note of it somewhere, so it can go on his bill."

"Oh. Right, yes, good idea." She reached past him and brushed the VDU with her fingertip. At once, a picture of a keyboard appeared on the screen. Oh, Theo thought, and felt vaguely ashamed of himself. "So," she was saying, "one bottle of – what was it?"

"Château d'Yquem 1932."

She was pecking at the screen with her fingernails, and various boxes were appearing and disappearing. "I didn't know we had any of that left."

"Just the one bottle."

"You're right." She'd brought up a screen labelled wine cellar manifest; and scrolled down a monstrous list of names. "There you go." She highlighted the box next to Château d'Yquem 1932 and changed the one to a zero. "You found it all right, then? It's a big cellar."

"I was lucky."

"You were, weren't you? Right, for future reference, here's the manifest, look; and these coordinates next to the name refer to this plan here." The screen changed to a diagram of the cellar, with each block numbered in what Theo recognised from his time at Leiden as a cunning variation on the Dewey Decimal System. "Just be sure to update the manifest every time you take out a bottle. Otherwise," she added with a grin, "it'd be chaos."

So much, he thought wistfully, for his haystack. "Right," he said, "I'll do that. It's an impressive collection they've got down there, isn't it?"

"One of the best in this part of Holland, apparently," she replied. "I don't drink the stuff so I wouldn't know. How about you?" She turned up the thermostat on her smile a degree or so. "Are you a wine buff?"

He kept perfectly still. "Me? No. My dad was, a bit. I'd just as soon have a beer."

"Me too. Or a coffee. I love coffee. How about you? Do you like coffee?"

She didn't look at all like the vanishing girl on the train, but in other respects there were distinct similarities. Any minute now, her thought, she'll be pulling out her maths homework for me to do. "Yes. I used to drink it a lot a while back. Not so much now, though."

"Same here. It's supposed to be not very good for you. But I do like it." She paused, the way a mountain lion does just before it pounces. "What made you stop?"

"Well." Instinctively he wanted to lie, but lying is so exhausting. It's like being nice to people. You can only keep it up for so long. "I used to be a scientist—"

"Ooh, how exciting."

"Or at least," he quickly amended, "I used to work in a sciency sort of place. And I had to do tricky maths problems, and the coffee helped me concentrate. Now, though—" He shrugged.

"I love science," she said. "I find it absolutely fascinating. What made you give it up?"

Gestures, of course, can lie for you as effectively as a bought-and-paid for politician. He lifted his invisible arm and said, "Accident. After that, well, I just didn't—"

He let the sentence drain away into the silence. She gave him a look of sympathy so deep you could've dumped radioactive waste down it and never had to worry about it again.

"That's so terrible," she said; and then, "I expect you don't want to talk about it," at precisely the same moment as he said, "I don't like talking about it." She smiled at him and said, "Of course, I do understand." Then, just when he thought he was home safe and she'd lost interest and was about to go away, she said, "So, where are you from? Have you got any brothers or sisters?"

Deep inside, he smiled. She'd overreached herself. Long experience had taught him that nobody, no matter how inquisitive or predatory, could bear to listen to him talking about his family for very long. He relaxed slightly, almost feeling sorry for her. "Well," he said.

He gave her the complete treatment. He told her about his father, the only son of Bart Bernstein. Pause. The Bart Bernstein.

"Who?" she obliged.

The Bart Bernstein, who'd written all those appallingly soppy sentimental ballads round about the time of the First World War. Since Bart was a shrewd cookie when it came to investing the proceeds of bestselling slush, his son had never done a day's work in his life, preferring to devote his considerable energies to annoying his wife and children. Eventually Mrs Bernstein decided she'd had enough and vanished without trace, leaving Bart Junior with two sons, Max and Theo, and a daughter, Janine. Max grew up to be a slightly more acceptable version of his father, and was generally well regarded until he accumulated a collection of gambling debts that even his father regarded as unconscionable and refused to pay; whereupon Max took the sensible precaution of making himself very difficult to find. But not difficult enough, apparently, because nine years ago, shortly before his father's death, the remains of a pair of his hand-made shoes and one DNA-identified tooth were found in a quicklime pit in Honduras. Janine Bernstein, meanwhile, was spending her share of her father's fortune on a tour of the world's premier rehab clinics, though to judge by results she hadn't found one she liked yet. The only reason she wasn't in prison was that they kept letting her out again, and when he'd written to her to ask for a loan to tide him over till he got on his feet again, shortly after he lost all his money in the Schliemann Brothers thing, her lawyers had written back threatening him with injunctions if he ever came within fifty miles of her. All in all, therefore, the answer to the original question was effectively No.

This was the point at which they always said, "That's dreadful, I'm so sorry," and Matasuntha was no exception. But every other woman who'd ever spoken those words to him used them to mean get away from me, you might be contagious. This time, he was at a loss to interpret them. About the only thing he was sure she wasn't trying to say was, that's dreadful, I'm so sorry, but that wasn't really much help. Intrigued, he smiled. "Well," he said, "that's the story of my life. How about you?"

"Me?" The question seemed to startle her a little. "Well, all I ever wanted to do ever since I was a little girl was work in a hotel."

"And?"

"Here I am." She beamed at him. "So you're a scientist, then," she said. "That's pretty amazing."

"What is?"

"Being a scientist."

"Oh, I don't know. If it was that difficult, most of the scientists I know wouldn't be able to do it. Anyway, like I said, I'm not one any more. They threw me out, I wasn't smart enough."

"You're just being modest."

"Not really. Modesty is when you tell lies." He stared at the phone, willing it to ring, but it didn't. Life can be so unkind. "So, what is it about working in hotels that you like so much?"

That slowed her up a little. "Oh, loads of things. Meeting new people, stuff like that." She was looking at him with her head slightly on one side. "I thought you said you gave up being a scientist because of the accident."

"I did. I caused the accident. That's why they fired me."

"Ah." In her eyes, buried deep, he thought he saw a little flash of triumph, as though she'd finally got what she'd come for. Damn. "Well, I mustn't hold you up any longer. It was nice talking to you. See you around."

She read me like a book, he told himself bitterly, after she'd gone away. And not just any book; one of the large-print editions they do for people with poor eyesight. I'm pathetic. And (he thought, with a sudden rush of panic) if she's really looking for Pieter's bottle and she's already searched the room, it shouldn't take her too long to figure out where it's hidden.

The thought of revisiting the wine cellar wasn't a cheerful one; his knees still ached from all those stairs, and it was a pretty spooky kind of a place. Never mind. He looked round to make sure nobody was about, and scuttled off through the door to the staircase.

The bottle was still there. He took it out of the rack, then hesitated. It was still a marvellous haystack. He found the useful broom, which was where he'd left it, then crossed to the furthest rack on the left. Six rows up, twelve bottles across from the right; he picked out a Cheval Blanc 1977 (whatever that was) and put Pieter's bottle in its place. The Cheval Blanc went where he'd got the Château d'Yquem from. Ten minutes' vigorous broom activity obscured his tracks. Job done.

When he got back to the desk, he found Call-me-Bill leaning against it looking deeply bewildered.

"There you are," he said. "Where have you been?"

"Toilet," Theo managed to reply.

"Oh." Call-me-Bill thought about that for a moment. "Oh, fair enough. But it'd be nice if you left a note or something if you're not at the desk. Better still, give me or Matasuntha a shout, so we can cover for you. It's really quite important, you know."

Theo mumbled an apology, which Call-me-Bill waved aside. "Don't worry about it," he said. "Just so long as you know for next time. I just came to tell you, your shift's over. I imagine you'd like to go back to your room and get some rest. You must be exhausted."

An hour sitting peacefully at a desk; well, that'd take it out of you, for sure. "Thanks," he said.

"Not at all. You're doing a great job."

Well, he thought as he climbed the stairs, anything's possible. Maybe the attrition rate among hotel desk clerks is on a par with junior officers in the trenches in the First World War, and just still being there at the end of an hour's enough to qualify you for the Silver Star. But he was inclined to doubt that. True, Mr Nordstrom had been a bit alarming, but all he'd actually done was ask for his key and a bottle of wine.

The elephant in the room can be ignored, with determination and practice, so long as it's content to sit quietly in a corner, doing nothing more energetic than gently massaging its neck with the tip of its trunk. When it starts trumpeting and crushing the furniture, the only sensible course is to give in and officially recognise its presence. There is, Theo formally admitted to himself, something profoundly weird going on around here. This is not a normal hotel, the people aren't regular people, it's got something to do with Pieter's bottle and a way of busting holes in the quantum partitions between alternate universes. If I was involved in any way, if I was still a physicist who gave a damn about all that stuff, I might be getting a little antsy at this point. Just as well I'm neither of those things, isn't it?

In denial, the voice of his former analyst muttered in the depths of his memory. Too damn right, Theo replied. And why not? Denial's the clove of garlic that keeps you from getting bitten. All around you, mystery and melodrama; but just so long as you've got your clove of garlic, you can carry on being the shoemaker in the little village at the foot of the mountain with the castle on it, and what the hell? Strangers may go up to the castle and not come back, but folks'll always need shoes, come what may. So long as you've got your clove, there's not a problem.

Provided, of course, that you don't get bored.

It's not something that the shoemaker needs to worry about, because there's always someone banging on his door with a seam that needs stitching or a heel that rubs. But a hotel clerk who gets off work at (he checked his watch) 4 p.m. and the rest of the day's his own, boredom is the maximum enemy. He lay back on the bed and closed his eyes, but he'd never felt wider awake in his entire life.

Suddenly, there was an impossibly loud bang, enough to shake the whole room and set the lights flickering. For a moment Theo was sure he was dreaming, reliving the moment when the VVLHC blew up (he did that quite often, for some reason); but then he heard voices shouting, doors banging, feet running, none of which featured in his all-too-familiar flashback. He slid off the bed, landing on the balls of his feet, and hurled himself at the door.

On the landing, the door of the room opposite was wide open, but there was nobody to be seen. The commotion was coming from downstairs. He hesitated for a moment, sniffed for smoke, then darted down the staircase as fast as he could go.

When he reached the lobby, he found out what had caused all the noise. A huge man – he didn't need to see the face to identify Mr Nordstrom – was lying on the floor in a pool of blood. Call-me-Bill was kneeling over him, twisting a tourniquet fashioned from Mr Nordstrom's idiotic cowboy tie around his blood-soaked elbow. Matasuntha was hurrying forward with a big black tin box. Another woman was tearing open a packet of gauze dressing. A shattered wine bottle lay on the ground a yard or so away.

"Dressing," Call-me-Bill said, tense but calm, not looking up; the woman Theo didn't know knelt beside him holding it, while he cut Nordstrom's jacket sleeve lengthways with a pair of scissors. "It's all right," he went on, "it's gone straight through and out the other side, and it's missed the bone. Thanks," he added, as the woman handed him the dressing and he pressed it carefully into place. "Bandage." Matasuntha took a roll of crêpe bandage out of the tin box and gave it to him; he gently lifted Nordstrom's arm and started to wind the bandage round it. "That was lucky. That could've been—"

Matasuntha cleared her throat loudly; Call-me-Bill looked up and noticed Theo for the first time. He froze for a moment, hedgehog-in-headlights fashion, then smiled and said, "Hi."

"Um," Theo said. "Is there anything—?"

"No, everything's under control, thanks." Call-me-Bill lifted the arm so that Matasuntha could fasten the bandage with a safety pin. "One of our guests has been in the wars a bit. You've met Mr Nordstrom, haven't you?"

"Um."

Mr Nordstrom lifted his head a little, groaned, "Good evening", and appeared to pass out. Theo tried to reply, but all that came out was a tiny squeak.

"Poor fellow slipped and cut himself on the bottle he was carrying," Call-me-Bill said. "Still, no harm done. He'll be right as rain in no time."

The pool of blood on the floor was half a metre square. "Ah," Theo said. "That's all right, then. Are you sure there's nothing I can—?"

"No, no, we're fine, you go on back upstairs and have a good rest." Call-me-Bill lifted his bright red hands and looked round for something to wipe them on. Matasuntha obliged with a towel. "Remember, breakfast's at seven to ten thirty in the kitchen. You know where that is, don't you? If not, ask Mattie, she'll show you the way." Matasuntha nodded and smiled brightly; she had blood on her cheek, like minimalist war paint.

"Right," Theo said. "I'll, um—"

"Yes, that's the ticket." All three of them were looking at him, not moving, clearly waiting for him to go away. "See you in the morning."

"Sweet dreams," Matasuntha said, and the woman he didn't know gave him what, if a smile was a sandwich, would have been the filling. He backed away towards the door he'd just come through. Mr Nordstrom came round and groaned, but they didn't seem to have noticed. It was as though they were trying to push him through the door using only their eyes.

Theo could take a hint, particularly when bludgeoned round the head with it. He turned, pushed the door open, and walked through it. Then he stopped and held perfectly still.

"Right," he heard Call-me-Bill snap, "on three. Mattie, get his feet. Dora, you got his head? Ready? One, two—"

Another horrible groan, then Call-me-Bill said, "It's all right, nearly there", followed by loud shuffling noises and the sound of a chair being knocked over. "Steady," Call-me-Bill warned someone. "And for crying out loud, somebody clear up that glass."

More shuffling; then Theo heard Mr Nordstrom moaning, "It was supposed to be Paris and it was Hanoi, didn't stand a chance," before Matasuntha cut him short with, "It's all right, we've got you," and someone kicked open a door.

Theo went up to his room, shut the door, looked to see if there was a lock or a bolt (there wasn't) and dragged the chair across to wedge under the handle. He wasn't a doctor (well, he was, but not of medicine), but he had an idea that it's gone straight through and out the other side, and it's missed the bone wasn't how you described an injury from a splinter of broken glass. Also, he remembered, now that he came to think of it, there hadn't been any kind of a stain on the carpet where the fragments of broken bottle lay, which suggested to him that the bottle had been empty. But, then, around here weren't they all?

Gunshot wounds, he recalled suddenly, had to be reported to the police, by law; but not nasty nicks you got off smashed bottles. That, he told himself, could well be part of an explanation that might eventually make some sort of sense. Paris and Hanoi, on the other hand, were beyond him entirely.

Clove of garlic, he thought. Even if Mr Nordstrom had got himself shot up in the course of some illegal activity, and Call-me-Bill, Matasuntha and the unidentified woman were in it up to their necks, it was still nothing at all to do with him. That, evidently, was how they wanted him to see it, he was only too happy to indulge them, and, really, there was nothing else to say on the subject. He glanced at his watch; three minutes past six. A little earlier than his usual bedtime, but it had been a rather wearing day, one way or another. He groped on the floor for the plastic carrier bag that held all his earthly possessions and found his copy of Greenidge and Chen's *Macrodimensional Field Inversion Dynamics*; ten times more effective than Nembutal, safe and reusable. He read five pages and fell asleep.

He sat up. It was pitch dark. Someone was sitting on the end of the bed.

"Who's there?" he said.

A light flared, and lit up a head. It had bright red skin, pointed Spock ears, a flat stub of a nose, shrunken cheeks, yellow eyes and no hair at all. It grinned, revealing a mouthful of needle-sharp cats' teeth.

"Max?"

He had no idea why he'd said that. The head sighed. "Do I look even remotely like your dear departed brother?" it said wearily.

"No."

"Well, then." The light grew brighter, and under the head he saw a squat, short body with long arms, sitting cross-legged an inch or so from his feet. It was wearing some kind of body armour made of overlapping steel scales, and its huge feet were bare, revealing claws instead of toenails. "Looks like I'm not him, then."

It was also holding a brown manila envelope. Theo felt an urge to grab at it, but the presence of the whatever-it-was appeared to have paralysed him, so he mumbled, "Give me that," in a high, squeaky voice instead.

"In a minute," the goblin replied. It looked at him, as though expecting something of him; then it sighed. "You were reading," it said. "Yes?"

Theo could feel the corner of Greenidge and Chen's *Macrodimensional Field Inversion Dynamics* digging into his side. "Yes. Yes, I was."

"And you fell asleep."

"Yes?"

The goblin clicked its tongue, which was brown and forked at the tip. "You had the bedside light on."

"I suppose so."

The goblin pulled an oh-for-crying-out-loud face. "The bedside light is off," he said, with exaggerated patience. "What does this tell you?"

Theo stared at him. "You turned it off?"

The goblin held up one hand. Claws, an inch long and twisted into spirals, in place of fingernails. "You seriously think I can manipulate a fiddly little switch with these? Oh come on."

A tiny scrap of scientific method, left behind from his previous existence, supplied the answer. "This is a dream. I'm dreaming."

The goblin put down the envelope and clapped its hands slowly four times. "Like British Airways," he said. "It was long and traumatic, but we got there in the end. Yes, this is a dream. I am not real. All right?"

Theo nodded. He could move again. "Hold on," he said. "If I'm dreaming, how come I know I'm—?"

The goblin scowled at him. "You just do, all right?" He picked up the manila envelope and tapped it with a claw. "This is good stuff, you know? Impressive."

"Thank you."

"Of course, you've forgotten to compensate for Heisenberg," it went on, "and here" – it stabbed at the paper with a claw – "you've written a three, but your writing's so bad you subsequently read it as an eight, so your calculations from that point on are garbage; a careless mistake, and quite typical, I might add, you really must do something about your slapdash attitude to details. Apart from that, though," it concluded with a nod, "not bad at all."

Theo blinked. Heisenberg, of course. And the misread 3 would explain why the last few lines had felt a little strained. "You're my subconscious," he said. "Really it's me figuring out what I did wrong."

The goblin shrugged. "If you say so," it said. "You're the doctor, as the expression goes." It put the envelope down on the bed and crossed its arms. "What are we going to do with you, I wonder?"

"You sound like my mother."

For some reason, that made the goblin grin broadly. "A word of warning. From," it added with a snicker, "your subconscious. Watch yourself."

"Excuse me?"

The goblin bent forward a little. "These people," it said, "are not what they seem."

Theo laughed. "You don't say."

He'd offended the goblin. It gave him a cold look. "All right, Mister Know-It-All, since you're so very clever, I'll leave you to draw your own conclusions from your extensive and accurate observations. Just don't come whinneting to me if it all ends in tears."

"Sorry," Theo said, and then he stopped dead. "Whinneting?"

"Whining," the goblin explained. "Complaining in a pitiful manner."

"Yes, I know. It was one of Max's words."

"Ah yes, so it was." The goblin shrugged. "Let's see. The embodiment of your subconscious mind seeks to give you sage advice, such as a caring elder brother might—"

"Max never gave a damn about me. Or anyone except himself."

The goblin nodded. "True. Anyway, we're drifting off topic. You want to be on your guard around these people. They're up to something."

"All due respect," Theo said carefully, "but I'd sort of gathered. What are they up to, do you know?"

"Me? I'm just your—"

"Pretend you aren't," Theo said firmly.

"Ah, well, in that case," the goblin said, "I'd draw your attention to the bottles, in particular the one left to you by Pieter van Goyen. Once you've got inside—"

There was a loud crash, and the goblin vanished. Theo sat bolt upright, and saw Call-me-Bill standing in the doorway, framed by the splintered wreckage of the door.

"Sorry if I startled you," Call-me-Bill said, with a pleasant smile. "Door must've been a bit sticky." He stepped over the shattered remains of the chair Theo had jammed the door closed with, looked down at it and shrugged. "Just thought I'd remind you, it's ten fifteen and breakfast finishes at ten thirty. Of course, I'm sure we could rustle you up an omelette or something if you want a lie in, but—"

"No," Theo said. "No, that's fine. I—"

"And when you've had breakfast," Call-me Bill went on, "if

you could see your way to doing an hour on the desk, that'd be grand. Cheers, then."

He smiled again and withdrew, and Theo vaulted off the bed, noticing in passing that the bedside light was on. He scrabbled in his carrier bag for his comb and dragged it through his hair, then shook the bag out on the floor searching for his razor. He shaved quickly and brutally, and was heading for the door when he saw the brown manila envelope lying on the bed, where he hadn't left it the night before.

He spent his hour on the desk in perfect isolation, which suited him just fine, since it gave him exactly the time he needed to fix the mistakes in his calculations that the dream-goblin had so thoughtfully pointed out. When he reached the last line, he paused. Leaving an armed bomb lying around isn't the smartest thing a person can do, even if it's lying around in a pocket, or hidden under a pillow, or sealed in a concrete silo at the bottom of the sea. At least two of the people in this hotel had taken a lively interest in his brown manila envelope, and he wasn't sure their motives were unimpeachably good. However, unless they were top-flight mathematicians, the incomplete formula would be useless to them. He, on the other hand, could solve the last line in a minute or so. He put the pencil and the envelope in his pocket.

No sooner had he done so than Matasuntha came in through the front door, holding a pair of secateurs. "Morning," she said. "Sleep OK?"

"How is he?"

"Sorry?"

"Mr Nordstrom."

"Oh, he's fine, I expect. I haven't seen him since last evening. Had breakfast?"

"Yes. Look, what exactly—?"

"What did you have?"

"Slice of toast and a coffee. What exactly happened last night? It looked like he'd been—"

"Just a slice of toast? That's not enough. You should try the scrambled eggs with smoked salmon and oregano."

Fine. "Tomorrow," he said. "I overslept this morning. Mr, um, Negative had to come and wake me up."

She nodded. "He's very good about that," she said.

"He didn't seem to mind, but I don't know if he was being sarcastic."

"Oh, Bill's not like that. Quite easy-going. Really, this isn't a bad place to work, you know."

He smiled at her. "You must've been up bright and early."

"No, I— What makes you say that?"

"Well." He looked at her. "Last night this carpet was absolutely soaked in blood, there was a great pool of it right here, where I'm sitting. And now there's not a trace of it. I assumed you'd been up at dawn with the carpet shampoo."

Just for a moment, a look of furious hatred shot across her face, like share prices on a ticker-tape machine. Then it was gone, leaving behind the unruffled surface of her smile. "We have cleaners for that sort of thing," she said. "And there wasn't very much blood. Mr Nordstrom slipped and cut himself when the bottle he was holding broke. Just a little nick, that was all. No big drama."

"Ah." Theo nodded. "That's all right, then. Presumably I imagined all the blood."

"Presumably." She put the secateurs down on the desk. "Well," she said, "I expect you need a break. I'll cover for you for a bit."

It wasn't a suggestion, more like an order. "Thanks, but I'm fine."

"Really, it's no trouble. Why not drop by the kitchen and have a coffee and a doughnut? They're very good."

He looked at her. A firing squad would've been friendlier. "That's extremely kind of you," he said, "but honestly, I'm fine. I don't want to give a bad impression if Mr Negative comes by."

"He won't mind. Trust me."

The last thing in the world he was prepared to do. On the other hand, he didn't really want to force the issue any further, and she had a grimly determined look in her eye that suggested physical force was definitely an option. "Thanks," he said, and stood up. "I'll do the same for you some time."

She smiled, surged past him and sat in the chair. "Or if you don't like doughnuts," she said, "there's always the apple turnovers."

He nodded. "I'll bear that in mind," he said, and withdrew.

The hell with it, he thought, as he finished his coffee in the deserted kitchen. Pieter's bottle.

He'd found a cup laid out for him on the kitchen table, along with a plate of doughnuts and another of apple turnovers. The coffee was freshly made, with milk, sugar and cream all within arm's reach. Who the hell had put them there he had no idea.

Pieter sent me here, he told himself; and Pieter was my old tutor and my friend. He fixed me up with this – he paused to clarify his thoughts – this extremely strange but basically not-too-bad job, and he left me the bottle. Oh yes, and it was supposed to be fun. Dangerous (Mr Nordstrom weltering in blood on the lobby floor) but a good laugh nevertheless. All right. Enough of the fooling around. Let's do it.

Down the long staircase, therefore, to the wine cellar. He turned on the light, and saw that the entire floor had been carefully swept, so that not a speck of dust remained anywhere. He thought about that for a while, then shrugged and put it out of his mind. His bottle was exactly where he'd left it, label uppermost, as far as he could tell untouched. He lifted it out, pocketed it and swiftly withdrew, taking care to turn out the light.

He went back to his room, to find the door had been replaced (not repaired; the paint was dry) and he had a new chair, of the same pattern but a slightly lighter colour wood. Wedging it under the handle didn't inspire quite the same level of confidence as it had done previously, but it was the best he could do. He sat down on the bed, put the bottle on the pillow and took out the manila envelope. Zero hour.

Presumably his subconscious mind had been chewing over the last line of the calculation while his conscious mind had been occupied with fending off Matasuntha and fretting itself stupid with vanishing bloodstains and similar trivia; he sailed through it with contemptuous ease, and there it suddenly was, on the paper in front of him, in his own abysmal handwriting. The formula; the key; the bomb. He stared at it, the way you sometimes stare at a familiar word that's suddenly stopped making sense. Then, with a sort of well-here-goes-nothing shrug, he picked up the bottle and carefully measured its length and width with his trusty Vernier caliper.

Well now, he said to himself, as he wrote the numbers and symbols out again; if H = 30.17 and D = 8.72, then according to the formula –

PART TWO

Message In A Bottle

He was standing under the broad canopy of a beech tree. It was a sensible place to be, because it offered the only shade for miles around, the sky was blue and the sun was very hot. He was surrounded on all sides by an ocean of ripe grain – wheat or barley, he couldn't be sure and he didn't really give a damn. He was holding the bottle in his right hand, which was visible. The clothes he was wearing were quite definitely not the ones he'd had on a moment or so before; in fact, he couldn't remember ever having seen them, or anything like them, except on the covers of the sort of books he didn't read; books with dragons and elves and heroes with swords and people whose names were split up with unexplained apostrophes. Not in Kansas any more. Um. So far, the only sound had been the jabbering of song thrushes and the distant cawing of rooks. Now he heard, far away and intermittent, the vaguely comforting drone of an aircraft. He looked up, and saw a white vapour trail, marking the passage of an airliner. He found it reassuring, because they don't have scheduled passenger services in those books he didn't read; therefore, normality still prevailed somewhere, even if it was only at twenty thousand feet above sea level. Then the airliner changed course.

It flew in a lazy half-circle; and although from his viewpoint it seemed to take a long time to trace its course against the blue background, once he'd taken relativity and all that stuff into account, he figured that the pilot was taking a hell of a risk banking and turning so steeply at such high speed; if he carried on like that, he'd rip his plane's wings off. But on it flew, describing an even tighter circle, followed by a loop and a dip and what was presumably something along the lines of an Immelman turn. Theo felt his jaw drop open. Even in a jet fighter, you'd be pulling so much G-force doing that, you'd black out. In a 747 –

He looked at the vapour trail. It was writing.

Just looking at it made him feel sick, but it was unmistakably writing; the first big loop was a capital C, followed by a small o, leading into an n; and now the lunatic was throwing his plane into another tight circle followed by a slingshot, to form the tail of a g. Skywriting, for crying out loud.

It was unbearable to watch, but he couldn't tear his eyes away. The letters continued to form; faster now, so God only knew what speed the plane was making. An r, an a, a t, a u; Congratulations.

Theo staggered backwards until he felt the trunk of the tree against his back; he slid down it and landed in a heap, sitting awkwardly on his left leg. Sure enough, the plane carried on tracing out Congratulations in white vapour against the relentlessly blue sky.

His first thought was, it's got to be the Nobel people. Somehow they've found out I've solved the Doomsday equation, and this is their way of telling me I just made the shortlist. Tempting though the hypothesis was, however, it didn't quite jive with what he knew about the Nobel Committee, who were serious, rather humourless folk, not given to flamboyant gestures. Besides, the plane was still busily writing – on your. No earthly use hypothesising in the absence of hard data. He leaned his head back against the tree and watched. And, because it was decidedly warm, and the tree was surprisingly comfortable, and the distant hum of the aeroplane had a certain soothing quality –

He woke up. He wasn't sure how long he'd been asleep, but it was long enough for the plane to have covered at least a third of the sky with neat, perfectly spaced and fully justified white lettering. Which said –

> Congratulations on your purchase of the revolutionary new VGI YouSpace hand-held portable pocket universe containment module, the ultimate in wish-fulfilment reality technology.
>
> Ever been told that you live in a world of your own? Now you can do just that, with YouSpace. Completely real, absolutely genuine, no annoying Virtual Reality gloves and goggles; lovingly tailored to meet your dreams and aspirations by the expert design team at VGI Parallel Universes Inc.
>
> YouSpace: a full-sized alternative reality small enough to carry in your coat pocket, big enough to hold an infinite number of galaxies (NB galaxies not included), entirely self-contained, with its own multiphasic timeline (so that you can spend forty years there in your lunch hour and still have time for lunch), accessed via the VGI XPX5000 E-Z-Port (TM), guaranteed for a lifetime and absolutely safe. All for $49.95*.

He tore his eyes away from the main text and found the footnote, in much smaller letters, hovering over a distant rocky outcrop;

> *Electromagnetic containment field sold separately; typically, basic VGI ZX7677 model retails at $ 8.8 bn; terms and conditions apply.

There's always something, he thought, and looked back at the main text.

YouSpace comes bundled with five default universes plus entry into the VGI Clubhouse (TM) shared universe (for social networking); your YouSpace unit can also accommodate up to 16 custom universes hand-crafted to your exact specifications by our design team. Although VGI makes every effort to ensure that its products are safe to use, it accepts no responsibility for the vicissitudes of fate, M-Space fluctuations or errors caused by careless or slipshod design. Very occasionally, universes may intersect and participants may find themselves in someone else's fantasy; in which case, they are urged to make their way as quickly as possible to the VGI shared universe, where company representatives will make the necessary arrangements to get them home.

VGI likewise can accept no responsibility for mishaps caused by the use of unlicensed software or the criminal activities of universe hackers. When purchasing additional universes for your YouSpace module, make sure you buy only licensed VGI products, and report all infringements, unlicensed copies and unauthorised intrusions to the company immediately.

YouSpace. You've got the whole world in your hand.

While he'd been reading, the airliner had flown straight over his head and was now busily annotating the sky behind the beech tree. He got up, walked round to the other side of the tree and read –

WARNING: The alternative realities accessed via your YouSpace unit are real and therefore potentially lethal environments. Caution should be taken to avoid edged weapons, firearms, orcs, giants, dragons, soldiers, mysterious one-eyed strangers, falling from a great height, diseases, deep water, fast-moving vehicles and animals, carnivores, bogs, quicksands, high-voltage electric currents, thermonuclear explosions, starvation, dehydration, jealous spouses, star-crossed love, political upheavals, earthquakes, mudslides, lava flows, tidal waves, snakes, bears, wolves, various species of insect, pitfalls, landmines, divine retribution, poison, obesity, alcohol, narcotics, old age, royal disfavour, assassination, envy, malice, evil, poetic justice, inflammable materials, lightning, unjust or corrupt legal systems, grief, longing, suicidal tendencies, sharks, crocodiles, blunt instruments, falling trees, collapsing masonry, rope bridges over deep chasms, direct impact from asteroids or other similar extraterrestrial bodies, ice ages, global warming, curses, witchcraft and entropy, all of which can cause severe injury or death. For detailed information on these and other hazards, consult literature available from manufacturer.

He stared at the white letters until they started to grow fuzzy and soft-edged. You missed out thin ice, he thought, not to mention killer jellyfish. His neck was sore from craning his head back, and the thought of sitting quietly in his room or behind the nice desk in Reception filled him with sweet longing. He looked round for a doorway, or a control panel, but there was nothing as far as the eye could see except ripening wheat.

There was that faint droning again. The plane was back. Instinctively he turned to face the only remaining panel of uninscribed sky. Sure enough –

INSTRUCTIONS FOR USE:

1 Input user code, password and your unique 77-digit PIN and product licence number

2 Set all NUM defaults to 0 before selecting PKP outlet port
3 Ensure RET definitions checkboxes are clear and all bouncers are disabled
4 Follow the instructions in the sky

Ah, he thought bitterly, I hadn't realised it was a Microsoft product. But the plane was still moving –

4 Alternatively, bypass start-up protocols

Definitely a Microsoft product –

5 For further assistance, shout Help

So he did that. Nothing happened. The plane had flown away, nobody came and there was no sound to be heard except the gentle tweeting of a songbird in the branches above his head. He slumped back down against the tree trunk and buried his head in his hands.

Nothing. Still nobody. The bird carried on singing.

After about twenty seconds, he lifted his head. The bird was –

"... And once you've done that, you can go home. Got that? Fine."

It was birdsong, but he could understand it. He jumped up, just in time to see a small brown bird fluttering out of the topmost branch of the tree.

"Hey," he yelled, "wait, stop, some back!"

The bird flew on, then banked, turned, spread its wings, glided, flapped twice and pitched on a twig above his head. "Well?"

"I'm sorry," he said. "I wasn't listening."

"Fine."

"Will you please," Theo said, "just say all that again?"

Pause. "All of it?"

"Yes. Please."

Three seconds' silence. "This time you'll listen."

"Yes. I promise."

"All right. Ready?"

"Yes."

"This is your last chance," the bird said sternly. "Really, I'm only supposed to say it once."

"I really am very sorry, and it's extremely kind of you to—"

"Yes, right, fine. OK, here we go. The most important thing you need to know is—"

Directly overhead, there was a rushing noise. A fast-moving shadow covered his face and a great dark shape burst into view, sailing through the air and vanishing behind the interwoven branches of the tree. Theo saw huge outstretched wings, talons, a beak like a meat hook and two perfectly round yellow eyes. There was a whacking sound, like a bat hitting a ball, and a sprinkle of small feathers was floating in the air like sycamore seeds, twirling as they drifted slowly downwards. With two beats of its absurdly broad wings, the eagle dragged itself out of its dive and launched itself upwards, a feathery bundle like a shuttlecock crumpled in its left claw.

"Hey!" Theo yelled. "Come back, I haven't—" Too late. The eagle was already no more than a T-shaped silhouette against the blue sky. A drifting feather brushed his nose, and he sneezed.

For a moment he stood quite still, frozen and stunned. Then he realised that his legs weren't capable of supporting him any more, and he folded at the knees and dropped to the ground.

Say what you like about Microsoft (and he did; oh, he did) but even their worst enemies couldn't claim that their key functions were prone to being snatched in mid-operation by questing hawks. He groaned, and brushed the feather away from his face. It stuck to his finger, and, as he struggled to remove it, he noticed that the red speckles of blood spattered on the feather's gossamer veins spelled out tiny words, which somehow came into focus and became legible as he stared at them –

> Access to Help is restricted to registered users only. To register, input user code, password and your unique 77-digit PIN and product licence number and follow the instructions in the sky.

On the other hand, he thought, why not hawks? If they could do malignant paperclips, they could conjure up hawks if they wanted to. But no. For one thing, the animation was too good.

"Help!" he yelled, lifted his head and watched the skies anxiously. Nothing.

So this was Pieter van Goyen's idea of fun, he thought bitterly. In fairness, his attitude was coloured somewhat by circumstances; he'd probably feel differently if he hadn't been stranded here, with only a sketchy idea of what was going on or how it was supposed to work. In spite of everything he couldn't help being impressed by the achievement, and the implications – for dimensional theory, M-space, the whole of quantum physics – were stunning. On the other hand, he couldn't help thinking that maybe Pieter could've found something slightly more useful to do with his discovery. It was a bit like inventing the wheel with the sole intention of building a superior golf buggy.

Never mind, he told himself sternly, about all that; what I need to do is find the way out of here. Which, apparently, I can't do; not without my user name, password, PIN and product licence number. He thought about that, and the few scraps of evidence he'd gathered so far about how this thing worked. Then he took a deep breath and shouted:

"HELLO! I'VE FORGOTTEN MY USER NAME, PASSWORD, PIN AND PRODUCT LICENCE NUMBER! HELP!"

He looked round. Just as he was about to give up hope, he felt a tiny pressure on the back of his right hand. He looked down, and saw a butterfly crawling from his wrist towards his knuckles. And, across the insect's outstretched wings, in tiny letters that grew as he looked at them –

Thank you for accessing VGI YouSpace HelpSwift. Your user name, password, PIN number and product licence number have been emailed to you at your registered address in your default reality.

The butterfly spread its wings and fluttered away before he could squash it, which was probably just as well. Never mind. He wasn't beaten quite yet. He took another deep breath, and called out:

"HELLO! I WANT TO ACCESS MY EMAIL! CAN I DO THAT FROM HERE?"

This time he wasn't in the least surprised when a dragonfly materialised a few inches from his nose and hovered for a moment, wings beating invisibly fast, before landing on the lowest branch of the tree. It crawled across a leaf, then flew away. And on the leaf it had chewed:

Accessing your email from a YouSpace pocket universe is quick and easy. Simply input your name, password, PIN number and product licence number, and you'll be forwarded to your mailbox instantly.

This time, when he shouted, there were no words, just a great deal of feeling. It relieved a certain amount of immediate stress, but that was all. He sat down under the tree and forced himself to get a grip. He'd got here, he told himself, by using straightforward, no-bullshit mathematics. The same agency, it stood to reason, should be able to get him home.

The idiotic costume he was wearing had no pockets; but there was a leather pouch attached to the belt, and, when he managed to get it off and prise open the drawstring, in it he found his handkerchief, a rubber band he remembered picking up off the reception desk, the magnifying glass, the pencil and the brown manila envelope. He sighed with relief and looked at it, trying to figure out how to reverse the effect. The obvious starting point was the seventh stage of the calculation, but he couldn't quite see –

He wrote a few lines, then realised he'd run out of space. He remembered that Pieter's letter was still inside, took it out and turned it over to use the back. And saw a scribbled note in Pieter's writing which he hadn't noticed before:

PS: you'll need a user name, password, PIN number and product licence number. These are as follows:

user name: pietervangoyen6

password: flawlessdiamondsoforthdoxy

PIN: 20485205720593724084503266384500923486 233458698743330503400564656452

product licence number: 1

MEMORISE THESE IMMEDIATELY. To input them, just say them aloud and clap your hands three times.

Regards,

P.

So he did that; and nothing happened.

He was about to break down and cry when it occurred to him that he'd logged on but he hadn't done anything yet. So he yelled "Help!"; and, a moment later, he saw a little man walk out of the edge of the corn and start trudging up the hill towards him. He was old and he had a limp, and he had to stop and rest twice, but eventually he dragged himself up level with where Theo was standing and dropped down at the foot of the beech tree, breathing hard.

"Are you—?"

"Just a minute, got to get my breath."

He was short, no more than four feet, with a Santa Claus beard and flyaway white hair under a stained and tatty jester's hat, and he wore black boots with tarnished silver buckles. His doublet was embroidered with question marks.

"You're Help," Theo said.

"That's me," Help wheezed.

"But a minute ago you were a—"

"Yes," Help said.

"There was a hawk, and—"

Help nodded. "Yes," he said. "Just because someone thought it'd be smart to use unregistered software. Only," he added, with a resentful glance in Theo's direction, "it's not the goddamn cheapskate user who gets eaten by the frigging hawk. Oh no. Right," he went on, sitting up and stretching. "What d'you want?"

"I want to go home," Theo said. "Now."

Help shrugged. "Who's stopping you?"

"I don't know how."

"You don't – oh for crying out loud. Hold on, though." He looked up at Theo and frowned. "You're not Professor van Goyen."

Here we go, Theo said to himself. "Um, no. I'm his heir."

"His what?"

"Heir. He left me this – this thing in his will."

Help looked at him as though he was talking in a language he didn't understand. "The professor's dead?"

"Yes. Didn't—"

Help sighed, a long and rather dramatic process in three acts. “Of course, nobody thinks to tell me. Oh no. I find stuff out as I go along, it’s more challenging that way. Dead? Really?”

Theo nodded.

Help thought for a moment, then shrugged. “Rest his soul,” he said. “So, what did he die of, then?”

“I don’t know.”

“You don’t know. Of course you don’t. Ah well. Leaving,” Help said briskly. “Piece of cake.”

“That’s easy for you to—”

“Usually,” Help went on, as if he hadn’t spoken, “a piece of cake. More precisely, a doughnut; though technically a bagel would do just as well.”

Can’t have heard that right. “Doughnut?”

“Yes, doughnut. You can buy them at any baker, patisserie or pavement café. In fact, the first thing you should do on arrival is go straight—”

Theo extended his arms. “Where, for pity’s sake? We’re in the middle of nowhere.”

Help sighed. “Just over the skyline there,” he said, pointing due north, “there’s a roadside vendor selling a wide range of food products, including doughnuts. Trust me, there’ll always be one somewhere, no matter where you end up, it’s hard-wired into the OS. Anyway, so, you’ve got your doughnut. Simply take it in your hand and lift it level with your eyes, and look through the hole in the middle.”

Theo waited for a moment, then said, “And?”

Help shook his head. “That’s it,” he said. “That gets you home.”

“A doughnut?”

“A doughnut. Any doughnut, so long as it’s round and it’s got a hole in it. Don’t,” Help added quickly as Theo drew a deep breath, “ask me how it works, it just does. So,” he added, as Theo shook his head in disbelief, “just to run over the salient points once more. Bakery or similar retail outlet. Doughnut. Lift, look and leave. Now, do you think you've got a handle on that, or would you like me to run through it again for you?"

Theo let the deep breath go. "No," he said, "that's fine, I'll give it a go and see what happens." He remembered something; the contents of his belt pouch. "I haven't got any money."

"Doesn't matter. Just say you want to look at it first. Sure, the baker'll probably think you're nuts, but three seconds later you're going to vanish into thin air right in front of his eyes, so really, image-wise, what've you got to lose?" He paused, while Theo treated him to a drowning-puppy stare. "I think it's a pretty neat idea, actually. Easy, quick, gets the job done, and in a YouSpace universe, anywhere you go you're never more than a hundred yards from a cake shop."

Suddenly, Theo remembered the excellent doughnuts in the hotel kitchen. "Fine," he said. "I'll just go and get one, then."

Help nodded. "You won't be needing me any more, then, so I'll just—" He mimed walking with his fingers. "We can pick this up next time you visit," he said.

Next time, Theo said to himself. Absolutely no chance of that. "Sure," he said.

"Right. Well, ciao for now." Help turned and trotted away down the hill, still limping, until he was lost to sight against the corn. Theo waited, to make absolutely sure he'd gone, then followed the line the old man had shown him. Sure enough, after about a quarter of a mile, he saw a canvas tent with a table in front of it. Behind the table stood a large, red-faced man in an apron, who was laying out loaves of bread. He looked up as Theo approached and smiled.

"Hello," Theo said. "Are you a baker?"

"That's right." The red-faced man nodded. "Like my

father before me. Sixteen generations, in fact. What can I do for you?"

The loaves smelt wonderful. Also there were lardy cakes, strudels, Viennese fingers, baguettes, apple turnovers, eclairs and macaroons. "Got any doughnuts?"

The baker's smile didn't falter, but it did sort of glaze over ever so slightly. "Yes."

"I'd like one, please."

"All right." The baker didn't move. "If you're sure."

"Oh yes."

"You wouldn't rather have a nice strudel? Gingerbread? Muffin?"

"Tempting, but I think I'll stick with the doughnut, thanks."

Still smiling, the baker nodded slightly. "You're the boss. One farthing."

Theo could feel his nerve breaking up. "Could I see it first, please?"

The smile was now a mask. "What for?"

"Oh, I just like to see what I'm buying."

"They're doughnuts," the baker said. "Just doughnuts. Precision-baked to Guild specifications. Which means," he added, "that each one is exactly the same as any other. Guaranteed."

This isn't going to work, Theo thought. "Humour me," he said.

Very slowly, without breaking eye contact, the baker reached behind him into the tent and pulled out a tray of doughnuts. "There you go," he said, keeping the tray well out of Theo's reach, "doughnuts. Just the one, was it?"

Theo swallowed. His mouth was as dry as a hot summer in the Kalahari. "If it's all the same to you, I'd like a closer look."

He could see the baker hesitate. "Look," he said, still holding the tray, "no offence, but you're not going to—"

"What?"

The smile was coming unravelled. "You're not going to do anything weird, are you?"

"Excuse me?"

"Like, well—" The baker's fingers tightened on the tray. "Like, well, vanish. Disappear. Nothing like that?"

"Good heavens, no," Theo croaked. "Perish the thought."

The baker breathed out through his nose. "I'm sorry," he said. "Like I said, no offence. But there's this nutcase comes round here. Short guy, fat, bald, talks funny. And every time, he asks to look at a doughnut, and as soon as I give him one, he vanishes."

"You don't say."

The baker shrugged. "I know it sounds screwy," he said apologetically. "Hell, it is screwy. I mean, people don't just vanish, it's not possible. Only this guy does. And it's starting to get to me, you know?"

"I can imagine."

The baker sighed, and rested the tray on the table. "Sometimes I wake up in the middle of the night and I'm thinking, am I going crazy, or what? People vanishing. I don't dare tell anyone – my wife, the guys down the Bakers' Guild, they'd think I was nuts or something. I'm not sure I could take it if it happened again."

Theo nodded. "But I'm not a short, fat, bald man," he said.

"I know. That's what's keeping me from smashing your head in with a baking tin. Because I swear, if that guy shows up round here again, that's what I'm gonna do. Sixteen generations of bakers, and nothing like that's ever happened before. Of course," he added, looking round and lowering his voice, "it wouldn't have happened under the old duke."

"Really."

"You bet your life. It's only since this new guy's been in

charge that – well, stuff's been happening. You hear about it all over, only folks are too scared to talk about it out loud. For fear of people saying they're crazy, you know?"

Theo nodded slowly. "Since the new guy's been in charge."

"Exactly. All kinds of screwy stuff. I'm not saying," the baker added quickly, "that he's not better than the old duke in a lot of ways, a whole lot of ways. Like, the emancipation of the serfs, ending the civil war, doing away with the whole droyt-de-seynyewer thing, all really good stuff, nobody's gonna argue with that, he's done a lot for the ordinary folks. Poor relief. Free visits to the doctor when you're sick, all that. Real enlightened. But."

"But?"

"That doesn't make up for the screwy stuff, that's what I say." The baker was sweating. "No way. Me, I'd rather have the old ways back and no crazy stuff. At least you knew where you stood, you know? Like, you take the bakery business, and these new laws."

"I'm not from around here," Theo said.

"Ah. Figures," the baker added, squinting at Theo's clothes. "Well, one of the laws the new duke passed, every baker in the duchy's got to have doughnuts available, any hour of the day or night, every day of the year, and there's got to be a bakery stall every half-mile along all the turnpike roads, we got a duty roster nailed up in the Guild house, it's murder. Plays hell with business, I'm telling you. But it's the law, so what can you do?"

Theo nodded sympathetically. "That's a very strange law," he said.

"You're telling me. I mean, take me, when it's my turn I've gotta set up my stall out in the sticks somewhere, no passing trade, complete waste of my time, I've got a perfectly good shop back in town, on which I got to pay rent, but instead I got to come out here, waste a whole day, maybe sell a couple of muffins and a slice of shortbread, if I'm lucky. And if I'm unlucky, that fat bastard comes along and vanishes at me. It's not right, I'm telling you. That's no way to run a duchy. Well, is it?"

"Barbaric, if you ask me," Theo said.

"You bet it's barbaric. And if you say no, I'm not doing it, next thing you know there's soldiers banging on your door in the middle of the night and you're never heard of again. That's tyranny, is what it is, and folks aren't going to stand for it, I'm telling you."

"That's right," Theo said, his hand creeping slowly towards the tray of doughnuts. "Someone ought to do something."

"That's what I keep saying," the baker hissed back. "Someone damn well ought to—"

With a degree of speed and agility he wouldn't have thought himself capable of, Theo lunged for the nearest doughnut. If the baker saw him do it, he wasn't quick enough to react. A split second later, the doughnut was in Theo's hand, moving through the air, drawing level with his eye. Through the hole he caught of fleeting glimpse of the baker's agonised face, then –

He sat up sharply, dislodging the bottle, which rolled off the bed and landed, with a thump but unbroken, on the floor. A faint crackle told him he was sitting on the manila envelope. His watch showed eighteen minutes past ten.

The envelope was noticeably thicker than it had been. He peered inside and found a glossy brochure. It was full of beautiful photos of exotic-looking places – beaches, mountains, forests, castles – and the accompanying text was in Russian. Oh well.

Not that it mattered, because nothing on earth would ever induce him to go through all that again. He wasn't at all sure what had just happened to him, but one thing he was certain about was that it shouldn't have, whatever it was; it had been weird and impossible, and as a scientist he refused to believe –

Blessed are those who have seen, and yet have believed. Some kind of really advanced computer simulation – no, he couldn't quite accept that, it had been too real, the smell of the warm earth, the slight stickiness of the doughnut . . . He rubbed his forefinger and thumb together. Sticky.

Talking of which – he looked down at his right arm, but there was nothing to see. He flexed the fingers. They were sticky too. But the watch on his left wrist appeared to be working perfectly.

Doughnuts, for crying out loud.

Reality? He couldn't quite accept that, either. The talking bird; the skywriting aircraft; the little man called Help. Stuff like that simply couldn't happen in real life.

(Yes, but if you had the technology you could have holographic projections doing impossible things in an otherwise perfectly real world. Or, since even the most conservative multiverse theories allow for an infinite number of alternative universes, why not a universe where the laws of physics are different enough to allow for talking birds, skywriting planes that don't rip their own wings off doing Ws and transphasic portals nestling inside everyday items of patisserie? Shut up, he urged himself, this isn't helping.)

He licked the ball of his left thumb. Traces of sugar.

Point made: no computer program, however advanced, could deposit traces of icing sugar on your fingers, not without teleportation, which is impossible. Therefore, somewhere over the doughnut, he'd touched a solid sugary sticky thing – a real one. And, if the doughnut had been real, so must the world it came from have been. *Sucroferens, ergo est*; it's sticky, therefore it exists, and all the king's horses and all the king's men, working double shifts and funded by a substantial grant from the

UN Weirdness Limitation Commission, couldn't put his comfortable Newtonian world model together again.

Oh boy.

Suddenly an image of Pieter van Goyen floated into his mind, smiling at him, his mute lips forming the words it's supposed to be fun. True, if Pieter was still alive and within arm's reach, he'd have strangled him for subjecting him to such a violent dose of Strange. On the other hand, if it really was really real –

Fun, he thought. Fun, for God's sake. Fun.

And why not?

He screwed his eyes shut, trying to remember what he'd seen written on the sky. The ultimate in reality wish-fulfilment technology. Five default universes, or concoct your own. Suddenly, he felt a desperate need for a detailed, comprehensive user's manual. A world of your own, for only $49.95.

He leaned forward and grabbed the bottle. It looked pretty much the same as it had done the last time he'd looked at it; a bottle, the label covered in tiny writing: no big deal. A hollow glass cylinder topped with an open-ended truncated cone, conventionally used for storing booze, ships, djinns and messages; just do the math, and immediately it becomes an infinite space containing infinite possibility. He turned it round in his fingers, rotating it like the Earth revolves around its polar axis. You, on the other hand, are going to have a really amazingly good life, thanks to the bottle. Enjoy it, that's the main thing. Pieter had said that. The wisest man he'd ever known, his friend. And why not?

He heard a rattling noise; someone was turning the handle of the door, not expecting it to be jammed shut. Theo panicked. His only thought was, where can I hide the bottle? "Just a second," he called out, and plunged the bottle between the pillows. Then he lunged for the door and yanked away the chair.

"The door sticks," Call-me-Bill said. "Sorry about that."

"No problem." Theo realised he was shaking slightly, but there didn't seem to be anything he could do about it. "What can I . . . ?"

"Time for your shift," Call-me-Bill said.

"Ah, right. I'll be there directly."

Call-me-Bill stayed exactly where he was. "If you wouldn't mind holding the fort till, say, midnight, that'd be grand."

Thirteen and a half hours. Still, he couldn't very well refuse. "No problem. I'll just—"

"Yes?"

He couldn't think of anything he could just do, to get rid of Call-me-Bill long enough to hide the bottle properly. "Shave," was all he could come up with.

"Don't bother, you're fine," Call-me-Bill said firmly. "Look, I hate to rush you, but there's nobody on the desk right now, and it's a sort of rule, the desk's got to be covered at all times. Otherwise it invalidates the insurance."

"Ah, right."

"So if you wouldn't mind going down there right away."

"Sure. I'll just—" No, he couldn't think of anything. "Just a second." He darted back to the bed, shoved his hand between the pillows, grabbed the bottle and crammed it in his pocket, doing his best to conceal it from sight. It was only after he'd done it that he realised he'd used his right hand.

"Look," said Call-me-Bill from the doorway, "I really don't want to hassle you, but—"

"On my way."

He squeezed past Call-me-Bill, who didn't move, then remembered the manila envelope. "God, sorry, won't be a moment." He squeezed past again, snatched up the envelope, and bolted, leaving Call-me-Bill standing in the open doorway of the room. He grinned as he clattered down the stairs. Let him search all he wanted; there was nothing for him to find.

The desk wasn't deserted after all. Matasuntha was sitting on it, swinging her legs, reading a magazine. It had a picture of an expensively dressed woman on the cover, and all the writing was in Russian. "There you are," she said.

"Yup. Sorry if I kept you hanging about."

She yawned. "That's all right." She closed the magazine and put it on the desk. "I'm just off into town," she said. "Can I get you anything?"

"No, thanks, I'm fine." She hadn't moved. "Don't let me keep you any longer."

She'd noticed the bulge in his coat pocket. From there, her eyes travelled to the corner of the envelope, sticking out from behind his lapel. "There's paper and pencils in the drawer," she said. "And a calculator, and log tables. In case you get bored."

"Thanks." He frowned slightly, realising what she'd just said. "Um."

"Well, you used to be a scientist, you said. You might want to calculate something."

He smiled at her. "Unlikely."

"But not impossible," she replied firmly. "Think of Einstein. He discovered relativity while working as a clerk in the patents office."

"So he did," Theo said. "Well, thanks for everything, and see you later. Have a great time in town."

Reluctantly she slid off the desk and moved away, clearly trying very hard not to look at the bottle in his pocket. "Bye, now."

"Bye."

He sat perfectly still and quiet behind the desk for what seemed like a million years, until he was quite satisfied that she'd really gone. Then he pulled out the bottle and looked at it. She wanted it, no possible shadow of doubt about that. So, he guessed, did Call-me-Bill, who was probably ransacking his room for it right now. He could understand why, now that he knew what it did. As soon as his shift was over, therefore, he'd have to hide it again. Not in the cellar this time; after his insight into the operation of the wine-cellar stock-control inventory, he had a feeling it wouldn't be safe there. Outside, in the bramble jungle? He didn't like that idea either. The depressing fact was that the enemy (it didn't feel quite right thinking of Call-me-Bill and Matasuntha in those terms; call them the opposition instead) most likely knew the geography of this place far better than he did, and would therefore be wise to all the potential hiding places. The alternative was to carry the bottle and the envelope with him everywhere he went. But what about when he was asleep?

He heard the front door open and looked up. The woman he'd last seen helping bandage up Mr Nordstrom walked in and came up to the desk. She smiled at him and said, "You're new here, aren't you?"

She was tall and slim, about fifty years old, with short dark hair; elegantly and expensively dressed. At a guess, Mrs Duchene-Wilamowicz, the other guest. "That's right," he said. "How can I . . . ?"

"Theo Bernstein." She nodded slightly. "Matasuntha told me about you."

"Ah. How can I . . . ?"

"And the name rang a bell," she went on, "so I looked you up. You're the man who blew up the Very Very Large Hadron Collider, aren't you?"

Whimper. "Yup," he said. "Would you like your key?"

"So." She gazed at him as if trying to decide whether to keep him or throw him away. "You're Pieter's friend."

Click. "You knew Pieter van Goyen?"

"I was married to him," she said. "For ten years. Gloria Duchene-Wilamowicz." She reached out her hand. He extended his left, but she shook her head. "The other one," she said.

"Ah." He switched hands, and they shook briefly, like diplomats. "You know about—"

"Pieter told me. We stayed in touch," she went on. "Fascinating," she added, releasing his hand. "It feels quite solid."

"It is," he said.

"What do you think happened to it?"

"No idea." She gave him a not-good-enough look, and he went on, "I mean, I've got theories, heaps of them. But—" Then, quite suddenly, a question bubbled up in his mind and slipped out through his lips before he could stop it. "Pieter never told me he was married."

She laughed. "I guess it slipped his mind. It usually did. He was a nice man, though, I liked him." She said it as if it was an achievement, like walking across Africa. "You were his favourite student," she went on. "He talked about you a lot."

"Did he?"

"Oh yes." She frowned a little. "I wish I'd listened," she added. "But then, if I'd paid any attention to what Pieter said, I'd have died of boredom inside of a year. Are you married?"

"Extremely," Theo said. "But not right now."

"It'd probably be OK now that you're not a scientist any more," she said kindly. "Seeing anyone?"

"No."

"Probably wise. Give it a year or so, if I were you. I heard of an ex-biochemist in Florida somewhere who was normal again eighteen months after quitting science for good, but it doesn't do to rush these things. So," she went on, looking at him a bit sideways, as if looking for a seam between his neck and his head, "what's one of Pieter's old students doing behind the desk at a fleapit like this?"

"Only job I could get."

"Ah. That figures. Actually, it's not too bad here. Bill's a nice guy, and little Mattie's just such a doll, don't you think? You could do worse," she added with a gentle smile. "In due course. When you're better. My key."

Matasuntha; just such a doll. No, he couldn't really concur with that; not even one of those Russian dolls which turn out to be half a dozen separate dolls, nested inside each other. "Sorry?"

"The key," she said gently, "to my room. So I can let myself in. Rather than standing outside in the corridor all night."

"Ah," Theo said, and pulled open the desk drawer. There was just the one rusty iron key in there this time. "There you go. Is there anything . . . ?"

"I don't think so. No, belay that. Get me a bottle of champagne. The Veuve Clicquot '77."

"Um," Theo said. "I'm not supposed to leave the desk unattended."

"No problem." She leaned over, grabbed the collar of his coat with a grip like a scrapyard crusher, and pulled him up out of his chair. Then she edged past him and sat down in his seat. "I'll mind the store while you're gone. See? No problem is insuperable so long as people are prepared to help each other."

Theo stood frozen for a moment. Then he nodded three times in quick succession. "Veuve Clicquot '77, coming right up. Um—"

Mrs Duchene-Wilamowicz sighed. "Row 9, stack 47, shelf 17B. On your left as you go in the door."

"Ah. Fine. Won't be long."

After all, he thought as he ran down the stairs, why not the cellar? It was huge down there, and now he knew about the catalogue system, he could make sure his hiding place was truly random. Then, once his shift was over, he could nip down again and retrieve the bottle, and –

Yes. Well. Think about that later. Right now, just concentrate on hiding it. Pieter's wife, for crying out loud. Probably just a coincidence; yeah, sure. Customers who believed that might also like to sample our extensive selection of guaranteed genuine three-dollar bills.

The cellar door creaked when he opened it, but it was just showing off; inside, no coffin draped in red satin, no bats, just a lot of wine, in racks. He found an empty slot, memorised the coordinates and took the bottle and the envelope out of his pockets. And hesitated.

After all, he told himself, his first visit had taken no time at all, literally. And that nice Mrs Duchene-Wilamowicz was minding the desk for him. And he needed to know – He turned over the envelope and looked at the equations, wondering what to do next; last time, he'd achieved access by solving the equation, and he'd already done that, so –

The flying knife missed him by an inch, sailed past and buried itself in the tavern door.

Fun, Theo thought furiously, and dived under a table. Pieter's idea of fun, he refined, as a heavy body crashed down about a foot from his nose and lay quite still. He couldn't see properly because the table was in the way, but was that an axe buried in the poor bastard's head?

He wriggled sideways, away from the body, until someone trod on the back of his left leg. That made him sit up, and sitting up made him bang his head on the underside of the table, and after that things were vague for an unspecified time. When the vagueness gave way to a searing headache, he lifted his head and peered out between the legs of a chair.

It was much quieter now; very quiet indeed.

Cautiously he crawled out from under the table and stood up. He was in a bar. Not the sort of bar he was used to, because, instead of glass-topped tables and chrome-legged neo-Bauhaus chairs, there were long wooden tables and the shattered remains of benches. The floor was covered in straw and bodies. A small dog was sniffing a pool of fresh blood with evident delight. Apart from the dog, he seemed to be the only living creature on the premises.

Fun, he thought. No, not really.

One of the bodies, a huge man in a leather jerkin, groaned and twitched slightly. Probably not a good idea to be the first thing he saw when he woke up.

At the far end of the room was a long wooden counter, with smashed jars and bottles on top. Sitting on the floor with his back to the counter was another enormous man in a leather jerkin. He was fast asleep, which was probably just as well, since someone had seen fit to pin him to the bar with two knives, driven through the fleshy parts of his ears.

Time to leave; but in order to do that, he needed –

One of the dead men had a moneybag on his belt. Theo hesitated for a moment, then knelt down and, feeling morally inferior to an investment banker cashing his bonus cheque, pried open the drawstring and helped himself to a handful of small silver coins. When he stood up again, he saw a small, round woman walking past him holding a broom. She didn't seem to have noticed the dead people. She was humming.

He watched her walk to the counter, hitching up her skirt as she stepped over a couple of bodies along the way, and start sweeping broken crockery off the bar top. He thought for a moment, then made his way to the counter and cleared his throat.

The woman looked up and smiled. "Yes, dear?"

"Excuse me," Theo said, "but have you got any doughnuts?"

She nodded, stooped and produced a tray of doughnuts from under the bar. "Farthing each," she said. "You're not from around here."

"No."

"On your holidays?"

Somewhere below him and to his right, someone groaned horribly. "Yes."

She nodded. "You'll be here for the flower-arranging festival, then."

"That's right." He spread the plundered coins out on the bar top. "Is that enough?"

"What for?"

"A doughnut."

She smiled at him and took one coin. "Where are you from, then?"

"South."

"Ah." That appeared to be all the explanation she needed. "While you're here, be sure to see the pig fighting. Tuesdays and Thursdays, in the market square."

"I'll make a point of it." His hand, his visible right hand, stretched out towards the nearest doughnut.

"We don't get many southerners," the woman was saying. Then she frowned and looked at him. "You remind me of someone, you know."

"Really." His fingertip made contact with the doughnut, in roughly the manner shown on the ceiling of the Sistine Chapel. It was slightly sticky, and he could feel individual grains of sugar.

"That's right. There was a young chap used to come in here a while back, looked just like you. Only he wasn't from the south. Easterner, he was."

"Well, then," Theo said. "Our family's lived down south for ninety-six generations."

"Max, his name was."

Theo snatched his hand away as though the doughnut was red-hot iron. "Max?"

She nodded. "Funny name. I guess that's why it stuck in my mind. Max as in maximum, you see, and him being so skinny."

There are hundreds of thousands of people called Max in the real universe, Theo thought, and no reason to suppose it's not exactly the same here. But his brother had been so thin, he was practically two-dimensional. "When did you see him last?"

"Now you're asking." She frowned and squidged her eyelids together; you could practically see the white mice running round inside the little wheel. "Can't say for sure. We get lots of people in here, you know."

Quite, Theo thought, and by the looks of it, most of them leave in wheelbarrows. A horrible thought struck him. "Was he – I mean, did he die here?"

The frown deepened, until you could've hidden a small elephant in it. "Don't think so," she said; but her tone of voice suggested a verdict on the balance of probabilities, rather than beyond reasonable doubt. "It can get a bit boisterous in here sometimes. You know, lads larking about."

The man pinned by his ears to the bar groaned, as if in confirmation. "But this Max character. He—"

"No, I'm pretty sure he made it," she said. "Because I remember Big Con – that's him there, bless him," she went on, nodding in the direction of a crumpled bag of bones near the fireplace. "I remember Con saying, you could chuck knives at that Max all day long and never hit him, cos he's so thin. No, I think he just stopped coming by after a while, for some reason." She looked at him. "You know him, then."

"What? I mean, I don't know. He could be someone I used to know, but then again, it could be someone else. Did he, um, come in here with anyone in particular?"

She smiled. "Oh yes," she said. "He was great pals with that wizard bloke."

"Wizard." He had to ask, but he already knew, with the resigned foreboding of an infant at the font who knows that his three elder brothers are called John, Paul and George, what the answer would be. "He wouldn't be a short, fat guy. Bald head."

"That's him," the woman said cheerfully. "Talks funny." She paused. "Like you do."

"He used to come in here with this Max."

"Oh yes. From time to time, you know. On and off."

"When was the last time you saw the wizard?"

"Not quite sure," she replied. "I think maybe he was in here last—" She stopped. She was looking over his shoulder. When she spoke again, she lowered her voice. "Don't want to seem unfriendly, but you might think about getting along. That's Mad Frad waking up over there, look. I don't think he likes you."

"What makes you say—"

"Well, he did throw an axe at you. Mind, you can't always tell with Frad. Sometimes when he wakes up, all he does is sit in a corner and sob for a day or so. Other times—"

"I'll be going, then," Theo said. "Thanks for the chat."

"Don't you want your doughnut?"

He'd forgotten all about it. His hand lashed out and connected, and the last thing he saw in that reality was the woman's face through the hole in the doughnut. And then –

"Sorry I was so long," he panted, slamming the bottle of Veuve Clicquot down on the reception desk. "I, um . . ."

"You've been seven minutes," Mrs Duchene-Wilamowicz replied, with a smile. "Not bad, considering."

"What? Oh, I see what you—" Memo from his brain; stop talking, before you embarrass yourself. "One bottle of champagne," he said. "Will there be anything else?"

She stood up. "No, that's fine. Thank you very much. I expect it'll be lovely and fizzy, after all that being shaken about." Looking past her, he saw that a couple of the desk drawers, the ones that stuck a bit, weren't properly closed, as they'd been when he left them. "Well," she said, "I'll leave you to it."

"Thanks for looking after the desk," he remembered to say. "Were there any messages?"

"Two," she replied. "I've left notes," she added, nodding towards two yellow stickies on the desktop. "Enjoy the rest of your shift. Doesn't time fly when you're having fun?"

He gave her back a thoughtful scowl as she walked away. Time flies, yes. Fun, no. That and the rummaged-in desk drawers, and the fact that she'd been Pieter's wife – obviously she knew something; equally obviously, it wasn't something to be admitted to or talked about openly, or else why all the sneaking about and room searching?

He sat back in the chair and thought about it all. Clearly she knew about YouSpace; so, in all probability, did Call-me-Bill and Matasuntha. It wasn't an unreasonable exercise in conclusion gymnastics to assume that they wanted the bottle. Fine, Theo thought. It's terrifying and potentially lethal, so why not let them have it?

If he'd been having this conversation with himself eight minutes ago, there'd have been no argument. Give them the stupid bottle. But things had changed since then. Sudden, unexpected and potentially troublesome as a Klingon battle cruiser at a garden party, echoes of Max were back in his life. Yippee.

Because of which, he really couldn't let go of the bottle just yet, not if there was any possibility, however remote, of finding out what had become of Max, not to mention what connection, if any, he'd had with Pieter van Goyen. Of course, the likeliest explanation was that it was all a con; a captivating little Easter egg snuggled into the program by Pieter to snag his attention and nestle there, the sweet-corn husk of doubt wedged between the teeth of curiosity. Ninety-nine per cent sure that that must be the true explanation; because he had no reason whatsoever to believe that Pieter and Max had known each other, or that Max could do any form of mathematics not immediately relevant to losing money in a poker game. Take ninety-nine from a hundred, however, and you're still left with one; just enough to persuade him to hang on to the bottle a little longer, and go back.

He glanced down at the yellow stickies, just in case. Flowers4U were terribly sorry, not a single chrysanthemum to be had this side of Nijmegen before Friday, so they were sending fifteen dozen white lilies instead, hope that's OK. Oh, and Janine had called, didn't leave a number, will call back.

Janine, he thought. That's funny. I had a sister called Janine.

Janine. He shuddered so violently he nearly fell off his chair. Needless to say it could perfectly well be a totally different Janine, just as the skinny Max in the horrible YouSpace bar could be a totally different Max. He grabbed the yellow sticky, glared at it, turned it over and scrutinised the back. No, he hadn't missed anything. Janine; neither a common nor an uncommon name; possibly, just possibly, his sister.

He thought about her. Blood is thicker than water; it's also sticky, messy and frequently a sign that things aren't going too well. Half reluctantly, he allowed his memory to present a medley of Janine's most characteristic moments. Janine aged nine, using his computer and her father's credit card to try and hire a professional assassin to kill her gym teacher; Janine aged fourteen, sad and angry because her boyfriend hadn't found a gift of one of her teeth, drilled and hung on a silver chain, a specially romantic Valentine gesture; Janine going through her political phase at age seventeen, again using Dad's card to buy ex-Soviet surface-to-air missiles to arm the Cockroaches Protection League; Janine, politely refused entry to her senior prom because of the axe imperfectly concealed in her corsage; Janine in her freak-religions era, in her full regalia as a priestess of Kali Ma; Janine, any age between nineteen and twenty-eight, in a plain white smock without pockets, swearing blind that this time she'd stay in the clinic and really get herself straightened out. Well, he thought. I do love my sister, really and truly; just not enough to want to be on the same planet as her, if it could be conveniently avoided.

And, if he wasn't mistaken, she felt the same way about him; hence the injunction, the terms of which were such that if she'd left a number and he'd returned her call, he'd have been liable to spend the next ten years in jail. What, he couldn't help wondering, might have induced her to change her mind? Not running out of money, because she knew he hadn't got any. Besides, even when her brain was so monstrously infused with chemicals as to render her technically no longer human, she'd always been ferociously shrewd with her investments, so the chances of Janine having gone bust were Paris-Fashion-Week slender. But, if it wasn't money, what the hell could it possibly be? And how could she possibly have found him?

Answer: it's not Janine, just someone with the same name. Even so; just his rotten luck to be away from the desk when the call came through.

Max and Janine too; all the little vampire bats coming home to roost. Or (ninety-nine per cent probability) not. He made a conscious decision not to think about it, and accordingly spent the rest of his shift thinking about nothing else.

Janine didn't ring the next day, or the day after that. He'd have known if she had, because he was on the desk from 7 a.m. to midnight both days –

"I'm really sorry," Call-me-Bill had said, "but we're short-handed right now, so we're all having to pull double shifts until it's all sorted out. You do understand, I'm sure." By the end of the second day, he was pretty sure he did understand, and it was nothing to do with staffing levels, which were exactly the same as before – Call-me-Bill, Matasuntha and himself looking after two guests who put in an appearance roughly once every twelve hours; apart from that, he might as well have been on the Moon. The explanation, he was more or less certain, had to do with Call-me-Bill and Matasuntha wanting him pinned down at the desk while they searched for Pieter's bottle.

Actually, he didn't mind terribly much. He was right next to the phone, so he'd be there when Janine rang, and while he was on Reception he couldn't sneak away into YouSpace, and when he got off shift all he wanted to do was crawl into bed and sleep. It was good, he tried in vain not to admit to himself, to have an excuse for not going there and following up the clue about Max. For one thing, it was fairly obvious it had to be a trap of one sort; it couldn't be more obvious if there were signs all over the stairs down to the wine cellar reading This Way To The Trap and Trap 50 metres. That wasn't enough to stop him following up the clue, but it did make him feel a bit of a fool. True, it was very boring sitting behind the desk all day with nothing to do, and he'd never really learned how to cope with boredom, which made him feel like he was being nibbled to death by tiny invisible ants eating his brain, a millionth of a gramme at a time. Given the choice between boredom and the only trap on Earth obvious enough to be visible from orbit, however, boredom wasn't so bad. And it gave him time to think the same agonising thoughts about his siblings, over and over and over again, which he wouldn't have had an opportunity to do if he'd been busy.

On the third day, Matasuntha brought him a sandwich around noon. She looked tired and irritable and she was covered in dust. "Eat," she grunted, and slammed the plate down on the desk.

"Thanks," he replied. "Keeping busy?"

For a moment he thought she was going to hit him. Then she climbed into a smile. "Cleaning the wine cellar," she said. "It's filthy down there."

The wine cellar. Where else? "That's a big job. It's huge."

"Yes." The smile held, like a pressurised cabin at fifty thousand feet. "You've been down there, then?"

"Couple of times."

"Well, you'll know how dirty it is."

"Quite. But at least you can always find what you're looking for." He smiled back at her. "Thanks to the inventory on the computer, I mean."

"That needs updating," she said. "My next job."

"Ah."

"You should count yourself lucky," she went on, gazing into his eyes like a cat at a mouse hole. "Sitting up here behind this nice clean desk while I'm down there, rummaging about among all those dusty old bottles."

He tried to do a nonchalant shrug. It came out as the sort of gesture you'd expect from a giant centipede trying to pass itself off as human. "Swap jobs if you like," he said. "You do the desk, I'll muck out the cellar."

"Sweet of you, but we'd better stick to the rota. Otherwise Bill won't like it."

When she'd gone, he realised he was sweating. Not, he was reasonably confident, that there was any immediate cause for concern. Thousands, tens of thousands of bottles; it'd take her weeks to pull each one out and look at the label. Time, though, was definitely on her side. Call-me-Bill could strand him here on the desk for weeks, months even, while Matasuntha fumbled about among the grime and the cobwebs. The sensible thing, therefore, would be to retrieve the bottle and find another hiding place; but he wasn't sure that'd be wise. He wouldn't put it past them to be staking the cellar out during his off hours, expecting him to do just that. What he really ought to do, he told himself gloomily, was go back into YouSpace, find out about Max, and then give them the stupid bottle and put them out of their misery. It'd be the humane thing to do (it'd be unfortunate if Matasuntha caught something nasty down there in all the dirt and grime, and her quest was clearly having a bad effect on her temper) and it'd mean he could stop worrying and get on with his life. As for the whole trap thing, he wasn't so sure about that any more. Not a trap as such; more likely some gag or practical joke Pieter had set up for him, under the bizarre impression that YouSpace was fun. A door with a bucketful of soot balanced on top of it, or something equally sophisticated. Get it over with, he told himself.

At a quarter to midnight, whcn the end was in sight and he could hear the mattress on his bed calling to him like a phantom lover, Mr Nordstrom came in. He was wearing full evening dress, the effect of which was spoilt rather by the torn trouser knees and the missing left sleeve. His hair, however, was neatly combed, and he appeared to be perfectly sober.

"Brandy," he said. "Remy Martin, quick as you like."

"I'm sorry," Theo started to say, "I'm not supposed to leave the—"

"I'll look after the goddamn desk," Mr Nordstrom growled. "Brandy. Now."

The toes of his shoes were scuffed, and could that possibly be a tooth embedded in the welt between sole and upper? "That'll be fine," Theo said. "Won't be a tick."

He scampered down the stairs, his mind racing. They'd assume he was on the desk, so they wouldn't be watching, but they must've given up searching and gone to bed by now, because even junior hotel staff don't have that sort of stamina. The perfect opportunity, therefore, to grab the bottle –

"What are you doing down here?" Matasuntha snapped at him as he walked though the door. "You're supposed to be on Reception."

She'd climbed up to the very top row of the tallest rack, apparently without a ladder, and was hanging by one hand and a very precarious foothold. In her other hand was a dusty bottle. "Mr Nordstrom sent me down for a bottle of brandy," he said. "Are you all right up there?"

"I'm fine."

"It doesn't look terribly safe."

"I'm fine," she practically shrieked. "Leave me alone." She was taking enormous pains not to look down, and he couldn't say he blamed her.

"Right, fine. Oh, the Remy Martin. Any idea?"

"Row C, stack 4, shelf 17."

Two coincidences. It was the next row along from where Matasuntha was perched, and it happened to be where he'd hidden his bottle. If he'd come along ten minutes later, chances were she'd have found it. A single fat drop of sweat trickled down his forehead and hung in his eyebrow, just inside his field of view.

"Thanks," he said. "Well, I'll let you get on."

He found the brandy easily enough, and, at the end of the row, Pieter's bottle, which he slipped into his pocket. Then he rolled a couple of bottles along half an inch or so to close up the gap. He looked up, and saw Matasuntha's three-inch heel pecking wildly at a shelf as she struggled to climb down. "Are you sure you're—?"

"Go away."

Fine. He got out of there quickly and sprinted halfway up the stairs. Then he stopped.

No time at all, in this universe. Well, why not? Then he could turn round, nip back, leave the bottle lying around somewhere obvious, where she couldn't help finding it, and that'd be the end of all that. And what a relief that would be –

Yes. It would. Really.

He put the brandy down carefully, then fished about in his pocket for the manila envelope. A moment later –

"I said," said the man in the hat, "you calling me a liar?"

It was a big hat; black, with a broad brim, casting a shadow over the man's face. In doing so it performed a public service. Thanks to the hat, all Theo could definitely make out was the man's piercingly bright eyes. That was more than enough to be going on with.

"Um," he said.

As well as the hat, the man was wearing an old-fashioned black suit and a bootlace tie. Oh yes, and a gun belt, in which sat an ivory-handled revolver, over which the man's gloved hand hovered like a mushroom cloud over a Pacific atoll.

"Say again?"

"Um," Theo repeated. "I mean, no. Definitely not."

The hat quivered slightly. "You saying you didn't call me a liar, son?"

"Absolutely not." Theo couldn't quite bring himself to

break eye contact, even though he was curious to find out what the heavy weight hanging from his own belt might be. That said, he had a pretty shrewd idea. "Wouldn't dream of suggesting such a thing."

The man under the hat was thinking. "So," he said, "you're saying that when I said you called me a liar, I was lying."

"Yes. I mean—"

"So you're calling me a liar."

"Um."

"Them's fighting words, stranger."

"What, um?"

The man under the hat frowned. "Yup."

"Really?"

"Yup."

"Oh."

"And in these parts—"

"What I really meant," Theo heard himself gabble, "was that when you said I called you a liar, you were quite justifiably mistaken, because I expressed myself so badly, for which I apologise. Really and truly. Really."

The man frowned, as though he'd taken a wrong turning several blocks ago and was trying to figure out where he was. "So," he said, "you're saying you didn't call me a liar."

"That's right, yes."

"You're lying."

Oh for crying out loud. "Well, yes, quite possibly. In fact—"

"I'm calling you a liar."

An old man who'd dived under a table a moment ago reached out a hand and retrieved his hat. A cat wandered across the floor, stood next to the man under the hat, looked up at him, arched its back, rubbed its head against his left boot, curled up and went to sleep. "Yes," Theo said.

"Yes what?"

"Yes you're calling me a liar, and yes I am one."

The man nodded. "We got our own way of dealing with liars in these parts, stranger," he said, with a degree of satisfaction mixed with relief. "We give 'em a wooden overcoat and a one-way ticket to Boot Hill."

"You don't say."

The man grinned. "Did you," he said with great pleasure, "just call me a liar?"

Sod it, Theo thought, and without really knowing what he was doing, he reached for his gun. The next millionth of a second was a blur; then there was a very loud noise, something bashed against the web of his thumb, making him whimper, and the hat wearer's gun flew out of his hand and sailed across the room.

There was a deadly silence, during which the cat got up and slowly walked away with its tail in the air. The man under the hat was staring at him in abject terror.

"Sorry," Theo said. "Butterfingers."

Very slowly, the man raised his hands and backed away. Theo looked round nervously, but instead of the traditional henchman with shotgun taking aim at the small of his back, all he saw was a bemused-looking man at a table near the window, staring dolefully at the ivory-handled butt of a revolver sticking up out of his bowl of chilli beans. Theo waited until his erstwhile opponent had retreated through the swing doors, then walked slowly and rather unsteadily to the bar.

"Whisky?"

He nodded enthusiastically. "And a doughnut."

"Coming right up."

He realised that he was still holding the gun he'd apparently disarmed the hat wearer with. He put it back in the holster. He had to have three goes at it.

The bartender was back with a half-tumblerful of whisky

and an elderly-looking doughnut. Theo scrabbled in his pockets, which were empty.

"Sorry," he said. "I don't have any money."

"On the house," the bartender said. "That was some mighty fine shooting, stranger."

"Was it? Oh, good." He lifted the glass, considered knocking it back in one, decided against it and nibbled at the meniscus like a tiny wee mouse. There was a brief moment of extreme disorientation, which he guessed was a bit like being sneezed on by a dragon. He put the glass down very carefully.

"Ain't many folks in these parts as'd stand up to Big Red," the bartender went on. "Leastways, not living. You're a mighty cool hand, mister, and that's no lie."

Oh please don't start all that again, Theo thought. "Awfully nice of you to say so," he muttered. "Look, I was wondering. Is there anybody in this town by the name of Max?"

"Max?"

"Yes. Short for—"

"Let me see, now," the bartender said. "There's Big Max, Little Max, Cheyenne Max, Little Big Max, Banjo Billy Max, Max the Knife and Max Factor. Would the guy you're after be one of them?"

"Um," Theo replied. "OK, how about a short, round man with a bald head?"

The bartender scratched his chin. "Might you be meaning Doc Pete?"

"Mphm."

"Hangs around with Nondescript Max at the Silver Dollar next to the livery," the bartender said. "I don't let 'em in here, see. They cause trouble."

There was a soft clunk, which Theo identified as the chilli eater by the window fishing the gun out of his dinner and placing it on the table. Trouble, he muttered to himself, as opposed to the peaceful equilibrium of the average uneventful day. "I can see why you wouldn't want any of that," he said. "Um, what kind of trouble?"

The bartender looked both ways, then bent forward and lowered his voice. "Weird stuff," he hissed. "Crazy stuff."

"Ah."

"It was getting so honest decent folk was scared to come in here." The bartender shook his head sadly. "So I told them, get out and stay out, and you can get your doughnuts someplace else."

Theo nodded slowly. "The Silver Dollar."

"Mphm. That woman as runs it, she just don't give a damn."

The customer by the window had finished his chilli, and put the plate on the floor for the cat to lick out. "Near the livery stable, you said."

"Turn left out of here, seventy-five yards on your right, you can't miss it."

The bar of the Silver Dollar was practically deserted. The only customer was a tall man, leaning up against the counter. His face wasn't familiar, but his hat was. He turned to stare as Theo walked in, recoiled in terror, looked around wildly for somewhere to run, lunged sideways, slipped in a pool of spilt beer, skidded five yards, crashed into a wall and slowly crumpled into a heap. The woman behind the bar gave Theo a startled look, then beamed at him. "Drinks on the house, stranger," she said. "Anyone who can throw a scare like that into Big Red—"

"Could I possibly have a glass of water, please?" Theo said.

"Water." She said it the way a professor of geography might say "Atlantis". "Sure. You want whisky in that?"

"Not really, no."

She turned and examined a row of bottles lined up on a shelf behind the bar, eventually picking one out. It was dusty and draped in cobwebs, and a peeling handwritten label read

WATR. She poured two fingers into a glass and slid it along the bar. Theo took a sip. It tasted of watered-down whisky.

"I'm looking," he said, "for someone called Max."

"Right. Would that be Crazy Max, Spanish Max, Big Little Max, Max the Axe—?"

"Nondescript Max."

"Oh, him." She frowned. "You just missed him. He was in here earlier with that other one."

"Short fat bald—"

"I threw them out." She peered at him closely. "You a friend of theirs?"

"Sort of."

"Door's right behind you, mister."

It was the same story in the Golden Garter, the Long Branch, the Birdcage and the Lucky Strike. That just left the Last Chance –

"Well," said the bartender, "there's Slim Max, Fat Max, Apple Max—"

"Nondescript Max," Theo said wearily. "Goes around with a short, fat, bald guy called Pete. They're weird."

The bartender nodded. "Wait there," he said.

He scurried off into the back; and, for the first time since he'd arrived in wherever the hell it was supposed to be, Theo felt a tiny spasm of hope. He wasn't kept waiting long. A few minutes later, the bartender was back. He'd brought some people with him. About twenty of them, including the sheriff.

"That's him," the bartender said.

They took him outside, put him on a horse and led him to the edge of town, where a single sad-looking tree stood beside the road. All of its branches had been sawn off except one, which stuck out at right angles, parallel to the ground. Why would anyone do that, he asked himself. Oh, he thought.

"Any last request?" the sheriff asked, as he threw the other end of the rope over the horizontal branch.

"Yes," Theo replied. "I'd like a doughnut, please."

"What is it with you people and doughnuts?" the sheriff asked; but he sent a runner to the Last Chance all the same. He looked surprised and hurt as Theo looked at him, through the doughnut's hole, just before dematerialising –

He landed on the wine cellar stairs and there was still a noose around his neck. He clawed at it with both hands until he managed to prise open the knot and drag it off over his head. It was, of course, his tie.

The hell with you, Pieter, he thought, as he tottered up the stairs on legs that seemed to have no bones in them; and also with you, Max, even though you're dead. When he reached the top of the stairs he couldn't bear to put the tie back on, so he stuffed it in his pocket.

"Your brandy," he said. "Sorry I was so long, but—"

Mr Nordstrom grabbed the bottle, ripped off the foil with his teeth, unscrewed the cap and swallowed five eye-watering mouthfuls. Then he wiped his mouth and put the bottle on the desk. "Why aren't you wearing a tie?" he asked.

"Um."

"Sloppy," he said. "Improperly dressed. I never take my tie off, no matter what."

Interesting mental images, for which he didn't have the time or the processor capacity. "Sorry," he said. "I won't—"

"Doesn't matter." Mr Nordstrom glugged another three mouthfuls. The bottle was a third empty. "Charge it to my room, all right?" He stood up, straight and perfectly steady. "Oh, there was a phone call while you were gone. I wrote it down."

The message, in immaculate old-fashioned copperplate on a yellow sticky –

Janine called. No message. Wouldn't leave number. Will call back.

Well, of course. She probably had private detectives watching the hotel through lenses the size of rhino horns; the moment he left the desk, they called her and she called him. It was the sort of thing she might just conceivably do too.

When he got back to his room, he found the door was locked, which surprised him since the last time he'd looked there hadn't been a lock on the door. But there was one there now. Also, a note –

Theo –

You must be sick to death of this rabbit hutch by now, so I've moved you to Room 9998 on the ground floor. It's much nicer.

Cheers,

Bill.

It was well after 1 a.m. by the time he eventually found Room 9998. He eventually tracked it down at the far end of a long corridor leading from the laundry, a huge vaulted chamber crammed with vast, silent machines. The door was open and the light was on.

His first reaction was that he'd come home. It took him a moment to figure out why. Then he realised. He'd been in a very similar room before; in fact, he'd spent a great deal of time there. He hadn't made the connection immediately because he'd never really noticed the room, only the stuff that was in it. Room 9998 was an almost exact replica of the static inversion chamber at the VVLHC complex; the place where the chain reaction had started, when he made his big mistake.

There were differences, of course. The static inversion chamber had been lined with a hundred and ninety centimetres' thickness of lead panelling and had housed the impulse matrix and the muon wave generator, along with twelve billion dollars' worth of computers and telemetry equipment. Room 9998, by contrast, was empty apart from a bed, a bedside table, an Ikea wardrobe, a single straight-backed wooden chair and a Corby trouser press. But the cathedral-high vaulted ceiling with the clear-glass observation cupola set in the exact centre were pretty much the same. The walls were bare plaster, but at regular intervals there were rows of plugged holes, where retaining bolts could once have held lead panels to the walls. There were also something like a thousand electric points set into the skirting; rather an extravagance for a room whose only electrical appliance was one table lamp, with a hundred-metre extension cable.

It made no sense, of course. But, in a cock-eyed sort of a way, it might explain why the corridor he'd just walked down was absolutely dead straight and lined with the same brand of ceramic tile that they'd used for the space shuttle project. And, of course, the projection range at the VVLHC.

Pieter's friend, he thought, in a sudden flash of intuition. And a very good friend he must have been, to have given Pieter space in his hotel to build a private, entirely unofficial replica of the VVLHC; several orders of magnitude greater than the more usual can-I-dump-my-scuba-gear-in-your-garage sort of favour that passes for an act of friendship between ordinary mortals. Fine. Even so. Passing over the question of why anyone would feel the need to build a pirate hadron collider out back of a hotel; why, having built such a thing, would you then dismantle it, strip out all the gear and convert it into a bedroom?

A very good question, but not one he felt up to answering after a very long day. He kicked off his shoes, flopped on to the bed and reached for the light switch. He pressed it. The light came on.

Theo sighed, got off the bed and set off on the long, long walk to the doorway to turn off the overhead light. When he got there, however, there was no switch. He paused, frowned and looked up. It took him quite a while to scan the vast ceiling, and he got a crick in his neck from tilting his head back, but his search left him with some valuable but disturbing data. There was no overhead light.

Nor were there lights on the walls, or angled spots set into the floor. The only light bulb in the whole place was the one in the bedside lamp. The light, almost painfully bright, was coming from the walls. In other words, the room glowed in the dark.

Some time after 4 a.m., Theo finally got to sleep, in a semi-derelict bathroom on the third floor. He'd taken twelve consecutive baths, and only stopped there because he ran out of soap. At 5.16 he was woken by Call-me-Bill, standing over him with a cup of coffee and a Danish pastry.

"There you are," he said. "We were worried. You weren't in your room."

Theo scowled at him. "That room," he said, "is radioactive."

"A bit," Call-me-Bill said. "Nothing to worry about, though. Don't you like it?"

"I just said, it's radio—"

"Apart from that."

Theo took a deep breath, then let it go. "I quit," he said.

"Excuse me?"

"I'm resigning. I don't want this job any more. I'm a tad fussy about my ambient radiation levels and I can't stand the weirdness. Sorry."

Call-me-Bill looked puzzled. "You're leaving?"

"Yes."

"You can't."

"Watch me."

"No, seriously," Call-me-Bill said, "you can't leave. Look. This'll explain."

From his coat pocket he produced a newspaper, rolled up tight into a tube. He flattened it out and pointed to a short column of text under a photograph of a scary-looking grinning lunatic. The headline read, Police Seek Suspect in Van Goyen Murder Hunt. The photo was an old one – Theo giving a press conference, the day before the VVLHC went online – but instantly recognisable.

"So you see," Call-me-Bill went on, "if you set foot outside the hotel grounds, you'll be arrested. It was on the TV news and the radio as well. It's just a shame they couldn't have come up with a better photo. This one makes you look like you've just stuck your fingers in a light socket." He gently tugged the newspaper out of Theo's hand, folded it and put it back in his pocket. "It'll all blow over soon enough," he went on reassuringly, "but till it does, you really ought to stay here, where you're safe. I did promise Pieter I'd look after you."

Theo opened his mouth, but it was as though someone had pressed the Mute button. Call-me-Bill smiled at him and gave his shoulder a friendly pat. "We'll keep you off the desk for a bit, though, just in case. Don't suppose you'll mind that, you've been pulling some pretty long shifts recently. Tell you what, why don't you give Mattie a hand sorting the linen? I can keep an eye on the desk, it's not like we're rushed off our feet right now."

Theo glanced sideways at him. "That's not what you said a few days ago."

"Ah, well, the rush is over now, for a bit. Gives us all a chance to catch our breath."

"What rush?"

"Good man." Call-me-Bill beamed at him. "And if you really hate 9998, we can swap."

"Sorry?"

"Swap," Call-me-Bill repeated. "I'll bunk down in 9998 and you can have my room. If you don't mind mucking in with all my junk, I mean. Not ideal, I grant you, but we're a bit pushed for space right now."

"Pushed for space? We've got two guests."

"Splendid." Call-me-Bill nodded decisively. "So, if you make your way down to the laundry room, I'll tell Mattie you'll be giving her a hand. No rush."

The laundry was a bit closer to the Room That Glowed than he'd have liked, and the grim, monolithic cast-iron-and-brass machines that stood silently in the corners gave him the creeps, although he couldn't for the life of him figure out what they were or what they did. He found Matasuntha standing in front of an enormous floor-to-ceiling cupboard. The door was open, and a ladder was leaning against one of the countless shelves.

"What kept you?" she said.

He'd come straight from his bathroom. "Sorry," he replied. "Look—"

"You can start," she said, "by getting down all the stuff from the shelves and putting it on the floor in neat piles so I can go through it all."

Every shelf – he lost count after thirty – was laden down with folded towels, sheets, pillowcases, eiderdowns, curtains.

There was enough fabric in that cupboard to make a loose cover for the Sun. "All of it?"

"All of it. Come on, don't just stand there like a pudding. Get on with it."

He hadn't actually seen the main reactor of the VVLHC overload, but he had an idea of what it must've been like. A bit like the indescribable build-up of pressure inside him when Matasuntha made her last remark. Fortunately, he knew about pressure. You can ignore it until it bursts and trashes mountains, or you can channel it into doing useful work. "Fine," he said. "I'll make a start, then."

"About time."

The top shelf was so far off the ground he could feel distinct symptoms of oxygen deprivation as he pulled out a crowded armful of blankets. He fought it, however, and clambered slowly back down the ladder. Matasuntha was writing something on a clipboard, with her back to him. He hesitated. He'd never deliberately attacked anyone in his life (YouSpace didn't count) and the last time he'd been in a fight, he'd been eight, and he'd lost. On the other hand, he felt that he'd exhausted all the usual diplomatic channels, and there simply wasn't time to get a UN resolution through the Security Council. Besides which, Russia would probably veto it. They usually did.

So, instead, he grabbed the nearest sheet, swung it through the air, like a Roman gladiator casting his net, and threw it as precisely as he could over Matasuntha's head. For a split second it floated, parachute-fashion; then it dropped, like a bursting bubble.

Matasuntha squealed like a pig and lashed out frantically with her arms. Theo was just wishing he hadn't embarked on this venture when suddenly the sheet collapsed and fell, quite empty, to the floor. Theo grabbed at it but he wasn't quick enough. Then something hit him on the back of the head, and the world went offline for a while.

When normal service was resumed, he found himself lying on the floor, face downwards, with his nose in a sheet. For a moment or so he simply couldn't think how he could possibly have got there. Then his aching head filled up with memories and he twisted himself over on to his back and looked up.

Matasuntha was standing over him, holding an ironing board. "What the hell do you think you're playing at?" she yelled.

His head was swimming. "You hit me."

"You chucked a sheet over my head."

"You vanished."

Slowly, she lowered the ironing board. "Yes, well. What was I supposed to do? You attacked me."

"One moment you were there, the next—"

"Yes, all right. Oh, get up off the floor, for pity's sake. I can't hold a civilised conversation if you're going to lie there all day."

He stood up. About halfway, a great wave of pain surged through his head and crashed against the back of his eyes, making him whimper. "Serves you right," Matasuntha said. "You scared the life out of me."

But not, apparently, for very long. "All right, I'm sorry," he mumbled, leaning hard against the cupboard door. "If I'd known you were going to dematerialise, I wouldn't have done it."

At that point, his knees gave way, and he slithered down the door and sat heavily on the floor, jarring his spine. All in all, he decided, he wasn't cut out to be an action hero. Apparently she thought so too; she clicked her tongue and said, "Just sit still for a minute or so, you'll be fine. Try and keep your head still, and if you throw up on my nice clean towels I'll stove your head in. All right?"

He nodded. The great surge of energy brought on by terror, confusion and frustration had all been used up in the failed attack. Now all he wanted to do was sit very still and quiet for the rest of his life, doing exactly what he was told and not getting hit with ironing boards.

"Out of interest," Matasuntha said, "why did you try and strangle me with a sheet?"

"I wasn't trying to strangle you," he said sadly. "I just want some answers, that's all."

"Answers?"

"Mphm."

She sighed. "Here's a tip for you. If you want answers, there's these things called questions. You ask them. It's the recognised procedure."

"Yes, but—" He couldn't find the energy to complete the sentence. "I said I'm sorry."

She was looking at him. "You reckoned," she said, "that the only way to get a straight answer out of someone around here was threats of physical violence."

"Something like that."

"Well." She sat down next to him on the floor. "I have days like that," she said. "It's when people keep giving you bizarre things to do and making completely arbitrary decisions that affect you directly, and when you ask for a reason they pretend they haven't heard you. I think that's called management. You get it in a lot of businesses, including," she added, "the hotel trade."

He nodded. "But we're not in the hotel trade, are we?"

She was perfectly still for a moment. Then she said, "No."

Once, many years ago when he was a kid, he bet his friend he could hold his breath for ninety seconds. He could remember the feeling of relief when he gave up on eighty-three seconds and breathed in. That was nothing compared to this. "Not the hotel trade."

"No. It's just a cover."

He took a deep breath, savoured it and let it go slowly. "What for?"

She was looking straight ahead. "You knew Pieter van Goyen."

"Oh yes."

"Fine. Well, Bill and me, we were his business partners."

"YouSpace?"

"I what?"

"Sorry," Theo said. "Ignore me. What business were you partners in?"

She frowned. "You know, I'm not entirely sure. It was something scientific and technical, and it was going to make us all very, very rich, but it was a bit against the law."

"A bit."

"Yup. Actually, that was your fault."

"Most things are, apparently. What did I do?"

She grinned at him. "Need you ask?"

"Oh. That."

"Yes." She pursed her lips. "Apparently, after your fifteen minutes of universal fame they brought in a worldwide ban on whatever it was you were doing. In case any more mountains got blown up, I guess. Which was a total bummer as far as we were concerned, because Bill and I had invested rather a lot of money in the thing Pieter was doing – building this place, for a start – and suddenly it looked like it was all about to go down the toilet."

"Hang on," Theo said. "You built a copy of the VV—"

"Not an exact copy," Matasuntha replied. "More a sort of tribute to it, if you get my meaning."

"Tribute?"

"We took the ideas we wanted and didn't pay anybody any money for them. That's one of the reasons we had to keep it quiet. Also, this international ban thing, after your little accident. Anyhow, it was all coming along quite well, and then

Pieter went and died on us, and now we're screwed. He hadn't finished doing the mathsy stuff, you see."

Theo nodded slowly. "So you needed me?"

Matasuntha laughed. "Oh, that was Pieter's idea. He said, if anything happened to him – and it was a distinct possibility, because this thing we're doing can be a bit unsafe—"

"As well as a bit illegal."

"A bit, yes. Anyhow, Pieter said, if anything happens to me, get a hold of Theo Bernstein, he's a total flake but a bit brilliant. Actually, I think it was some stuff you did that we were paying tribute to." She gave him a sweet smile, then went on, "Of course, once you'd trashed the big Swiss thing, obviously nobody was going to give you a job selling matches in the street. So Pieter set it up for you to come here if anything happened to him, and then we'd sort of trick you into finishing the mathsy stuff. I'm really not supposed to tell you that," she added. "Bill'll be livid if he finds out. But what the hell," she said, flicking her hair away from her face with intent to cause irrelevant thoughts. "I figure, if we carry on pissing you off like we've been doing, you'll up and leave anyhow, and then we'll really be screwed. Bill's my uncle, by the way, in case you were wondering."

He hadn't been, but now she mentioned it – no, definitely not. He waved his visible hand towards the huge machines in the corner. "So all this junk—"

"Isn't for doing the laundry with, no. Again, you'd have to ask Uncle Bill about it, and probably he wouldn't know, because Pieter saw to all that. What Uncle Bill mostly did was write cheques. He's got really good at doing that."

"And Room 9998?"

She pulled a sad face. "That was where it was all set up," she said. "Of course, when Pieter died we closed it down, stripped out all the gear and crated it up in these enormous lead-lined boxes. It's all stored in some warehouse right now, until we can get it back up and running. But we had to switch it off, because it was leaking a bit."

He glared at her. "A bit."

"More than a little but less than a lot. Uncle Bill's got a little gadget, if the leak gets too bad it makes this squeaking noise. It's fine now."

Theo felt slightly reassured; as a passenger in a plane spinning out of control towards the ground might feel on fastening his seat belt. "A Geiger counter."

"Whatever. Uncle Bill would know. Anyhow," she went on, "that's all there is to it, really. Mr Nordstrom and Mrs Duchene-Wilamowicz are sort of the financial side of things. We had to bring them in when our cash flow got a tad constipated. You don't have to worry about them, they're basically no bother. Nordstrom was in business with Uncle, and Mrs D-W's a sort of cousin."

Theo nodded slowly. "And the vanishing?"

"Excuse me?"

"Just now. You vanished."

"Ah." She blushed slightly. "I can do that. God only knows how, we certainly don't. Pieter thought it was maybe something to do with the same effect that did that to your arm, but if you ask me he was just guessing. It's useful sometimes, when I can control it. But it can be a pain as well. Tends to happen at moments of heightened emotion." She looked down at her hands. "It makes it hard for me to keep a steady boyfriend, among other things. But what the hell."

Theo thought for a moment, but thinking was like wading through piranha-infested porridge. "Are the police really after me?"

"'Fraid so," she replied. "For which, I have to say, you've got Uncle Bill to thank. His bright idea for keeping you from wandering off. I'll talk to him about it," she added, "because I think it's a bit mean, framing someone for murder. He doesn't usually do stuff like that, but he's been under a lot of pressure since Pieter died, what with all the money and everything."

She made it sound like he'd borrowed a lawn mower and brought it back with one of the little plastic knobs broken off. "Where on earth did he get that much money, anyhow?"

"Oh, it's not his. Well, not really his. He's got this hedge fund thing. I'm not entirely sure what that means."

"It's where a lot of rich people put money in a fund to buy hedges," Theo said. "Then they sell the blackberries and make an absolute killing. Of course you know what a hedge fund is."

She glowered at him, then shrugged. "Anyway," she said, "he took a bunch of money out of that, and then he borrowed some from Nordstrom and the Duchene woman, but that's nearly all used up now. Which shouldn't be a problem, provided we can get this thing working."

"It'd help if you knew what it was," Theo said warily. "I mean, it makes a difference, where the mathsy stuff's concerned."

"Does it?"

"Oh yes. You need a completely different set of equations if it's supposed to be a quantum particle accelerator, say, than if what you're trying to build is the last word in pencil-sharpeners. As you well know." He tried to fix her with a steely glare, but it was a bit like trying to nail custard to a wall. "Admit it," he said. "You were the girl on the train."

"What train?"

"You can't only vanish, you can change what you look like as well. And that's creepy."

She gave him a puzzled look. "What girl on what train? I really don't know what you're talking about. I don't ever travel on trains, I get motion sickness."

The horrible possibility that she was telling the truth seeped into his mind like water through a ceiling. Nevertheless, he told her about the girl on the train; her beauty, her friendliness, her interest in quantum physics and the bloodcurdling manner of her departure. "That was you, wasn't it?"

But instead of guilty or defiant, she just looked confused. "Sorry," she said, "definitely not me. Until very recently I thought string theory was trying to explain how balls of wool get knots in them without you even touching them. And I've spent half my life trying to change how I look, and I still can't get my hair to stay straight for more than ten minutes. Which means," she added with a frown, "there's somebody else out there who knows about all this stuff." She looked at him. "That's bad."

"And who can disappear?"

"Apparently. Honestly," she said, looking straight at him, "it wasn't me. And if it wasn't me, it had to have been someone else. That's logic, that is."

He didn't want to believe her, but he didn't seem to have any choice. "If you say so," he said. "All I'm interested in is what you want me to do. And if I do it, will your uncle call off the police so I can get out of here?"

She actually looked hurt when he said that. "I'm sorry," she said. "I always said we should be straight with you instead of messing you around, but Uncle Bill reckoned if we did that, you'd want a huge great cut of the profits."

Theo told her where Uncle Bill could insert the profits, and she replied that that would certainly call for an innovative approach to money-laundering before they'd be able to spend it. "I know we haven't exactly got off to a good start," she went on, "but that's no reason why we can't make friends and cooperate. Anyway, you can't leave. You know too much now." She got to her feet and gathered up an armful of towels.

"While you're deciding what you're going to do, you can help me with all this lot."

"Why? This isn't a hotel."

"No, but Uncle Bill would like to think you still think it is. I'm not supposed to have told you anything, remember?"

"That still doesn't mean I have to fold towels."

"If you don't, he might fire you."

Arguing with her was like one of those games where you've got to jiggle a little plastic box around until all the little ball-bearings have settled in the holes. He'd always hated them and he'd always got one for Christmas. "Fine," he said. "It's not like I've got anything better to do. But you're going to talk to your lunatic uncle and get the police off my back. Otherwise, I suggest you buy yourself a really good calculator."

Folding towels for the next four hours gave him time to think. Although Matasuntha wasn't the sort of person he'd usually believe if she told him he was breathing, he had the feeling that parts of what she'd told him were probably the truth. Pieter had lured him here as a backup; well, that he could believe, though he wished he couldn't. Also, the girl on the train hadn't been Matasuntha, and she didn't appear to know about YouSpace. In which case, Pieter and Call-me-Bill's secret, illicit project was something else; and YouSpace –

Didn't fit in anywhere. Something else Pieter was playing around with, nothing to do with Matasuntha or Uncle Bill. Pure coincidence? Sure, and the soft swishing overhead was the lazy wing beats of the flocks of circling pigs. Refusing to touch with a ten-foot pole the issue of how come a hedge fund manager was also a top-flight quantum physicist – one that he'd never heard of – he tried to come up with some reason why Pieter should've inflicted that terrible plaything on him at the same time as enticing him here to do cutting-edge mathsy stuff. He batted the idea round in his mind until his synapses were raw, but he could squeeze out only one possibility. Max. YouSpace was Pieter's way of passing on some information about Max, while making it impossible for anyone who couldn't solve the impossible equation that got you inside the bottle to intercept it.

As a hypothesis, it was still about as likely as free universal healthcare in the United States, but it was all he could think of. For one thing, Max was dead, had been for years. Therefore, anything to do with him could hardly be particularly urgent. Had Pieter known Max? No evidence for that whatsoever. His original hypothesis was that Pieter had dropped false hints about Max purely in order to lure him into YouSpace. That still made a kind of sense; turning it on its head, so that the Max stuff was both real and important, made no sense at all. In fact, he'd be inclined to reject the whole theory out of hand, except that it was the only one he'd got. Also, there was a nagging feeling at the back of his mind that there was something; hopelessly vague but just strong enough to keep him from walking out on the whole horrible mess, changing his name and making a new life for himself in Ulan Bator.

Nothing for it; he was going to have to try YouSpace again. As soon as he made the decision, a heavy weight seemed to press down on him, making him wonder if being stuck where he was with a bunch of devious lunatics was really as bad as all that. Or prison, even; he could go to the police and they'd put him in a nice quiet cell for a few months until they figured out that he couldn't possibly have killed Pieter, during which time he could catch up on his reading, sew a few mailbags, nothing taxing or bewildering, and no being suddenly plunged into unexpected life-threatening situations where everybody knew what was going on except him. It was tempting, no question about that. But –

Screw you, Max, he thought. But.

"Where are you going?" she asked, as he headed for the door.

"Toilet."

"Oh." She frowned at him, as though he'd just claimed a day off for the funeral of his sixth grandmother. "Well, don't be long."

"I'll be as long as it takes," he replied with dignity, and bolted.

"I'm sorry," said a voice in his head, "Could you repeat that?"

He stared. This wasn't –

Not in his head. In his helmet. "Mission Control calling Alpha One. Please repeat. Over."

In front of him, through the glass of his helmet visor, he saw a red desert meet a pink sky. He turned his head, and the movement nearly knocked him off his feet. He staggered, left the ground for a split second, and landed gently.

"To refresh your memory," the voice said, "you got as far as one small step for. You were saying?"

"Shit."

Pause. Crackle. "Um, you might care to rephrase that. Bear in mind, there's two billion people watching this live back home."

"Where the hell," Theo asked, "is this?"

"Um. Mission Control to Alpha One, are you experiencing difficulties, over?"

Very carefully, Theo moved his head about ten degrees left. "This isn't Earth."

"No, Alpha One, that's the point. Look, are you feeling OK? Any dizziness, nausea—?"

"Jesus Christ," Theo yelled. "Get me out of here. Now."

Two sharp crackles. "Alpha One, this is Mission Control, we're having technical problems, so we're signing off, we'll get back to you soonest." Crackle. Buzz. "What's the matter with him, is he nuts or something? He's fucking lost it, man, what do you mean, the mike's still—?"

The voice cut off abruptly. Theo looked down at his legs, and saw that they were covered in silver-foil trousers, which made him feel as though he really belonged in an oven. The boots were also silver, and huge. His arms were covered in the same material, and both of them were visible. He lifted his left foot, and it seemed to want to rise up in the air and float away.

Mission Control, he thought. Oh God.

He stared at the red desert, which was nothing but sand dunes, as far as the eye could see. Very carefully he turned round and looked behind, and saw what was presumably his landing module. It didn't inspire confidence; a silver and white box on four frail, shiny legs, like a spider made out of biscuit tins and cardboard. I'm supposed to fly all the way back to Earth in that, he told himself. Yeah, sure.

Something nudged his leg, which made him jump. Not, with hindsight, the most sensible reaction; he soared his own height off the ground and nearly flipped over before sinking slowly back down again. As he touched down, he saw a creature, squatting in the sand, looking at him.

The first thing he noticed was the eyes. There were eight of them, in two bunches of four, like shiny black grapes, and they were set in an upside-down pear-shaped head that tapered steeply to a point. The creature's head was slightly larger than its body, which was supported by three stumpy legs and from which hung four long, spindly arms. What he could see of its skin was green; the rest was covered in what looked like dark blue cloth, and around its foot-long neck was something that looked disconcertingly like a fat, drooping bow tie. It raised a nine-fingered hand and waved at him.

Little green men. Bug-eyed monsters. Oh please.

He edged round until he was facing the pathetic-attempt-at-a-spaceship thing and took a long step towards it, only to find he wasn't moving. He looked down and saw a thin green hand wrapped round his ankle.

In space, proverbially, no one can hear you scream. So that was all right.

At the third try, he managed to yank his leg free of the hand, but that only made matters worse; once loose from his anchor, he sailed swiftly and gracefully through the whatever-passed-for-air and collided, head first, with the lowered ramp of the spaceship. He must have hit it at just the right angle; the foot of the ramp bounced and lifted, and all he could do was watch as it swung upwards and latched itself shut, about ten feet off the ground, sealing the spaceship as tight as a can of beans.

You clown.

The voice was inside his head, not his helmet, so it wasn't Mission Control. At first he assumed it was his inner voice, the one that had taken over the job of nagging him when his mother left home. But it didn't sound like the voice, with which he was all too familiar. Not that it –

It's all right. I've got a ladder. But you want to be a bit more careful.

That wasn't right; because his inner voice didn't have a ladder. He pushed himself up off the ground with his hands, sat up and looked back. The little green man was standing next to him, shaking his head.

I'm assuming you've got a key or an access code or something.

He stared. The little green man's lips weren't moving,

mainly because he didn't have any. Of course, for an entirely telepathic species that wouldn't be an insuperable problem –

He concentrated harder than he'd ever done before, and thought, Are you talking to me?

Yes. And there's no need to shout. Look, if you've locked yourself out I know a guy with a cutting torch, but that's going to make a mess of your flying-in-the-sky-thing. Did you really come here from another world in that heap of shit, by the way? You must be brave as two short planks where you come from.

You can hear me.

Well, yes. Oh, and why don't you take that stupid hat off? You'll be far more comfortable.

I can't. I need it to –

Bull. The atmosphere here is 78 per cent nitrogen, 19 per cent oxygen and some other stuff. I'm not a zoologist, but your brain says you should be fine with that.

How do you—?

When I said take the helmet off, a chemical analysis of your home atmosphere flashed across your subconscious mind. I compared it with the local stuff, and it looks like it's basically OK. Therefore losing the goldfish bowl should be no big deal, and then we can have a civilised conversation. How about it?

Yes, but—

Also, those other aliens that look like you can breathe our air just fine.

The sun chose that moment to rise, flooding the desert with red light the precise colour of strawberry jam. It was probably just a coincidence.

What other aliens?

The ones that look just like you.

Theo hesitated; then he fumbled for the catches of his helmet. In the end, the alien had to help him. That's better, isn't it? said its voice in his head, as he breathed in a lungful of air that tasted overpoweringly of soap, with a hint of maple syrup. It also made his head swim slightly, like whisky on an empty stomach. Now you can have a G'ntyhtruhjty cake.

A what?

The alien pulled its face off; or, rather, it lifted a tubular flap of skin up over its head, to reveal a sort of compartment, inside which was what looked very much like a doughnut, except that it was green. It lifted the doughnut out and put it on one of its stick-insect fingers, like a grossly oversized ring. Then it pulled the flap down again. A G'ntyhtruhjty cake. We offer them to guests as a token of friendship and hospitality.

Ah.

Refusing to accept a G'ntyhtruhjty cake is a mortal insult that can only be avenged through the complete annihilation of the offender's tribe, or in your case, species, the voice pointed out. Go on, you don't actually have to eat it. Stick it down your jumper and have it later.

There were no pockets in the space suit, so Theo hooked it over a projecting toggle on his chest. Thanks, he thought.

Don't mention it. Well, I guess you'll be wanting me to take you to our leader.

Not really, no.

Oh. You sure? He's not that bad once you get to know him.

I'm sure he's very busy, and I wouldn't want to be a nuisance. No, I'm rather more interested in the other aliens you mentioned.

Really?

Yes.

The alien scratched the top of its head with eighteen fingers. Let me get this straight. You came all this way in that bizarre contraption just to talk to a couple of your own kind.

Yes.

You don't want a guided tour of the therion reactors, or a trip along the Hanging Canyons of Foom?

Later, perhaps. First, though, I'd quite like to see these two aliens. How many of them are there, by the way?

Two. A tall one and a very tall one.

The alien was maybe four feet, so that wasn't much help.

Did they happen to mention their names?

Long pause. What's a name?

Fine. Could you just tell me where I can find them, please?

No. But I can take you to them, if that'd be any use.

That'd be fine, thank you, he thought fervently; and the alien pulled open its shoulder (this time it wasn't quite so bad) and took out a little green box. It pressed a couple of buttons, and a panel on the box slid open. From it, the alien took a tiny little plant in a tiny little flowerpot, and a tiny little bottle, the contents of which it poured over the plant.

Won't take a moment, the alien said.

The plant started to grow. Ten seconds later, it was about the size of a mature apple tree. Two more seconds, and Theo hurt his neck looking up at it.

A bit slow today, sorry about that.

Under his feet, Theo could feel the tree's roots disturbing the ground as they forced their way down. Meanwhile, enormous blossoms formed on the tree's lower branches. The petals fell away, revealing long bean-shaped pods, which lengthened and swelled until they were the size of a two-man canoe.

You might want to step back a bit.

Just in time; one of the pods quivered and fell to the ground, splitting open lengthwise to reveal a shiny, sticky, open-topped green sports car. With a single frog-like hop the alien jumped in and prodded something; the car started to purr like a cat. Get in, said the voice in Theo's head. It's not far.

The passenger seat was a bit too small, and Theo had to perch on top of it, clinging to the dashboard with both hands. Ready? He nodded, and the car sprang into the air.

A true scientist would have kept his eyes open, but Theo felt much happier with them shut, and he kept them that way for the next ten minutes, even when the alien prodded him in the thigh and urged him to look down and see the magnificent groves of washing-machine trees, which it claimed were one of the wonders of the continent. A slight bump suggested that they'd landed, but Theo wasn't taking any chances. Only when all sensations of motion had stopped and the alien said we're here did he open one eye about half a millimetre.

They were in a city. In fact, if it hadn't been for the pink sky, the pink, red and mauve buildings and the blood-red sidewalk, he could have believed he was back home. The streets were deserted –

Well, of course they are. It's the middle of the day.

– which was probably no bad thing. The alien hopped out of the car and told Theo to do the same; then it pressed a button and the car began to wither, until there was nothing left but a pale green papery husk. The alien screwed this up into a ball and dropped it into a nearby trash can. Come on, it said, and waddled away up the street so briskly that Theo had to break into a jog to keep up.

This is the Old Town, the alien was saying, some of it's almost two years old. They're on about clear-felling all the way up to the Broadwalk and replanting with affordable low-cost social housing, but I say the hell with that. Some people have no sense of history, you know? Right, we'll try in here first. It paused outside what was unmistakably a bar, and looked up at Theo with a solemn expression in its eight dark eyes. You want to watch your step a bit in here. Folks are pretty easy-going as a rule, but there's limits, you know? Just take it easy, and it'll be fine.

Take it easy in what way exactly? Theo thought furiously, but the alien had pushed open the door and gone in, so he took a deep breath and followed.

There's always a scene in westerns where the stranger walks into the saloon and the whole place goes dead quiet. The effect is diluted slightly on a planet of mute telepaths, but any loss of intensity was more than made up for by the fact that every one of the drinkers at the bar had four pairs of eyes to stare at him with. All of them except one.

Hey you, said a different voice in his head. Can't you read?

There was, of course, no way of knowing who was thinking at him, though he had an idea it wasn't going to matter terribly much in the long run. He looked round for the alien he'd come in with, but the space where it had been standing was now ominously empty. Several of the bar aliens were getting slowly to their feet.

I asked you, can't you read? You stupid or something?

I'm sorry, he broadcast as hard as he could; and no, I can't read your—

More chairs scraped. It says, no aliens, the voice translated helpfully. Reckon you'd better leave, while you still can.

Oddly enough, Theo had been thinking precisely the same thing. He reached for the alien doughnut he'd hung on the front of his suit, but it wasn't there.

It's all right. He's with me.

It was another voice in his head; but this time it was a voice, not an array of verbalised thoughts. He spun round, lifting six inches off the ground in the process, and saw –

"Hello, Theo," Pieter said. "Fancy seeing you here."

PART THREE

Somewhere Over The Doughnut

"You're dead," Theo said. They were sitting in a back room, on tiny kindergarten chairs, around a table on which rested a green bottle, two green cups and a plate of the weird green doughnuts. "Am I?" Pieter said. "Well, yes, I suppose I must be, if you're here." He frowned. "Pity," he said. "Oh well. Comes to us all in the end, I guess. How did it happen?"

"I don't know," Theo admitted.

"You don't know. Fine." Pieter shrugged. "But you got my legacy, obviously."

"Yes."

Pieter grinned. "And what do you think of it? Isn't it great?"

Yes, he told himself, that's all very well, but if I strangle Pieter, how am I going to get back home? So, reluctantly, he didn't. Instead, he said, "No."

Pieter stared at him. "You don't like it?"

"It's horrible." The words burst out of his mouth like water from a cracked pipe. "Three times I've used it so far, and each time I've nearly been killed in a bar. If that's your idea of a good time, then—"

He broke off. Pieter was gazing at him out of huge round eyes. "You mean to say you haven't reset the narrative parameters?"

"What?"

Pieter swelled up like a bullfrog, then started to laugh. It took him quite some time, during which Theo nearly burst a blood vessel staying calm. "You haven't, have you?" Pieter said eventually. "You've left them set on default."

"If you say so."

"My God." Pieter wiped the tears out of his eyes with his sleeve. "You halfwit, the default settings are an anti-tamper device. If you go into YouSpace without resetting them you're launched into a life-threatening scenario designed to scare you shitless. Didn't you read the manual?"

"What manual?"

"I didn't leave you a copy of the manual?"

Theo's fists were starting to hurt. "No, you didn't."

"Ah. Well, never mind. Now you know. First thing when you get back, reset the narrative parameters in MyYouSpace. Then you can choose whatever you like. Personally, I always like to start off waking up in bed with a beautiful woman I've never seen before, but it's entirely up to you. All you have to do is—"

"Pieter," Theo interrupted firmly. "What's all this about my brother Max?"

Pieter frowned at him. "You've got a brother? I didn't know that."

"Max. He died, years ago."

"I'm sorry. Were you close?"

"Pieter." His head was beginning to throb, but he ignored it. "Everywhere I go in this portable nightmare of yours, people tell me you and Max are hanging out together. What the hell is all that about?"

Pieter rubbed his chin with his fist. "I'm sorry, I haven't the faintest idea. I never knew you had a brother. You never told me."

"Didn't I?" Suddenly, Theo couldn't remember. It was

possible. His brother had never been a subject he'd been happy talking about. "But in that case, if you didn't—"

He got no further. At that moment, the door flew open and five aliens burst into the room. They were holding silvery things, sort of like small fire extinguishers. When Pieter saw them, he reached inside his coat for something; whatever it was, he wasn't quick enough. Dazzling jets of plasma shot out of the fire extinguishers and splashed over him. For a split second Pieter was perfectly still, bathed in white fire. Then he shrivelled, like a leaf on a bonfire. His body became a cinder, the cinder became ash, which lost its shape and crumbled in a neat pyramid on the floor.

Theo watched as the aliens shifted their weapons and pointed them straight at him. Fortunately, he saw them through the hole in one of the weird green doughnuts.

When his shift was over, he found a note for him from Call-me-Bill on the reception desk, telling him that he was now in Room 1. This turned out to be the whole of the third floor. It was quite nice, if your idea of a cosy little nest is the Metropolitan Museum of Art; the main thing was, there was a bed. He fell on it and was asleep as soon as he touched the mattress.

He was woken by what at first he thought was a growling noise, but which proved to be a phone on the bedside table. He grabbed it, mostly to make it shut up, and moaned, "Yes?" into the mouthpiece.

"Theo?"

He'd never woken up so fast in his entire life. Usually, his progress from asleep to awake was slow and gradual, like Man evolving from plankton. This time, though, all the lights in his head came on instantly. "Janine?"

"You total shit, Theo."

Yes, it was Janine all right. "Hey, sis. Long time no—"

"Shut the fuck up and listen." Pause. Janine had forgotten what she was going to say. "Anyhow," she said, "how are you? How's tricks?"

"Fine." He frowned. Why had he just said that, when it was patently untrue? Force of habit, presumably. "How about you?"

"Awful. Everything sucks. I got kicked out of the clinic, my probation officer hates me and Raoul left me for a seventeen-year-old waitress."

"Apart from that."

"Lousy. Anyhow, what do you care? You never gave a damn about me."

He remembered something. "I thought I wasn't supposed to talk to you. The injunction—"

"Screw the injunction." Another pause. "Theo, I'm frightened."

He opened his mouth, but all the words had been repossessed by the Vocabulary Bailiff. All of them except one. "Sis?"

"I'm frightened, Theo. Shit, I'm goddamn terrified. I think I'm going crazy."

Well, he thought. "What makes you think that?"

"I—" Three seconds' silence. Three seconds is actually quite a long time. "I'm, like, hearing voices."

Again. "I thought Dr Ionescu had you on medication for that."

"Not those kind of voices, you idiot. I thought—"

"Yes?"

"I got a phone call. It sounded like Max."

His turn; four seconds. "Remind me," he said, in a fake-casual voice he hated himself for. "Which one was Raoul? Wasn't he your tai chi instructor?"

"That was Ramon. Theo, I heard him. I heard his voice."

He felt as though he was standing in front of a door, through which he definitely didn't want to go. "How did you find me?" he asked.

"What?"

"How do you know where I am? Where did you get this number from?"

An impatient click of the tongue, crisp as a bone snapping. "I've got you under twenty-four-seven surveillance."

"You what?"

"I've been doing it for years," she replied impatiently. "Oh for God's sake, Theo. If I'd known you were going to make a fuss about it, I wouldn't have told you."

"I'm not making a fuss," Theo replied gently. "Just out of interest, though, why?"

"To protect myself, of course. Don't think for a second I don't know."

"Don't know what?"

She laughed, harsh and cold. "About you conspiring with that asshole Ionescu to get me certified insane and locked away so you can get hold of my money. So, naturally, I have you followed. Look, do we have to go into all that right now?"

In the past he'd tried counting to ten before saying anything. Then it had crept up to twenty, then twenty-five. "Sorry," he said. "I mean, for what it's worth, that's a complete figment of your imagination, but—"

"You see? Now you're saying I'm delusional. Fuck you, Theo, I should've known better than to expect any help out of you."

"Sis—"

Click. Whirr. He sighed, put the receiver back and waited. Ten seconds later, the phone rang again. He picked it up. "Hi, sis."

"You're a total bastard, Theo."

"If I was a total bastard, you wouldn't be my sister."

"Theo."

"Sorry. Look," he said, before she could start up again, "about this phone call. You're sure it was Max's voice?"

"Sure I'm sure."

"So tell me about it. What happened?"

Pause, while she collected her thoughts. Considering the dreadful things she'd done to her brain over the years, it was still in remarkably good shape. The little brain that tried. "I was sitting by the pool," she said, "and Lise-Marie – you remember her?"

The vulture-like French Canadian woman who guarded access to Janine with the single-minded ferocity of a dragon in Norse mythology. Like any near-death experience, hard to forget. "Yup. And?"

"Lise-Marie said, there's a call for you, and I said, who is it? And she said, your brother, so I assumed it was you, so I said, put it through. And it was—"

Long pause. "Max," Theo said.

"You think I'm crazy."

"No," Theo said. "Not this time."

"Theo—"

"Sorry, sorry. So what did he say?"

Long silence. Just when he'd begun to worry, she said, "Hi, Jan. That's what he said. And I said, who the hell is this? And he said, come on, Jan, don't you recognise me? And then I screamed and threw the phone in the pool."

Like you do. "Ah."

"Who the fuck else ever called me Jan, Theo?"

Nobody; at least, not twice. "So what did you—?"

"I think I wasn't very well for a bit after that," Janine went on, "because the next thing I remember was waking up and Ionescu standing over me saying it'd probably be best to leave the straps on for a while. And then he asked me who the call was from."

"Right. And what did you say?"

"I said it was from you. Well, I wasn't going to say I'd just been talking to my dead brother, was I? He'd have thought I was nuts, I'd have been put away. I do not trust that man.

Theo pursed his lips. Dr Ionescu was brilliant and, in his opinion, longer-suffering than Lebanon, but it didn't do to tell Janine that. "Fine," he said. "When was this, exactly?"

"What? Oh, two days ago, maybe three. I've been trying to get through to you, but your people keep pretending you aren't there. You know how hurtful that is?"

"You could've left a number."

"What, and have you harassing me? No way." Another pause. "You believe me?"

"That it might've been Max? Actually, yes, I do."

"So you don't think I'm crazy."

"No."

A very long pause. "You're just saying that to make me crazier," Janine said. "You think that if you encourage me in my delusions it'll be easier to get me put away. Dr Ionescu—"

"Janine. I believe you."

"Yeah, right. Why?"

"Because—" He clamped his mouth shut just in time. Because people in an alternative universe keep saying Max has been seen with my dead friend Pieter. "Because you're my sister, and I know you," he said. "Sometimes you do some rather injudicious stuff, but basically you're as sane as I am. So, if you say you heard Max, I believe you. Simple as that."

"Really?"

"Really."

Yet another pause. Then: "What the hell do you mean, injudicious? What have I ever done that—?"

"Well," Theo said, "having me followed, for a start."

"You're upset about that, aren't you?"

Upset. Oh boy. "A bit, yes."

"I bet you're thinking, she must be crazy, to do something like that."

"Janine."

"Yes?"

"Promise me," he said. "If you hear – well, if you hear that voice again, call me, will you?"

"OK."

"And getting the call traced might not be a bad idea."

"For fuck's sake, Theo." She was starting to feel better, evidently. "Of course I did that. All my calls are traced, naturally. But it was from a cellphone, they couldn't get a fix, not even which country he was calling from."

That he could believe. "And if he calls again, for crying out loud, talk to him. OK?"

"Yes, Theo."

"And then call me."

"Yes, Theo." Pause. "Look, about the having-you-followed thing."

Theo sighed. "It's all right," he said. "Don't worry about it."

"You won't tell Dr Ionescu, will you?"

"No."

"You really really don't think I'm crazy?"

"Really really."

"It gets so hard sometimes."

"I bet."

"You're just saying that," she snapped, and the line went dead. He put the phone back slowly, as if afraid of waking it up.

When he reported for duty in the laundry room the next morning, there was nobody there, and all the sheets and towels and pillowcases had vanished. The machines were still in place, but although he crawled all over them trying to figure out what they were supposed to be for, he ended up no wiser than he'd been when he started. He couldn't even tell if they ran on electricity or something else. He gave up after an hour and went back up to Reception, but there was nobody about. He sat down at the desk and turned the computer screen so he could read it. The screen flickered into life, and he typed YouSpace user's manual into Google, just in case. Did you mean . . .? Google asked him reproachfully. He smiled and shook his head. Then, slowly and methodically, he went through the computer, looking for anything that might give him a clue about what was going on. There were lots and lots of files in lots and lots of folders. They were all password protected, but since there was a yellow sticky attached to the monitor with the word PASSWORD on it, followed by Flawless Diamonds Of Orthodoxy, and since the one password opened all the files, that wasn't an insuperable problem. Opening the files, though, just made things a tiny bit worse. Nearly all of them were in languages he didn't understand, some of them in alphabets he'd never seen before. The few in English were mostly to do with laundry collections and the contract for emptying the septic tank. There was one that looked hopeful; it was a list of words, in three columns, and the first three words in the second column were –

Bandits
Cowboys
Spaceman
But directly under those were
Nosebleed
Lyons
Ramayana

August
Thereafter
– which didn't exactly inspire confidence. Nevertheless, he printed out a hard copy of the list and put it inside the manila envelope. Then he stood up and looked round until he saw what he'd been searching for.

It was a small box on the wall, painted red and with a glass front. He looked around for a suitable heavy object, found a fairly chunky desk stapler, and used it to smash the glass. The result was one of the loudest noises he'd ever heard, including the VVLHC blowing up.

For a surprisingly long time, nothing happened. Then Call-me-Bill came charging down the stairs, wearing a tuxedo and pyjama bottoms, yelling, "Where's the fire?"

Theo smiled at him. "There isn't one."

"What?"

"There is no fire."

"What?"

Theo pointed at the alarm and tried to mime switch-it-off, which turned out to be harder than he'd anticipated. Eventually, though, Call-me-Bill must have got the general idea, because he opened a panel next to the box and pressed a button, and the horrible noise abruptly stopped.

"Where's the—?"

"No fire."

"But you—"

"That," Theo said pleasantly, "was just to get your attention. Sorry if I startled you."

"You lunatic," Call-me-Bill panted, sitting down on the edge of the desk and grabbing at his forehead. "You scared me half to death. I thought the building—"

"Well, it isn't," Theo said briskly, "so that's all right, isn't it? Now, while you're here, I'd like to ask you about a few things. Would that be OK?"

"I could've had a heart attack," Call-me-Bill said helplessly. "I could've died."

"Ah well, omelettes and eggs." He smiled. "If it's the hoax element that's bothering you, I could really set fire to the hotel, it'd be no trouble. I'm good at destroying buildings, you see. Especially," he added cheerfully, "large hadron colliders. Hell, with all the kit you've got downstairs, I could fix this place so good, they'd have to cordon it off for ninety years."

Call-me-Bill tried to back away, but the desk was in the way. "You're nuts," he said.

"Nuts," Theo replied calmly, "not fired. Well? Do I still have a job or don't I?"

"Um." Call-me-Bill was breathing hard, and it made his throat wobble, like a bullfrog. "Obviously you're upset about something. Is it the room? You can move back to your old room if you'd rather, I just thought—"

"Oh come on," Theo said, and he felt a strange calm sweep over him, like the hole in the middle of a cyclone. "I just threatened to blow up the hotel."

"I promised Pieter van Goyen—"

"About Pieter." There had been many questions jostling about in his mind, fighting to jump the queue, but now that the name had been spoken out loud, he knew exactly what he wanted to ask. "How did he die?"

"What?"

"He's dead, right? So, what happened to him?"

Call-me-Bill wriggled backwards on the desk. "You mustn't fool around with the fire alarm, you know. It's a serious breach of health and safety. We could get closed down."

"This isn't a hotel," Theo said firmly. "What happened to Pieter van Goyen?"

Call-me-Bill sagged, like a tyre with a slow puncture. "There was an accident," he said, "at the lab. It was very quick, he wouldn't have suffered."

"That's nice. What sort of accident?"

"They were testing some new piece of apparatus." Call-me-Bill was sort of stroking the side of the desk. "I don't really know what it was, something to do with teleportation, I think, or it might've been antimatter. Anyhow, two people saw him go into this acceleration chamber thing, and then there must've been a freak electrical surge or something, because the power suddenly came on, and there was this blinding white light, and when we managed to switch it off and get inside, he wasn't there."

Theo pursed his lips. One stray pronoun. "And?"

"Well," Call-me-Bill went on, "it was a sealed chamber, lined with thirty centimetres of lead. They did tests, of course, and there were a few residual traces of DNA. And a sock," Call-me-Bill added, "with his monogram, PVG. Trouble is, only Pieter really knew exactly how the machine worked, so—"

"The lab," Theo said. "At the university, presumably."

"Not as such, no."

"Here. In the basement."

Call-me-Bill nodded slowly. "Once the police and the government people had finished investigating, we cleared it all out, naturally, and closed the project down. That's when we decided to turn the place into a hotel. Well, you know, great big building in its own grounds, handily situated for road and rail links, it seemed like a good idea."

Theo shook his head. "You didn't close it down," he said. "You and her – is she really your niece, by the way? Not that it matters."

Call-me-Bill nodded. "My sister Morgaine's daughter," he said.

"And the police. Are they really looking for me?"

"No," Call-me-Bill said, looking away. "Sorry, that was Mattie's idea. She thought you might walk out, you see. She's got a bit of a ruthless streak, she gets it from her mother."

Theo took a deep breath. "Pieter's not dead, is he?"

"Excuse me?"

"He's gone somewhere, but he's not dead. You or your weird niece accidentally sent him somewhere. Well?"

"He's dead all right," Call-me-Bill said, and the sweat on his forehead sparkled like dew in long grass. "I told you, he went into the chamber and he didn't—"

"You sent him somewhere," Theo repeated, "and you need me to get him back."

Call-me-Bill's head lifted, stayed still for a moment, then dropped back; up-down, up-down twice, as if someone was controlling it with strings. "Mattie told you."

"No, I figured it out for myself. You see, I—" He stopped, trying to think of the right words. "I had reason to believe Pieter was still alive."

Now the unseen puppeteer swivelled Call-me-Bill's head sharply round to the right; a bit too sharply. Any more, and it could easily have come off. "What? What do you mean?"

"I talked to him."

Call-me-Bill was breathing deeply in and out through his nose. "When?"

"Today."

"Where?"

"Ah. Long story." He tossed a mental coin, which came down and balanced delicately on its rim. So he had to make a conscious decision. "The term YouSpace mean anything to you?"

There was a long silence. Then Call-me-Bill actually grinned. "We weren't going to call it that," he said. "In fact, I thought we'd decided, but Pieter always was a stubborn bastard. He'd thought up the name, you see, and once he'd set his heart on it— Yes," he went on. "You could say that."

"Your niece doesn't know about it."

"Not under that name," Call-me-Bill replied. "But she knows about it all right. Question is, how do you—"

"Another long story," Theo cut him off. "But I saw Pieter van Goyen in YouSpace earlier today. Very much alive."

Call-me-Bill leaned forward to sink his face into his hands, lost his balance and sort of toppled-come-slid off the desk. He stood up, looked down at the desk as though he was more hurt than angry, and sat down again. "There you are, then."

"He's dead," Theo said. "I watched him die."

Call-me-Bill's mouth dropped open, and the colour drained from his face, as though someone had turned a stop-cock and Essence of Pink had come squirting out of the overflow. "Are you serious? You saw—"

Theo nodded. "He was disintegrated by bug-eyed monsters with ray guns," he said. He paused, then added, "Do you believe me?"

"Oh yes," Call-me-Bill said, his mouth moving awkwardly, as if he'd just had an injection at the dentist's. "Default setting 3, Alien Planet." He lifted his head, and Theo could see he was close to tears. "What happened?"

"I'm not entirely sure. I'd met Pieter and we'd just started to talk when these aliens burst in and shot him. They were just about to shoot me when I did the doughnut thing and escaped."

"Doughnut thing?"

The dropping penny sounded like a brass cannon falling down a mineshaft. "You know, the way you get out in a hurry. You don't know, do you?"

"Never been in there," Call-me-Bill replied. "I don't know how."

"Ah." Theo smiled at him, just to be annoying. "Well, it was pretty unambiguous. He just sort of—"

He broke off, as if fingers were tightening around his throat. It had just occurred to him; Pieter had been alive, and the man he'd seen disintegrated had been the real thing. They looked at each other.

"I'm sorry," Call-me-Bill said at last. "I know you two were close."

"Yes. You too?"

Call-me-Bill sighed. "He taught me when I was an undergraduate," he said. "Amazing man. Of course, I wasn't what you'd call his prize pupil. I only got in because my dad built them a new library. But Pieter – I don't know, we just sort of hit it off. And then, after I got chucked out for being useless, we sort of stayed in touch. He used to send me postcards."

"Postcards."

Call-me-Bill grinned. "Picture postcards," he said. "Niagara Falls. I think he must've bought a big box of them, because they were always the same one. I don't think he ever went there, though. Anyhow, he'd write dear Bill and then best wishes from Pieter, and leave the rest blank."

Theo could imagine Pieter doing that; wanted to stay in touch but didn't have anything in particular to say. He tried not to remember the look on Pieter's face when the plasma hit him.

"Anyhow," Call-me-Bill said with an effort, "about five years ago I got a call from him. It was basically, hi Bill, how are you, and can you let me have a billion dollars? I said I haven't got a billion dollars and he said well, how much have you got, and that's how it started."

"What started?"

Call-me-Bill sighed. "Now that," he said, "is a very good question. I asked him, of course. Well, you would, if you're investing an eight-figure sum. He grinned at me and said not to fuss about that. I told him I was just an old worrywart and I'd quite like to know. He said it'd make us all rich. I said, Pieter, I am rich and I'd quite like to stay that way. Then he laughed and changed the subject."

"But eventually—"

"Eventually." Call-me-Bill sat up a little straighter. "He explained it, and I could just about follow; a way of accessing alternative realities, at will. A hundred bespoke Disneylands in your coat pocket, and all of them actually real. By then we'd built the accelerator and most of the machinery, so it was a relief when he told me it was – well, a toy. About the only sure-fire money-spinners these days are toys and bombs, and I was starting to think, with him being so damn coy all the time, it had to be a bomb. But a toy was fine. It was like being in on the ground floor for PlayStation."

The toy that had killed Pieter. Still, on balance, better than a bomb. Nearly everything is.

"Anyway." Call-me-Bill was stroking the desk again. "We carried on with the construction work, while Pieter did the maths. Then, just when we thought we were getting there, Pieter said he'd run into a snag. Well, more like a brick wall." Call-me-Bill scowled, then went on: "He came swanning in, sat down where you're sitting right now, and told us that the whole thing was impossible."

"Ah."

"'Ah' is putting it mildly. I'd just sold nine major TV networks and an airline to pay for all the junk in the cellar, and Pieter blithely announces that the laws of physics wouldn't let us go any further. I was just weighing up different ways of killing him when he said, of course, that's not an insuperable problem."

Theo frowned. "But you just said—"

"Yes. And I forgot to mention, I made him put the maths up on that screen there, and we went through it together. He was quite right. The quantum phase realignment shift matrix we needed was quite simply impossible, in a Newton–Einstein–Hawking universe. Anything we projected outside our universe would be untraceable, and therefore to all intents and purposes lost for ever. It'd be like dropping a grain of sand out of an aeroplane and then landing and trying to find it again. You could go, but no way in hell could you ever come back."

Not an insuperable problem, huh? "Go on."

"Well, I'd more or less narrowed the choice down to strangling him or bashing his head in with a brick when he did that sort of wise-frog grin of his and said, well, it's obvious what we've got to do now; and that's the point, I'm afraid, where I started whimpering, and it was quite some time before he could persuade me to stop.

"The key proviso, he said, was in a Newton–Einstein–Hawking universe; which was a nuisance, he said, because that was precisely the sort of universe we live in, so achieving anything here was pretty much out of the question. But, he went on, as we all know, other universes are available. Somewhere, in the infinite diversity of the multiverse as hypothesised by Tegmark, Vanchurin and Wheeler, there must be one where what we want to do is not only possible but as easy as switching channels on your TV. So, all we needed to do was relocate the base of operations to this other, more amenable universe, and we'd be home and dry. This one where we are now would then be just another parallel reality, readily accessible from our new HQ. He said it'd be no different from moving a corporation when you don't like the local tax laws or business regulations. You shift the office overseas, and carry on trading just like you used to, but without having to pay stupid amounts of tax or obey a bunch of fatuous local laws. And once he'd found a nice user-friendly universe, getting there wouldn't be a problem; the bugger would be getting back again, except that it wouldn't be an issue because of the YouSpace technology, which would deal with all that, because in a non-Newton, non-Einstein, non-Hawking universe you could do that sort of thing, no trouble at all. He made it sound like getting round the no-smoking rule by stepping outside into the street."

Call-me-Bill paused for a moment, allowing Theo to catch up with his breathing, which he'd neglected for longer than he'd realised. For a moment there, it had been like listening to Pieter, when he was in one of his brainstorming moods, the same sensation of travelling faster than light straight into the Sun; we can do this temporarily overriding do we actually want to do this, or will it get us all killed. Gradually, though, the enchantment faded, and common sense came plodding breathlessly in its wake, like an overweight amateur running a marathon. "He actually did it," he asked helplessly, and Call-me-Bill nodded.

"We'd built a prototype of the quantum phase realignment shift matrix acceleration chamber," he said. "In the room out back of the laundry."

"The one that glows in the—"

"Yes, that one. Anyhow, he set the controls, so all I had to do was push a button when he gave me the signal. He told me exactly what'd happen. There'd be this blinding blue glow, he'd sort of flicker at the edges, like he was made of sand and the wind started blowing, and then he'd vanish, at which point my job was to switch everything off pretty damn quick and get the hell out of there before my face melted and ran down my shirt front. And it all went just like he said it would, and that was the last I saw of him."

"And?"

Call-me-Bill sighed and rubbed his eyes with thumb and forefinger. "That was Phase One," he said. "Phase Two would be Pieter arriving in the non-Newton-et cetera universe, setting up the YouSpace generators and using them to get back here. That was two months ago." He paused and frowned at his hands. "As you know, linear time doesn't pass in YouSpace. He should've been back here a split second after he left."

A subtle blend of nausea and terror rinsed out Theo's mind, leaving it empty for a moment. Then he said: "But YouSpace is working."

"Oh, we know that," Call-me-Bill replied with an unhappy grin. "So obviously he got there, and he set up the machine. Which sort of begs the question, why didn't he come back? And now," he added, with a catch in his voice, "you tell me you saw him get blasted by aliens with death rays." He shook his head slowly, three times. "That was the whole point about YouSpace. It's not a simulation, it's not virtual reality, it's real. Which is a great selling point, the total authenticity of the experience and so forth, but if you saw Pieter get killed, then he's dead. And that's—"

Theo didn't need to be told what that was. "I'm sorry," he said.

"You're sorry." Call-me-Bill pursed his lips. "Flow, my fucking tears. You see, not only have I lost my dear friend and mentor, I can also kiss goodbye to three-point-three-six-five billion dollars. You know why?"

"Um."

"Because," Call-me-Bill went on, "and you may just have noticed this when you tried out the useless bloody thing, there is no users' goddamn manual. Which makes it," he carried on with rising anger, "not just useless but horribly, horribly dangerous. You noticed?"

Theo shivered. "I noticed."

"Well, there you are. You see, Pieter was going to do a manual, but he got carried away with the jump to the other universe thing and he never got round to writing it. He knew how it all works, but we don't. Accordingly, we're shafted. We've got this amazing product we can't do anything with. It's like you're sitting in the cockpit of a jet, fifty thousand feet up, and you don't know if the green button on the dash is the landing gear or the ejector seat."

It was a while before Theo trusted himself to speak. "So," he said, "what are you going to do?"

A hungry look spread across Call-me-Bill's face. "We," he said, "meaning Mattie and me, we aren't going to do anything. You, on the other hand, are going to be busy."

"Me?"

"Oh yes. Pieter always said, there's only one man alive who could understand all this shit; meaning you. What you're going to do is, you're going to figure it all out from first principles, and then you're going to write the manual."

"Me?"

"You and no other," Call-me-Bill said grimly. "Originally, the idea was to send you in there to find Pieter and bring him back, but that's not going to happen now, apparently. So; Plan B. If I were you, I'd sharpen my pencil and put fresh batteries in my calculator, because you, my friend, are about to reinvent the goddamn wheel."

On the positive side, he wasn't having to pretend he was working in a hotel any more. This meant he didn't have to waste hours and hours sitting behind a desk in a deserted lobby. As far as the positive side went, though, that was more or less it.

The negative side, now; there was a lot of that. There was being cooped up in the room provided for him to work in – tiny, windowless and furnished with a chair, a table, a calculator, a moderate amount of air for breathing purposes and nothing else, so he couldn't possibly be distracted – with nothing to disturb him apart from Call-me-Bill barging in every fifteen minutes bleating, "Have you done it yet?" There was the problem of the work itself. Call-me-Bill had handed him a printout of the calculations he'd found on Pieter's laptop after his disappearance. It had taken both of them, and an improvised stretcher and a car jack, to get the printout on to the table. Plenty of material to work on, therefore; the only problem was that it made no sense whatsoever. He sprained his brain for a week trying to find a way in before he realised what the problem was –

"Variable base mathematics," Call-me-Bill repeated. "What—?"

Theo gave him a terrible smile. "It means it keeps switching," he said. "From base ten to base four to base sixteen, sometimes in the same line. Which means two and two could equal four, or ten, or eleven, and you've got no way of knowing which base you're in from one moment to the next. Presumably there's a reason for it, but I can't figure out what it is."

Call-me-Bill frowned, then smiled at him. "Very good," he said. "Carry on."

So on he carried, by the simple expedient of ignoring the problem and believing. This didn't come easily. When two and two made five, all his instincts yelled at him to stop, go back, find the error and correct it. Instead, he forced himself to have faith, so that if two and two made five, that was all right because Pieter said so. Once he'd trained himself to do this, a thin, frail thread of understanding began to stretch itself, like a spider's web in sub-zero temperatures, from one page to the next. The variable bases, he discovered, were necessary because each line of maths might well be operating in two or three or more alternative realities at the same time. In a bizarre way, though, that actually helped, after a while. Outbreaks of base six, for example, indicated activity in the primary default alternate reality – the one where he'd jumped in just after the horrible bar fight, presumably – while the cowboy-saloon reality seemed to happen mostly in base nineteen. After three weeks of battling with this garbage he was beginning to have a shadowy idea of what Pieter had been trying to do, but still no clear picture of how he'd done it, or which sheets of single-spaced mathematical symbols represented Pieter's working notes towards writing a user's manual.

"It's like this," he explained to Call-me-Bill, after a particularly fraught progress meeting. "Suppose I'm a single-cell amoeba and you want me to evolve into Einstein. Well, at the rate I'm going, in a year's time, with a lot of luck, I might just be a sea cucumber."

Call-me-Bill gave him an agonised look. "That's not good enough," he said. "The money—"

Theo said something intemperate about the money and what Call-me-Bill might like to do with it. "It's useless," he went on. "God only knows how long it took Pieter to do all this stuff. And he knew what he was doing, and he was a genius."

Call-me-Bill looked at him. "So, how long—?"

"Fifty years. Maybe. If I manage to keep this pace up without turning my brain to glue, which," he added with a scowl, "doesn't seem very likely. If you ask me, your best bet would be to cut your losses and turn this place into a hotel. You could make good money if you could get a slice of the conference trade."

Somehow, Call-me-Bill didn't find that idea very appealing, so it was back to the printouts and the calculator for another excruciating week, at the end of which Theo realised there was something else at work in there, something he hadn't identified yet, without understanding which he was simply wasting his time; at which point he kicked off his shoes, smashed the chair against the wall until there wasn't a big enough bit left to hold on to, and spent the next eight hours folding sheets of printout into paper aeroplanes.

And then it hit him, suddenly and without warning. So simple. So utterly and completely deranged, but so very simple.

"Think about it," he urged Call-me-Bill, who was looking at him nervously, as though expecting to have to defend himself with a chair at any moment. "In an infinite multiverse, there's got to be some reality somewhere where all this shit is actually perfectly normal and as clear as a bell. So; we go there, we do the maths, we reconstruct the user's manual, we use it to get home. What could possibly go wrong?"

Call-me-Bill was trying to avoid sudden movements. "Fine," he said, "in principle. So, how precisely do you figure on finding this other reality and getting there?"

Theo beamed at him, which for some reason made him even more nervous. "Leave it with me," he said. "I expect I'll think of something."

And think of something he most certainly did. Sitting on the floor with his back to the wall, with paper aeroplanes floating lazily past his head and fluttering gently to the ground, he thought of many things; the gentle chatter of a brook in spring, the patter of rain on rooftops, the breathtaking fractal beauty of birdsong and apple cores, and the many and complicated things he'd like to do to a wide variety of people, starting with his parents and working bloodily and methodically through the cast list of his life until he got to Matasuntha and Call-me-Bill. It helped, but not nearly enough.

Maybe he drifted into some sort of sleep; not the refreshing kind that knits up the ravelled sleeve of care and makes you such a trial to your hungover fellow workers, not quite the accidental doze you slide into on train journeys or during earnest films with subtitles; his body was at some kind of rest but his mind must've been redlining, because when he snapped out of it, he knew exactly what he was going to do next. He was dimly aware that the conclusion he'd reached was a culmination of a long and painstaking internal debate, which he'd missed out on because he'd been asleep. Not that it mattered. He was perfectly happy to take it on trust, because it seemed so obvious.

I'll ask Max, he told himself. Max will know.

He went from sitting on the floor to lying on a bed, in a darkened room. A faint blade of orange light shone through a crack in the curtains, enough for him to see that he wasn't alone.

Whoever she was, she was lying with her back to him. A glimmer of light from the window shone on an unruly sea of golden hair. He remembered what Pieter had said about the way he liked his YouSpace visits to start. Well, he thought.

She sighed softly and wriggled round to face him, and for the first time in a long time he found himself thinking that Pieter hadn't been such a bad guy after all. She opened her eyes and smiled at him.

"Fancy a doughnut?" she said.

For some reason, he found it hard to speak. "A—"

"You do like doughnuts, don't you?"

"Love 'em," he whispered hoarsely. She grinned, hopped off the bed and returned with – why was he mildly disappointed? – a plate of doughnuts, golden brown and sugar-frosted. He picked one up and held it; then she kissed him, and it sort of slipped his mind.

"So," she said. "I think that settles it, we are going to be friends. It's so important, isn't it, to be on good terms with the people you're going to be working with?"

"Absolutely," he whimpered. "All the latest studies on workplace interaction stress the value of a warm and cooperative ambience."

She picked up a doughnut and nibbled the rim with her small, white teeth. "When they told me I was going to be working with Professor Pieter van Goyen – the Pieter van Goyen, the guy who designed the Quite Ridiculously Huge Hadron Collider, I thought, wow, this'll be awesome. And then I thought, what if he's some stuffy, flaky old guy who only cares about the project? I thought, that won't be a lot of fun."

"And?"

She laughed and bit a chunk out of the doughnut. "Let's say you've set my mind at rest on that score, Professor."

Her eyes were the colour of mint leaves. "Excellent," he said. "So, um, what's your overview of where the project's at right now?"

She giggled and tried to stuff doughnut in his mouth. He dodged, and she kissed him instead. "I think it's coming along just fine," she said. "Particularly now that Max has fixed that thing with the Heisenberg collimator."

"Max—"

"Yes, I know." She gave him a sympathetic grin. "He's a pain in the ass, but you've got to admit, he's good at what he does. And so long as he carries on doing it," she added, with a faintly feral glint in her eye, "that means we get some time to relax and, um, pursue other interests. Don't know about you, but that suits me just fine."

She reached out and put her hand on the back of his head, drawing him towards her. He didn't exactly resist, but she stopped and looked at him. "What?"

"Max," he said. "I don't know anything about him. Do you—?"

She shrugged. "What's there to know? He's a workaholic and a flake, with below average social skills and personal hygiene issues. But you know that, for Christ's sake. You taught him for five years."

"That was some time ago," Theo managed to say. "People change."

She shook her head. "Not Maxie. But hey, who gives a damn? And anyhow, from what I hear, compared to his brother, he's Prince frigging Charming. Just be glad we got the lesser of two assholes."

"His brother," Theo said quietly.

"You know, Theo. The clown who blew up the—"

"Oh, right. Him."

Thanks, Pieter. She was looking at him a little oddly.

"Didn't you teach him too?"

"Yes, but I prefer not to dwell on it."

She laughed. "Don't blame you. I seem to remember meeting him once, at the Leipzig conference. Little bleary-eyed guy with a stammer and a runny nose. I can't understand how you managed to put up with him for five years."

"Ah well," Theo said, having first ungritted his teeth. "Time, the great healer. Anyhow, let's not talk about him."

"Let's not talk at all."

He was sitting on something. The doughnut. "I need to see Max," he said. "Now."

"Now?"

"Yup. I've just thought of something that won't wait. Where do you think he'd be at this time?"

She gave him a long, cool look. "In bed with a glass of milk and a learned journal," she replied. "Not like you. Why, is that what you'd rather be doing?"

He managed to squeeze her out a smile. "You wouldn't happen to have his address and phone number?"

She sighed. "Wait there," she said, got up and left the room. A shame, he thought, a great big shame, but what the hell. Business before pleasure. Exactly why business had to come before pleasure, especially given that linear time wasn't passing as far as he was concerned, he was at a loss to say.

"Here." She threw a cellphone in his lap, and dictated a number. The phone rang. Max, he thought. My God. Max.

"Hello?" But it was a woman's voice.

"Um, is Max there, please?"

Pause. "No."

It had been the sort of pause you get when the person answering the phone turns away and mouths are you here? and the person you want to talk to pulls a face and shakes his head. He frowned. "Are you sure?"

"Course I'm sure. It's not exactly a grey area."

"Sorry, of course. Um, when's he likely to be back?"

"Couldn't say. Who is this?"

His tongue was between his teeth, shaping the th of Theo. "Pieter van Goyen."

"What? Sorry, Pete, didn't recognise your voice there. It's Marge."

"Ah. Look, can you give him a message, please? To call me, ASAP."

"Sure. Where are you?"

Excellent question, referring back to an earlier question, your place or mine, which he hadn't been there for. "This number," he said, ignoring the ferocious scowl that earned him from whatever her name was, whose phone he was presumably using. Oh well, never mind.

"I'll be sure to tell him. Ciao, Pete."

He killed the call. She was glaring at him.

"Sorry," he said, handing her the phone. "But it's important."

"In that case," she said, pulling on a robe, "you should've said to call you back at home, because that's where you're going. Right now."

In the background he could hear the faint, mocking crackle of burning bridges. Oh well. "Yes, right, I'm sorry, I didn't think."

"For crying out loud, Pete. It's hardly rocket science."

"Pity. I'm good at that."

He headed for the door. She cleared her throat. "Far be it from me," she said, "but aren't you going to put some clothes on?"

"What? Oh, right." He looked round, and the dim amber light picked out a tangle of discarded garments, at least some of which must be his, in a heap by the window. Burning with the special embarrassment that only happens when you're dressing on suffrance before getting thrown out, he fumbled for the other sock, decided he could probably do without it, and dragged his pants on. Probably, he told himself, this wasn't how the scenario played out for Pieter. Still, he'd had the manual, even if it was only inside his head.

The phone rang.

She scowled at him. "You'd better answer it," she said.

He grabbed it from her outstretched hand. "Hello?"

"Pieter?"

Max's voice. For God's sake.

He straightened up fast. "Max?"

"Yes. Who is this?"

She was still glaring, so he turned away, facing the window. He looked up and saw the sky. It was dark blue, with a round fat full moon. "Max, it's me."

"What?"

"It's me, dammit. It's—"

And then his voice jammed in his throat and he couldn't breathe or move. Something horrible was happening to him. He could feel his face stretching, as though his nose and mouth were plastic and they'd melted, and someone was drawing them out like strings of fondue. His ears were changing too, the skin around them was being squeezed like a toothpaste tube into a strange, inappropriate shape. He wanted to yell, but his tongue was swelling in his mouth and,

for some unfathomable reason, he couldn't take his eyes off the moon.

"Pieter?" There was terror in her voice. "What the hell are you doing?"

Then he did yell, because something was bending his knees the wrong way, but inexplicably the bones didn't snap under the intolerable pressure, and now, instead of hinging forwards, they hinged back –

"Pieter!"

His eyes still fixed on the moon, he raised his hand (his visible right hand) until he could see it, on the edge of his field of vision. It was covered in thick grey hair, which doubled in length as he watched. Suddenly the blockage in his throat cleared; he breathed in, and the shock of a million new smells, all overwhelmingly rich and detailed and crammed with information, made his head swim. He gasped and, as he closed his automatically opened mouth, he felt long, sharp teeth digging into what had been his lower lip.

He heard her scream, but she needn't have bothered; the smell of her fear was so much more informative, and it made his mouth water. He watched her back away; she was clear when she moved, but when she stood still she was just a blur. He felt a strange twisting movement just above his bottom, and realised with a deep pang of embarrassment and shame that it was his tail, wagging.

A werewolf, for crying out loud. Pieter –

Meanwhile, though, the poor woman was clearly terrified out of her wits, and he couldn't allow that to continue. He decided against a reassuring smile, because when a man opens his mouth and displays all his teeth, that's fine, but when a wolf does it, the message thereby sent isn't quite the same. Never mind; a few reassuring words would have to do instead.

He said: Don't worry, it's perfectly all right, I won't bite you. What came out from between his teeth, however, was a clear, high-pitched howl that scared the life out of him until he realised it was him doing it. She, meanwhile, was scrabbling at the door handle, too paralysed with fear to make it turn. All in all, he couldn't help thinking, not an improvement.

(And all the while, a nagging little sub-routine in the back of his mind was asking; why a werewolf, Pieter, where the hell's the fun in that? A vampire, maybe; it's just possible to understand the kick to be got from the dapper clothes, the swirly cloak, the subdued lighting, the necks of swooning girls. But you'd have to be profoundly weird to want to spend your leisure time moonlighting, so to speak, as a part-time dog.)

"Hello? Hello? What the hell's going on there?"

The phone was now lying on the floor, with Max's voice bleating tinnily out of it. He grabbed for it, but he had nothing to grab with; his fingers had gone, and all he had was stupid little stubs with claws sticking out of them; sensational for ripping and tearing flesh, not so great for holding stuff with. Max, he shouted into the mouthpiece, don't hang up, it's me. But that wasn't what came out. His howl blended with the woman's scream in an unintentional form of counterpoint; then she managed to get the door open, and scrambled through it.

He rolled on his back and thrashed his head backwards and forwards until he could feel the phone under his ear. It was making the long drone that tells you the call is over. He whimpered, squirmed and kicked until he was on his feet – four of them, goddammit – and tried to figure out what to do.

Leave, you idiot. Get out, now. Fine. A slight twitch of his nose told him exactly where the doughnut was; also what it was made from, how old it was, who had baked it and when they'd last had sex – it was on the bed, slightly squashed but still in one piece. Wonderful. All he had to do was lift it up and look through the hole –

Um.

Making the wolf body do what he wanted wasn't easy. It was a bit like trying to fly a plane for the first time, blindfolded, with large jellyfish superglued to each fingertip. It wasn't like crawling on hands and knees, because his hind legs were convinced he was standing upright, and trying to make them walk in a straight line was like the first time you try and reverse a car with a trailer. He could smell the doughnut to within a thousandth of an inch, but because it wasn't moving he couldn't see it, only a vague pixillated area, like people's faces on TV when they don't want to be recognised. He tried to jump up on the bed, but the wolf's hindquarters were far more powerful than he'd anticipated, and he found himself sailing through the air and splatting himself against the opposite wall.

Come on, he ordered himself, you're a top physicist, you can do this. He sat (good boy, sit!) and tried to work out the geometry of the problem, but it proved to be harder than he'd thought. Something to do with a different degree of depth perception; distances were different, somehow, and the pre-loaded wolf software in his head kept telling him to forget about looking for the doughnut, just smell it and pounce. He tried that and ended up in the corner of the room, in the wreckage of a small table, with a lamp flex tangled round his neck like spaghetti on a fork.

No wonder, he thought, werewolves are so aggressive. Five minutes of this, and Gandhi would be ready to rip someone's throat out. He stood up – he was just starting to get the hang of the tail's function as an aid to balance – and fixed his full attention on the fuzzy patch that was the doughnut. Then he opened his jaws and got a firm grip on the bedclothes, while his mind ran the calculations: velocity, mass, vector, air resistance, delta V. It wasn't easy – being a quadruped, the wolf instinctively calculated in base four – but he made the best estimate he could manage, dug his claws into the carpet, and tugged hard.

It worked. The bedclothes shot towards him, the doughnut flipped up into the air and immediately became properly visible. He jumped, jaws open, tracking the doughnut in flight and adding forward allowance, not forgetting to compensate for the delay in its trajectory due to the Earth's gravitational field. There was an audible click as his teeth clashed together, but he was definitely holding on to something. He landed and squinted down his nose, and saw a semicircular blur in the foreground of his vision. All right!

The urge to chew was almost overwhelming, but he forced himself not to. He dug deep inside and excavated all he could find of Theo Bernstein. The next bit was going to be the tricky part.

He could hear voices: angry, scared, men shouting orders, the banging of car doors. Not the sort of thing you want to hear when you're a to-be-shot-on-sight monster cornered in a room with only one door. Think, he ordered his brain, but all it seemed capable of recommending was hurling himself at them and tearing them into tiny shreds, which he really didn't want to do. On the other paw – no, hand – he had to do something; in a universe where werewolves and humans coexist, it was only logical to assume that on every cop's belt there was at least one clip loaded with silver bullets. Nothing for it; he'd have one chance, and that'd be it.

Deep breath; then he lowered his head and lifted it sharply, opening his jaws to let the doughnut sail up into the air. It rose, spinning like a space station, and hung for a moment, waiting for gravity to notice it, rotating around its central hole. A fraction of a second later, the door was kicked open and the Special Werewolf Squad burst in. Through the sights of their silver-bullet-loaded machine guns they glimpsed a flying doughnut with what appeared to be a single red eye set in the middle like a ruby. Then they opened fire, but all they managed to shoot was a wall.

"Oh, that," Call-me-Bill said. "Yes, I remember him talking about it. He'd been at an airport, and the only book on the bookstall that didn't have a pink cover was *Twilight*. I guess that's where he got the idea from. Anyhow," he went on, before Theo could express himself fully on the subject, "I take it from what you just said that you're not quite there yet."

"No."

"Never mind." Call-me-Bill clicked his tongue and smiled. "Keep at it, I know you'll get there in the end."

Maybe traces of the wolf had come back with him through the doughnut's eye; he growled, and the hair on the back of his neck bristled slightly. "It's pointless," he said. "It's like there's some kind of built-in mechanism. As soon as I'm about to find out something useful, horrible things happen and I just about escape with my life."

"Could be," Call-me-Bill said thoughtfully. "Pieter was keen on his security protocols. I expect that when you find out the proper start-up procedure, that sort of thing won't happen any more."

He thought hard over the next few days. It had been Max's voice, no question about it. Why, though, was he surprised by that? If YouSpace could project him into parallel universes, then it followed that there were versions of reality out there somewhere in which Max hadn't died. If he'd survived, he'd be, what, thirty-six; in an infinite multiverse, there'd be an alternative world or two in which Max had never gone off the rails to begin with. Instead, he'd become a physicist, worked with Pieter van Goyen, was now leading a dull, blameless life advancing the sum of human knowledge. True, that version was so profoundly weird and unlikely that it also allowed for the existence of werewolves, but never mind. Infinity is infinite.

In which case, a sort of Max was out there, alive, well and modestly flourishing. Two points to consider. One, would such a Max be his Max in any meaningful sense? Two, did he really want to make contact with any variant or avatar of his infinitely annoying brother? Point one was a bit too metaphysical for his taste, but point two was well worth serious consideration. Provided Max was safe and well and capable of fending for himself, did he really want to see him again? Well?

There was a voice in his head that said: come on, he's your brother, dammit. There was another voice that said: exactly. The first voice said: he's your own flesh and blood. The second voice said: so's Janine. The first voice said: you and Max have got unfinished business to sort out. The second voice said: yes, I never did get around to ripping his lungs out with a blunt spoon, oh well, never mind. The first voice said: be serious, can't you? The second voice said: I am serious, believe me.

The first voice said: Max might know how to make YouSpace work. The second voice said: how unlikely is that? The first voice said: about as likely as werewolves. Exactly, said the second voice, and realised it had walked right into that one.

Yes, said the second voice, rallying bravely, but the only reason you want to get YouSpace working is so you could see if Max is out there somewhere. Not the only reason, said the first voice, but its heart wasn't in it; there's the money as well, if we can get this thing working and make it safe to use, it could be huge, it could be the biggest thing in home entertainment since –

The second voice said: hm.

Some money would be nice, the first voice said. Well, wouldn't it?

Put like that, the second voice had to concede, there was a case to answer. And besides, the first voice went on, it's not like you've got anything better to do, is it? I mean, before all this started you were sleeping on the slaughterhouse floor and shovelling guts all day, just to stay alive. This is better than that, surely. The second voice muttered something about lynch mobs and werewolves, but the first voice pretended it hadn't heard.

Yes, but it's dangerous. You could get –

Theo sat up straight. He'd remembered a scene he'd walked in on, something he hadn't been supposed to see: Mr Nordstrom lying on the floor in Reception, soaked in blood, with Call-me-Bill and Matasuntha and Mrs Duchene-Wilamowicz trying to stick him back together before he fell to bits. And what was it he'd said?

Mr Nordstrom was in his room: Room 3, third floor. It actually looked like a perfectly normal hotel room, right down to the upper half of a pair of trousers sticking out of the wall-mounted trouser press like a blue pin-striped tongue. Mr Nordstrom looked at him, scowled and said, "Yes?"

"Hi," Theo said. "Can I come in?"

"Why?"

"Because this isn't a hotel, I'm not a desk clerk, you're not a guest and the wine cellar sure as hell isn't a wine cellar."

Mr Nordstrom nodded. "I can let you have five minutes," he said, and pushed open the door.

As he walked in, Theo looked round until he saw what he'd been looking for. He recognised it at once, even though he'd never seen one before. Once he'd postulated its existence, figuring out what it'd look like hadn't been too difficult.

"Pieter van Goyen?" he asked, as he picked it up.

"Yes, Pieter made it, and for Christ's sake be careful with

it." Mr Nordstrom reached out a hand to take it from him, but Theo held it just out of reach.

"Let's see," Theo said. "You put the bottle in this end here, right? Yes, and then you plug this flex into the wall, and this end here—"

"That's the projector," Mr Nordstrom said. "It projects the image of an archway on to any flat surface, like a wall."

"And that's the way in?"

Mr Nordstrom nodded, and he handed the machine back to him. "And it works?"

"Oh, it works just fine," Mr Nordstrom said, taking it and putting it carefully down on a table. "So long as you've got pre-loaded capsules to go in it."

Theo smiled and sat down on the bed. "That's what all those bottles in the cellar are, aren't they?"

Mr Nordstrom frowned. "You don't know?"

"No, so I'm working it out for myself."

"Bill hasn't—?"

Theo shook his head. "Bill hasn't told me and I haven't asked," he said. "I have the feeling that truth percolates through Bill the way water does through the human kidney. It goes in as truth and comes out as something quite like it, but not exactly the same." He grinned. "Shoot."

"What?"

"Talk. Tell me stuff. Or I'm leaving."

Mr Nordstrom glowered at him, then sank down in a chair. "Fine," he said. "You know about the parallel universe project?"

"Let's assume I do. Bits. Who are you?"

"You don't – right, fine." Mr Nordstrom looked hurt. "I'm Jake Nordstrom, CEO of Heartless & Amoral Capital Investments. I've put three billion dollars into this."

"Ah."

"Which is awkward, since I only have two billion dollars."

"Ah."

"The other billion – well," Mr Nordstrom went on, "you get the idea. What else do you want to know?"

"The bottles."

Mr Nordstrom nodded. "Each bottle contains five standard hours in an alternative reality. You put the bottle in the machine, the arch appears, you walk through, you're there. Then you come home."

Theo steepled his fingers. "The other day," he said, "you were nearly killed playing with that thing."

"That's right." Mr Nordstrom didn't sound too bothered. "Somehow, I got the wrong bottle. I was expecting a Paris bordello circa 1898. What I got was heavy street-fighting in the closing stages of the Vietnam War. We're still trying to figure out how it happened."

"That may have been my fault," Theo said. "You see, I wanted to hide this" – he took Pieter's bottle out of his pocket, then put it back again, just in case Mr Nordstrom got ideas – "and the wine cellar seemed like a good idea. I moved a few bottles around. Presumably—"

"Yes." Mr Nordstrom breathed out heavily through his nose but didn't move. "You weren't to know, I guess."

"Quite. You'll notice, I'm managing to cope with the guilt pretty well. I figure, if people don't tell me things, I can't be expected to know them. Right?"

"That bottle . . ."

"Yes?"

"Bill told me. Pieter left it to you, in his will."

"So he did."

"Properly speaking, it belongs to me."

Theo sighed. "You know, if circumstances were just a little different, you could have the frigging thing. All it's done so far is try and kill me."

"Ah. Safety proto—"

"So people keep telling me, yes. But I need it, for now, anyway. When I've done with it—" He shrugged. "So, the sooner I get what I need, the sooner you get the bottle. Understood?"

Mr Nordstrom gave him the sort of look you might expect to see on the face of a tiger which, as it's about to pounce on a quivering fawn, notices that the fawn's just pulled a gun on it. "Sure," he said. "What else can I tell you?"

Theo shrugged, picked up the bottle-reader again, turned it upside down, and put it back on the table. "Mishaps aside," he said, "this gadget seems to work pretty well."

"It's all right, I suppose," Mr Nordstrom said. "But it has significant drawbacks. You see, it's not real."

Theo raised an eyebrow. "So?"

Mr Nordstrom smiled. "It's like the difference between sex and masturbation. This machine isn't that much better than your garden-variety virtual reality, except you don't have electrodes up your nose. What's in the bottles is five hours taken at random, remotely, from a parallel universe. You've got no control over who you are in it, what you can do there, what's going to happen. Pieter had some way of—" He paused and scratched his chin. "Well, it's a bit like drilling a hole in a barrel and siphoning off a bit of what's inside. He didn't have to go there, he could do it from here. But he was doing it blind. So, it's pot luck. You could get five hours of thrilling adventure and extreme sensual pleasure, or you could end up with five hours of speeches from a party conference. People aren't going to pay good money for that."

Theo grinned. "I can imagine."

"Also," Mr Nordstrom went on, "it's prohibitively expensive. One of those bottles costs best part of a million dollars, and Pieter couldn't figure out a way of bringing the unit cost down. That's why he decided we had to move on to phase two."

"YouSpace."

"I thought we'd decided we weren't going to call it that. Anyway, yes. That was the plan. This is really just a dead end."

"You seem to like it."

Mr Nordstrom laughed. "Well, I paid for it," he said, "I figure I might as well get some use out of it. But it's pretty poor stuff, mostly. Apart from the Vietnam thing, I've been to a fairy-tale world where dragons exist and magic really works . . ."

"Interesting."

"It should've been, yes. But I spent five hours as a clerk in their equivalent of the Inland Revenue. Or there was the one where women outnumber men six hundred to one. I had high hopes of that."

Theo's eyes widened a little. "Yes?"

"Oh, it was all right," Mr Nordstrom said, "if you enjoy spending a morning alone on a fishing boat in the middle of the ocean. No control, you see. You've got to be able to jump in at the right time and place, or the customer simply won't want it. It'd be like having a TV that insists on making you watch the Ring cycle live from Bayreuth."

Theo thought for a moment. "When you got back from Vietnam," he said, "you were in pretty bad shape."

"Ah." Mr Nordstrom smiled. "That time, we got lucky. Well, luckyish. Nineteen ninety-six Merlot. It's five hours in a hospital in the twenty-seventh century. Unfortunately we've only got a few bottles of that left." He pulled a face. "We started off with two cases. Like I said, you just don't know what you're letting yourself in for when you go through that arch."

Theo pursed his lips. "It sounds like hours of boredom punctuated with brief incidents of violence and fear," he said. "What's the fun in that?"

"Why do Canadians watch ice hockey? Something to do, I guess. Besides, like I told you, I paid for it. Well." He frowned. "I embezzled the money that paid for it. It'll be me that gets slung in jail when the auditors figure out where it's gone. So, why not?"

Theo wasn't listening. Something Mr Nordstrom had said had set off a chain reaction in his head. Pieter left it to you in his will. Perfectly true; but the YouSpace bottle hadn't been all he'd inherited –

A small bottle.

A brown manila envelope.

A pink powder compact.

An apple.

"And anyway," Mr Nordstrom was saying, "seventy million of that ninety-two million was what Fedeyevski, you know, the Russian oligarch, ripped off from some mid-eastern dictator, who skimmed it off oil company sweeteners, so who that really belongs to I'd really hate to have to guess . . ."

The apple; he could understand that, just about. An apple that stayed perfectly fresh after weeks in a safe deposit box; some kind of stasis field, presumably a by-product of Pieter's alternate universe research, intended to pique his curiosity and point him in the right direction. Sorry, Pieter, I was too dumb or too preoccupied to pick up on that one. But the powder compact –

"And twelve million of that is the CEO's cut from a pharmaceutical company's slush fund, which I was supposed to have invested in armaments R&D, there's this outfit in New Mexico who figure they've found a way round the small print in the Geneva Convention so they can produce mustard gas, provided they don't actually call it that . . ."

The powder compact. He could remember picking it up and slipping it in his pocket at the bank, but, after that, he couldn't recall having seen it. At the time, he'd subconsciously rationalised it as a souvenir or something, most likely a memento of some lost love. Now he came to think about it, though, Pieter hadn't been a lost-love kind of guy. If he'd kept anything to remind him of a long-ago moment of ecstasy and passion, it'd most likely have been a Snickers wrapper.

"I said," Mr Nordstrom growled at him, "what are you going to do?"

Excellent question. "Sorry, what?"

"Have you been listening to a word I've said?"

Theo nodded. "Several," he said. "But I skipped most of them, because they didn't seem to be important. Well, thanks, got to go."

He stood up, but Mr Nordstrom was quicker. He stood between Theo and the door, scowling horribly. "You've got to get this thing working, understand? All that money—"

"Oh, money," Theo said cheerfully. "Can't buy you happiness, you know. You look at my sister. She's got loads of it, and she's miserable as hell. Would you mind moving eighteen centimetres to the left? That's the ticket."

He raced back to him room. His jacket was hanging on a hook behind the door. He grabbed it and plunged his hand into each pocket in turn. He didn't find a pink powder compact, but he did come across something of approximately the same size and diameter. A hole.

He sank down in his chair and grinned, mostly because grinning is easier than crying, and he felt the need to conserve his strength. It served him right, of course. He should've realised the significance of the wretched thing earlier – assuming it had any, of course, and was something other than a receptacle for pink powder. Not that it mattered now. He had no idea how long the hole had been there, so the compact could be anywhere between here and the bank. He could look for it, of course, but that would require energy and enthusiasm. Right now, if energy and enthusiasm were money, he'd be Greece.

He looked at his room – the desk, the mountain of small paper darts made from Pieter's printout – and decided he needed to be somewhere else for a while. Just for a split second, he considered taking to the bottle. He could sort of see the attraction of a restful hour in an alternative reality at a time like this; a universe in which Pieter van Goyen had died at birth, for example, or a place in which the loudest sound ever recorded was a leaf drifting down to the forest floor. But there was no chance that the bottle would take him anywhere like that, so he wandered down to the lobby instead.

Matasuntha was sitting at the reception desk. Pointless, he thought, because now he knew what was going on, what was the point of pretending this place was a hotel? She turned to give him a reproachful look, then shrugged and smiled. "How's it going?"

"Nowhere," he replied.

"Not your fault."

"What?"

"It's not your fault you can't figure out how to make it work," she said. "If you ask me, Uncle Bill's being pretty unreasonable asking you to. But he's desperate, bless him."

"I know. All that money."

She nodded. "I don't think he'd be so worried if it was just his money," she said. "But it's mine, and Mr Nordstrom's, and Mrs Duchene-Wilamowicz'stoo. He feels responsible."

"Indeed." Theo perched on the edge of the desk. "That drip-drip noise you can hear is my heart bleeding." He sighed; he felt he ought to be hostile and unpleasant, but it was too much effort. "Losing lots of money isn't that big a deal," he said. "Trust me, I know all about it."

She grinned at him. "It's made you a better person, right?"

"Well, no. It's made me a thinner, shabbier, more miserable person stranded in a pseudo-hotel with a lot of lunatics because he's got nowhere else to go. Apart from that, though, it's not so bad. As you'll find out for yourself quite soon, I imagine."

"Thank you so much." She gave him a sort of mock-frown. "Well, I'll try and handle poverty with the same grace and dignity you're showing. Aren't I lucky to have such a splendid role model?"

"You bet. I had to make do with Gandhi and St Francis of Assisi, which probably explains why I'm such a mess." He stopped short and stared at her. "What are you doing?"

She looked up at him. "My face, what does it look like?"

"Where did you get that?"

"What, this?" She held up her powder compact for him to inspect. "Actually, I'm not sure."

"Think."

"Lancôme?" She squinted at the compact. "No, definitely not. Too pink. Now I come to think of it, I found it. On the floor, down in the wine cellar."

He swooped like a hawk and snatched it from her hand. "Hey," she said, but he was holding it up to the light, looking for –

"Do you mind?" she said. "I haven't finished with it yet. I've got one half of my face glossy and the other half matte."

"Start a fashion," Theo snapped. He'd found something. "In the drawer, there's a magnifying glass. Quickly."

She scowled at him, but he wasn't looking, so she fished out the glass and handed it to him. "Well?" she said. "What's so earth-shatteringly urgent?"

"P V G," Theo replied. "There, see for yourself." He handed her the glass and the compact. "Looks to me like it was scratched on with a pin or a compass point or something."

"Stupendous," she said. "I still don't quite see why I can't powder the other side of my nose."

"P V G. Pieter van Goyen." He breathed out slowly

through his nose. "It's mine," he said. "Pieter left it to me in his will."

"Fancy that. Other people get houses and money."

"It was in my pocket. I forgot about it till just now, and then I found there was a hole and it must've fallen through."

"Aren't you lucky I found it, then?"

"Yes," he admitted. "Thanks."

"You're welcome. Now can I—?"

"What? Yes, sure. No," he amended quickly, snatching it back from her. He felt for a catch or something to open it, but there didn't seem to be anything like that. Matasuntha watched him for a while, then sighed. "Give it here," she said.

"No. It's mine."

"All right, it's yours. Now give it here and I'll show you how to open it."

He hesitated. "I can manage."

"No you can't."

"I'm a quantum physicist," he muttered, scrabbling with his fingernails at the seam. "I can open a goddamn powder compact—"

"You're a man," she replied. He sighed, nodded and handed it to her. She opened it and gave it back.

"Thanks."

"No problem. Tie your shoelaces for you later, if you ask nicely."

He was staring into the mirror in the lid, but all he could see there was a bewildered idiot, and he could look at one of those any time he liked. He picked out the little pink sponge thing, but under it there was only pink powder. "Is that it?"

"What?"

"There aren't any hidden compartments of anything?"

"Well, usually there's a network of tunnels leading to the hinge. No, of course not."

He stared, then breathed out slowly through his nose, misting the mirror. "Sod it," he said. "I was so certain I was on to something." He looked away. The idiot was now a blurred idiot, and it was getting on his nerves. "I thought, maybe Pieter had hidden a message or something—"

"Look."

The mirror was demisting itself, and, as the cloud dissipated, he saw that the idiot had gone. In its place –

"The magnifier, quick," he snapped, but she was already holding it out. He grabbed it and screwed up his eyes to read the tiny words on the screen. "Is this normal?" he asked.

"No," she replied. "Move your head, I can't see."

It occurred to him that maybe he didn't want Matasuntha reading Pieter's hidden message to him over his shoulder. But it was too late to do anything about that now, not unless he wanted to make an official declaration of war. He moved his head a little. "You can read that?"

"Mphm."

"You must have eyes like a hawk."

"Small, round and yellow. You say the sweetest things."

He moved the glass closer, and the words came into focus. His breath caught in his throat as he made out –

YouSpace 1.1
User's Manual

"Oh, my God," Matasuntha said softly.

Theo moaned quietly. "I've been carrying it around with me all this time—"

"Correction," she pointed out. "You dropped it. I found it."

"Yes, well." He frowned. "What happened? Why didn't it do this when you opened it?"

She shrugged. "At a guess, DNA recognition security protocols. It only came on when you breathed on it."

"Ah, right." He stared a moment or so longer, then scowled. "It's stuck. How do I make it scroll down?"

"I don't know, do I?" She clicked her tongue. "You're the science wiz, as you never seem to tire of reminding me, you figure it out."

He tried. He prodded the hinges, stroked the rim with his fingertip, tapped on the lid, ran his fingernail over the mirror: nothing. The original message grinned back at him unchanged.

"This is hopeless," he snapped. "Useless frigging thing—"

"You're going to hit it now, aren't you?"

"What?"

"Well, like I said, you're a man. You've done the swearing-at-it thing, so hitting's obviously next. Try talking to it."

"Don't be so—" He stopped. Then he cleared his throat and said, "Next." Immediately, the screen cleared and was replaced by a column headed List of Contents. He didn't turn his head; but he could feel her smirk burning the skin on the back of his neck. "Right," he said. "Let's see." He moved the glass forward again and said aloud: "Getting Started."

The screen changed. The phone rang.

Theo froze. The phone rang again, and Matasuntha picked it up and said, "Hello?" He shook himself, and crouched forward to read the next menu, as Matasuntha said, "Who's calling please?" in her best receptionist's voice. 1.1. Security protocols –

"It's for you."

"What?"

She was holding the phone out for him to take. He scowled horribly at it. "Take a message."

"I don't think so."

He made a terrible sighing noise, then grabbed the phone and snapped, "Yes?"

"Theo Bernstein?" A man's voice, unfamiliar.

"Yes. Look, I'm really busy right now—"

"Armed police. We have the hotel surrounded."

YouSpace isn't the only place where a fraction of a second can last for years. A fraction of a second later, he managed to mumble, "You what?"

"Armed police. Throw out your weapon and come out with your hands up."

Matasuntha gave him a sympathetic shrug. A nice thought, but it didn't really help much. "I haven't got a weapon," Theo said.

"Oh. Hold the line, please."

"I think Uncle Bill's got a baseball bat you could borrow," Matasuntha whispered. "If it'd make things easier."

"Hello? Mr Bernstein?"

"Hello, yes?"

"Are you quite sure you haven't got a weapon?"

"Yes."

"In that case, come out with your hands up."

"But—"

Click, whirr. Theo stared at the phone, then put it back. "I thought you said—"

"Mphm. I thought so too. Maybe Uncle Bill changed his mind or something." She shrugged. "You'd better go out," she said. "I'll get Uncle Bill and we'll come down to the station and sort it all out, I promise."

He looked at her, then at the compact in his hand. He really didn't want to, but –

"Here," he said, "you take this. Look after it, all right?"

"Thanks." She took the compact, picked up the sponge and started dabbing at her nose. "Well, go on, then," she said. "Otherwise they'll be kicking the door down."

He turned to go; she stood up quickly, darted in front of him and kissed him hard on the mouth. "Try not to get shot," she said. "Promise?"

Theo nodded dumbly and headed for the door. He opened it and peered outside. There didn't seem to be anybody about. Feeling more than a little foolish, he lifted both arms above his head, like a Chicago voter in a show of hands, and walked forward.

"Hold it right there," said a voice. "And don't try anything smart."

There was something about the voice. It was doing its best, bless it; the words were rasped out and bitten off, with a definite attempt at menace, but the voice itself was high and thin. "Hello?" Theo called out. "Where are you, I can't—"

"Shut it," quavered the voice. "All right, throw down your weapons and—"

"Um," Theo said. "We've been through all that already, I haven't got any."

"Positive?"

"I think I'd have noticed."

A clump of the head-high nettles that grew up through the tarmac of the hotel drive parted, and two men came out. One of them was well over six feet tall, fair-haired, skinny, roughly seventeen years old and fitted with the biggest ears Theo had ever seen on a human being. He was eating a sandwich. The other man was tiny and somewhere between ninety and a hundred and six, and wore a jet-black curly wig that wasn't on quite straight. It made him look a bit like a freeze-dried Elvis. "Don't move," he said. "Or we'll drop you where you stand."

Theo stared at him. "You're not a policeman," he said.

The old man gave him a wounded glare. "Thirty years," he said. "Best motor pool superintendent they ever had. And once a cop, always—"

"And neither is he."

The old man looked sheepish. "That's my grandson," he said. "Learning the business, he is. Good lad, very keen."

The good lad finished his sandwich and produced another

one from his pocket. "Lunchbox, they call him," the old man said resignedly, "because he's always stuffing his face. But keen as mustard, really."

The boy gobbled the last mouthful and immediately switched to standby mode. Theo lowered his arms and massaged his triceps. "And you're not armed," he pointed out. "Are you?"

"Technically, no. But don't you try anything," the old man added quickly, "or he'll do you. He could snap your neck like a twig if he wanted to."

The boy carried on doing his impression of a radio mast. Theo sighed. "What's all this about?" he said.

"We got this for you." The old man poked his glasses on to the bridge of his nose, rummaged in his pockets and produced a matchbox, an appallingly filthy handkerchief, a crumpled paper bag and a folded sheet of paper, which he thrust in Theo's direction. "Summons," he said.

"What for?"

"Breach of injunction," the old man replied. Theo shrugged and stepped forward to take the paper; the old man shrank back, and Lunchbox stepped neatly behind him. Theo took the paper and unfolded it.

"Oh for crying out loud," he said. "*She* phoned *me*."

"None of our business," the old man whimpered, "we just do as we're told, so don't go getting violent. I just got to say the word, and he'll do you, like I said."

Lunchbox was unwrapping a chocolate Swiss roll. "Fine," Theo said. "So, Janine sent you."

"The plaintiff," the old man said.

Theo raised an eyebrow. "No offence," he said, "but I'd have thought she could've afforded better. I mean, look at you."

"Bugger that," the old man said angrily. "We're the best, we are. Twenty-five years in the trade, mate, seen it all, trouble is our business. For crying out loud, Arthur," he added, without turning round, as Lunchbox took out his phone and started texting furiously, "not when we're on a job, all right?"

Lunchbox took no notice. The old man shrugged. "Anyhow," he said, "you've got your bit of paper and that's due service, so there's no point trying any rough stuff, and even if you did—"

"I know," Theo said, "neck snapped like a twig." He folded the paper and put it in his pocket. "Have you two been watching me?"

The old man nodded. "Kept you under surveillance ever since you got here," he said. "Don't get out much, do you?"

"You'd be surprised," Theo replied. "Look, could you please ask Janine from me to make up her mind? Either she never wants to see or hear from me again, or she can call me, that's fine. Let me know what she decides, all right?"

"Not up to us, is it?" The old man looked vaguely shocked. "You don't catch us telling the client what to do. You want to ask her something, write to her lawyers."

"Ah. I'm allowed to do that, am I?"

"Try it and see. Anyhow, don't let us keep you. Come on, Arthur," he added, as Lunchbox unwrapped an individual pork pie. "You'd think he'd be as fat as a barrel, but look at him."

Theo went back inside. Matasuntha had gone, but the powder compact was still on the desk. For some reason, that made him feel happy. He picked it up and went back to his room.

She was there, sitting in the one chair, stirring a cup of coffee. "Hi," she said. "You didn't get shot then?"

"Apparently not. What are you doing here?"

As he said the words, he saw that there were two coffee mugs on the desk. "I had every confidence you'd beat the rap," she said. "Milk and sugar?"

"They weren't real policemen."

She grinned. "Thought not. I took the call, remember? And I don't think there's many ninety-year-old policemen, or at least not assigned to the SWAT teams. Who was it?"

He explained, about Janine and the injunction, and was rewarded with an appropriately bewildered look. "Your sister's having you followed?"

"I tell myself it's a sign of affection, like the way some cats bite you to the bone," he said. "But I don't think it is, really."

"No?"

"No. I think it's because she's sick in the head and fundamentally nasty. But what the hell, nobody's perfect."

She gave him a second and a half of sympathetic grimacing, then said, "You found the compact?"

"Yes."

"I left it," she said, "so you'd see how honest and trustworthy I am."

"And it's DNA-encoded so only I can make it work."

"That too. Well? Let's see it."

He sighed. On the other hand, said a small voice in his head, it'd be quite nice to have some company for a change, instead of having to do it all on your own. He thought about that, and could see the merit in it. That said, he recognised that small internal voice. It was the same one that had urged him to propose to his third wife. But, he rationalised, getting rid of her would be more trouble than letting her stay. "Here," he said, and put the compact on the table.

She was frowning. "That's so weird," she said, and he realised he'd been using his invisible hand. "Can't you put a glove over it or something?"

"Sure," he said. "But all that'd happen would be, I'd be wearing an invisible glove."

"Whatever." She shrugged, then gave him an accusing frown. "Oh, and you never answered my question."

"What? Which question?"

"Milk and sugar?"

"What? Oh. Yes."

"Milk and sugar."

"Yes."

"Help yourself." She pointed at a carton and a small bowl of sugar lumps, and bent her head over the compact. The mirror reflected her face, and that was all. "Presumably we can download this into a laptop or something," she said, frowning.

"No idea," Theo replied, putting his mug on the desk and leaning over her shoulder. "I think I'd better have the chair," he said.

"Fine." She stood up, and he took her place. Now she was leaning over his shoulder, and the ends of her hair were just touching his cheek. He tried very hard to ignore that. "Right," he said briskly, "here goes." He licked the tip of his index finger and pressed it to the glass of the mirror, which immediately brought up –

YouSpace 1.1
User's Manual

"Next," he said, and when the list of contents appeared, he said, "Getting Started." The screen cleared, a tiny red horse galloped across his face, and a page of text stood out on a white background.

"You need a PIN number," she said in his ear.

"Already done that," he said.

"What is it?"

He pretended he hadn't heard. "What I want to know," he said, "is how you cancel the security protocols. The ones that keep landing me in life-threatening situations."

The screen cleared again, the red horse cantered across the bridge of his nose, and –

6.2.1 Cancelling security protocols.

In order to cancel the security protocols, wish for the security protocols to be cancelled.

"Is that it?" she said.

He shrugged. "Is that it?" he asked. The screen cleared, and –

Yes.

"Oh well," Theo said. "Right, then. How do you choose where you want to go?"

27.6.13 Choosing where you want to go.

In order to choose where you want to go, choose where you want to go.

"We've got to try this," she said. "It can't be this easy."

"What, now?"

"Got anything else you really need to do?"

He frowned; then he took the bottle from his pocket. "I'm not sure about this."

"Don't you trust me?"

Her hair was tickling the side of his neck. "Do you get upset when people lie to you?"

"Yes."

"In that case, I trust you." The bottle was resting on a nest of his fingertips. "The hell with it," he said. "Where would you like to go?"

"I don't know. My mind's gone a complete blank."

"Mine too." He closed his eyes. Somewhere nice, he thought. Oh, and deactivate the security protocols.

Somewhere nice . . .

He opened his eyes and saw a seagull.

Somewhere nice. He could feel the warmth of the sun on his face, and sand under his bare legs. Lying beside him, in a bikini, was a woman with long red hair. He could only see the back of her head, but that was all he needed to see –

"Amanda?"

"Mphm." It was her all right. Nobody else in the world could do that soft sleepy grunt of utter contentment. Quickly he glanced down. His right hand was still visible, and there was a wedding ring on its fourth finger.

"Honey," he said, "what's the date today?"

She told him. She was quite right too.

He couldn't have moved if he'd wanted to. Somewhere nice . . . Somewhere, a time and a place, where the VVLHC hadn't blown up, he was still married to Amanda, and they were lying on a beach together in the sun. And – because that was what was so very different about YouSpace – it was real –

The sky, he noticed, was emerald-green.

She grunted again, and he realised he was staring at her right shoulder blade. He'd always been ridiculously fond of it, though when he'd mentioned the fact she'd accused him of being weird. And all he'd done was think somewhere nice.

If it's real, he thought, I don't have to go back.

He lifted his head, just to make sure. He didn't recognise the beach, but it was everything a beach should be: a perfect interval between the blue sea and everyday life, a thin golden ribbon of calm joy. So, if the VVLHC hadn't blown up, presumably he still had his job. And – his mouth went suddenly dry – the money. Maybe, if he was quick, there'd be time to get all the money out of Schliemann Brothers before the crash –

About fifteen yards away, he saw the back of a man's head, just visible over the top of a colossal sandcastle. It was blond and curly, and it had enormous ears. He blinked, then shifted a little, just enough so that he could see round the side of the sandcastle. Sure enough; there were Lunchbox, in swimming trunks, eating a bacon, lettuce and tomato roll, and the old man, in a raincoat and a scarf, screwing a long lens into a camera body. Well, he thought, almost perfect. But close enough can be good enough, sometimes. Behind him, he heard a crunch, which he recognised as the sound of someone biting into an apple.

Amanda growled and turned over. He smiled at her. She smiled at him. And then her face froze.

"Theo," she said, "who the hell is that?"

She was looking past him. He wriggled round, and saw Matasuntha, wearing two pieces of string and biting into an apple. She smiled, waggled her fingers and said, "Hi, Theo."

Amanda moved like a cobra. She sort of slithered and reared up out of the sand, and the look on her face was one he'd seen ever so many times before, though never quite at this level of intensity.

"Um," he said.

It was what he'd always said, and it had never done him any good. In fact, he remembered, it was surefire guaranteed to make things much, much worse. "Well?" she snapped. "I'm waiting."

"I'm Mattie," Matasuntha said. "Who are you?"

There's never a doughnut when you want one. "I'm his wife," Amanda said, in a voice you could've preserved mammoths in. "For the time being, anyhow."

Matasuntha frowned. "You never said you were married. I'm not sure I'd have come here with you if I'd known you were—"

"Theo—"

And then he saw it: fifty yards or so down the beach, under a canvas awning, a man in a white T-shirt, frying doughnuts over a portable gas ring. "Just a moment," he said, swooping and grabbing Amanda's handbag. "Won't be long."

When he got back, twirling the doughnut round his finger, Amanda and Matasuntha were more or less where he'd left them. Amanda snatched her bag back from him and lashed out at his ankle with her foot. He swerved to avoid her, darted behind Matasuntha, who turned her head to look at him, and smiled at them both. "I'm going now," he said.

"Theo," Amanda said. "If you leave now, don't bother coming back, you hear me?"

He ignored her. He was smiling straight at Matasuntha, who finally got the point. "Theo," she said. "How do you—?"

"Ah," he said. "That'd be telling. Well, have fun, you two. I feel sure you're going to be great friends."

The doughnut was a circular frame for a miniature of Matasuntha Suddenly Worried, but not for very long.

He just had time to sit down and put his feet up on the desk. Then she was back.

"You bastard," she said.

She looked different: pale, thinner, hair tangled and bedraggled, fingernails bitten short. "Hi," he said, as she dropped to the floor, sat with her back to the wall and pulled her shoes off. "You got home all right, then."

"Eight weeks," she spat at him. "Eight weeks I was stranded there, you total—"

"But you figured it out in the end, I take it."

She shrugged. "I don't know. I was rummaging about in a dustbin looking for something to eat, there were some cakes and things, I picked one up to see if it was edible, and here I am. No thanks," she added bitterly, "to you. How could you?"

Theo gave her a pleasant smile. "Oh, I don't know. Maybe the same way you made Amanda believe we were having an affair. You might care to explain that."

"Isn't it obvious?" She was massaging the soles of her feet. "If I hadn't, you'd have stayed there, right?"

"Yes," Theo said crisply. "And why the hell not?"

"Because we need you here." She picked up her shoes and threw them across the room. "Here, give me the compact, I need to do my face. I spent four nights sleeping on a bench in the bus station."

He hesitated, then snapped the compact shut and tossed it to her. She caught it one-handed, without looking. "I may forgive you," she said, "if you bring me food, right now. And coffee," she added, with a catch in her voice. "You know how long it's been since I tasted coffee?"

So he went to the kitchen, where he found Call-me-Bill busy at the stove.

"Potato dauphinoise," he said. "How's it going?"

Theo hesitated. Of course, he'd get all the news from Matasuntha soon enough. "Hopeful signs," he said.

"Great." Call-me-Bill poured cream into the pan from a large jug. "How hopeful?"

"Cautious optimism."

"That could mean anything," Call-me-Bill said. "Like, if it wasn't for cautious optimism, I wouldn't bother getting out of bed in the morning."

Theo opened some cupboards until he found a tin of corned beef, which he opened and turned out on to a plate. "Any coffee going?"

Call-me-Bill nodded at a pot on the stove. "Oh, there was a phone call for you. I took a message."

"Who from?"

"I think he said his name was Captain Zod."

There was a crash as the plate hit the floor. "Captain—"

"Zod. That's an Albanian name, isn't it?"

Theo stooped, gathered up the corned beef with his fingers and stuck it in his pocket. Then he grabbed the coffee pot and ran out to Reception. On the desk was a little yellow sticky: Captain Zod, and a number.

He called the number. It rang and rang.

"What kept you?" she demanded, as he returned breathless to his room. "I was just about to start gnawing the edge of the desk."

He fished the corned beef out of his pocket. It had crumbled into three clods, which had acquired a surface coating of grime and bits of fluff. She didn't seem to mind. "Is that coffee?" she asked with her mouth full.

"Yes. Damn, I didn't bring a cup."

"No matter." She grabbed the pot, put the spout in her mouth and tipped her head back. After a long interval of glugging she sighed and wiped her mouth and chin with her wrist. "I think," she said, "I'll be all right now. It was close, but—" She stopped, and frowned. "Who are you calling?"

Theo had the phone to his ear. It rang and rang. After fifty-six rings, he gave up.

"Well?"

He sighed and perched on the edge of the desk. "When I was a kid," he said, "about ten years old, my brother was eleven, we were nuts about *Star Trek*."

"Not to worry," she said. "You grew out of it, that's the main thing."

"We used to play this game," Theo went on. "I was Captain Sherman of the Dauntless. My brother Max was Captain Zod of the Fremulan star destroyer Ob."

"Really?"

"Mphm." He handed her the yellow sticky. "The thing is, it was a secret. Nobody else knew."

She looked at him. "That's Uncle Bill's writing."

"Yup."

She frowned. "What about your sister? She must've known."

He shook his head. "She hated *Star Trek*. *Star Wars* fan."

"That would explain a great deal. So, not her, then."

"No."

"And you tried the number."

"No reply."

She took another swig from the coffee pot, then stood up wearily. "Mind out of the way," she said, elbowing him gently aside so she could sit down at the computer. "Now then."

"What are you doing?"

"Tracing the call." She played a piano concerto on the keys, and a screen full of numbers appeared. She glanced down at the yellow sticky and typed. "Uncle Bill has friends in low places. Right, here we are. Your call – oh."

"What?"

"Came from a payphone in a bar in Caracas," she said. "Sounds to me like someone's jerking your chain. You sure it couldn't be your sister?"

He shook his head. "Thanks for trying." He sighed, and took her place on the floor. "Why is it," he said, "I'm never here to take my calls?"

"You ought to get a cellphone," she replied, tapping keys. "You want the address of the bar?"

"Not particularly." He played back how he'd said that in his mind, and added, "Thanks for offering, but I don't think it'd help."

"He left the number. He wants you to call him back."

"I doubt it." He could feel his temper slipping away from him, like the last glimpse of land before it sinks below the horizon. "I think someone's been to a parallel universe where he's still alive. He's got Max to tell him about the *Star Trek* thing, and now he's playing mind games with me."

"Why would anyone—?"

"I don't know, do I?" The bump and wrench, like a tooth being pulled from an anaesthetised gum, had been his temper finally letting go. He didn't particularly want to be angry right now, but it seemed he had little choice in the matter. "It's a hypothesis," he said. "That's what scientists do. They think up something that sort of fits the facts, and then they see if they can prove it. If they can be bothered. I'm not sure I can, to be honest."

"He's your brother."

"Was my brother. And you know what? I never liked him much." He paused. It had never occurred to him to wonder why, until now, when the answer suddenly turned up on his mental doorstep. "He cheated."

"What?"

"He always cheated," Theo said. "At everything. Even when we were playing *Star Trek*. There was a bit where you had to throw a dice, and his always seemed to roll off the table on to the floor, and he'd pick it up and say it was a six before I had a chance to look." He listened to what he'd just said, and laughed. "Not just that. He cheated at every damn thing, and he still always lost."

"Sounds like he's trying to cheat at being dead."

"He'll lose. He always loses. You know, if sometimes he won, I could've forgiven the cheating."

There was a pause; then she said, "None of this would matter if it's really just someone pretending to be him."

"That's cheating too," Theo said furiously. "Like when he paid some guy to pretend to be him in an exam. Now he's getting someone to do his living for him."

"Did he pass the exam?"

"No. The guy he paid didn't know spit about higher maths. Got sixteen per cent."

Matasuntha was nodding slowly. "I can see how you'd lose

patience with someone like that. Still." She shook her hair out of her eyes. Amanda used to do that, but not quite the same way. On balance, he preferred how Matasuntha did it. "He's dead. That's final. Nothing can change that."

There are moments in every great scientist's life when a light comes on, illuminating shapes previously indistinguishable in the dark. Sometimes there's apples and bathwater and tramcars to give a little nudge, though they usually miss out on the glory; when did you last see a copy of The General Theory of Relativity, by A. Einstein and A. Tramcar? Theo wasn't like that. "What did you just say?"

"What? Well, just that your brother's dead, and nothing can—"

"I'm not so sure about that."

She gave him a sweet and simple smile. "Right," she said. "He's not dead. Instead, he's emigrated to the Isle of Avalon, along with Elvis and JFK and Princess Di, and every now and again he pops over to Caracas to make annoying phone calls. Next he'll be talking to you from your microwave. Come on, Theo. They found an actual body."

"No, they didn't. All they found was one tooth."

She frowned at him. "I'd forgotten that. You think—"

"He was mixed up with some nasty people," Theo said. "And he was Pieter's ex-student. And Pieter was ridiculously kind-hearted sometimes and a lousy judge of character. He liked some really uselcss people."

"You mean your brother?"

Theo nodded. "I never could understand why. I mean, Max never did any work, he spent his whole time boozing and doing drugs and demonstrating a totally unreconstructed attitude towards sexual politics. Basically, all he did was buy drinks for people and have a good time."

"And you can't see why Pieter liked him."

"No, it's a complete mystery. But . . ." Theo closed his

eyes for a moment. "Consider this. Max is at the end of his rope, he needs to get far, far away and make himself very hard to find. Pieter, meanwhile, is at a crucial point in his experiments with alternative universes. He needs to send someone over there, to see if it works. Like putting a monkey in a spaceship and blasting it into orbit. Actually, that's a very good analogy."

"Max was the monkey."

"Mphm. Not quite as intelligent and far less self-disciplined, but considerably more expendable. They fake Max's death, and Pieter sends him to Somewhere Else."

Matasuntha frowned thoughtfully. "And there he still is."

"Presumably."

"Then who's phoning you from a bar in Caracas?"

The history of science doesn't record the moments of hesitation and doubt; as, for example, when Archimedes' wife yelled at him for slopping water all over the bathroom floor, or Mrs Newton said, "So an apple fell on you. So what?" You have to extrapolate that there were such moments, and the genius in question rose above them and moved on. "I don't know, do I? Maybe it's someone who knows what happened and thinks I know where he is. Maybe he's found a way to come back."

"YouSpace."

One of only three in existence. Leaving two unaccounted for. "Maybe."

She took the lid off the coffee pot and peered inside. "This isn't any good," she said. "Can a human being die of caffeine deprivation? Let's not find out." She went out, and came back a few minutes later with a fresh pot, two mugs, a carton of milk and a sugar bowl.

"Better now?"

"Marginally," she replied, pouring coffee into both mugs. "Milk and sugar, right?"

He nodded. "You think Max may have got hold of a YouSpace bottle?"

She lifted her mug and gobbled energetically. "Well, you can find out easily enough," she said.

"Can I?"

"Sure. Go there."

"What?"

She gave him an even-you-should-be-able-to-understand look. "Tell the bottle you want to go to the universe where Max is hiding out," she said. "Simple."

Two voices in his head; one shouting Yes, the other yelling No. "Hold on, though," he said. "Multiverse theory."

"Excuse me?"

He took a moment to think it through. "Multiverse theory states that in an infinite multiverse there's a universe for every possibility. Thus, if I formulate the possibility of a universe where Max is hiding out in YouSpace, it'll exist and I can go there. Question is, would it have existed if I hadn't conceived of it, or am I calling it into existence just by thinking about it?"

"Oh, for crying out loud."

Fair comment. "I was only trying to think of every possible outcome, just in case—"

"Drink your coffee before it gets cold."

For once, the bad thing he was being urged to forestall had already happened; the coffee was tepid, and she'd put in too much sugar. "I still don't like the idea," he said.

"You don't want to find out if your brother's still alive?"

"I meant the whole idea of fooling around with alternate realities," he said, though she'd been closer to the mark than he felt comfortable with. "I mean, for all we know there could be the most appalling consequences we haven't even begun to imagine. Trust me," he added bitterly, "I know about what happens when things go wrong."

She looked at him. "Yes, and every time a butterfly flaps its wings, there's a risk of hurricanes in Kansas. What are you going to do? Tour the Amazon with a can of bug spray? If everybody thought like you, nobody'd ever do anything."

"Yes, but—"

"And what happened to you," she went on mercilessly, "was because you made a mistake. You got it wrong. You screwed up. Try not to screw up this time, and it'll be fine."

The foul taste in his mouth was probably only the coffee. "Fine," he said. "That's your considered judgement on messing around with the nature of causality."

"Pieter van Goyen thought it was OK."

And there she had him. He closed his eyes, then opened them again. "All right," he said. "But first I'm going to do the maths. Properly, not rushing. And then I'm going to check it, five times, maybe six. And then—"

He yawned. "Sure," she said. "That'd be sensible. Maybe you should get some rest first, you look dead beat."

She had a point. He did feel tired. In fact, for two pins he'd close his eyes again and take a nap right now. "I think I might just lie down for a moment," he said.

"You do that."

He looked across the room to the bed. It was ever such a long way away. The floor, on the other hand, was much more conveniently situated, and he could get there simply by falling. So he did that.

"Sorry," she said, reaching over him and picking up the powder compact. He started to protest, but a yawn took control of his face and stretched it till the skin burned. "Happy landings," she added, as she picked up the bottle. "Now, then—"

"Wha—?"

"Take care," she said (and her voice came from a long way

away, filtered through a lot of thick soggy mist, which swirled inside his head.) "And no hard feelings, OK?"

In the beginning was the Word.

Hardly likely, is it? In order for it to be a word, it would've had to belong to a language; otherwise it'd just have been a random, meaningless noise – zwwgmf, prblwbl, bweeeg. You can't have a one-word language; words need context. Therefore, of all the things that could possibly exist in isolation at the Beginning, a word is the least plausible. All right, back-burnerise the Word for now, let's try something else.

In the beginning was (say) the Mouse; fine, except that unless some primeval crumbs happened along pretty soon thereafter, it'd quickly have become first a hungry, then a dead mouse, and the universe would've fizzled out almost immediately.

In the beginning was the Lump of Inert Rock; better, except that everything we know about rock tells us that it's the end of a process rather than the beginning. It's cold lava or dried, compressed mud, or the shells of a billion tiny shellfish squashed up tight. In the beginning was the Lump of Inert Rock is like saying the empty packet came before the breakfast cereal.

In the beginning was the Ball of Burning Gas; now perhaps we're getting somewhere, because you might argue that bits of that ball exist to this day, in the form of stars, scattered about the place like a teenager's possessions, and that could be taken as some kind of corroborative evidence of something, even if it's just that God is eternally fifteen years old.

It's still a hell of an ask, though. Since nobody was around to see it, how can anyone really know? Walk into any courtroom and listen to the witnesses, and you'll soon learn how very, very difficult it is to prove anything, even with the help of the time-burnished machinery of the law and half a dozen extremely well-trained and well-paid lawyers. The ball-of-burning-gas idea, like the lump-of-rock, mouse and word hypotheses, basically relies on blind faith; and, if you're going to believe in something, the word is a far more elegant and intellectually pleasing choice than a boulder or a fireball.

Even more elegant, not to mention more democratic and egalitarian, would be to say that they're all true. If we posit a multiverse rather than a mere universe, it's not only possible but logically inevitable. In multiverse theory, everything exists (somewhere, over the rainbow, presumably, but the best academic authorities have yet to tackle the issue); the only limitation on perfect clarity is our limited ability to imagine. But, just because we can't conceive of a functional word- or mouse-originated universe, that doesn't mean to say it isn't out there somewhere, six degrees up and three left from the indigo band. That'd be like saying that a black cat in a coal cellar doesn't exist until we turn the light on.

He woke up on a rocky plateau overlooking a dark blue lake. Overhead, a white sun blazed in a cloudless sky. For some reason he was wearing what looked like a pilot's flight suit. His head hurt.

He stood up, felt dizzy and sat down again. That bloody woman, he thought. Drink up your coffee before it gets cold.

Standing up was a little bit easier the second time. He looked around, but there was nothing to see except blue water on one side and brown rock on the other. No doughnut vendors anywhere.

Why the hell had she done it? Payback, because he'd left her stranded on the beach with Amanda? A plausible enough hypothesis, except she wouldn't have had time, surely; she'd only been gone a few minutes, to refill the coffee pot. Long enough, he decided. And there was no need to speculate in depth about her motivation in marooning him, because he'd done precisely the same thing to her, not so long ago. A spectacularly dumb move on his part, he couldn't help thinking, except that at the time he'd been so angry –

In the distance he could just hear a faint sound of voices. So that was all right, then. In a moment, when he'd caught his breath and finished thinking murderous thoughts about Matasuntha (he didn't want to have to rush that part) he could stroll over and find the statutory doughnut seller, and then he could leave. No problem.

That was, of course, the difference. He knew how to get home, and she knew he knew. He'd left her to figure it out for herself, and she'd only made it back by sheer fluke. Considered in that light, her stranding him here was little more than a prank, and he probably deserved it. In fact, he was only feeling angry because she'd made a fool out of him. How she'd laugh when he got back – in her terms, a fraction of a second after he'd left – and how helpful it'd be to their working relationship (he told himself) if he took the joke in good part. Query: would he feel this way if she hadn't kissed him before he went off to face the old man and his idiot grandson? He thought about that, and decided not to think about it any more.

He yawned. It was really quite pleasant here. The sun was bright, the rocks were warm and the blue water of the lake was crystal-clear. You could spend a lot of money and waste many, many hours being publically humiliated in airports and end up at far worse places. A beach umbrella and a long, cool drink would be nice. He wished for them, but that didn't seem to work. Well, it wouldn't, would it? Once you were here, the experience was real. That was the whole point.

A cool breeze, just enough to be refreshing, blew across the lake, ruffling the surface. Because time didn't pass inside YouSpace, he could stay here as long as he liked and lose no time at all. He lay back on the rock and absorbed sunlight like a lizard for a while. There would definitely be a public demand for this product, he decided, if it could be made to work safely and reliably. Or even if it couldn't, he reflected; after all, Microsoft did OK, and their stuff –

The voices were getting closer. Damn, he thought. He was enjoying the solitude, and a large party of tourists would spoil the mood. He looked round. It was a huge lake; plenty of space for them and for him, without anybody having to share. He stood up, but he couldn't see anyone. The voices were coming from just over the horizon, where a gently inclined sand dune slouched against the sky. From the top of the dune, he ought to be able to see where the tourists (Germans, probably, or Italians, if the racket was anything to go by) were coming from.

The sand was a bit awkward to walk on, but he made the top of the dune without undue effort and looked across a wide valley. About two hundred yards away was a cornfield, on the edge of which he could make out tiny figures. They didn't seem to be heading his way. In fact, they seemed to be happily engaged in playing in the corn; an odd thing to do, even for holidaymakers. His curiosity piqued, he set off down the slope to get a closer look.

Halfway down, he made out an interesting sight: a red and white striped awning, in the middle of nowhere. As an old YouSpace hand, he reckoned he knew what that was: the local doughnut outlet. Not a bad idea, he told himself, to get his doughnut now, while he thought of it, just in case there was a problem. He altered course a few degrees and headed for the doughnut stall.

He'd covered half the distance when it occurred to him to look back towards the cornfield. He could see the people rather more clearly now. There was something weird about them. For one thing, they were dressed oddly. He stopped for a more deliberate view. They looked like actors or fashion models – they were all young, strikingly tall and uniformly blond – but for some reason best known to themselves they were dressed up as cavemen. Also, they weren't playing in the cornfield. They were robbing it.

Curious behaviour. They were grabbing handfuls of wheat ears and stuffing them in their mouths. There was, of course, some logical explanation, probably involving a New Age colony or a music video, but the image was disturbing enough to make him quicken his pace towards the doughnut stall. After all, the werewolf scenario had seemed normal enough until the full moon butted in and spoiled everything. He'd had a nice relaxing half-hour, he decided, and it was time to go. No point in ruining an otherwise pleasant experience by hanging around too long or getting involved.

He broke into a gentle trot and arrived at the doughnut stall very slightly out of breath. Under the shade of the awning he could see a long trestle table covered with trays of doughnuts, eclairs, cream horns, buns, cupcakes and flapjacks, which reminded him that he'd skipped a meal or so recently. He couldn't see a stallholder, so he reached for the nearest doughnut –

Something slammed against the side of his head, and he dropped forward, banging his chin on the edge of the table as he fell. The world had gone all soft and runny, and he heard a voice, above and behind him.

"Damn humans." The voice sounded more weary than angry. "It's time they did something."

"In broad daylight too."

Um, he thought, but he wasn't up to doing anything more energetic than lying still and groaning.

"It's wearing clothes."

"I swear they're getting worse." He heard the sound of a cellphone being dialled. "Hello? Put me through to Pest Control, will you? Thanks, I'll hold."

"Never seen one in clothes before."

It wasn't sounding good. With a substantial effort, he wriggled round and saw two animals.

No he didn't. At first glance he'd taken them for animals, but that was because he'd just had his brains shaken up by a powerful blow to the head. Not animals. The word zoomorph floated into his mind from somewhere (he couldn't help being impressed at his own resilience; how many people could come up with zoomorph a few seconds after being bashed stupid?) Animal-shaped, but not animals as such. More like –

"Look out, it's coming round."

Cuddly toys. Two of them. One of them was bear-sized and sort of bear-shaped, except that no bear ever looked anything like that, or ever had fur that distinctly unnatural shade of orangey-lemon, or wore a little red jacket two sizes two small for its shoulders, or had eyebrows. By the same token, the other one wasn't a tiger, because tigers don't stand upright, or have anomalously humanoid jaws and pink noses. That was it, he suddenly realised; that was what was so terribly wrong. They weren't just unnatural, or anatomically impossible. They were cute.

"Yes, hello?" The tiger was talking into a phone pressed to its ridiculously implausible ear. "Yes, I'm calling from the doughnut stand at BY129865, we've got a rogue human, could you send a team to—? Right, yes. Only, hurry, will you? We've got it cornered, but it looks pretty lively. And . . ." The tiger hesitated. "It's wearing clothes. Yes, really. OK. Thanks."

Then Theo recognised the voice, and it was as though a door had opened, or a light had come on. He knew these creatures. He'd known them all his life.

"Tigger?" he said. "Pooh?"

The bear nearly jumped out of its skin. The tiger froze. "It's talking," it whispered.

"Like hell it is," the bear replied, in a high, brittle voice. "It's just barking."

"It said our names."

Slowly and cautiously, the bear reached out and grabbed a hammer. "Some of them can do that," it said, trying to sound casual and failing dismally. "People train them to repeat names and simple phrases. My cousin Paddington had one once that could sing all four verses of 'Bear Necessities'. Didn't mean it could talk, though. Didn't make it intelligent."

The tiger was grimly maintaining eye contact. "If it moves," it said, "bash its head in."

This isn't right, Theo told himself, it's people dressed up in costumes, like at Disneyland. But he knew instinctively that there was nothing even remotely human under the fur. Another memory stirred; a film, this time. His mouth was completely dry, as if he'd slept with it open.

Behind him, he could hear screams, and gunshots. The bear relaxed. "It's the patrol," it said. "They'll be here in two shakes."

"You think they'll be able to catch it?"

"Maybe. Or maybe they'll just shoot it, who gives a damn?"

I do, Theo thought, and remembered he was a scientist and a mathematician. Let x, therefore, be the time needed for a hammer y held in the paw of a bear P to move the distance Z between the bear's chest and the head of a human T moving from A to B. Assuming an average speed s for the hammer and s1 for the human –

He did the equation, and got the result s1 = 2.16 metres/second. He wasn't sure he could move that fast, but it was probably worth a try.

"Hey, it's getting away!" the tiger yelled as he streaked past. He felt the slipstream of the hammer just behind his ear, but not the hammer itself. He ran.

As he powered up the slope, he realised his tactical error. Instead of running away, he should've lunged forward, towards the doughnuts. Damn. There was, however, no chance of going back. Obese and anatomically unworkable it might have been, but the bear had amazingly fast reflexes. Without the element of surprise and the additional element of horrified bewilderment, he'd never have made it past them. He put his head down and made himself run faster, until he reached the top of the slope, where he lost his footing in the soft sand, slipped and fell. Hauling himself to his feet, he looked up and saw –

The humans on the edge of the cornfield were under attack. A dozen enormous jet-black mice, on horseback, were riding round them, shooting from the saddle with carbines. Some of the mice wore red trousers, the others had blue dresses and enormous pink ribbons on top of their heads. The humans were screaming, scattering wildly as the mice pressed home their charge. One or two of them fell and didn't get up.

Disneyland, Theo thought. Oh shit.

Over to his left he heard a mechanical rattle, the sort of noise you get when you rack the action of an automatic rifle. He turned and saw a horse standing a few yards away. On its back was a huge black mouse, blue-skirted and pink-ribboned. It was looking straight at him down the barrel of its gun.

"No," he yelled. "Minnie, no!"

The mouse froze. A slow frown creased its incongruously

pink forehead. Theo opened his mouth to shout again, but something hit him so hard he was knocked off his feet. The sound wave, moving appreciably slower than the bullet, reached him just before he blacked out.

His head hurt.

He opened his eyes and saw that he was in a cage; wrist-thick bamboo poles lashed together with rope. Very gently he put his hand to the side of his head. His hair was sticky.

Across the room, on the other side of the bars, an enormous duck was sitting on a stool. It wore a blue sailor jacket and a bonnet with dangling ribbons, and it was nursing a rifle. It was looking past him, as if trying very, very hard not to see him.

"Excuse me," Theo said.

He could've sworn he saw the duck wince ever so slightly. Apart from that, it didn't move, just carried on staring dead ahead as though its life depended on it.

"Um, excuse me. Donald, isn't it?"

This time, he saw the duck's hand-like wing tighten on the grip of its gun, and maybe its huge oval eyes widened a little; anyway, they hadn't blinked once. All in all, he got the impression of a duck determinedly not hearing voices coming from a human in a cage. The plan he'd been working on withered and died. This wasn't a duck that could be reasoned with.

A surge of pain in his head made him lie back, and he stared at the bare wooden rafters for a while, trying to fight off the panic that was gradually, relentlessly, working its way into his mind. He'd never really thought about death before, except in a vague, objective kind of a way. He was aware that it existed, but so did Omsk; both of them were distant, irrelevant and not particularly attractive, and he had no intention of visiting either of them. The thought that he might die alone, pointlessly, unnoticed, unaided and quite possibly at the paws of viciously predatory cartoon characters would never have occurred to him, and he was entirely unprepared to deal with it.

But then, dealing with stuff had never been his strongest suit; he'd always preferred to run away, and right now he could see no reason to change the habits of a lifetime. The obstacles in his path consisted of a bamboo cage and an armed duck. What, he asked himself, would Einstein have done? Or Niels Bohr?

"Help!" he shouted. "Guard!"

The duck didn't move.

"Guard!" He paused, then added, "Aargh!"

The upper and lower mandible of the duck's beak were moving slightly, as if it was muttering something to itself over and over again under its breath. "Help!" he yelled. "Heart attack! I'm dying!"

Slowly, the duck turned its head and stared at him. It didn't need to say anything; words, indeed, would probably have ruined the effect. "Sorry," Theo mumbled, "false alarm. I'm fine now."

The duck gave him another second and a half of the stare, then moved its head away and carried on contemplating the opposite wall. Theo lay down on the floor and curled up in a little ball. It seemed the sensible thing to do.

Some time later, he heard voices and looked up. The duck was on its feet, rigidly to attention, wing-feather-tips brushing its temple in a millimetre-perfect salute. The two newcomers didn't seem to have noticed. One of them, a blue-grey donkey with a lilac belly and a bow tied to its tail, was taking readings with some kind of instrument that whirred and flinked tiny red and green lights. The other, a tiny deformed-looking pig with the body of a pink wasp, was filling a syringe from a brown glass bottle.

"Leave us," the donkey said to the guard, which saluted again and left the room. The pig squirted a tiny drop of something blue from the needle of its syringe, and put the bottle away in a big black bag.

Really not good, Theo decided. He reckoned he could probably take the pig, if he caught it unaware, but the donkey was big and mean-looking, and the guard would be only a shout away. He had no idea what was in the syringe, but he'd been around the scientific community long enough to figure that it probably wasn't anything he'd want inserted in him. He stayed where he was and tried to look as though he was fast asleep.

They came across and stood a few feet from the cage, gazing at him as though he had little dotted lines tattooed on his skin. Then the pig said, "I don't know, it looks perfectly normal. Its hair's not the right colour, but that could be ordinary genetic mutation."

"The clothes," replied the donkey. "Where'd it get them?"

The pig leaned forward to look. "Some kind of military uniform."

"Not one I recognise. And the shoes. Look at the shoes. What kind of feet do you suppose would fit in shoes like that?"

Valid point. The animals he'd seen so far either had bare, rounded stubs at the end of their legs, or else wore footwear like plump cloth bags tied at the ankle. How any of them could stand up without falling over was a mystery to him. He tried to shuffle his feet under him, but it was clearly too late for that.

"The shoes," the donkey went on, "clearly weren't made for any sentient species known to us. But they were made. They appear to be the product of sophisticated manufacturing techniques, maybe even mass production. Therefore somebody made them." It glanced down at its scanner again, and its frown deepened. "Ask yourself," it said. "Who made them, and what for?"

The pig rubbed its vestigial chin. "Some people like to dress up their pet humans in quaint costumes," it said. "Maybe—"

"And it talks," the donkey said grimly.

The pig looked up at it. "Surely not."

"That was what the report said." The donkey looked at the door to make sure it was closed, and lowered its voice. "Surely you can grasp the significance. A talking human, wearing unfamiliar clothes and bizarre footwear, suddenly appearing out of nowhere. If it means what I think it means . . ."

The pig looked terrified. "The Catastrophic Origin theory," it whispered. "But surely—"

"That's what we're here to find out," the donkey said. "Now, I suggest we start by administering the hydroglycobarythane, followed by an incremental series of electric shocks."

In spite of himself, Theo made a soft whimpering noise. Both animals turned and stared.

"I think," the piglet said in a horrified whisper, "it can understand what we're saying."

The donkey nodded slowly. "So do I," it said. "Of course, we can test that quite easily using tetracyanic acid and a simple thumbscrew."

"Um," Theo said loudly, "sorry to interrupt but I couldn't help overhearing, and if it'd save you the trouble, then, yes, I can understand you. Well, not the hydroglycowhatsit stuff, because I'm not a chemist, but the general sort of gist of things, no problem—"

The donkey's head shot up. The pig made a terrified

squealing noise and scrabbled in its bag, producing a small but efficient-looking handgun. "Let's shoot it now," it said quickly. "We can get all the answers we need from dissecting it."

"Calm down, Professor," the donkey said quietly. "And put that thing away, for now at least. I assure you, the cage is quite robust, and the guard is close by. We're in no danger."

"Physical danger, perhaps not," the pig muttered darkly. "Spiritual danger, on the other hand—"

"Come now," the donkey said, and its lips curled in a sort of smile. "You're supposed to be a scientist. It's not going to eat your soul, you know. That's just a story."

The pig seemed a little bit calmer, but it was still holding the gun. "Quite," it said. "And as a scientist, I know that folk tales and legends often have a solid foundation in fact. If that – that thing makes the slightest attempt to cuddle me, I'm shooting first and rationalising afterwards, is that understood?"

"Of course. If you have to shoot, though, try and avoid the head. I'm particularly keen to examine the upper hippocampus, and I can't do that if you've spattered it all over the opposite wall."

"Um, excuse me," Theo yelped desperately, "but really, there's no need. I'm a scientist myself, I can tell you what's inside my head without you cutting it open."

The pig squeaked loudly and darted behind the donkey, aiming the gun at Theo between the donkey's ears. The donkey opened its mouth once or twice, then said, "You're a scientist?"

"It's just some words it's picked up listening to its owners," the piglet muttered. "I say shoot it now, before it does something to our brains."

The donkey wasn't listening. "You mustn't mind my colleague," it said slowly, "he had a strict orthodox upbringing, you know, stories about Before, when humans ruled the world. I won't let him shoot you—"

"Thanks," Theo gasped.

"Unless absolutely necessary. Tell me," the donkey went on, gently easing the pig backwards with one of its hind legs, "where are you from? Come to that, what are you?"

"Um."

"I'm sorry?"

"It's a long story," Theo said cautiously. "Are you by any chance familiar with Everett's work on relative state formulation?"

"That does it," whimpered the pig. "I'm going to count to three, and then—"

"Be quiet," snapped the donkey. "Say that again, will you?"

"Relative state formulation," Theo repeated. "It's the basis of modern multiverse theory. Put simply—"

"Multiverse," the donkey said slowly. "Now there's a word you don't hear every day."

"I've never heard it," squeaked the pig. "It sounds silly. How can you have a multiuniverse? I mean, the universe is like, everything, right? So how can you . . . ?"

Without looking round, the donkey lashed out with its hind legs, hitting the pig square in the chest and hurling it across the room. There was a soft thud as it smashed into the wall; then it dropped to the floor like a cushion and lay still.

"Now then," the donkey said briskly, swishing its beribboned tail, "we don't have much time. I'll have to think of a plausible story to tell the guard, but that won't be a problem. Between you and me" – the donkey was nibbling at the ropes that held the bamboo rods together – "the ducks aren't the pinkest ribbons in the drawer, if you get my drift."

Theo backed away until the cage stopped him. "What are you—?"

"Breaking you out of here, what does it look like?" the

donkey said with its mouth full. "Unless you want to stay here and get vivisected by the scientific community. Sorry, I neglected to consult you on that. Well?"

"On balance," Theo said, "no, not really. But—"

"That's all right, then," the donkey said, spitting out a mouthful of chewed-up fibres. "Now, if you'd be so kind as to give the bars directly ahead of you a good sharp kick."

There was a crash as the cage collapsed. A couple of bamboo rods bounced off Theo's head, but they were light enough not to bother him; just as well, since his head was spinning enough already. "Well," the donkey said, nuzzling through the pig's pockets, "are you coming or not?" It teased out a fat wallet with its teeth and tossed it through the air at Theo, who dropped it. "In there you'll find a security pass," the donkey said. "That's it, the bright blue one. We'll need that. Now," it went on, "get the pig's clothes and put them on."

The pig was dressed in a sort of giant nappy. "That's silly," Theo said. "I'll never pass for Piglet. The ears are all wrong, for one thing."

The donkey sighed. "Fine," it said. "Stay here." Then it frowned. "You called it—"

"Piglet," Theo said. "From *Winnie the*—"

The donkey gave him the most intense stare he'd ever been subjected to. "*Pooh*," he said. "Yes. You're going to have to tell me how you know that. But not now," it added, pulling itself together. "Get dressed, then put Piglet in the cage, what's left of it. And keep your mouth shut, whatever you do."

A little later, while Theo struggled desperately to keep the nappy from sliding down round his ankles, the donkey went to the door and pushed it open a crack. "Guard."

Theo couldn't see the duck, but he could hear its voice. "Sir."

"There's been a dreadful accident," the donkey said. "The

human broke out of its cage and attacked us. I managed to subdue it, but my colleague is badly hurt. I shall take him to the Owl for medical treatment. You must stay outside this door and not let anyone pass until I return. Is that understood?"

"Sir."

"Very good. Carry on." The donkey backed into the room. "Right," it whispered, "In the pig's bag there's a roll of bandage. Wind it round your head and face, and then I'll help you with the arms and legs. Quickly."

"And remember," the donkey added, as Theo, mummified except for a narrow slit for his eyes, scrambled on to the donkey's back, "you're dying, so groan a bit. But don't overdo it."

The duck didn't even look at him as they went past. Various bears, rabbits, baby deer, bipedal gun-toting dogs and generic small cuddly mammals turned to stare at them as they crossed the compound, but the donkey kept calling out, "Medical emergency! Radiation!" as they passed, so they had a clear run as far as the checkpoint gates, which were guarded by two elephants with huge ears, little yellow caps and shotguns.

"Medical emergency," the donkey said.

The elephants didn't move. "Papers."

"My colleague here was standing right next to the reactor core when it blew," the donkey said. "He's suffering from massive radiation exposure. For pity's sake, don't get too close."

"Papers."

"He's already starting to mutate," the donkey said. "I need to get him to the university, we've got equipment there that might save him. Don't look," he added, as one elephant leaned forward, "it's horrible."

The elephant stretched out its trunk and twitched aside a fold of bandage from Theo's face. "My God," the elephant said, "he's right." It shrank back and shouldered arms. "Pass," it said.

Half a mile from the compound, the donkey stopped, looked back and said, "Right. We're clear. Get the hell off me."

Theo slid to the ground and started clawing at the bandages, which had been driving him crazy. It took him a minute or so, but eventually he was free of them, at which point he became painfully aware that he was wearing nothing but the pig's bulbous pink nappy. He cringed, and tried not to think about it.

"Come on," the donkey said. "We've still got a long way to go."

They walked in silence for a while. The donkey was tense, forever craning its neck to look around for pursuers or patrols. "I figure we've got an hour's start on them," it said eventually. "Then someone's going to come looking for Piglet and me. And then the candy floss is really going to hit the fan."

Theo had been meaning to ask. "Why?" he said. "Why did you rescue me?"

The donkey gave him a long, sad look. "Because you're not the first sentient talking human I've come across, is why," he said. "And because I'm a true scientist. I may hate the truth with every bit of kapock of my stuffing, but I can't deny it's true. It's a little thing called integrity, I don't suppose you have it where you came from."

"Well," Theo said. "Actually, yes. Sort of."

"Really? You surprise me." The donkey stopped and glowered at him. "I'm inclined to doubt that," it said.

"Oh?"

"Oh yes. Because," it went on, "if sentient talking humans really exist, then it's more than likely that there's a grain of truth in the old stories. In which case," he added, "I ought to kick your arse from here to the Hundred Acre Wood." An agonised expression passed over his face. "Look," he said, "I've got to ask. Are you him?"

"Who?"

"Christopher Robin."

Theo shook his head slowly. "Not as such, no."

The donkey breathed slowly in and out. "Thought not," he said. "Too old, for one thing. Also, I resolutely refuse to believe in the existence of Christopher Robin. You could say that's the cornerstone of my very being."

"Nope," Theo said, "I'm not him."

"Ah."

"But he was real," Theo couldn't resist adding. "He grew up and ran a bookshop somewhere in the west of England. Died about fifteen years ago."

The donkey groaned and said nothing for a while. Then it stopped again. "And the rest of it?" it said. "Is it true?"

"I don't know. What are you talking about?"

The donkey looked away. "That once upon a time, your kind enslaved my kind, treating them as toys and playthings, until finally – after the Great Machine blew up and laid waste your entire civilisation – we rose up, burnt what was left of your cities to the ground and slaughtered you by the million, until there were so few of you left that you wandered into the woods and mountains and reverted to wild, senseless animals. Well?"

"The first bit, yes," Theo said. "Sorry about that, by the way. The other bit, um, not yet."

The donkey looked at him. "Not yet?"

"Not where I come from."

"But that doesn't make sense. All this happened hundreds of thousands of years ago."

"Um," Theo said.

The donkey stared at him for a moment, then suddenly nodded. "Multiverse theory."

"That's right."

"You're from a different—"

"Yup."

"Ah." The donkey looked faintly relieved. "So what you mean is, you're from somewhere that might, if a highly speculative theory is correct, be a universe parallel to our own in certain respects, but which almost certainly differs from it in others, and might therefore differ in regard to the existence of Christopher Robin and the historical reality of the so-called Age of Degradation. Yes?"

"I suppose so."

"Excellent." The donkey cheered up immediately. "So long as it's just a theory, I can more or less live with it. Right, let's get moving. We haven't got all day, you know."

They followed a winding path down to a long, broad, sandy beach. Behind it a steep granite cliff reared up to the sky, from which a cruelly hot sun beat down on them. They walked across the sand for about a mile, and came to the mouth of a cave.

"In there," the donkey said, nodding his head at the cave mouth. "Right, this is where I leave you." He hesitated, then added: "Good luck."

"What about you?" Theo said. "You can't go back. What are you going to do?"

The donkey shrugged. It was the gesture he'd been born for. "Don't worry about it," he said. "It's only me, after all. I expect I'll wander aimlessly around for a bit and then I'll die."

Instinctively Theo reached out a hand to give the donkey a consoling pat, but it shrank away and scowled horribly at him. "Don't even think about it, human," it growled.

"Sorry. I was just—"

"Yeah, right. Next thing you know, you'll be wanting me to sleep on your pillow. Now get out of my sight, before I decide to turn you in to the authorities."

Theo lowered his hand. "I understand," he said. "And I'm sorry, I didn't think. Thank you," he said. "You're a true scientist, Eeyore."

The donkey's lower lip quivered. "You're just saying that because I sacrificed everything to save your worthless life."

"Yes."

"Think nothing of it," the donkey said gravely. "Well, so long."

Theo turned quickly away and plunged into the cave. It was dark, and it took him a while for his eyes to adjust. Eventually he saw a rocky floor and a roof fringed with stalactites. And a suitcase.

He blinked. It was a nice suitcase; pigskin, with chromed buckles. It had been around. There were scuff marks, and a couple of flight labels. On the lid, level with the handle, were initials in gold: MCB.

The C stood for Cornelius.

A little voice in his head said: I really wish I wasn't wearing a pink nappy at this point. He ignored it, cleared his throat and said, "Max?"

No reply. He took a step forward and tried to open the suitcase, but it was locked. He sighed and, feeling suddenly and comprehensively weary, sat down on the floor.

"Theo."

He jumped up and spun round. A tall, thin figure stepped out of the shadows at the back of the cave. There was a sudden dazzling flare of flame, clouded by drifting blue smoke. The man had lit a cigar.

"Max?"

"Hi, Theo. What kept you?"

Max stepped forward. He was wearing an elegant white silk suit, a white shirt and two-tone fawn and brown shoes. His hair – a trifle longer than it used to be – was beautifully cut and combed, but uniformly silver-grey. It suited him, of course. Everything always suited Max. If he slipped and fell in a slurry pit, it'd only be a matter of time before slurry started featuring heavily in the latest collections from Diesel and Ralph Lauren. A cigar the size of a torpedo jutted out of the corner of his mouth.

"Max."

"Theo."

"You fucking evil fucking bastard," Theo said. "Why aren't you dead?"

Max removed the cigar and smiled at him. "Pleased to see you too, Theo. And don't call me a bastard, it's disrespectful to our mother." He took a long pull on the cigar and threw it away. "What is that thing you're wearing? It looks like a—"

"Max."

"Yes, I think we've established that. Sit down, for crying out loud, and have a drink."

Without looking, Theo backed away until he tripped and landed on his backside. Max leaned back into the shadows and produced a canvas director's chair, in which he perched gracefully. From his inside pocket he drew a silver flask. "Remy Martin," he said, unscrewing the cap. "You can't get it here, of course, so I'm having to make it last. No? Suit yourself." He took a neat swig from the flask and put it away. "Well," he said, "I'd like to say how good you're looking." He frowned. "But I'm addicted to the truth, so I can't. You look like shit. How's Amanda?"

It took Theo a moment to remember the name. "She left me."

"Pity. She was too good for you, of course."

"How the hell do you know about Amanda? You died before we got married."

"I try and take an interest," Max replied. "Also, I'm not dead." He yawned, and took out a cigar case. "I tried to call you but you weren't there."

"Max, you complete shit," Theo said gently, "what are you doing here?"

Max lit his cigar with a gold Zippo. "I guess you could say resting. That's what actors call it, when they can't get a job. Fortunately—" He puffed at the cigar. "My needs are few and simple. The Seven Dwarves bring me food." He smiled. "They seem to have got it into their heads that I'm Walt Disney, which makes me sort of like God in their eyes. Of course they're sworn to secrecy, so they won't tell the others. And the donkey knows about me, of course. I like him, he's a doll." Smoke streamed down through his nostrils. "I expect you'd like me to tell you how I got here."

"I think you should," Theo replied. "And then I can kill you."

Max smiled indulgently. "You're just saying that," he said. "Well, let's see, where to begin?"

"How about my favourite part? The bit where you died."

"Ah, but I didn't." Max smiled. "That was just make-believe. You may recall, I'd got myself into a bit of a jam."

"You faked your own death."

Max opened his mouth, put a finger under his top lip and lifted it to show a gap. "I keep getting false ones fitted," he said, "but every time I move somewhere new, they vanish. No dentists here, of course, or at least not human ones. Actually, I don't think they have teeth here. In fact, you hardly ever see them eat. And I don't think they ever shit. Probably don't have the right plumbing."

"You faked your death," Theo repeated. "Then what?"

Max sighed and tipped ash from his cigar. "Well, I was at a bit of a loose end, really. My family had more or less disowned me." He gave Theo a reproachful look. "I couldn't really trust any of my so-called friends not to give me away to the bad guys. All I could think of was Pieter van Goyen. He'd always liked me, you know. I wasn't sure what he could do for me – like, college professors don't have a lot of money – but I had this feeling that a smart guy like that would be able to think of something. And he did."

"YouSpace."

Max shook his head. "We decided not to call it that," he said. "Too sort of bland. But yes. Or, at least, the first prototype of the technology that'd lead to YouSpace. Pieter warned me, he said it was all mostly theoretical and there was no way of being sure it'd work, let alone getting me back again. But I didn't really have too many options at that juncture. So I said yes, please, and off I went."

His cigar had gone out. He paused to relight it, then went on: "In retrospect, I was really lucky. I mean, I could've landed up anywhere. But where I ended up was this kind of cute agrarian idyll, sort of like Switzerland only warmer. A peasant family took me in, fed me and looked after me and all. I stayed there for about three months. But then there was a spot of trouble."

Theo waited a few seconds, then asked, "What?"

"The daughter got pregnant. Shame, she was a nice kid. Anyhow, I had to get out of there in a hurry, so I wandered around for a bit, ended up in a biggish town, got a job in a bank. Well, they called it a bank. It was all pretty medieval. Abacuses instead of computers, you know? I did my best to fly straight, but I guess the temptation was too much for me. I'm forced to conclude I have a rather low temptation threshold. Not my fault, I was born that way."

"You stole from the bank."

Max shrugged. "I'd been a tad unlucky playing cards at the tavern," he said, "and, really, it was like taking candy from a kid. Only some bastard must've told on me, because they found out and I landed up in jail. That was bad," Max added, with a shiver. "Positively medieval. Well, I had a bit of the money still stashed away, but when I tried to make a deal with the warders, they couldn't understand what I was talking about. Do you know, in that universe they had no idea of the concept of bribery and corruption?"

"You soon taught them, though."

"You bet. Once they'd caught on, they thought it was a great idea. After that, I travelled for a while. You know me. Restless."

"One jump ahead of disaster, you mean."

"Restless," Max repeated firmly. "I hate to vegetate. Actually, I'd hooked up with this sort of band of pirates when Pieter found me. He'd figured out the next step in the technology, you see; a stable gateway."

Theo frowned. "What, you mean like horses could go in and out?"

"Stable," Max said sternly, "as in staying put for more than ninety seconds. So, first thing he did was come and look for me. It took him a while, but he was able to trace me by scanning the resonance pulses for my unique molecular key. Just as well he showed up when he did, actually, because by then the pirates were sort of miffed at me, for some reason."

"People can be so unreasonable," Theo muttered darkly. "What did you do, lose their ship in a poker game?"

"Anyway," Max went on, "Pieter gave me this." From his jacket pocket he produced a bottle. At first glance, it looked like one of those miniatures you get in hotel minibars and on planes. When Theo looked more closely, however, he saw there was a tiny little globe floating near the neck of the bottle. If he peered really close, he could just make out Australia.

"Cute, isn't it?" Max said. "The globe is in fact the acceleration chamber. Originally it was going to be a clock, and the particle diffuser was going to be a little cuckoo that came out on a spring. But the first time he tried it, the cuckoo accelerated to three times light speed and shot down a News

International satellite on its way out of planetary orbit. The bottle's safer."

"That's a—" He realised there was no technical term, and for a moment he was struck dumb. A scientist without jargon is like a glider on a still day. "A YouSpace module," he improvised. "Like the one I've got."

Max's eyebrows shot up. "You've got one?"

"Well, yes. Pieter left it to me in his will."

"Pieter's dead?"

Years ago, Theo had been trapped at the bar at a conference by an obnoxious semiconductor expert who insisted on telling him about a strip club in Amsterdam where the girls all wore shimmery sort-of-thin-stuff (the right word was diaphanous, but Theo couldn't be bothered to tell him) dresses; and when the lighting guy did some clever thing with the overhead spots, the light changed direction and it was as though they weren't wearing anything at all. Annoyingly, that was what Max reminded him of at that particular moment; the angle had shifted just a little, and suddenly there was Max, deprived of his layers of camouflage and armour, a small, frightened man who's just realised that the last bus has left without him. "Yes," Theo said. "Didn't you know?"

"He can't be. I saw him only a week ago."

"I saw him die," Theo replied quietly. "He was killed by space aliens in a bar. They shot him with a ray gun. There was nothing left."

"My God," Max said. "And you're sure it was . . . ?"

"Him? Oh yes. Remember, I knew him much longer than you did. It was Pieter all right. The real Pieter. He's dead all right."

"Christ," Max said. "That's bad. You know what that means?"

"His second Nobel prize will have to be posthumous?"

"I'm stuck here, is what it means," Max said furiously. "I

can't get out. That thing" – he jabbed a finger at the miniature bottle – "has packed up, it doesn't work any more. Brilliant for holding ten cc's of the liquid of your choice, fuck-all use for anything else." Suddenly he frowned, then turned his head and stared at Theo with a desperate look on his face. "Just a minute, what am I saying? You got here, right? So, you must have a working YouSpace bottle. Well?"

"Yes."

"There you are, then." Joyfully, Max punched his left palm with his right fist. "You can get us both out of here. I always knew there was some purpose to your existence."

"Not got it with me, though."

"What?"

Theo smiled at him. "Matasuntha – you know her? Right, fine. Matasuntha put knockout drops in my coffee and stranded me here. The only way I can get back again is if I look through the hole in a doughnut."

A tragic look appeared on Max's face. "Theo, please," he said, "don't crack up on me now, you're all I've got. What are you talking about?"

"A doughnut," Theo repeated calmly. "Or, apparently, a bagel, though I haven't tried that yet. And don't ask me how or why, but it does work. You hold it like this." He mimed holding up a doughnut. "And you look through the hole in the middle, and, bang, you're home."

Max's face had crumpled into a little sad mask. "Theo, if you're jerking me around, so help me I'll strangle you. A doughnut."

Theo nodded. "Apparently it's sort of hardwired into the OS that, wherever I go, there's always a shop or a stall selling doughnuts within easy walking distance of where I arrive. Actually, that's true, at least so far. There was one here."

"So? Why didn't you—?"

"Staffed by Disney creatures," Theo said. "They called the

police, or whatever the killer mice are supposed to be. That's how I got caught."

"You idiot," Max said sadly, and for a split second Theo actually felt guilty, until he remembered who he was talking to. "Doughnuts, for crying out loud. I've been here over a year and I've never seen any doughnuts."

Theo shrugged. "Get your dwarf buddies to bring you some," he said.

"I could ask them, I guess," Max said doubtfully. "Mostly they bring bread and cheese. You have no idea how heartily sick I am of bread and cheese. Tell you what," he went on, "soon as we get back, you're going to buy me a five-course dinner at Delmonico's. I can tell you right now what I'll have, I'll start with the—"

"You'll be lucky," Theo interrupted him. "I'm broke."

"Bullshit. You got my share of Dad's money as well as your own."

"Ah," Theo said, and told him about Schliemann Brothers. Max stared at him for a moment, then uttered a long, low groan. "You moron," he said. "Of all the half-witted—"

"Max—"

"All right." Max sat up straight and clenched his hands into fists. "Us fighting won't help anything, let's just concentrate on getting out of here, and then we'll figure out what to do." He frowned, then said, "How about Janine? She hasn't lost her share, has she?"

"No. In fact, she's—"

"That's OK, then," Max said. "Janine'll see me right, she always liked me best. So, doughnuts." He clasped his hands together, index fingers pressed to the sides of his nose; his habitual thinking pose. It always made you think you were in the presence of genius in action, which shows how gullible people can be. "In case the dwarves can't provide, we need a Plan B. You say there's a doughnut stall close to where you came in?"

"Yes, but there are these psychotic Disney animals—"

"For Christ's sake, Theo, don't be such a worrywart. You always did make such a fuss about doing the simplest little thing. No wonder Dad used to get so mad at you all the time."

"Dad did not—"

Max raised his hand. "Not to mention," he said reproachfully, "always having to have the last word. I guess it was unrealistic of me to imagine you'd have changed since I saw you last. Still, you ought to try. You owe it to yourself."

"Max." Theo stood up slowly. "You know, I've been thinking. I'm not sure about this parallel-universe-alternate-reality thing. I don't see how it could possibly work."

Max sighed. "Theo," he said, "this is not the time for—"

"Because," Theo went on firmly, "if multiverse theory is right and there really are an infinite number of realities out there someplace, then somewhere there'd have to be a universe where you aren't a shallow, self-obsessed, feckless, obnoxious, arrogant, poisonous little shit. And I just can't believe in that. Moons made of green cheese and worlds supported in the branches of giant ash trees, yes. A bearable Max, no way. It's just not possible. So long."

"Where are you going?"

"To get a couple of doughnuts, where d'you think?"

"Fine," Max grunted, relighting his cigar. "Don't be all day about it."

Outside, the sun was skin-flayingly bright and hot, conspiring with the white sand to burn the inside of his eyelids red raw. He stomped along the beach for a while, trying to remember which way he'd come, until he came to a massive outcrop of rock jutting out almost to the edge of the sea. He walked round it, and saw a statue.

Once, he guessed, it must've been twice the size, but drifting sand had buried it up to its waist. It was a mouse: twenty feet tall, with circular ears and a cute button nose the size of a diving bell, its lips drawn back in a frozen, sneering grin, its long, elliptical eyes scoured blank by centuries of drifting sand and sea spray. Theo stood and gazed at it for a moment, then shrugged, gave it the finger and trudged on.

After an unspecified time, he staggered, dropped to his knees and rolled over on to his side, unable to go any further. The sea was only a yard or so away, and it looked cool and soothing; he wriggled across to it crab-fashion and plunged his aching feet into the water. The salt bit into the cracks and scratches; the pain startled him out of a vague, resigned doze he'd begun to drift into, and probably just as well. Falling asleep out in the open under a sun that hot would be one way of ending all his troubles, but there might still be a better one.

There was something bobbing in the water, a yard or so out. He watched it for a while, unable to summon up the mental energy to identify it. Then a wave lifted it a little, and he realised it was a bottle. That made him laugh out loud. It would be perfect, he decided, if there was a message in it, but of course there wouldn't be. It was just a bottle: junk, litter, pollution. If he was home, or if he gave a damn about this rotten planet, he'd feel a spurt of moral indignation about that. Right now, though, he simply couldn't be bothered.

But the bottle stayed roughly where it was, bobbing energetically up and down like a dog with its lead in its mouth, demanding to be taken for a walk. A bottle, he thought. Actually, a useful commodity. Fairly soon he was going to get dehydrated. If by some miracle he found a source of fresh water, a bottle would come in handy. Groaning self-indulgently (but why not? Nobody there to see) he crawled into the delightfully cool water and reached out until his fingers closed around the bottle's neck. He lifted it up and looked through it. There was something inside.

A message in a bottle. Oh please.

On the other hand, why the hell not? He unscrewed the cap and shook the bottle; the wedge of brown paper slid forward and lodged in the neck. He looked around for something to winkle it out with, but the seashore was depressingly short on toolkits. In fact, the only artefact beside the bottle within visual range was Piglet's nappy, secured with a safety pin . . .

Even then, it took him ten minutes' worth of patient and not-so-patient fiddling, scrabbling, teasing and high-octane bad language before he was able to get his fingernails closed on a tiny corner of paper and draw the message out. He dropped the bottle and the pin and unfolded the message. It was a map.

To be precise, it was a map of the beach; because there was the Mickey Mouse statue, there was the rocky pillar, and there was a cross, correlating exactly to his present position, marked U are Hear. Proceeding from the cross was a dotted line, which sprawled and wandered around the beach in a series of long, lazy curves until it reached a crudely drawn O, above which was written donuts.

He looked back at the beach and saw the dotted line. It was composed of the footprints he'd made getting there and retrieving the bottle. The O marked the spot where he'd stood and stared up at the statue. He scowled at the map, then screwed it into a ball and threw it away. Being rescued is one thing, but nobody loves a smartarse.

Gathering the folds of the nappy in his right hand (he couldn't now find the safety pin) he retraced his steps until he was standing once again in the shadow of the colossal mouse. A seagull perched on the mouse's left ear spread its wings and launched itself into the air, complaining bitterly about the inconvenience. He knelt down and started scrabbling in the sand with his fingers.

Almost immediately, he connected with something. It proved to be a small tin box, olive-green, on whose lid was stencilled in white, property of US Government, along with a serial number and a hazmat symbol that suggested the box had once contained weapons' grade plutonium. He was inclined to doubt that, somehow. He flipped off the lid and saw a doughnut.

Gingerly he prodded it with his forefinger. It was soft enough to be fresh, and still faintly warm, glistening with frying oil. He picked it up, taking care to keep it sideways on, so he wouldn't inadvertently look through the hole. He hesitated. His moral duty was to take it back to the cave, where Max was waiting. He hesitated a bit longer.

He's your brother, said his conscience, but even it didn't sound terribly enthusiastic. I know that, he thought, and I'm glad he's alive after all, I guess. But he's all right here, isn't he? I mean, the Seven Dwarves are bringing him food and presumably doing his laundry, or else how come his suit is so spotlessly, immaculately white, and at least here there aren't Mob hitmen gunning for him, like there would be back home. Would I really be doing him a favour, taking him back into harm's way? Surely it'd be better, kinder, to leave him here for now, go back, figure out a way of taking him from here to a more suitable parallel universe, where he could be safe and happy and a very, very long way away . . .

Well?

His conscience didn't reply immediately. Perhaps it was wrestling with its conscience, and so on and so forth, like two mirrors facing each other. That was the sort of thing that happened when Max was involved. When it finally spoke, the best it could come up with was Yes, but.

That, however, was enough. He sighed, stood up, took a firm grip on the hem of the nappy and headed for the rocky outcrop.

As he rounded it, he felt something whistle past his cheek; swishswishswish, the sound a bullet makes as it spins in flight. A fraction of a second later, he heard the bang. He looked up and saw a bunch of red-jacketed bears on the edge of the cliff. A spurt of sand kicked up a yard or so to his left; another bang. Oh hell.

He turned to run back the way he'd just come, but he could hear shouting, someone yelling orders. They were behind him as well as in front. Quickly, he assessed the distance to the bears on the cliff: four hundred yards, at least. A moving target at four hundred yards was a pretty tall order. Letting go of the nappy and letting it slide to the ground, he picked a line across the beach and started to run.

He'd never been much of an athlete, even at school, but the gunshots and splashes in the sand motivated him in a way that a succession of PE teachers and coaches had never quite managed. I'm going to make it, he was just thinking, when a dappled whitetail fawn rose up out of the dunes on his left, about twenty-five yards away, and drew a bead on him with a slide-action shotgun. He skidded to a halt, his feet scouring ruts in the sand, just as the fawn fired. He felt the slipstream of the shot charge, a welcome breath of air on such a hot day. Behind him he could hear hooves thudding. Another volley of shots from the bears on the clifftop bracketed him with admirable precision. For a split second he considered plunging into the sea and swimming for it; just then, half a dozen mermaids burst up through the water and aimed at him with spear guns. Out of the corner of his eye, he caught a glimpse of three elephants, their huge ears flapping like wings, flying directly at him out of the sun.

He grinned.

There's conscience, and there's brotherly love, and there's getting your head blown off. Sorry, Max, he said to himself, and slowly raised his hands in the universal gesture of surrender. All it took was a slight tilt of the wrist to bring the doughnut into line. Through the hole in the middle he saw an elephant bank into an Immelman turn, and then –

PART FOUR

Doughnut Go Gentle Into That Good Night

As he fell out of nowhere, his head hit the side of the desk, which meant that the crucial quarter-second during which he'd have had the element of surprise was wasted in suffering pain and feeling dizzy. By the time all that stuff had run its course, it was too late. Oh well. "Hi," she said. "Well?"

He looked up at her. No doubt about it, she was a beautiful woman, with captivating eyes and a lovely smile. A pity she was going to die so young. "You—"

She wasn't listening, or even looking at him. She was waiting for something; something that hadn't happened. Suddenly, Theo knew what it was.

"He's not coming," he said.

"What?"

"Max. He's not coming."

Actually, it was far better than merely killing her. The look of pain on her face would've touched a heart of stone, provided that it hadn't just escaped by the skin of its teeth from a posse of blood-crazed Disney folk. "What? He's not—"

For a moment he was tempted; but he was a scientist, devoted to the truth. "He's not dead, if that's what you mean. He's still there. I got out, he didn't."

"You left him there." She was very beautiful when she was angry, but beauty isn't everything. "Your own brother."

"I tried," Theo said. "But I got ambushed by the bad guys. I nearly didn't make it."

She didn't seem all that interested. "You left him there," she repeated. "Oh, swell."

Slowly and painfully he picked himself up off the floor and leaned against the desk. All the unaccustomed running about had taken its toll. At least he had proper clothes again. "So," he said, "you and Max. I should've guessed."

She dropped into the chair and buried her face in her hands. "I should've known better than to rely on you," she said. "A perfectly simple, straightforward little job."

Somehow, though, he found he couldn't be angry, not now that he knew. Women under the influence of Max, he was aware from long experience, weren't responsible for their actions. Still, there was one point he felt he had to clear up. "You kissed me," he said.

"Yes. Well?"

"You kissed me," he repeated, "to get a sample of my DNA, so you could get past the security lockout on the powder compact. That's how you were able to send the message in the bottle, and the doughnut. Well? Yes or no."

"Yes."

"And you're Max's—"

"Yes."

"Fine." Which, he realised as soon as he'd said it, wasn't true at all. It wasn't fine, not by a long chalk. But, by the same token, it wasn't her fault. You could no more blame girls for catching a dose of Max than you could find fault with trees for squashing houses when blown down by a high wind. "Well, I'll be going now, then."

Her head shot up like the price of gold in a recession. "You what?"

"I'm leaving. Well, you don't need me any more, do you? You can get into the powder compact, which means you can read the YouSpace manual, which means you can figure out how to make it work, which means you can go and rescue Max yourself, which means—"

"You can't just leave," she said.

"Why not?"

"We need you. You're the only one who can understand all this shit."

Theo smiled at her. "By all this shit, presumably you mean Pieter van Goyen's epoch-making advances in quantum physics?"

"Yes."

"I'm leaving," he repeated. "I think I'll give the animal slaughtering business another try. You meet a better class of people."

"Uncle Bill won't let you. He knows people."

Theo nodded. "So do I," he said. "I know you, and your uncle Bill, and my brother Max. That's why I'm leaving. I thought I knew Pieter, but nobody's right all the time. Have a nice day."

He'd got as far as the door; he'd put his hand on the doorknob. "Please don't go."

She was good. Not quite in Max's class when it came to pathetic wheedling, but you couldn't blame her for that. She was good enough, which was all that mattered.

"Here's the deal," he said. "I'll help you rescue my worthless jerk of a brother, and then you and he can make each other thoroughly miserable while I go and try and salvage something from the wreck of my life. Agreed?"

She nodded brightly. "Sure," she said. "You won't regret it, I promise you."

"You'd be amazed what I can regret if I put my mind to it.

She laughed. He recognised the distinctive timbre. It was the noise a girl makes when she's laughing at a joke her boyfriend's just made; she hasn't actually got the joke, or she doesn't think it's particularly funny, but she's doing the best she can. From Matasuntha, it sounded dangerous, and it occurred to him that if Max was rescued and restored to her loving arms, it wouldn't be all that long before he started thinking wistfully of the quietly idyllic life he'd led in the cave, being waited on hand and foot by Sneezy, Happy, Sleepy, Dozy, Bashful, Grumpy and Doc. In fact, if ever a couple truly deserved each other, they did. You'd need a far darker imagination than Theo could lay claim to in order to dream up any punishment more exquisitely suitable.

"First, though," he said, with an entirely authentic yawn, "I'm going to get some sleep. Please go away, using the door provided."

She was smiling at him. In any number of parallel universes, many of them only slightly different from this one, he'd have liked that a lot. "Sure," she said. "I'll tell Uncle Bill we're nearly there, he'll be thrilled."

"Oh, and the powder compact."

"Yes?"

"Leave it on the desk on your way out."

She paused and looked at him, and he couldn't quite read what her face was saying. "I was going to see if I could download—"

"Leave it," he said. "On the desk."

"OK." There was a slight click as she put it down. "I just thought, I could study it for a bit while you're resting. One less thing for you to do."

"That's very sweet of you, but no thanks."

"Suit yourself." She hadn't moved. "Anything else I can help you with?"

"There's one thing you can do for me."

"Yes?"

"Go away," Theo said firmly. "That'd be a major contribution to the success of the project."

"That's not a very nice thing to say."

Theo grinned sadly at her. "That's the trouble with the truth," he said, "it's got such appallingly bad manners. Tall rectangular thing over there, hinges on one side, opening and shutting mechanism on the other. Let's see if you can figure out how to make it work."

She still didn't move. "Why are you so keen to get rid of me all of a sudden?"

He broadened the grin into a beautiful smile. "Because I don't like you," he said. "Bye."

She shot him a high-velocity sigh, stalked to the door, dragged it open, walked through it and slammed it behind her. It was a magnificent slam, executed with plenty of wrist and forearm to achieve the maximum terminal momentum, and the aftershock vibrated right through the wall, into the bookshelf over the desk, right down to the bottom shelf, on which she must at some point have placed the YouSpace bottle. It quivered for a moment, walking a millimetre or so towards the edge like an old-fashioned washing machine. Theo only noticed it as it quivered over the point of no return. He dived, his invisible arm extended, grabbing at it as it finally toppled and dropped into empty air. It was a splendid effort, and fell only a couple of centimetres short.

Theo crunched down on to the desk, heard a crack and felt first his elbow and then his head bash against something hard. The impact jarred his bones and rattled his teeth, but he barely noticed. He was totally preoccupied watching the YouSpace bottle tumble once, twice through the air before catching the edge of the desk. There was a snap, like a bone breaking, and suddenly the carpet was littered with little bits of broken glass.

"And another thing." Matasuntha was standing in the doorway. Whatever the other thing was, it never got mentioned. She was staring at the emerald shrapnel on the floor.

Her mouth was open, but no sound came out for quite some time.

"It's no good," Theo said for the fifteenth time. "You can't mend it."

Uncle Bill looked up at him hopelessly. He had splinters of glass stuck to his fingers with superglue. "It says on the label, sticks anything," he said.

Theo nodded. "In this reality, yes. But there's an infinite number of realities where it doesn't, and they were all in the bottle. By the way, you're kneeling on the tube."

"What? Oh." Uncle Bill frowned, looked down and tried to stand up. The carpet swelled up round his leg like a blister, but he stayed on his knees. "Maybe if we tried duct tape—"

Theo sighed. "Believe it or not," he said, "there are some eventualities where even duct tape won't cut it. Sorry, but this won't work."

Matasuntha made an impatient gesture, emphasised by the large sliver of bottle glued to her wrist. "All right then," she said. "If you're so goddamn smart, what do you suggest?"

"Give up," Theo said sweetly. "Forget it. Find something else to do. I know," he went on, "how about turning this place into a hotel?"

"The hell with that," Matasuntha snapped. "We're so close. You actually went there, and we've got the user's manual—"

"Hold it," Uncle Bill said urgently. "That's it, the user's manual. Look and see what it says. Under broken bottle."

Theo shrugged, took the powder compact from his pocket, opened it and traced his finger down the mirror. "Hey," he said, "there's an entry for that. If the bottle gets smashed."

Uncle Bill surged up to look over his shoulder, but the carpet held him fast; he toppled and landed on his hands. "Well? What does it say?"

"Just a second." Theo was scrolling down. "Here, yes. Buy a new one. Right." he snapped the compact shut and pocketed it.

"The answer's obvious," Matasuntha said. "He'll have to make one from scratch."

An overwhelming urge to laugh hit Theo like a fist in the midriff. "You're kidding," he gasped. "Oh, please tell me you meant that as a joke."

"You've got Pieter's notes," Uncle Bull said. "You were his student. I don't see why you shouldn't give it a try."

"You're crazy. Tell him he's crazy," he snapped at Matasuntha, who gave him a cold stare in return. "Go on, tell him."

But Matasuntha was studying him, as if he was half a worm she'd found in an apple. "Of course he can do it," she said. "He's smart. They wouldn't have put him in charge of the hadron collider if he wasn't pretty damn smart."

"I blew it up."

"Because you're careless," Matasuntha replied. "You can be careless and smart at the same time. No, what you're thinking of doing is going off somewhere and making a YouSpace thing all for yourself, cutting us right out of the deal.

"She's nuts," Theo yelled. "Tell her, she's nuts. I have no interest whatsoever in your stupid, lethally dangerous—"

"You wouldn't." Uncle Bill was looking at him with the sort of expression Mother Teresa might have worn if she'd caught one of the novices raiding the petty cash. "That's so low."

"Oh, for crying out loud." Theo sat down on the floor and buried his head in his hands. "Fine," he said. "If that's what you think, I'll try it. Doomed to failure," he added, "a complete and utter waste of time, but so what? Anything so long as you stop looking at me."

For three days and most of three nights, Theo stared at Pieter van Goyen's notes. He might as well have been gazing at the sun, because the experience left him dazzled and blind. No doubt about it, Pieter's work was utterly brilliant – the equations danced and sparkled on the screen, sometimes surging forward like a tidal wave, sometimes shearing off at an angle like a shoal of tiny, transparent fish – but, after seventy-two hours in their company, he was forced to the conclusion that he now knew considerably less about quantum mechanics than he had when he started. All he could say for certain was that Pieter had succeeded, and that what has been done once can be done again. The notes, however, were to all intents and purposes useless.

Fine.

At dawn on the fourth day, he switched off the screen, put the notebooks carefully away in a drawer, grabbed a blank sheet of paper and a pencil and decided to figure it all out for himself, from first principles. It was a fine and noble moment, which lasted for about three seconds. Then he looked down at the paper and saw that it was still blank. So he drew a small blue dot, and wrote above it, You Are Here.

That didn't help at all, so he drew a bottle round the dot, and then some wavy lines to represent the sea on which the bottle was floating; it was now a ship, in a bottle, on the sea, the ship being the message. He turned the paper over and drew the bottle sticking up out of the sand on a beach (he drew a sandcastle to make it clear where it was supposed to be). The idea was that someone, typically a poor but deserving fisherman, would come along and give the bottle a brisk rub, at which point the genie would come whooshing out and solve all his problems –

At this point he paused and wondered if he'd finally flipped, or whether this was an Einstein's tramcar moment, the point at which a homely analogy floodlit the runway on which divine inspiration could touch down and taxi smoothly to a halt. Six minutes later, he folded the paper into an aeroplane and sent it sailing gracefully across the room. He then spent two hours reading up the lives of great scientists on Wikipedia. That didn't help much, either. Then he turned off the screen and sat in his chair, pretending to be dead. Death, he reflected, was probably like playing the piano; the only way to get really good at it is to practise extensively beforehand.

He'd got to the stage where he couldn't feel his toes when a tiny noise made him look up. It had come from the direction of the door, which he'd locked to avoid interruption. The key was turning in the keyhole.

Keys don't usually do that, except in Spielberg films. He'd just made up his mind to go and investigate when the door opened and two men burst in. One of them was short and very old. The other was young, tall, blond, windmill-eared and eating a sandwich.

"You two," Theo said. "What—?"

The old man gave him an apologetic smile. "Sorry about this," he said, then nodded to his grandson, who grabbed Theo by the lapels and lifted him up so violently that his head banged hard on the ceiling. There was a beautiful firework display that nobody else could see, followed by –

Theo opened his eyes and groaned. "Lunchbox," he said.

The young man gave him a shy smile, then took another

bite of his individual pork pie. There was a sharp jolt, as the van went over a pothole.

"You awake, Mr Bernstein?" The old man turned round in the driving seat to look at him. Theo, who could see past him and through the windscreen, yelled, "Look out!" The old man waggled the steering wheel, the van lurched, and a lorry horn dopplered past over to their left. "You feeling OK, Mr Bernstein? Sorry about this."

"Keep your eyes on the road!"

"No worries, Mr Bernstein, I been driving fifty years, never had an" – the van swerved so ferociously that for a moment it flexed like a drawn bow – "accident. It's all right, you're perfectly safe."

By now, Theo was painfully aware of the handcuffs and the rope around his ankles. "No I'm not," he shouted back. "Stop the van now. I mean it."

The young man was peeling the foil lid off a yoghurt. "Sorry," the old man said, "but we got our instructions. Your sister wants to see you. Urgent."

"Fine. Tell me when and where, and I'll take the bus."

"Don't you worry, Mr Bernstein, we'll be there in an hour or so. How's the head?"

"Hurts like hell."

"Sorry about that. I told the lad, there was no call for him knocking you out like that. Trouble is, he don't know his own strength. Say sorry to Mr Bernstein, Art."

The young man took the plastic spoon out of his mouth and made a noise like a bumblebee in a padded box. "He says he's sorry," the old man said. "He's a good lad really, and, anyhow, I promised his mother. You just lie still and relax, Mr Bernstein. Rest your head."

The old man must have stood on the brake at this point, because the van compressed like a spring. Theo slid forward until his feet collided with the back of the passenger seat;

then his unsupported head bumped against the hard floor. The fireworks display started up again, but he wasn't in the mood. There's a time and a place for whooshing red rockets and swirly purple and green Catherine wheels, and this was neither. Unfortunately, he couldn't see a way of getting the old man to stop without getting all of them killed. Unless –

"Excuse me."

"Hm?"

"Would you mind very much slowing down a bit? Only, I get travel sick, you see, and—"

"What? Oh, right." The van slowed down (a horn blared behind and to the side, but all in a good cause this time) and Theo felt a wave of relief wash through him. Over the last year he hadn't enjoyed his life very much, but apparently he wasn't quite ready to die just yet. Life, he decided, is a bit like an optimist reading a Martin Amis novel; he keeps going, no matter what, just in case it gets good towards the end. "Art, give the gentleman a paper bag, just in case."

Lunchbox fished in his pocket, uncrumpled a bag and laid it on Theo's chest like a floral tribute. "Thanks," Theo said, "but I can't use my hands, you see, so—"

"Good point," the old man said. "Art, I think we can do without the cuffs."

It took Lunchbox quite some time to find the key. It turned up eventually, buried under three film-wrapped bricks of ham and tomato, two more of BLT, four rather squashed Swiss rolls, a book-sized wedge of cheese and three Snickers bars. Then he looked down at Theo's hands and frowned.

"His right hand's invisible," the old man said. "Take off the left one and perhaps you'd be good enough to do the other one yourself, Mr Bernstein. He's a good boy, but not what you might call practical."

The removal of the handcuffs opened a new range of options, all of which Theo reluctantly dismissed. Lunchbox might be skinny and dimmer than a hotel corridor light bulb, but he'd proved strong enough to bash Theo stupid just by lifting him a little too enthusiastically. The old man had slowed down a bit, but kicking the van doors open and jumping out still didn't appeal terribly much. It looked, therefore, like he was on his way to see Janine. At least he'd arrive without cramp or pins and needles up to the elbows.

"What does my sister want to see me for?"

"No idea, sorry," the old man said. "All we was told was, fetch him over here immediately. I expect she just wants to talk to you a bit."

Theo nodded slowly. "Tell me, Mr – sorry, I didn't catch your name."

"That's all right, Mr Bernstein. Don't worry about it."

Oh well. "Tell me," he repeated, "if Janine were to order you to, well, kill me, let's say, and dump my body out at sea, for example, you wouldn't do that, would you? I mean, I can see you're basically good, decent people, with standards. You'd never dream of doing anything like that, I can tell."

A short and rather awkward silence; then the old man said, "The way I look at it, Mr Bernstein, there's no use worrying about stuff. I mean, for all you or I know, the planet could get hit by an asteroid and then that's all of us gone, just like that. If you start thinking about things, you'd never be able to sleep at night. Would you like something to eat, Mr Bernstein? Art, give the gentleman a sandwich."

The look of terror that covered the young man's face would have melted the heart of a tax inspector. "Better not," Theo said quickly. "Like I said, motion sickness. Not a good idea."

"Ah. Right, well, if you change your mind, just say."

Theo shuffled around a bit until he was able to prop himself up against the van doors. His head hurt every time the old man braked suddenly or swerved, but eventually he dropped into a vague half and half doze, which was considerably more restful than watching Lunchbox eat. In his semi-conscious state he was dimly aware of a cellphone warbling, and the old man saying something about being just a little bit behind schedule but otherwise all according to plan, and ETA at the designated transfer point in twenty minutes, and a bunch of other stuff that Theo couldn't be bothered to follow. He was just about to drift into a proper dream, probably the one where he was back at his old school and he'd just been elected pope by a full conclave of the Roman Catholic Church, and nobody would believe him because he was only eleven, when –

Somebody was prodding his shoulder.

"Wake up, Your Holiness." Prod, prod. "Here, Nev, gimme the plant mister, the silly old bugger's out like a light."

He opened his eyes. A cardinal, in a red cassock and mozetta, was bending over him holding a plastic water-squirter bottle. He had an earring in his left ear.

"You're Australian," Theo said.

The cardinal sighed. "That's right, Your Holiness. Now, sit up and put your teeth in, and then it'll be time for your call to the Kremlin. You know how the Tsar gets if he's kept waiting."

Over the cardinal's shoulder, across a long and richly furnished room, Theo could see a huge open window. It looked like he was on the top floor of a very high building, and the view was magnificent; a vast expanse of blue water under a cloudless sky, at the edges a horizon fringed with skyscrapers, the Sydney Harbour Bridge –

The cardinal was offering him a gold plate, on which rested a set of false teeth. "Am I the Pope?" Theo asked.

"That's right, Your Holiness."

"What are we doing in Australia?"

Sigh. "You live here. We're in the Vatican." The cardinal turned his head and spoke to someone beyond Theo's range of vision. "Two of the pink pills today, I reckon, Nev. Can't have him talking to the Tsar in this state, probably start a war."

Theo wriggled. The chair he was sitting in was huge, and his feet weren't touching the ground. "The Vatican's in Rome," he said. "Why are we—?"

"Was in Rome," the cardinal sighed, "till 1973, when the hadron collider blew up and Italy got buried in ash. Then we moved, remember? Now, take your pills and you'll be just fine."

An acolyte thrust a silver saucer with pink pills on it in his face. He dodged it. "The Tsar?"

The cardinal rolled his eyes. "That's right. You're finalising the partition of Brazil, remember? No, you don't, do you? Better have one of the blue pills as well, Nev, or we'll be here all flaming day."

"What Tsar? There is no Tsar. There was a revolution—"

"Bloody hell, he's off again." The cardinal shook his head, making his earring swing wildly. "Listen, Your Holiness. You're Pope Wayne XXIII, we're in Sydney, in the Vatican, it's 2016 and you're in the middle of negotiating who gets Latin America south of Guatemala with the Emperor of bloody Russia. You need to pull yourself together, Wayne mate, or there's going to be tears before bedtime."

Theo wasn't having much luck with words, but numbers still seemed to make sense. Twenty sixteen. The future. In which case –

"Sorry," he said, and grinned. "I remember now."

The cardinal relaxed. "That's fine, Your Holiness. Man of your age, it's only to be expected. Now, if you'll just take your pills, we can decide the fate of Christendom without making a right royal bog-up of it."

"Yes, of course." Theo nodded wisely. "But first, if it's all right, I'd quite like something to eat."

The cardinal looked uncertain. "You sure? You know what happens if—"

"Yes," Theo said, and gripped his hands on the arms of his chair. The gesture wasn't wasted on the cardinal, because he nodded to the acolyte. "Fetch his Holiness a Vegemite sarny, Nev, quick as you like."

"Actually," Theo said firmly, "what I'd really like is a doughnut."

The cardinal's face hardened. "Come on, Your Holiness, you know what the doc said. No doughnuts, under any circumstances."

"Oh. In that case, how about a b—?"

"Or bagels. Or Polo mints. He told you, remember? One more doughnut, it'll be the death of you."

A surge of panic swept through Theo. "Look," he said, "I'm the Pope and I want a doughnut. Now. And that's ex cathedra."

"I'm sorry, that's not – get that, will you, Nev?" the cardinal said, as a phone rang somewhere. "Doctor's orders," he went on. "No doughnuts and no bagels, or he won't be responsible."

"I forgive him," Theo said grimly. "You too. Plenary absolution, provided I get my doughnut now. Understood?"

The acolyte was back, holding a phone. "It's the Tsar," he mouthed.

"Buggery." The cardinal pulled a sad face. "All right, give it here. The pills," he hissed.

"Not unless I get a—"

"All right." The cardinal grabbed the phone. "Please hold for His Holiness, Your Majesty." He held the phone out to Theo, who raised his eyebrows. The cardinal mouthed Yes, all right, and Theo took the pills from the saucer, popped them in his mouth and stuffed them in his cheek with the tip of his tongue. Then he took the phone and said, "Yes?"

"Theo?"

"J—" He managed to choke back the rest of her name just in time. Janine's voice. "Speaking."

"Theo, you total shit, where are you? We've been looking everywhere."

The acolyte had left the room, but the cardinal was still there. Never mind. As soon as the doughnut arrived, he'd be out of there. "I'm in the Vatican," he said. "In Sydney."

The cardinal groaned and turned away.

"You what?"

"In the Vatican. Sydney, Australia. So, you wanted to talk to me."

"What the hell are you doing there? You should be on the planet of the Disney creatures, rescuing Max."

Theo opened his eyes very wide. "You know about that."

"Of course I do, I'm not stupid. What the hell are you doing in Sydney?"

"I'm the Pope."

The cardinal made a low moaning noise. "What do you mean, you're the—? Oh, forget it," Janine said. "Stop pissing around and go and get Max, right now."

The acolyte was approaching. He held a golden salver, in the exact centre of which was a doughnut. Theo leaned forward and grabbed at it, but the acolyte held it just out of reach. Then the cardinal handed him a note on a scrap of paper: not till you've got us Porto Alegre.

Fine, Theo thought, if that's what it takes. "I insist you let us have everything south of the Serra Geral," he said. "Otherwise, the deal's off."

The cardinal nodded approvingly. "You what?" Janine said.

"I mean it," Theo said firmly, his eyes glued to the doughnut. "What? Yes, that's fine. I'm glad we were able to agree on that. So, if you can picture a line running approximately fifteen degrees forty-five minutes south—"

"Theo, unless you go and rescue Max this minute, I'm going to have you killed, do you understand me? I mean it."

The doughnut was still just beyond the furthest extent of his arm. "And how am I supposed to go about doing that exactly?"

"Easy. Just do what you usually do. Go there, get Max, come back."

"What I usually do," Theo repeated. "You don't know how it works, do you?"

"Of course I do."

Years of experience; he knew when she was lying. "Which is why I ended up here," he said, "instead of the planet of the Disney creatures."

The cardinal let out a low whimpering noise and grabbed the phone from Theo's hand. "G'day, Your Majesty," he said, "sorry about this but His Holiness would appear to have had a heart attack. He'll call you back soon as he's feeling better. Cheerio." He pressed the kill button so hard he splintered the casing, and dropped the phone on the floor. "That does it," he snapped. "Sorry, Wayne, mate, but this time you've gone too far. Nev, get me the Archbishop of Wangaratta."

Quickly, Theo did the mental arithmetic; distance, time, velocity, angle. Then he lunged.

He almost made it; almost, but not quite. Later he realised that he'd been basing his calculations on the length of his arm in his home universe, whereas in this one it was 0.9 centimetres shorter. His nails scraped the edge of the salver, but that was as close as he got. Then he overbalanced and hit the floor. "The doughnut," he screamed. "Give me the doughnut."

The cardinal was staring at him with a mixture of loathing and pity. "Nev," he said, "His Holiness is having some kind of seizure. Lock him in the dunnee and call Doc O'Shaugnessy."

Respectful but extremely strong hands attached themselves to the front of Theo's robes and hauled him to his feet; then the floor and ceiling changed places for a while, as Theo was carried across the room and dumped in a toilet. He tried the door, but it wouldn't open; presumably Nev had wedged it shut with the back of a chair. Marvellous.

After that, not much happened for quite some time. It was rather a nice toilet, as toilets go; it had a marble floor and gold-plated taps, and the paper was purple, monogrammed with the papal crossed keys. Theo put the seat down and sat on it, and waited for someone to come and let him out.

There was a mirror, which was interesting; the face that stared back at him was more or less his own, but about forty years older. He didn't feel that old, so presumably the transformation was entirely superficial. His right arm was visible, and he was wearing a big, chunky ring; if he ever got home again and managed to take it with him, it'd be worth good money, but he was fairly sure he wouldn't be allowed to keep it. That, after all, would be something nice, and YouSpace didn't seem to work like that.

Janine, he thought. Janine and Max. That's the problem with being human. We have brains capable of figuring out the universe to a thousand decimal places, we can build machines as tall as mountains or as tiny as specks of dust, we can prise open atoms like walnuts, we can calculate the weights of distant stars, manipulate nature, ride on super-sophisticated fireworks out beyond the atmosphere, we could blow up our own planet in the time it takes to blow your nose; there's practically nothing we can't do, except choose our relatives. Everything else: no bother, piece of cake. But the one thing that'd do more to alleviate stress and grief and give us a head start in the pursuit of happiness is entirely beyond us, further than the Andromeda galaxy, more elusive than the Higgs-Boson. No wonder there isn't a Nobel prize for putting up with your family. They wouldn't be able to find anyone to give it to.

He was here, presumably, because he'd been dreaming about being made pope; his subconscious mind must've instructed a YouSpace device to find a reality in which that could happen, and the bottle had sent him here. From that it followed that Janine had such a thing; also, that she didn't know how to use it, or she'd have sent him directly to the Disney planet. One disturbing factor was the doctor's prohibition on doughnuts, bagels and Polo mints. That suggested to him that someone was determined not to allow him to escape before he'd completed his mission – finding Max – and logic required that that person should be Janine. But if she could program in such a sophisticated element as no-doughnuts-or-bagels, why couldn't she work the YouTube bottle herself? That didn't make a whole lot of sense. Of course, Janine's actions had never been exactly rational. How many Janines does it take to change a light bulb? Three: one to rip the socket and flex out of the ceiling, one to burn down the house to punish it for popping a bulb, and one to complain that the other two are out to get her. Even so. Curious.

Meanwhile, there was the small matter of how he was going to get out of here and back to where he belonged. He closed his eyes and pictured the doughnut he'd been so close to grabbing. It proved that there were doughnuts in this reality, in this building; the question was, how to get his hands on one. Unless –

Ten seconds later, a promising hypothesis went down in flames. The hole in the middle of a toilet seat didn't work –

"Um, Your Holiness."

Nev the acolyte was standing in the doorway. Theo could see him quite clearly, through the hole in the toilet seat. "Yes?"

"Doctor O'Shaugnessy's here," said Nev. "If you'd like to follow me."

"Sure." Theo got up, closed the lid, straightened his robes and followed Nev into the throne room. There was a man standing with his back to them both, gazing out through the picture window at the magnificent view; a short, bald man with shoulders so sloping and dandruff-flaked you could've used them to stage the Winter Olympics.

"Thanks, Nev," the man said. "You can leave us to it. I'll shout if I need you for anything."

Nev only took a second and a bit to walk to the door, open it and close it again after him. For Theo, it felt like an eternity: long enough to grow stalactites from the ceiling and hold a glacier race right around the Equator. Eventually, though, the man turned round to face him.

"Hello, Theo," he said.

"Pieter?"

Pieter van Goyen smiled at him; the same twinkly-hippo smile he remembered from – what was it? A thousand years ago? – when his most desperate problem was how to explain why the assignment he was supposed to be handing in somehow hadn't got started yet. "I never realised you wanted to be the Pope," he said. "Is this a new direction for you, or something you've always aspired to?"

"You're dead."

Pieter grinned. "No, I'm not," he said.

"You're dead. I saw it. They shot you with a ray gun. You disintegrated."

"Ah." Pieter did that hands-raised-fingers-spread gesture. "That."

"Yes, that."

"Your trouble is," Pieter said kindly, "you don't think. You assume. I hoped I'd cured you of that back in your second year, but obviously not."

"Pieter . . ."

Pieter looked round, located a chair and sat in it. There was a faint creaking noise, but somehow the chair held, banishing any doubt that they were in a wholly different universe. "You visited one of my default realities, yes?"

"If you say so. Look—"

"Not a particularly attractive place," Pieter went on. "Bizarrely improbable aliens in a setting all too obviously derived from the cantina at Mos Eisley. Did it occur to you to ask yourself why I'd choose to make something like that a default? No," he went on, as Theo started to make not-interested noises, "clearly not. Well, try it now."

Angrily resentful at being given homework at a time like this, Theo jammed his brain into gear. "Because it's the only universe where some specific thing can happen."

"Warm."

"A law of physics doesn't apply."

"Warmer."

Click. "Teleportation," Theo barked. "It's a universe where it's possible to teleport."

Pieter clapped his hands together once and pointed at him. "A long and bumpy ride, but you got there in the end."

"And the ray guns—"

"Were real ray guns," Pieter said, "if you'll excuse the apparent paradox. Fortunately, when I'm there, I carry a teleport activator key with me at all times. I beamed out. Simple as that."

Theo suddenly felt terribly weary, as though he was just about to run out of fuel. "All right," he said, "I guess that accounts for it, and you really are still alive—"

"Thank you so much," Pieter said gravely.

"That doesn't explain," Theo went on, with a last flicker of rage, "why you won't let them give me a doughnut."

"Ah."

"Doctor's orders. Apparently you're the doctor. Why?"

Pieter wriggled a little in his chair, and there was a faint splitting sound. "Because I wanted to keep you here until I found you," he said. "Which wasn't easy, believe you me. Honestly, Theo, of all the Vaticans in all the autonomous Papal States in all the multiverse, why did you have to choose this one? It's so hopelessly obscure it barely registers. You do realise, this whole reality is posited on Rupert Murdoch converting to Roman Catholicism in 1962, following a profound spiritual experience on the road between Rockhampton and Toowoomba. In order for that to happen, they've had to do without the Internet, the Russian Revolution and forty-eight per cent of the Renaissance. Oh, and the Roman Empire celebrated its 2,750th anniversary in 1999. They had a procession and a sherbet fountain, and fifty Seventh-day Adventists were thrown to the lemurs."

"Lemurs?"

"Health and safety. You can see why it took me a while to track you down. Talk about off the beaten track. In probability terms, this is the sticks."

Amazing how Pieter could make him feel guilty. "I'm sorry," he said. "I was dreaming."

"You dream about being the Pope?"

"On this one specific occasion," Theo protested. "I was back at school, and—"

"Ah." Pieter nodded. "And some idiot initiated a YouSpace field—"

"I thought you weren't going to call it that."

"While you were still asleep and dreaming, so your unconscious mind directed the parameters index locator wizard to find a reality in which you could be the Pope." Pieter's face cracked into a grin. "This one. Showing just how screwed up the universe would have to be before you'd get elected to high ecclesiastical office. Rather reassuring, actually, if you care to look at it from that perspective. Anyhow," he went on, fishing in his inside pocket and producing a cigar the size of a medium torpedo, "no harm done. You're here, I'm here, we can get down to business. Oh, don't worry," he added, as he lit the cigar and blew out a cloud large enough to asphyxiate most of San Francisco, "one good thing about this universe. Nicotine is good for you. Trust me," he added, "I'm a doctor."

Theo fanned a clearing in the smoke with his hand, just enough that he could see Pieter's face. "I take it you want something."

Pieter looked hurt. "Oh, come on," he said. "One little thing I want you to do for me, after everything I've done for you."

"Such as."

"Oh, let me see. I got you a job, left you YouSpace, the most amazing recreational tool in human history, which will make you the richest man who ever lived. Well?" he smiled. "How am I doing?"

Theo gave him a cold stare. "As far as the job goes," he said, "I was happier hauling guts in the slaughterhouse. The YouSpace thing is utterly terrifying and horribly dangerous, and you can insert it in a region of negative solar activity. Also, you brought Max back into my life. And Janine. Thank you so fucking much."

"Janine," Pieter repeated. "Ah yes, that charming sister of yours. How does she fit in?"

"She knows Max is alive. She's got one of your magic bottles. She sent me here to find him."

Pieter frowned. "Just a moment," he said. "Rewind that last bit. She sent you here."

Theo shrugged impatiently. "Well, not here specifically. But she wants me to rescue Max and bring him home. So she had me kidnapped, and she put me in her YouSpace thing—"

"Her YouSpace thing."

"Yes. Mine got broken, which as far as I'm concerned is no great loss, thank you all the same. There was this planet where—"

He stopped short. The look on Pieter's face had drained all the language out of him. Pieter was scared. "What?" Theo demanded. "Why are you gawping at me like that?"

Pieter did a shut-up gesture with his hands. "Slowly, and try and be coherent, just for me. Your bottle got broken?"

Theo nodded. "Matasuntha—"

"And your sister's got a bottle, and she kidnapped you."

"I just said—"

"And presumably she doesn't know how to use it, because without the user's manual—"

"I guess so."

"Oh, my God."

Some people panic easily. They lose their cool so often and so readily that they'd be well advised to wear it round their neck on a bit of string, like a librarian's glasses. Pieter, though; Pieter had never, in all the years Theo'd known him, displayed anything remotely resembling anxiety, doubt or fear; not unless you counted the time he'd run out of coffee at 3 a.m. in the middle of the summer vacation, when all his neighbours were away. To see the look on his face right now was like asking God a question and being met with a blank stare and a shrug. "Pieter?"

He'd gone white, and his eyes were huge. It made him look like Gollum on a bad few-remaining-strands-of-hair day. "You do realise what this means."

"No, of course not. Nobody ever explains anything."

"It means," Pieter said, and his voice was high and slightly shrill, "we're stuck here. Both of us."

Did not compute. "No, it doesn't. There's doughnuts, in the kitchen. There must be. They brought me one, only—"

"They won't work," Pieter yelled. "For God's sake, Theo, didn't you read the user's manual?"

"Yes. Well, sort of. Skimmed through it."

Terror made Pieter look slightly bigger and considerably thinner, for some reason. Also a lot older. "If you'd taken the time to read the manual," he said, "you'd know that the interface transit retrieval talisman is personalised to each individual module—"

"Excuse me?"

"Each bottle's made differently," Pieter translated scornfully. "So that only the registered owner and people in actual physical contact with him can use doughnuts to go backwards and forwards. It's a security measure."

Theo would quite like to have told Pieter what he thought of his various security measures, but he decided that the situation was already fraught enough to be going on with. "I see," he said. "No, actually I don't. How does that—?"

Pieter sighed. "It was to stop the locals in other realities you happen to be visiting from accidentally straying into ours every time they happened to look through the hole in a doughnut. Otherwise there'd be chaos, obviously, thousands of doughnut eaters from alien realities suddenly materialising on the streets of our major cities. That's why it's so vitally important that you only travel through your bottle. Use someone else's, and the doughnuts won't work. You'd be stranded."

When the going gets panic-stricken, the panic-stricken get going. The solution popped neatly into Theo's mind without him even having to think. "But that's OK," he said. "You got here through YouSpace, right? So, you've got a bottle. We get a doughnut, I grab hold of you, we both go home. Simple."

Pieter gave him a long, sad look. "I had a bottle."

"Yes? And?"

"I left it to you. In my goddamn will. And you broke it."

Image the hot shower you'd been looking forward to all day turned out to be iced water. "The same—"

"Yes." Pieter closed his eyes. "As it clearly states in the manual, each unit can be registered with up to three authorised users." He sighed, and shook his head. "How do you think I got here? Walked? Got the bus?"

"But—" Theo realised he'd finally had enough, even from Pieter van Goyen. "For crying out loud, Pieter, explain. Otherwise—"

"What?"

Theo forced his face into a grim, hard expression. It was like getting your foot into one of your eight-year-old daughter's shoes. "Otherwise," he said, "I'm going to go out there and be the best possible pope I can be, and you can spend the rest of your life treating German measles. It wouldn't be so bad," he added cheerfully. "Better than cleaning up in the slaughterhouse, anyway."

"In Australia?"

"Better than the slaughterhouse," Theo said firmly. "I've been thinking for some time I ought to settle down, make something of my life. The Papacy wasn't quite what I had in mind, but what the hell. I could really make a difference, being pope."

"So could a ring-tailed possum flying an airliner. Look, we both know you're bluffing."

Theo scowled at him, then made the sign of the cross. "*Pax vobiscum*, scumbag," he said. "Oh, and you're fired. I've felt for some time I need a personal physician with integrity and compassion. Not to mention a medical degree."

Pieter sighed, then shrugged. "Fine," he said. "After all," he added, "it's not like we're going anywhere in a hurry." He looked down at the cigar between his fingers, which had gone out, and relit it. "We need coffee," he said. "Medical emergency. There's a bell around here somewhere. You ring it, and some clown comes and takes your order. Ah. This'll do."

There was indeed a small silver bell, resting on a beautiful leather-bound Bible, next to a silver candlestick, in which a fat white candle dimly flickered. The combination stirred something in Theo's memory, but he couldn't be bothered to follow it up. He shook the bell and it tinkled, and a moment later Nev the acolyte appeared. "Your Holiness?"

"Coffee," Pieter said. "Strong. Lots."

"Your Holiness," Nev repeated. "Is that wise?"

Theo shrugged. "He's the doctor," he said. "He says it's OK."

Nev continued to stare at the bell in Theo's hand, and the candle, which had gone out. "You don't think it's a bit, well, extreme?"

"What, coffee?"

"Excommunicating the whole of Sydney."

Theo frowned, then looked back over his shoulder through the picture window. Ah, he thought. Bell, book and candle. Oops. "Did I just do that?"

"Afraid so, Your Holiness."

"Butterfingers," Pieter muttered. "His Holiness just had one of his funny turns," he went on, as the cardinal appeared in the doorway. "I'm sure he didn't mean anything by it. He gets these sudden incontrollable rages, and then, wham, eternal damnation from Wollongong to Gosford. I'll give him something for it, he'll be fine soon. Meanwhile, some coffee would be nice, if it's no bother."

Nev and the cardinal backed out slowly, taking care to maintain eye contact until the door was safely shut behind them. "Thanks, Pieter," Theo said. "Thanks a lot."

Pieter shrugged. "When you decide to make a difference, you don't muck about." he said. "I think your chances of staying here and living a nice, quiet life aren't quite what they were. I'm not quite sure what's involved in getting rid of a pope who's gone out of his gourd, but there's bound to be a proper procedure." He smiled, then added, "Don't ever threaten me, Theo, it's rude and I don't like it. Understood? Splendid. Right, what do you suggest we do now?"

"I don't know, do I?" Theo yelled. "I just want to go home."

"Can't, sorry." Pieter gave him a look you could've crushed diamonds with. "Not if the bottle's broken."

"The phone." A tiny spurt of hope. "We could use the phone."

"What, to order in pizza?"

"To call Janine. My sister."

Pieter shook his head sadly. "All right," he said, "it's possible there's a version of your sister in this reality. But she won't know what's going on, and she most definitely won't be able to get you home. Obviously you haven't been listening to a word I've said, or you'd—"

"She rang me," Theo said. "Just now."

If Time is a piece of cheese, the two seconds that followed were fondue. "I beg your pardon?"

"She called me. Everyone thought she was the Tsar, naturally—"

"Of course. Easy mistake to make."

"—but it was her, I talked to her, she told me to find Max. Then the cardinal grabbed the phone and told her I'd had a heart attack, so I didn't get to ask her how she'd got me here. But if she got me here, she can get me back. Can't she?"

Pieter hadn't breathed for quite some time. "Not sure," he said. "Depends."

"On what?"

"Well, it looks like she's got a YouSpace bottle," Pieter said, puffing at his cigar, which had gone out again. "So in theory, yes. But I doubt very much if she knows how to work it."

Theo grinned. "Maybe not," he said. "But you do."

"Yes," Pieter said. "I do, don't I? Good thought."

"It'd be like those aeroplane disaster movies, where the guy on the ground tells the complete novice how to land the plane."

"Um. Bad analogy."

"So all we've got to do is call her back."

"Of course. Got her number, have you? Bearing in mind that it's absolutely impossible to send a telephone signal of any sort across the transdimensional vortex."

"She did it," Theo said simply. "So it's possible. And I don't need her number." He picked up the phone. "All I have to do is press the call-you-back button and we're there."

"Theo." Pieter's face was as unreadable as *On Chesil Beach*. "I think you may just have had a good idea. Hard to accept, I know, but we are, after all, scientists. Well, don't just stand there like the Prune-King's daughter. Do it."

Slowly and carefully, Theo flexed his fingers, making sure they all worked. It was still rather weird, being able to see them again. "All right," he said. "On one condition."

"Theo—"

"One condition. Just one. Otherwise, we stay here and learn to love Aussie Rules Football. Well?"

"Whatever."

"The condition is," Theo said gravely, "you explain."

"What?"

"Everything."

"Oh, that. Yes, if you like. Now, press the damn button."

Feeling a bit like the President after the Russian premier has refused to take back what he just said about motherhood and apple pie, Theo placed the tip of his finger over the button, until he could just feel the texture of it, and applied gentle but consistent pressure. There was an agonising pause, followed by the dial tone.

"Well?"

"Quiet, it's ringing."

Four rings; five. Then a male voice Theo didn't recognise said, "Ja?"

"Hello. I'd like to speak to Janine, please."

"Huh?"

Deep breath. "Janine Bernstein. Could I possibly talk to her, please?"

Pause. "Zis is Kurt. Vat you vant?"

Pieter was pulling the sort of face the human skin wasn't designed to cope with. "Please may I speak to Janine Bernstein. Please."

"She not here. She gone out. Zis is Kurt. Vat you—?"

"Do you know when she's likely to be back? It's very important."

"She gone out. I ott-chob man. She not tell me ven she come back. Vy ze hell she tell me anyzing. I not care. I chust vurk here."

Theo tried to count to ten. He got as far as three. "Is there any way you could get a message to her? It really is extremely –"

"I write note. She not read. She never read note. I write anyhow, is vaste of time. I write note."

Pieter was making faint mewing noises, like a sick cat. "Can you please tell me the phone number?"

"Vas?"

"The number. The phone number I'm calling on right now?"

"Vy you ask? You know number. You calling on number. Vot you ask me for?"

"Please?"

"I not know number. I chust vurk here. Is lousy job. I cut grass, vosh vindows, take out trash, I not gottdamn social secretary. You get off ze line now. I go."

"Please tell her," Theo said desperately. "Theo called. About Max. Urgent. Really, really urgent."

"I write note. Vaste of paper. She not read. I go now."

The click, and then the whirr. Theo slowly put the phone down. "She's out," he said. "I left a message."

"That's it, then," Pieter said. "We're screwed. We're going to be stuck here for the rest of our lives. In Australia."

"No we aren't." Theo said firmly. "Janine will get my message and call us back, and then—" He gave up. "You're right," he said. "We're screwed. Oh well."

"Oh well?"

"It's not so bad," Theo said. "At least it's the twenty-first century and the people are human. Think about it. We could be stuck where Max is."

Pieter shrugged. "That's not so bad, either. There's humans living on the southern continent. They're all princesses. No men, just a load of rich, lonely young women in sparkly dresses. There are definitely worse places, trust me."

"Yes, well. Max isn't there, is he? He's stuck in a cave surrounded by furry animals with automatic weapons."

"In accordance with the fundamental human right to keep and arm bears. Yes, I know. Old but gold. He'll be all right, don't worry. Besides, I thought you didn't give a damn."

Theo shook his head. "I don't like him but I don't want him killed. He's my brother." He sighed. "It's a very special relationship, you know? No, I don't suppose you do."

"Actually, that's how I feel about my sister. Two parts a sort of mystical union of souls, three parts constant unbearable irritation. Also, I never know what to get her for her birthday." Pieter sat down on the papal throne and relit his cigar for the third time. "You could knock through that partition wall there and turn this whole wing into a bowling alley."

"She'll call us," Theo said. "I mean, she wants me to find Max, she'll be on that phone any moment now. Not that she gives a damn about me, but where Max is concerned—"

"Theo," Pieter said, "forget it. We aren't going anywhere. Did I tell you about the time-decay thing?"

"The what?"

"Ah." Pieter nodded slowly. "Key piece of information. It's in the manual, of course, but since you couldn't be bothered to read it—"

"Pieter."

"Fine, right. As you should've figured out for yourself, the YouSpace acceleration effect subjects organic matter to extreme prototachyonic inversion stress. That's fine so long as you're inside the bottle's ambient baryon field, and returning to your reality of origin purges all the prototachyons out of your system, so it's no bother at all once you're home. But if you leave the baryon field, which happens if, to take an example purely at random, you're stranded because the bottle's got busted, the build-up of antiprototachyonic radiation in your body tissue quickly leads to cellular degradation resulting in nucleotide dysfunction and catastrophic failure of protein cohesion." He paused, took in Theo's blank stare and translated, "You go all runny, then you fall to bits. Or at least," he added with a slight shudder, "that's what's in store for me. You're probably OK. As far as we know, the bottle that brought you here is intact."

Theo stared at him. "You're going to—"

"Yup. In about a hundred and forty hours. They'll have to bury me in an ice-cream carton. Same goes for Max, of course. Hence," he added, blowing out a dense blue cloud, "my apparently flippant and devil-may-care demeanour, imperfectly concealing a very real sense of shit-scaredness and existential terror."

"Pieter," Theo whimpered, "we've got to do something."

Pieter smiled. "I am doing something," he said. "I'm sitting on the Throne of St Peter smoking a good cigar. It won't help any, but neither would anything else, so why the hell not?"

"Janine—"

"Is not going to call," Pieter said firmly. "Stop torturing yourself with false hopes and accept the situation. Prepare yourself for the inevitable. And you might start looking round for a bucket or something. I'd hate for my mortal remains to soak away into the carpet."

The phone rang.

"It's her," Pieter screamed. "Out of the way!" He launched himself out of the throne, shouldered past Theo, grabbed the phone and yelled, "Yes?"

Theo tried to take the phone from him, and got a hand in his face. "What?" Pieter was saying. "What? No. Who is this? No, sorry, but – no. Get off the fucking line, Your Majesty, we're expecting an important call. Yeah, and yours too." Slam.

"That wasn't Janine, then," Theo said.

"No." Pieter hobbled back to the throne and sat down heavily. "Just the Tsar, about some idiotic treaty. I told you, didn't I? She's not going to come through for us. So stop deluding yourself and . . ."

Ring. Ring.

This time, Theo beat him to it by a clear thousandth of a second. "Hello? Janine?"

"Hi. This is a free message. Right across the country, thousands of people just like you are paying too much for their personal loans. Call us now for a really great deal on—"

Dimly, Theo was aware of movement, and a hand gripping his wrist. "Don't throw the phone," Pieter was shouting at him. "We may still need it. Don't throw the phone."

"What?" The red mist that had covered his eyes started to dissipate, and he let Pieter take the phone away from him. "That wasn't Janine," he said.

"I'd kind of gathered."

"She's not going to call, is she?"

"No."

"And now we can't call her back, because she's not the most recent caller any more." Suddenly he felt as though a great weight had been lifted from his shoulders; he'd been let off having to hope, and now he could relax into despair. "We're screwed. You're going to die. There's nothing we can do."

"Mister Tactful," Pieter said. "I wonder, though."

Hope is a bit like bindweed, or Russian vine. Just when you think you've killed off the last root, there it is, back again. "What?"

"Do you think they've got any booze around here? They must have. I wonder how we go about getting hold of some."

"Pieter."

"Well, why the hell not? What can a person do in a hundred and forty hours? He can watch the whole of *Star Trek Voyager* on DVD, or he can get really, really, really stonked."

"Pieter—"

"True, both options would leave you regarding death as a merciful release, but—"

"Pieter!" He hadn't meant to shout. "Pull yourself together, for crying out loud. Think of something. You're a Nobel Laureate, aren't you? You invented this horrible thing. You can't just crawl away and get drunk. It's—"

"What?"

"It's what Max would do."

"Ah." Pieter grinned. "Great minds." He picked up the little silver bell and shook it ferociously. A moment later, Nev appeared. "We want a drink," Pieter thundered at him. "For medicinal purposes. Now."

Nev looked at Theo, who hesitated, then nodded. "Right," Pieter said. "What've you got?"

"Would Your Holiness like to see the wine-cellar inventory?"

"The hell with wine," Pieter said, but Theo shushed him. Three little words. "Wine cellar inventory?"

"Yes, Your Holiness. It's very extensive. In excess of ten thousand bottles."

Theo smiled. "Fetch," he said.

"That's not the way to go about it," Pieter protested, as Nev withdrew. "Wine's all very well for polite social occasions, but for the genuine, all-out, peel-back-a-million-years-of-evolution experience, you need the hard stuff."

"Hush," Theo said gently. "Ah," he went on, as Nev reappeared with a large loose-leaf folder, "let's see what we've got here." He looked up and down the columns of names and dates, but nothing rang a bell. Not to worry. "I think we'll try the Château Cheval Blanc 1961. Thank you, Nev. Go in peace."

"I don't know what's got into you," Pieter growled, as Nev scuttled away. "Don't you understand? I don't want fruitiness, body, a faint tang of woodsmoke and a great nose. I want to get drunk."

Theo gave him a sweet and gentle smile. "Trust me."

"Trust you? The man who blew up the VVLHC?"

The smile died instantly. "You please yourself," Theo said. "You can stay here, get smashed, practise medicine, turn into soup, do what the hell you like. I plan on going home. You don't have to come. In fact, right now I'd rather you didn't."

"But—" What happened then was really rather fascinating. Pieter's lips continued to move for a second or so, presumably carrying on with the protests and the abuse, but no sound came out. Then he frowned. "You don't think—"

Theo nodded. "Yes."

"But what possible reason can you have for believing . . . ?"

Theo shrugged. "I don't know," he said. "Intuition. Instinct. A pattern gradually beginning to emerge. Anyhow," he added, "it's worth a try. And if I'm wrong, the worst that can happen is we get to share a bottle of nice wine."

"But—"

"Put it this way," Theo said. "A piece of string has two ends. Otherwise, it's not a piece of string. OK?"

"What's string got to do with anything, for crying out loud?"

Theo knew that if he was proved wrong he was going to regret this moment. But what the hell? It's not every day you get to be intolerably smug to a Nobel prizewinner. "String's got to do with everything," he said. "I'd have thought you'd have known that, being a professor. And put that horrible cigar out, it's giving me a headache."

Pieter glared at him, then ground out the butt on the arm of the throne. "You've changed," he said.

"Thank you."

Theo turned his back, walked to the window and gazed out at the view: the sea, the soaring buildings, the impossibly blue sky. True, it was a world in which Russia was still ruled by a Tsar and the Vatican stood where the Sydney Quay Deli ought to be; also, if Pieter had been telling the truth, the Internet hadn't happened and Europe was still ruled by the Caesars. Even so, from up here it looked habitable and survivable, if he didn't melt down to the consistency of thick minestrone over the next few days. Compared with how the world had looked the day after the VVLHC, the other Big Bang, it wasn't so bad. And, if he stayed here, he'd be free of YouSpace, that nasty little room where he'd bashed his brains out trying to do impossible maths, Max, Janine, Matasuntha's Uncle Bill, not to mention Matasuntha herself –

Yes. Well.

– Max, Janine, Matasuntha's Uncle Bill and the entire scientific community who reckoned he should've been coated in honey and pegged down over an anthill because of the harm he'd done to the popular conception of the sciences. That was an awful lot of bad stuff to leave behind in one go. Catastrophic change can sometimes have its good side. Having all your teeth pulled out at once isn't so bad if all of them were giving you toothache.

Nev was back, with a cobwebby bottle, a corkscrew and two glasses. Theo looked at the bottle for some time, then said, "I don't know how you do this."

"Simple," Pieter replied. "Pull the cork. If it's a single-use spatio-temporal dislocation module, the vortex effect automatically engages, and you're drawn into the dysperistaltic field, and there you are. If it's not, you tilt the bottle to roughly thirty degrees to the horizontal and aim the booze at a glass."

Theo went to get the bottle, but his hand was shaking. "You do it."

"If you like. If it's corked, though, we send it back. Agreed?"

Pieter slit the foil, drove in the corkscrew, wound it and pulled. There was a soft pop. Nothing happened. They looked at each other, then Pieter bent over the bottle and stared down into the neck. "Shit," he said, "it's just wi—"

* * *

Somewhere, far away down the beach, a radio was playing. The tune was familiar, but the words were slightly different:

Now everybody's got an ocean
Across the USA
Because of global warming,

The floods are here to stay.
They went and melted both the ice caps;
Stupid USA.

Oh, Theo thought. Not promising.

For some reason, Pieter seemed to have got there earlier; he was sitting in a striped blue and white canvas chair under a huge red umbrella, sipping a margarita. He was tanned, with blobs of white zinc cream on his nose and chin, and his feet were bare. He looked up, scowled and shouted, "Theo? Where the hell did you get to?"

"I just got here. Where is this?"

Pieter's wrath evaporated instantly. "Minneapolis," he replied. "Merry Christmas, by the way."

"Huh?"

"It's 25 December," Pieter said. "You're just in time for the hog roast."

"Minneapolis?"

Pieter nodded. Above his head, the sun was a white disc in a kingfisher-blue sky. Theo felt a drop of sweat roll down his nose, and wiped his forehead. "Ah," he said.

"Exactly. Christmas Day in Minneapolis, and it's ninety-two in the shade on the beach. Give you three guesses what's different about this reality."

"You sure it's not just the future?"

Pieter shook his head. "Time travel is impossible," he said confidently. "Trust me, I'm a physicist. Not here, though. Here, I'm Honest Pete Tomasek, joint owner of the Minneapolis Yacht Marina and Country Club." He frowned again. "You're my business partner. Which reminds me: there's a raft of cheques and stuff for you to sign. You'd better see to it ASAP."

"What the hell," Theo demanded, "are we doing in Minneapolis?"

Pieter yawned, twiddled the little wooden stick in his drink, drew it out and licked it. "You were right about the bottles in the Vatican cellar being single-use spatio-temporal dislocation modules. God only knows how you knew, but you knew. Where you went wrong was your choice of vintage. Still, on balance, this is better than where we just came from."

Little wheels were turning in Theo's head. "How long have you been here?"

"Three weeks," Pieter replied. "Just long enough to settle in and learn the ropes. I like it here."

"Three weeks. Shouldn't you be cream-of-physicist soup by now?"

Pieter beamed at him. "Yes. And I'm not. Which suggests there's something about this place that counteracts the degradation effect. Personally, I'm guessing it's to do with the damage to the ozone layer. Massive exposure to unfiltered UV light." He shrugged. "It'd probably be a good idea if I steered clear of Kryptonite while I'm here, but otherwise I can't really see a problem. Hence," he added, "the cheerful outlook and jovial demeanour. Have a drink. They mix the sneakiest margarita."

"Pieter," Theo glanced up at the sky. "We can't stay here. It's a dying planet."

For that he got a don't-be-a-fusspot gesture. "It's not that bad. They've got at least ninety years before the ambient radiation quotient reaches lethal. Also," he added cheerfully, "they've got me. If I invent some brilliant fix for the climate change thing, I can save the planet and really clean up financially. Or I could just sit here and veg out in peace. Don't you love it when you've got options?"

Theo looked at him. I'm not the only one who's changed, he thought. Or maybe it's just that rose-tinted spectacles don't work properly in an atmosphere saturated with the wrong kind of light. "Pieter."

"Hmm?"

"When I was your student," he said, "I looked up to you. I admired what you'd achieved. I respected you as a scientist and a human being. And now you're saying you don't give a damn, not unless you can make a lot of money out of global catastrophe."

Pieter gave him a sour look. "Blow it out your ear, Grasshopper," he said. "Don't you get it? We're stuck here. We tried your million-to-one long shot, and, guess what, it didn't work. No wine cellar, I checked. And there's no way your lunatic sister can call us, because that's impossible. We're stranded on, as you so rightly point out, a dying planet. The moral high ground's a bit different when there's self-induced floodwater lapping round the foot of it. There's nothing left to do here, Theo, it's too late. So." He sipped his drink and smiled. "The hell with it. Eat, drink and be insufferably self-righteous about other people's mistakes, for tomorrow they fry. Isn't that what being a scientist's all about?"

"Pieter—"

"Besides," Pieter went on, slamming his glass down on the table, "I'm beginning to have serious doubts about science in general. I mean, look at this place. Look what they've done to it. And who made it possible? Well?"

"Pieter—"

"People like me, is who. People with vision and imagination combined with knowledge, determination, passion and an infinite capacity for taking pains. Geniuses did this, Theo. Not fools, not people who count on their fingers and move their lips when they read. Idiots could never have figured out how to turn oozing black sludge into cheap energy, or designed the internal combustion engine. No, that took the finest minds the human race has ever produced. If we'd left it to the dumb-as-dogshit farmers, all this would be a golden ocean of frigging grain."

"Pieter—"

"Don't," Pieter snapped furiously. "Don't you dare say I'm wrong, because—"

"Wouldn't dream of it," Theo said meekly. "I just wanted to tell you, I know that woman."

Pieter blinked at him. "Uh?"

"That woman over there. Tall, smartly dressed, about fifty. She's something to do with Matasuntha's Uncle Bill."

"It's possible, I guess," Pieter said. "I mean, this friend of yours could have an exact equivalent in this universe. But the odds against running into the mirror-reality double of someone you know are so vast I never even bothered to consider it."

"She's waving at us."

"No, that's impossible," Pieter said firmly. "The odds against knowing the mirror-reality double of someone you know are—"

"She's heading this way."

"What?"

"She's coming to see us. She's got a wine bottle."

Pieter's head slowly turned. "Does she know about—?"

"Oh yes."

Pieter sat bolt upright so fast he poked himself in the eye with one of the spokes of the umbrella. "That's crazy," he said. "Why would anyone in their right mind want to come here?"

"What?"

"The bottles," Pieter said. "They were sort of like the Mark One version of YouSpace. Each bottle is a one-off return trip to a pre-selected alternate reality."

"I know. So?"

"So," Pieter said, "when I chose them, I picked nice places. The sort of place you'd want to go to. Vacation spots. The sort of place, in other words, that this isn't. So how in hell has one of my bottles brought her here?"

"Hold on," Theo said. "You've been here before?"

"God, no," Pieter replied. "It was all strictly theoretical. What I mean is, I calculated the probability needed to access a given alternate reality, and programmed the bottle's guidance parameters accordingly. I didn't test-drive the things."

"Think about it," Theo said. "One of your bottles brought us from the Vatican to here."

Pieter looked blank. "I suppose it did, at that. Except that those bottles were in an alternate reality, so – oh, the hell with it, I give up. Why does everything have to be so complicated?"

Coming from Pieter, that was a bit like George W. Bush saying, Why don't people check their facts before plunging into things? Even so, Theo couldn't be bothered to comment. The woman, who was quite definitely Mrs Duchene-Wilamowicz, in an elegant navy-blue suit with matching navy court shoes and shoulder bag, was bearing down on them with a look on her face that would've stopped a runaway train. Theo was about to call out to her when he noticed that Pieter had wriggled ninety degrees in his chair and was trying to hide his face behind his hands; curious behaviour, even by his standards –

"Mr Bernstein."

– but so what? He turned and gave his rescuer a huge smile. "Mrs Duchene—"

"What the hell do you think you're playing at?"

Ah, he thought. Hostility. Not to worry, though. He'd been in deep trouble so long he was thinking of making it his domicile for tax purposes. "Am I glad to see you," he went on. "How did you . . . ?"

Mrs Duchene-Wilamowicz sat down and put the wine bottle on the table. "Guesswork," she said. "An extremely speculative long shot. Honestly, we've been worried sick about you. What were you thinking of, going off like that without telling anyone? Oh for pity's sake, Pieter," she added, "get a grip."

Pieter winced and edged round, but avoided eye contact. "Hi, Dolly," he said sheepishly.

Theo had to ask. "You know him?"

Pieter was about to say something, but he got a direct hit from a stare that would've done wonders for the planet's ice-caps, and subsided into meek silence. "It was Matasuntha's idea," she said. "He's an idealist, she said. Try the global-warming planet. Don't be ridiculous, I told her, nobody would be that stupid. But she insisted, and here you are."

"Global . . . ?"

"Yes. The planet where they reversed global warming. That's why you're here, isn't it?"

"Um."

She frowned. "We assumed you might come here so you could find out how they did it. Just the sort of quixotic stunt you'd be capable of, she said. "Mrs Duchene-Wilamowicz raised an eyebrow. "That's not why you're here. Oh well, not that it matters. Come on, I'll take you back. And then you can go and fetch Max."

Theo didn't mean to make a loud whimpering noise. It just slipped out. "Max?"

"Yes, Max. Your brother. Your brother, who you abandoned in a cave surrounded by dangerous animals."

"It wasn't his—"

"Quiet, Pieter." A click of the tongue, like a bone snapping. "I suppose you'll want to come back too. Really, you're not safe let loose on your own."

Pieter mumbled something. The word sorry was in there somewhere. Meanwhile, three words had just percolated through into Theo's brain. "Reversed global warming?"

"Yes, that's right."

Theo looked out across the bay, where gulls circled over

the Minnesota Sea. “Um,” he said, “I don’t think so. Otherwise, this lot wouldn’t be quite so under water.”

“That’s what it’s supposed to be,” Mrs Duchene-Wilamowicz said briskly. “There was supposed to have been a catastrophic disaster caused by the malfunction of a large-scale scientific experiment, which raised the ambient temperature by twelve degrees. Oh well.” She shrugged. “Pieter must’ve made a mess of his arithmetic. Wouldn’t be the first time. Come on, then, if you’re coming.”

She probably owns dogs, Theo thought; she’s used to that level of obedience. “Just a moment, though,” he said. “Why are you so concerned about my stupid brother? Why is everybody—?”

“Later,” Mrs Duchene-Wilamowicz said firmly. “We don’t want to be stranded here, do we?”

Theo nodded his head so vigorously he nearly became the first man to hang himself, standing up, without a rope. “Absolutely,” he said. “How do we do that, exactly?”

Mrs Duchene-Wilamowicz opened her bag and took out a pair of reading glasses and a cork. “It’s written on here,” she said. “Different every time, which is annoying.”

“It’s all to do with the parallel vector index,” Pieter said defensively. “It’s one of the things that made me decide the one-off modules were a dead end.”

Mrs Duchene-Wilamowicz made a very soft grunting noise, presumably signifying scepticism. “Right,” she said, putting the cork and her glasses back in her bag and snapping the clasp shut. “We need a waiter.”

“Of course we do,” Theo said. “What the hell for?”

“To take our order, of course.” She lifted her head, and instantly a young man in dark trousers and waistcoat came racing up to the table, holding a small notebook, thereby confirming Theo’s initial impression of Mrs Duchene-Wilamowicz. He’d already decided that she was one of those quiet, forceful women. Now he knew she was a waiter-whisperer as well. It all fitted.

"Right," she said. "To start, we'll have prosciutto, olives, roasted garlic, peperoncini, artichoke hearts, rocket pesto, Milanese salami and thinly sliced mozzarella, with a very light dressing of virgin olive oil."

"*Si, signora*. And to follow?"

"Lasagna verde, vermicelli, capellini, fusilli lunghi, tagliatelli and stuffed manicotti. But," she added, skewering the waiter with a look that would've pierced tank armour, "we want all that at the same time as the first course. That's very important. Do you understand?"

"*Si, signora.*"

"And on separate trays," Mrs Duchene-Wilamowicz went on. "That's very important too."

"*Si, signora.*"

"Both courses simultaneously, but separate."

"Si. And wine?"

"No." She nodded, releasing him, and he scuttled away. Mrs Duchene-Wilamowicz breathed a little sigh, and folded her arms tightly. "I do hope he's got that straight," she said. "You never can tell with waiters."

"Um, have we got time for lunch?" Theo asked warily. "Only, I thought we were in a hurry to get back."

"We are. Pieter," she snapped suddenly, "what are you doing?"

Pieter was writing frantically on the only surface available – the back of his left hand. "Not now, Dolly," he said. "I think I'm on to something."

"Pieter."

Yes, a remarkable woman, able to materialise waiters and quite possibly calm thunderstorms and raise the dead. But was she powerful enough to command Pieter van Goyen? Apparently she was. "What?"

"You're up to something. What are you doing?"

Pieter scowled, then put down his pen. "Actually, it was something you said."

"I rather doubt that. What did I say?"

"The planet where they reversed global warming," Pieter replied. "As it happens, I remember programming that particular bottle, purely as an intellectual exercise. I never imagined it'd be anything like this."

"And, clearly, you got it wrong," Mrs Duchene-Wilamowicz replied. "Hence, as Mr Bernstein pointed out, all the water."

Pieter smiled and shook his head. "No, it came out just right," he said. "This is the planet where they found out how to put right the damage. It must be. I found it."

"Hm."

"But," Pieter went on, "like you say, it hasn't happened yet. Therefore, it's going to happen, at some point, most likely in the very near future."

"I'm sure that's a great comfort, Pieter. Meanwhile—"

"My program," Pieter went on, somehow managing to override her command protocols, "was designed to put a visitor down at the most interesting place and time for any given venue. Therefore, we've arrived at the point where they make the great discovery. Stands to reason. Inevitable."

"If you say so, Pieter, dear." Mrs Duchene-Wilamowicz made a show of looking round. "I have to say, though, it's not looking particularly likely."

"You think so?"

"Oh come on," she said. "This is hardly the sort of place where you'd expect to find a scientific genius doing epoch-making work."

Pieter lifted his head and gave her a beautiful smile. "Well," he said. "Not if you will insist on interrupting me."

The effect was as though she'd just found a dead frog in her terrine of venison. "You—"

"Obvious when you think about it," Pieter said cheerfully. "I'm the key element in the program. I come here, solve the problem—"

"Pieter."

"And as soon as I realised that," Pieter went blithely on, "as soon as I knew I was bound to succeed, I had this really rather wonderful idea. You see, basically, what you need is two huge great refrigeration units, one at each pole. What's the main active agent in refrigeration? Propane gas. And what vast untapped natural resource lies directly under Alaska and Antarctica? Whopping great oil fields. So, all you'd need to do is—"

Mrs Duchene-Wilamowicz let out a long but entirely dignified sigh. "When we get back home," she said, "I'll have to write to all the encyclopedias, because the Great Wall of China will no longer be the largest man-made structure on the planet. Your ego—"

"Dolly." Pieter's voice was quite quiet, but it shut her up instantly. "Young Theo here was just lecturing me on what a waste it'd be if I didn't use my exceptional talents in the service of mankind—"

"Not quite how I put it," Theo mumbled defensively, but he still got scowled at.

"Well," Pieter went on, "for once he's quite right. I'm here at this place, at this time, for a reason."

"Manifest destiny," Mrs Duchene-Wilamowicz said sourly.

"If you like, yes. I was sent herc by a superior power. Me," he added happily. "Not someone you argue with. Well, you do, of course, but that's just your incredibly bossy nature. No, it's quite plain. I ordained that I should come here and do this thing. So, obviously, it's my duty."

"Oh for pity's sake," Mrs Duchene-Wilamowicz said. "Well? What do you want?"

The waiter, who'd appeared with a tray in his hand, shrank back a step. "*Signora*—"

"What? Oh, put it down. And where's the pasta? I told you, simultaneously."

"*Si, signora. Un momento, per favore.*" He darted away and came back a few seconds later with a second tray. When he was a yard or so from the table, Mrs Duchene-Wilamowicz barked "Stop!" He stopped. "Put the tray down, and go away."

The waiter put the tray down carefully on the ground, backed off a few paces, then turned and fled. Mrs Duchene-Wilamowicz examined both trays for a moment, then turned to face Pieter. "So," she said. "You want to stay here, is that it?"

"Yes."

"Fine. I wash my hands of you. You can stay here, work your miracles and rot, for all I care. Just don't expect me to come traipsing round after you when you realise you're stuck here for ever."

Pieter grinned. "Oh, I'll be fine," he said. "Theo'll come back for me, won't you?"

"Um," Theo said.

"Of course you will. Dolly," he went on, "exactly what do you think you're doing with those trays?"

She was holding one tray directly over the other, lining up the edges with total precision. "Really, Pieter," she said. "A genius like you. You ought to be able to work it out from first principles."

Pieter shook his head. "Not a clue, sorry."

"Ah well." She paused for effect, then went on: "According to the instructions on the cork, in order to get home we need to trigger a massive carbon-oxygen implosion. The only way we can do this in this particular reality is the total annihilation effect brought about by the collision of pasta and antipasta. So—"

"Dolly—"

She looked at him. "Goodbye, Pieter," she said..

"Dolly, I was kidding. The instructions were meant as a joke. What you really need to do is—"

Mrs Duchene-Wilamowicz let go of the tray. There was a crash, the sound of splintering crockery –

"Dolly—"

– followed by an ear-splitting roar and a sheet of white flame that blotted out everything.

"Oh," Theo said, as his head stopped spinning. "It worked."

He'd felt better. There had been the heat of the flames on his skin, the indescribable sensation of being poured uphill into the mouth of a narrow bottle; and then this. He took a deep breath, staggered, caught himself just in time and subsided, with some degree of control and dignity, on to the carpeted floor.

"Well, of course it worked," Mrs Duchene-Wilamowicz said. "I followed the instructions on the bottle. Not what most men would have done, of course, but I have this strange belief that instructions are put there so you'll know what to do. Must you sprawl on the floor like that, by the way? It's so hard to have an intelligent conversation with someone in a different plane."

Floor. Well, yes, she had a point there. "Sorry," he said, and tried to stand up, but his knees wouldn't take his weight. Fortunately, the carpet was deep and springy. "Where is this?" he said.

"Home. Well, sort of. Our reality."

He had another go. This time, he made it, but only because someone helped him. He swung round to find out who his unseen assistant might be, and –

"Lunchbox."

The tall, thin young man smiled awkwardly and made a grunting noise that might just possibly have been some sort of articulate speech. Theo yelped and tried to pull away, but Lunchbox's hand was locked round his elbow. Where he kept his muscles was anybody's guess, but he quite definitely had some.

"Don't make a fuss," Mrs Duchene-Wilamowicz said briskly, "you'll only hurt yourself and it won't do a bit of good."

"But that's not right," Theo blurted out. "Lunchbox is one of Janine's goons, surely."

The look on the young man's face made him feel desperately guilty, as though he'd just kicked a baby wolf cub. Mrs Duchene-Wilamowicz clicked her tongue. "The term you're groping for is private enquiry agent," she said. "We don't use the G-word, it's not polite. Arthur, dear, you don't have to grip quite so tightly. Mr Bernstein isn't going to run away."

The pressure on his elbow relaxed slightly, allowing a tiny trickle of blood to squeeze down into Theo's almost completely numb forearm. "Where is this?" Theo repeated. "I don't recognise it."

"This is my daughter's house," Mrs Duchene-Wilamowicz said. "It'll be your place of work from now on. Sorry, didn't I tell you? You're working for me now. After all, someone's got to keep you on the ball. You're very bright and a good physicist, but you lack focus."

"You can't do that," Theo yelped. "You can't just steal me."

"Why not? Besides, it's not stealing. You don't belong to anyone."

"I belong to me."

"You don't count. Also, you want to help. You want to get Max back. He's your brother."

They train dogs easily enough. Go about it the right way

and you can transform a tail-wagging, face-licking man's best friend into an implacable killing machine just by saying one word. But you couldn't do that with humans, surely.

Maybe you could. It would all depend, presumably, on the word. Three letters, proper noun, beginning with M, rhymes with 'fax' –

"Screw Max. The hell with Max. I hope they catch him and feed him to the cuddly warthog from *The Lion King*. May meerkats feast on his decomposing—"

He stopped, but only because Lunchbox had stuck a sandwich in his mouth. It took him three seconds to choke and another two seconds to spit it out, by which time his fury had abated a little, and curiosity had elbowed its way in front of the mic. "What do you care about my useless brother, anyhow? Why is everybody obsessed with that lying, swindling, pathetic—?"

Lunchbox sighed tragically and produced another sandwich. Theo took the hint and lifted his free hand in token of surrender. And noticed something.

Mrs Duchene-Wilamowicz was way ahead of him. "It's back," she said. "Your invisible hand."

"No, that's not—" Theo stared at it, then shook his head. "We're still in a YouSpace world, aren't we?" he said. "You're playing games with me."

"Wait just a moment. You'll see."

Theo's eyes were still fixed on his hand. Was it just his imagination, or was it getting paler? White, pearly white like a light bulb, translucent. "No!" he wailed, but it was no good. He could see the opposite wall through the outline of his metacarpal.

"Radiation," Mrs Duchene-Wilamowicz said. "You did know that, didn't you? That's what happened to it when the hadron collider blew up. I imagine when you heard the blast or saw the flash, you instinctively raised your hand to shield your face. Which, on reflection, was probably just as well, or else your normal blank expression would've been blanker still."

"That's right, I—" Theo's head snapped up, and he stared at her. "Radiation?"

She nodded slowly. "Rather a stiff dose, I'm afraid. As far as living on borrowed time is concerned, you're the oncological equivalent of the Eurozone. However – oh, pull yourself together, for pity's sake."

Theo looked at her, but all he could see through the tears was a sort of blurry, splodgy mass. "However?"

"That—" She nodded at his hand, which was now just a cartoon outline sticking out of his shirt cuff. "That is an extremely hopeful sign. You see, every time you translocate to an alternative reality, a portion of the radioactive contamination is leeched out of your system. One or two more trips, and—" She shrugged. "No guarantees," she said. "This is all practically unexplored territory, medically speaking. But it's your best chance. After all, why else do you think Pieter left you the YouSpace technology?"

Theo's head had been doing a lot of swimming lately, enough for it to be in serious contention for the 2016 Olympics. This one, though, had it doing butterfly stroke. "Pieter knew—"

"Of course he did. How do you suppose I know about it? Because Pieter told me. It was his way of making it up to you."

Dead silence, apart from the strange, otherworldly sound of Lunchbox eating a Jaffa Cake. "Making it up to me for what, exactly?"

"For blowing up the Very Very Large Hadron Collider."

"Um, no. Other way round, surely. It was me who blew up the VVLHC."

"No."

"Yes. It was me. Really it was. I moved the decimal place—"

The rest of the sentence melted away, like snow on a hot flue. What was it, Theo couldn't help wondering, about this woman, anyhow? She had a knack of making him feel like he was five years old and had just flushed the keys to Daddy's new Mercedes down the toilet. All she'd done was press her lips a tiny bit closer together and, well, look at him, and he felt a sudden urge to sit down and write out I Must Not Talk In Class five hundred times.

"My mistake," she said eventually. "I said just now you were a good physicist. Obviously not."

"That's right. That's why I blew up the—"

"You did not blow up the Very Very Large Hadron Collider. Oh, for crying out loud," she added impatiently, "did it never occur to you to check the figures? Yes, you made a boo-boo with your sums. Yes, you moved the decimal point the wrong way. But if you'd bothered to go back and do the maths again, you'd have realised your mistake wasn't anything like enough to blow the whole shooting match. The worst that would've happened was it'd have tripped a fuse and knocked it out for a day or so. Arthur, you can let go of him now. I think he's changed his mind about wanting to run away."

Lunchbox let go of Theo's arm, which lolled bonelessly from his elbow and dangled, unnoticed. "But that's not right," Theo said weakly. "I mean, I—"

She was right, though. Even as he'd been speaking, his mind had been running the calculations, and she was right. There had been three fail-safes and two redundant systems standing between his misplaced dot and total meltdown. He'd been so quick to assume that it had been his fault, he hadn't even considered them. "Hold on," he whispered. "If I didn't—"

She looked at him and didn't say a word.

"Pieter?"

She nodded.

"No. No, I'm sorry, but that's just impossible. Pieter may be a bit of a jerk sometimes, and slightly more self-centred than a centrifuge, but he could never make a mistake like—"

"It wasn't a mistake."

Lunchbox ate a sausage roll, two Garibaldi biscuits and an apple. Then Theo said, "What?"

"It wasn't a mistake," Mrs Duchene-Wilamowicz said. "It was deliberate. He needed to find out the maximum acceleration stress factor for the antigravitic buffers before he could use the same technology for the single-use module project. The wine cellar," she translated helpfully. "Anyhow, the only way to do that was by destruct testing. So, he blew up the VVLHC." She smiled at him. "And blamed it on you."

The top of Theo's head was a tooth, and his brain was an abscess. "No."

Mrs Duchene-Wilamowicz shrugged gracefully. "It's the truth," she said. "And I know it's true, because Pieter told me so himself. All your misery and unhappiness, the shame, the disgrace, your wife leaving you, the whole thing, is all Pieter's fault. All of it."

"No." He wanted to hit her, and presumably it showed, because Lunchbox hurriedly gulped down half a cherry Bakewell and flexed his long fingers. Theo didn't notice. "And even if you're right, it wasn't all his fault. I mean, it wasn't Pieter that made Schliemann Brothers go bust."

She cleared her throat. "Actually," she said, "yes, it was. Schliemanns had lent twelve billion dollars to a private consortium working on a roughly similar project to Pieter's. When the VVLHC blew up, the other backers pulled out, the consortium folded and Schliemanns had to file for bankruptcy. Two birds with one stone, as far as Pieter was concerned. He got his test results and put his only rivals out of business, and you took the blame, got irradiated and lost all the money you inherited from your father. He's smart, my brother."

Enough is enough. With a wail of horrified fury, Theo lunged at her. She sidestepped neatly, and for a moment he seemed to hang in the air, like Tom the cat in the cartoons when he runs off a cliff. Then Lunchbox hit him over the head with a solid-steel thermos full of French onion soup, and for a while all his troubles seemed so far away.

PART FIVE

One Empty San Miguel Bottle To Bring Them All And In The Darkness Bind Them

Subconsciously, he didn't want to wake up. What, me, his inner being said to his awareness-of-self, go back out there and deal with all that weird, crazy shit, when I could stay in here where it's nice and snug and nobody wants to tell me anything or make me do stuff that screws up my world view to the core? Get lost, said his inner being. Go pester someone who gives a damn.

But, apparently, he had no say in the matter; and so, some indeterminate time later, he opened his eyes and –

(He's smart, my brother. Oh boy.)

– saw a pair of flowery chintz curtains drawn across a window, set in a wall with brightly coloured wallpaper figured with nursery rhyme characters. There, for example, was Humpty Dumpty, sitting on a wall, looking uncannily like Dick Cheney; there were the three little pigs in their house of straw, on the point of finding out that good ventilation isn't always an unalloyed blessing; there was Mary and her lamb, and –

He pulled his arm out from under the sheets and stared at it. Not visible. So he was in his native reality, at least. Small mercies.

"How are you feeling?"

The voice came from his left, and he was horribly afraid he

knew who it belonged to. He rolled over, sighed and said, "You."

The old man beamed at him and nodded. "Young Art's just nipped out to get a bite to eat," he said, "so I'm kind of minding the store, so to speak. Talking of which," the old man went on, "I do hope you're not going to get violent again, because I am authorised to use lethal force if absolutely necessary."

"What do you—?"

"Sorry." The old man tugged at something in his ear. "Hearing aid's playing up," he explained. "Say again?"

"What do you mean, lethal – forget it," Theo sighed. "Look, where am I? What the hell is going on?"

The old man gave him a sympathetic half-smile half-frown. "Sorry," he said. "Need-to-know basis, that is. If I told you, I'd have to kill you."

"You'd have to—"

"Say what?"

"Doesn't matter," Theo said, and let his head rest gently against the pillows. They were wonderfully soft, perhaps the most luxurious things he'd ever felt. A person could go to sleep, lying on pillows as soft as that.

"Art wanted me to tell you, he's really sorry he had to hit you like that."

"Why? Did he spill his soup?"

"He's a good boy. Mr Bernstein, really he is," the old man said passionately. "He's not usually violent, you know, in fact he's very sensitive and creative. You should see the drawings he done when he was a kid. Trees and sheep and all that. His mum's still got them stuck up on her fridge."

He rubbed the back of his head with his invisible hand. "Sure," he said. "Quite the young Damian Hirst. Where does he put it all, by the way? He should be fat as a pig."

"It's his glands," the old man said sadly. "They never been right, his glands, but he never complains."

"How could he? His mouth's always full of sandwiches."

The old man couldn't bring himself to answer that, and looked away. So did Theo, who was scanning his immediate environment for something he could use as a weapon. The old man looked reasonably harmless, but Theo had seen enough martial arts movies to know that the deadliest fighters on the planet are doddery ninety-year-old Chinese. The old man didn't look Chinese, but the way his luck had been running lately, he wasn't inclined to take chances. Unfortunately, the most lethal object within arm's reach was a large pink stuffed rabbit, with a satin bow round its neck and a sort of twisted Anthony Perkins look on its face that sent a cold shiver down Theo's spine. So what. Necessity is the mother of invention, which probably explains why invention's father left home on the pretext of buying a newspaper and hasn't been heard of since.

"So," Theo said, "where exactly are we? Oh, I forgot, you can't tell me that."

"Sorry, Mr Bernstein."

"How about telling me who you're working for?"

"Sorry, Mr Bernstein."

"Well, I know the answer to that one. Mrs Duchene-Wilamowicz, obviously. You had enough of my sister, then."

"No comment."

"God knows I don't blame you. She was bad enough when she was ten. Tried to letterbomb the local zoo as a protest against man's inhumanity to small furry animals. Would've succeeded too, except she hadn't quite appreciated that not all fertilisers make good explosives. What they got was an improvised timing device strapped to a bottle of Baby Bio."

"That's very sad, Mr Bernstein. Probably she was unhappy at home."

"No more so than the rest of us," Theo replied, yawning and stretching, and in the process grabbing the horrible rabbit with his invisible hand. "My mother had the good sense to clear out, but the rest of us were stuck there: me, Janine, Max and Dad. It wasn't a good combination. We got complaints from the vipers' nest next door saying we lowered the tone of the neighbourhood."

"Is that right?"

"You bet." Slowly, without breaking eye contact, he dragged the rabbit under the covers. "On balance, I guess Max was the worst, but Janine came pretty close, bless her. She never liked me, I don't know why. It's not like I ever did anything to deserve it. Quite the opposite. I was always the one trying to keep her from getting into trouble. Don't do it, I said, you'll regret it later, it'll all end in tears. But Max kept egging her on."

"Some people are funny like that, Mr Bernstein. Not me. I like everybody."

"Me too. Well, everybody except Max. As far as Janine goes, I try very hard not to bear a grudge. Mind you, when it rains I try not to get wet, but sometimes you can't get your coat on in time, you know?"

"I got a sister myself. We've always got on very well. Would you like to see some photos?"

"Freeze." With a snake-like movement, Theo pulled Disturbed Rabbit out from under the bedclothes and thrust it at the old man as though it was a gun. "There's an improvised explosive device hidden inside this toy," he said. "Try anything and I'll blow us both to hell."

The old man frowned. "You sure, Mr Bernstein? I been here all the time and you only just woke up. There wasn't time."

"I work quickly."

"Improvised out of what, exactly?"

"I'm a physicist," Theo snarled. "It was physicists who split the atom, remember? Well, this thing's crawling with atoms."

"Yes, but—"

"Listen," Theo said. "You know the Very Very Large Hadron Collider? I blew that up using nothing but a pencil and a scrap of paper. Don't mess with me. I mean it."

"Now then, Mr Bernstein. Don't do anything stupid."

"What, like rescuing my brother? No chance. That's why I'm getting out of here. In one piece, for choice, but if not, in lots and lots of little tiny bits." He gave the rabbit a wild shake, and its ears waggled alarmingly. "I'm going to count to three, and then—"

"All right." The old man's eyes were wide with fear. "Don't blow us up, Mr Bernstein, young Art could be back any minute, I promised his mum I'd look after him. Please, Mr Bernstein."

Grinning, Theo clambered out of bed, the rabbit gripped firmly in his outstretched hand. "I'm going now," he said. "But first, you're going to answer a few questions. Who are you working for?"

"I can't tell you that."

Theo pushed the rabbit into his face. "One."

"Mrs Duchene-watsername. Honest."

"Thank you. Where are we?"

"I don't know. Really I don't," he added, as the rabbit's ears danced like treetops in a gale. "I got given one of those SatNav things, it said turn left here and take the second exit, I just did like it said. Some place out in the country, is all I know."

Theo gave him a ferocious scowl, but he was fairly sure the old man was telling the truth. "Where's the car?"

"Round the back. Keys are in the ignition."

"Fine. You're a hostage. Move."

"Mr Bernstein."

"Don't be a hero, old man," Theo said. "Think of Art. Think of all the bacon sandwiches he'll never eat if he's blown to kingdom come."

"It's not that, Mr Bernstein. I just thought, you might want to get dressed first."

A valid point. "Don't move, all right?" Theo said. "Stay absolutely still. Don't even breathe."

"Right you are."

Theo looked round. "You wouldn't happen to know where my clothes are, would you?"

"In the wardrobe, Mr Bernstein."

"Thanks."

"No problem."

It was awkward, putting on his trousers and shirt with just the one invisible hand while brandishing Disturbed Rabbit menacingly with the other. Worth it, though. The alternative – staying put and having to cope with what he'd learned – didn't bear thinking about. With any luck, his old job at the slaughterhouse might still be available. When he thought about it, those happy, stress-free days before he'd ever heard of YouSpace, the nostalgia was almost too much to bear. "Right," he said, fumbling the last button into its hole, "we're off. And don't try anything, understood?"

"Whatever you say, Mr Bernstein."

Theo waited for a moment, then snapped, "Move!"

"Sorry, I was waiting for you."

"You go first. I follow you."

"Ah, got you. Sorry. This is all new to me, I never been a hostage before."

"That's perfectly all right," Theo said. "When you're quite ready."

"Where are we going, exactly?"

"The car," Theo said.

"Sorry?"

"The car."

"Right, yes. You want me to drive?"

"Yes. No. You sit in the back and stay absolutely still and quiet. Got that?"

"Loud and clear, Mr Bernstein."

The house was huge. He'd felt twinges of agoraphobia the first time he'd been shown round the VVLHC site (the echoing man-made caverns, the vast, perspective-twisting white-tiled tunnels), but that was nothing compared to this place. God could've played hide-and-seek there and had a really boring time. What made it ever so slightly worse was the décor: pink, white and pale blue, with satin tiebacks on every curtain and enough scatter-cushions to fill the Mariana Trench. There was only one person in the world with taste that bad, and he'd known her all his life.

"Nearly there. Mr Bernstein," the old man wheezed, as they clattered down a grand pink-marble staircase into a sitting room the size of Syntagma Square. "We can get out through the french windows and on to the drive, then round the side and we're there. Mr Bernstein?"

Theo had come to a dead stop. He wanted to get out of there, in roughly the same way a bullet is anxious to leave the barrel of a gun, but there was a noise coming from the other side of a door, and somehow he couldn't move past it without confirming his suspicions. He knew that noise. Only one thing had ever sounded quite like that.

"No, Mr Bernstein, you really don't want to—"

But Mr Bernstein really did. He opened the door, and saw –

It all made sense, now he saw it. The whole house had been built around it, leaving a huge space in the middle, in which stood – well, you'd have to call it the Very Very Very Very Large Hadron Collider, or maybe even the Ridiculously Big Hadron Collider's Big Brother. He was standing on the outer circumference of a circular room, looking up at the underside of a dome. Every surface was panelled with mirror-polished titanium alloy plating, and around the curved walls coiled a glowing blue transparent tube, spiralling upwards like a compressed spring. Far away in the dead centre of the chamber stood a glass and steel tower, glowing Mordor-green, partially masked by a swirling cloud of dry ice. The hum came from under the floor, ran up through the soles of his feet and out into his fingertips and the ends of his hair. In the distance, a machine voice was counting down: a million and thirty-six, a million and thirty-five. Ten feet away from him stood a small aluminium trolley, on which rested a laptop, some diagnostic equipment, a pair of lead gloves and an empty coffee mug marked World's Best Dad.

He looked down at his hands. One was invisible. The other was slightly translucent.

That wasn't good. With what little self-control he had left he pulled himself together, turned round and headed for the door, only to find that he wasn't alone. Five more or less human shapes in dull grey metallic suits were lumbering towards him, their faces indistinguishable behind the visors of their goldfish-bowl helmets. He had a feeling they weren't there to sell him souvenirs.

The cell was small the way the collision chamber had been big. He could stand up if he ducked his head, but why bother? Instead, he sat on the concrete bench and stared at the door, which was lead-lined and a metre thick. There wasn't a window or even a light bulb, but he didn't need one. He could see perfectly well by his own pale blue glow.

There are worse ways to die than massive radiation poisoning. Four of them; and they're no fun, either. Right now, he didn't feel too bad. In fact, he felt perfectly fine, apart from the cramp, hunger and a pressing need to go to the toilet. Of course, it was only a matter of time before the first symptoms made themselves felt, and then that'd be it.

Meanwhile, if he was really lucky, he might have just enough time to try and make sense of it all and fail miserably. Better, on the whole, not to bother. Let's just sit here and think about nothing at all.

He was just getting the hang of thinking of nothing at all when the door opened and the goldfish-bowl-heads bustled in. They grabbed him, put him on a gurney, stuck a bag over his head and took him for a long ride.

"Really, Mr Bernstein. What are we going to do with you?"

What a question. "I'm not sure," he replied into the darkness. "You could try a really thick lead coffin and dumping me at the bottom of the sea, but that'd be a bit harsh on the local fishermen. Other than that, it's a problem. Luckily, not mine."

Something tugged at the back of his head, and he was blinded by a star going supernova. It turned out to be a single low-wattage light bulb. "Hello, Mrs Duchene-Wilamowicz," he said. "You shouldn't be here, you know."

"You idiot," she said. "You were told not to go in there, and what did you do?"

I know who you are, he thought. But there's no point going into all that now. "Look who's talking," he said. "In case you hadn't noticed, I'm glowing blue all over. The surgeon general has determined that glowing-blue people are bad for your health."

She raised an eyebrow. "I'm touched by your concern."

"Oh, you know what they say. Thicker than water. In my case right now, of course, maybe not."

She nodded slowly. "You've figured it out, then."

He was mildly offended. "I should damn well think so," he said. "You haven't exactly made it difficult. More a case of saturation bombing with bloody great hints. I have to say," he went on, "as far as I'm concerned, this isn't a joyous experience."

She shrugged. "Too late to do anything about it now," she said. "Anyhow, let's get on with it."

"Excuse me?"

"You're going back to the Disney planet," she said. "To save Max."

Theo grinned. "No I'm not."

"Yes you are."

"No I'm not."

"Yes you—" She closed her eyes and breathed out slowly. "Let me spell it out for you," she said. "You've been exposed to a lethal dose of van Goyen's radiation—"

"Good name," Theo said. "Classy."

"Your only hope of survival," she went grimly on, "is purging the radiotoxins by means of quantum displacement via the YouSpace device. As you're now aware, we've reconstructed the YouSpace technology here in this building. We've reverse-engineered the guidance system software from our analysis of the single-use bottles. All we're lacking is an understanding of how to operate the software."

"The user's manual."

"If you like, yes. The only person with that knowledge, apart from Pieter van Goyen, is you."

"Not quite," Theo interrupted. "Matasuntha—"

"Very well, the only person apart from her. The point is, we have the car but you've got the keys. And if you don't go now, you're going to die, thanks to your idiotic—"

"Right, thanks, I get the point." Theo shook his head sadly. "Where's the bottle?"

"Bottle?"

"The YouSpace bottle. You said you'd made one."

Exasperated hissing-kettle noise. "I said we'd built a van

Goyen Accelerator," she said. "You saw it. The big shiny thing that made you sick. That's it."

Theo gave her a horrified look. "I can't use that," he said. "All I know about is using the bottle Pieter left me. The one that got broken. Without it, the user's manual won't work."

"Try it."

"I can't," Theo snapped at her. "It'd be like trying to steer a car with a rudder. It can't be done."

Mrs Duchene-Wilamowicz narrowed her eyes. "Wing it," she hissed.

"Fine." Theo shrugged. "In that case, I'll need a piece of paper and a pencil."

Mrs Duchene-Wilamowicz nodded, and a goldfish bowl produced the back of an envelope and a biro. "Now push off," Theo said. "I need to concentrate."

Mrs Duchene-Wilamowicz hesitated, then made a shooing gesture. The goldfish bowls withdrew. "You too," Theo said. "I can't think with you peering over my shoulder."

"Try."

"No, really. It's not something I can do with people watching. I promise I won't run away."

She gave him a look as long and cold as a Canadian winter. "Please yourself," she said. "I'm warning you, though. Don't mess with me. I want Max back, alive, in one piece. Once you've done that, I really don't give a damn what happens to you. Understood?"

Theo smiled. "Perfectly. Goodbye."

She looked at him, frowned, shook her head and left the room. Theo spent the next twenty seconds flushing her out of his head. Then he looked down at the piece of paper.

I can do this, he told himself. After all, Pieter did it. And I think I know how.

He closed his eyes, took the pen in his invisible hand and

rested it lightly on the paper. Suppose, he told himself, just suppose I'm Pieter van Goyen. I want to do something, but I know for a fact that it's impossible. Well, yes; impossible in this reality, because it breaks all the local laws of physics. But the multiverse is infinite. Therefore, every possibility, however impossible, exists somewhere within it. Therefore, somewhere, there's a parallel reality where the rules are completely different, and this thing I want to do is as easy as sneezing in a pepper factory.

What I want to do is travel from one version of reality to another. Can't be done; not here. There, it's a piece of cake. I'm not there, I'm here. But if I was there, it'd be ludicrously simple for me to travel from there to here, and back again. And if, while I was at it, I happened to collect myself and give myself a lift back to there, it'd save me all the effort, pain and frustration of doing all the maths and stuff here, only to find that what I'm seeking to do can't be done.

The multiverse is infinite. Therefore, somewhere, there's a version of reality where (a) the rules are completely different, and (b) reality-hopping is as straightforward as climbing aboard a bus, and (c) I'm already there. Being me, I know that I desperately want to be collected and given a lift. True, in so doing I'll create a spatio-temporal paradox resulting in a feedback loop and possibly endangering the entire quantum continuum, but what the hell. Like I give a damn. After all, didn't I blow up the VVLHC and dump the blame on my poor, long-suffering former student just so I could test out a theory? When you're me, none of the rules apply.

In which case –

He looked down. The pen and the envelope had vanished. In their place lay a small green bottle. Tightly curled and stuck in the mouth was a scrap of yellow paper. He teased it out, unrolled it and read –

Hello, you.

Fine. The Disney planet, he thought, and closed his eyes.

In the beginning was the Word.

To understand the operation of the multiverse, we have to know what that Word was; because everything thereafter came from, was posited on, relied on, followed on from it. Without the Word, the rest of the Sentence can't possibly make any sense. For example, if the rest of it is shut the door, we can't do anything until we know whether the Word was please or don't.

Finally, thanks to extensive research by a dedicated team of scholars in a reality long ago and far away, we now know what the Word was. We even have the primordial punctuation that goes with it.

The Word was Help!

He opened them again.

Then he closed them, mumbled "Oooh", and groped wildly for the handrail he'd briefly glimpsed before the view got too much for him. A gust of wind made him stagger, and he screamed.

Then he opened his eyes and looked sideways. Not down, because he didn't want to have to think about what he was standing on, which appeared to be nothing at all, or what was under nothing-at-all, which was a very distant prospect of royal-blue sea. The sideways view wasn't much better. He could see blue sky, a fat white fluffy cloud, and what looked like a very large quantity of matchsticks, arranged vertically, under a massive bank of red and white balloons.

He shifted his feet just a little. Nothing-at-all was solid and smooth. Very carefully, he lifted his left foot and lowered it again, clipping nothing-at-all with his heel and making a noise like a minimalist tap-dancer. Glass. He was standing on glass.

Standing on glass, and there was a wooden handrail, which he was holding on to with two solid, visible hands. Tightening his grip until his tendons started to hurt, he leaned his head back and looked up, at the underside of a balloon.

He opened his mouth and yelled "Doughnut!", but he couldn't hear his own voice. Besides, he remembered, doughnuts wouldn't work. They'd been specific to Pieter's bottle, which was broken.

The balloon, he noticed, was connected to the glass floor by four ropes; correction, four cables or hawsers. Allowing for perspective, he guessed they were roughly as thick as his waist. A floor (albeit glass), a handrail and a balloon no smaller than the dome of the Kremlin. He tried to find that reassuring, but another gust of wind made the whole structure sway.

When it settled again, he looked down through the floor. That and a distinct feeling of giddiness (altitude sickness) led him to estimate his height above royal-blue sea level at approximately twenty thousand feet. Christ!

Moving very slowly and deliberately, he wrapped his arms round the handrail and clasped his hands together. The rail felt reasonably solid; some kind of wood, planed and varnished. He felt as though he'd just run ten miles uphill wearing a rucksack full of bricks.

Someone was coming. A tiny figure was making its way along a row of matchsticks – correction, a far-away glass floor – heading in his direction. Whoever it was, the figure seemed to be walking at a perfectly normal pace, the way people walk on the ground. He shouted "Help!" at the top of his voice a couple of times, but he might as well have been starring in a silent movie. The distant figure gradually drew closer. It was wearing a duffel coat, a scarf and a red bobble hat.

Deep breaths, he told himself. Deep, slow breaths, and for crying out loud, don't let go. He tried to move his feet, but they skidded on the glass, lost traction and slid out from under him, leaving him hanging from the handrail by his elbow. Something warm trickled slowly down the inside of his right trouser leg. The best he could say for it was that it probably wasn't blood.

Hello.

He looked up, and saw a face. Part of a face; not very much, sandwiched between the scarf and the bobble hat. He could see a small pointy nose and two bright blue eyes. The voice was inside his head.

"Help," he whimpered. Mute button still on, no sound.

Are you all right?

The voice in his head was female. He had no idea how he knew that, because the words were feeding directly into his brain without any sound at all. Also, he couldn't see a mouth, but the scarf hadn't moved. Te-

Lepathy, yes. You're not from around here, are you?

Concentrating very hard, he tried to think: HELP. GET ME DOWN. The eyes narrowed, implying a puzzled frown. You what?

I SAID HELP. HELP. GET ME DOWN.

My God. You're a –

(Bizarre feeling of someone groping about inside his head for the right word)

– not-telepath. Well?

He nodded.

Seriously? You can't –

He swung his head slowly from side to side.

Really?

Numerous studies, including Ostrogorsky (2006), Baumann and Stern (2009) and Denkowicz and Chang (2012) have concluded that telepathy is impossible. In our universe, at any rate. Theo nodded until he felt a definite twinge in his neck. The eyebrows shot up and vanished into the red wool of the hat. All right. Let's see. Um. OK, try this. Don't try and do words. Just think.

He thought: Think?

Think.

Think. Think think think.

No, think.

I am thinking, you stupid woman.

Ah, got something. Irritation. You're annoyed about something.

Suddenly, Theo felt very, very tired. Nevertheless, he ushered everything else out of his mind and imagined –

Himself. Himself, falling. Not all that difficult to do, actually. Himself, letting go of the handrail and slipping through the gap between the rail and the floor he couldn't actually see, and falling, arms flailing, legs kicking –

Oh for heaven's sake. It's all right. You're perfectly safe.

Head swivelling helplessly from side to side, mouth wide open in a wordless, silent scream –

Don't be such a baby. Come on. Let go of the rail and take my hand.

He looked at her. She wasn't holding on to the rail. Instead, she was leaning forward slightly, holding out her pink-woolly-mittened hand. On her feet she wore grey sheepskin boots, standing (apparently) on thin air poised twenty thousand feet over an unspecified ocean.

I haven't got all day, you know.

Ah, the great leap of faith. The ones you get to hear about, of course, are the ones that don't end in long drops and messy landings. History tends to skate over those: the aeronautical pioneers who proved that it's not possible to fly simply by jumping off tall buildings flapping your arms like a bird. For every Wright Brother there are ten thousand equally earnest believers who got scooped up and buried in jars, and whose memories weren't preserved by succeeding generations, because nobody wants to admit they're descended from an idiot. On the other hand, it was painfully obvious that he couldn't stay where he was indefinitely: his fingers were getting numb from continuous feverish gripping, and he had cramp in both legs from hanging at an awkward angle. Oh well, he thought. He let go, grabbed wildly with his left hand and closed it tight around a full set of slim, wool-covered fingers.

Good boy. Now stand up. There, now. What was so difficult about that?

It's a million miles to the ground and I'm standing on a thin sheet of glass, and – Well. Now she came to mention it, nothing, really. Simple. Straightforward. Easy as falling off a –

Whoa. Steady.

Easy, and let's not mess with images of falling off anything. Instead, he equalised his weight on both feet, straightened his back and imagined himself saying, Thank you.

You're welcome. Now, let's get in out of the wind, shall we? It's a bit nippy out here.

She turned and walked, and he followed, keeping his eyes glued to a small area of duffel coat covering the place between her shoulder blades. Occasionally, roughly every thirty steps, he felt his foot skid a little on the glass. Ignoring it was possibly the hardest thing he'd ever done.

Just when he'd resigned himself to spending the rest of his life staring at six square inches of coat, she stopped. He adjusted his focus, and saw that she was standing in front of a door. It was just eight planks nailed to a couple of crossbars, but when she pushed it, it opened. He followed her through it, and suddenly there was a visible floor instead of blue water. His head swam and he staggered, and fell back into, of all things, a chair.

"Here we are" said a female voice. "Sit down and make yourself at home. I'll get you a nice hot cup of tea."

"You're talking."

"Of course I am." She'd gone into another room. "It's much easier talking than thinking. But you've got to think outside because the wind's so noisy."

The voice he was hearing wasn't anything like the voice he'd imagined to go with the words condensing inside his head. It was younger, higher, more ordinary – someone you've just met in the street, as it were, rather than a goddess or a guardian angel. He considered the room he was in. Bare wooden walls. Some kind of fibre matting on the floor. A low wooden table, with a wooden bowl of apples and slightly brown pears. The chair he was sitting in and two others. No electric light, just a sort of Venetian blind arrangement set in the ceiling like a skylight. No metal of any kind to be seen anywhere.

"Nice place you've got here," he said.

"What?"

"Nice . . ." She was looking at him with her head on one side, like a bewildered dog. "Doesn't matter. Where is this?"

"You don't—?"

"No."

"I see. What's the matter with you?"

Where to start; oh, where to start? Fortunately, a stray seed of inspiration floated in through his ear, took root and blossomed. "Amnesia," he replied. "Guess I must've hit my head or something." He dabbed behind his ear. "Ouch," he added, by way of corroboration. "I can't seem to remember anything."

She nodded. "Right," she said.

"You don't seem surprised."

"Well, we had that other case this time last year."

"That other case."

"Yes. Over on the East Float. They found this man clinging to the rail, and he couldn't remember anything at all; not his name, or which Float he was from, or which sect he belonged to. They had to tell him everything."

"Everything?"

"Everything."

"I'd like that," Theo said passionately. "Do you think you could see your way to . . . ?"

She pursed her lips. "Everything?"

"Oh, yes please."

She thought for a moment, then sighed. "Oh, all right, then." She took off the hat and the scarf, revealing a small, pretty face and an absurd amount of wavy red hair. "Drink your tea," she said, "and I'll tell you everything."

It all started (she said) about a thousand years ago. A thousand, or two hundred, something like that. We don't actually know, and who gives a damn?

Anyway, something really bad happened down on the surface. Some people think it was a war, others say it was chemicals or something, or it could have been scientists doing an experiment that went badly wrong. Anyhow, there was this very, very, very large explosion, and nobody could live on the surface any more. If we stayed on the land or the sea, we'd all die. So that just left the sky.

You're not drinking your tea. Yes, it's supposed to taste like that. We like it.

Luckily, there was like a thirty-year window where we could make all the necessary preparations. So, they had a big meeting, all the survivors from all the old countries, and they figured out what to do. The idea was, Venice-in-the-sky. We don't actually know what that means, but it must've meant something, or they wouldn't have called it that, would they?

It works sort of like this. There are four Floats, OK? Each Float hangs from something like a million fifty-thousand-litre helium-filled balloons. We call them the Bubbles. Now, it was clear from the start that we'd never be able to go back down to the surface again, so either we had to take stuff with us, or else it had to be sustainable; that was the key word, sustainable. It meant, we had to be able to make it or grow it twenty thousand feet up in the air.

The big breakthrough, which made it all possible, was aeroponic cultivation. Basically, that's where you grow stuff in air rather than dirt. The idea had been around for a long time but nobody bothered with it much, because dirt was easier, apparently. Anyhow, we grow all our food that way. And, of course, the rubber trees.

Oh yes. Vital.

Well, everything, really. We use the wood for repairing the Floats, building houses, making all the stuff we use. The rubber is what we use for the Bubbles, and for cars and lorries and all that, and waterproof roofs. We twist the bark into ropes, and we rot down the leaves and everything that's left over to make methane to power the generators. Nearly the whole of the South Float is covered with rubber plantations, and there's about two thousand hectares on the East Float as well.

And that's about it, really. You're born into a sect: gardeners, rubbersmiths, carpenters and sunlighters. I'm a gardener, I work on the smaller cabbage farm on North 36C. It's a bit of a hike, this being East 607J, but I've got my own car, so it's no bother, really. Of course, when I was little I wanted to be a sunlighter, everybody does when they're little. Very glad that particular dream never came true, thank you very much.

What? Oh, right, you don't know. The sunlighters are the

poor devils who look after the Bubbles. Very glamorous, of course, and everybody thinks you're wonderful, but you'd have to be nuts to actually do all that stuff. Well, I'll give you an example. If you're a sunlighter, after five years in the job they give you a medal – real metal – and a big house and a pension for life. Or that's the theory, anyway. Nobody's ever survived long enough.

Anyhow, that's really all there is to it. Nothing much ever happens, you see. Everybody's too busy doing their work to make things happen. Once a year we all get together on South Float and drink a cup of tea, eat a rice bun and sing the national anthem, but otherwise one day's pretty much like all the others. And of course, everybody knows everybody, and there's just the Floats, unless you get really bored, in which case you can take your car and drive to Mount Everest; that's the only point on the surface anyone ever goes to. They reckon you can stay there for fifteen minutes and it won't do you any harm. But it's a three-month drive, so you've got to be really desperate. I've been twice. Actually, there's not much there, just the pointy top of the mountain and a little platform you can stand on. But it makes a change.

Say what? Legal system? Oh, you mean laws, yes, that's right, we were told about all that stuff in school. Fancy you remembering about laws, when you've forgotten absolutely everything else. Well, we don't have them any more, of course. Don't need them. Basically, everybody gets on really well with everybody else, so . . . All right, yes, if six people sign a declaration saying you're horrible, then they push you over the edge. But nobody's been horrible for, what, two hundred years or something. We're all really nice to each other. Why wouldn't we be?

Theo swallowed carefully; his mouth had gone dry. "No idea," he said. "I try to be nice to everybody all the time. At least," he added quickly, "I'm sure I do, though of course I can't remember. But if I wasn't nice to people, they'd have chucked me off the edge years ago, so it stands to reason I'm nice, doesn't it?"

She gave him an odd look. "Well," she said, "that's all I can think of to tell you. How was the tea?"

"Delicious."

"We make it out of rubber-tree bark chippings mixed with finely ground maize husks. Just as well you like it, because that's all there is, besides water."

"I like water. I expect."

She looked at him some more. "You know," she said, "it was really weird, about the other guy."

"Oh yes?"

"Mphm. I mean, like I said, everybody knows everybody, so you'd think, if someone showed up who'd lost his memory, it wouldn't be long before he got recognised by someone who knew him. Or at the very least, the other people in his sect would wonder where he'd got to, or his family, come to that. But the other guy, he's been here a year and nobody knows who in sky he is. To begin with we all thought he must be a sunlighter who'd fallen off a Bubble and bumped his head. But nobody in Sunlighter Guild's ever seen him before."

"Maybe he's from—" Theo paused. "Somewhere else?"

She laughed. "There isn't anywhere else, silly," she said. "For heaven's sake, we'd know about it by now if there was. Unless you believe in little green men from Mars, of course. But he's not green. Nor," she added with a tiny frown, "are you."

"Um. I mean no, definitely not. I'm sure I'm really quite ordinary and nice, if only I could remember."

"I'm sure too," she replied, with a slightly forced smile.

"Anyhow, I think the best thing we can do is take you down-float so you can meet the Duty Officer. He'll know what to do."

"Duty . . . ?"

"Oh, it's just a name left over from the old days," she said casually. "It means whoever's in charge. We all take turns, you see. Each one of us, just for one day. There's never anything to do, of course, you just sit in a big chair and look important. I'm due for my turn in twenty-six years, four months and three weeks come Thursday."

"I see," Theo said. "And whoever's turn it is today will know what to do with me?"

"Of course," she said, "he's the Duty Officer. Come on, we can go in the car."

Theo suddenly felt a tremendous reluctance to get out of his chair. "Go out there, you mean."

"Well of course out there, silly. He's not going to come to us, is he? It's only a four-hour drive. I can drop you off on my way in to work."

Drop me off, Theo thought. "I really don't want to be any bother to anyone," he said. "Why don't I just stay here and try very hard to remember what I've forgotten?"

She narrowed her eyes. "Don't you want to meet the Duty Officer? Most people do. He's the most important person on the Four Floats."

Theo grinned feebly. "Well, in that case," he said.

You can't help feeling just a tad pathetic and sad when it takes you every last scrap of your courage and moral fibre to face something that's just another stage in someone else's daily commute. Hop in, she thought into his brain, as he teetered on the edge of the invisible platform, looking down in terror at what appeared to be four planks of wood hanging from two pink balloons. All around him, the wind screamed and howled, tugging at his shirt like a bored child. It was a yard from the edge of the glass (he could just see it, a slight refraction of sunlight against the blue backdrop of the far-too-distant sea) to the nearest plank. She skipped the distance lightly, then turned and scowled at him. Come on, I'll be late for work.

One small step for a man. One giant leap of faith for a man on the verge of falling a very long way and then going splat. He closed his eyes and hopped, making the little raft shake horribly. She grabbed his hand and pulled him off the edge into the middle. Scaredy-cat. Well, yes.

He opened his eyes. She was standing behind him, engaged with a device that looked a bit like an old-fashioned mangle; she was turning a big wheel with a handle, and a couple of large wooden cogwheels were slowly going round and round. It occurred to him that he ought to offer to help, but that would involve standing up and moving, and besides, it might come across as chauvinistic. He stayed where he was.

She gave the wheel one last turn, then pressed a little wooden lever at the side. At once, a broad wooden propeller he hadn't previously noticed began to spin at the back of the mangle, and the raft shot forward. She pounced like a cat and landed next to him, kneeling on the planks.

Off we go.

Mostly to keep from looking down, or sideways, which was almost as bad, he studied the mechanism she'd been messing about with. After a moment or so, he figured it out. The gear-train and the flywheel turned the propeller, which made the raft go. What drove them, and what she'd been winding, was a foot-wide, anaconda-thick rubber band.

Well, yes. Of course it works. Yes, you've got to wind it up again when it runs down, but so what? Well, you think of something better, then, if you're so clever.

Desperately, Theo tried not to think of an internal combustion engine.

Oh, that's just silly. That'd never work in a million years. For one thing, it'd blow up.

Well of course it would. Silly me. What on earth could I have been thinking of? (Well, this –)

Oh. Oh, that's clever. So that'd stop the gas coming through all at once. And that bit there goes round and round, and the burnt gas gets pushed out through that tube there. Gosh.

Theo groaned. He didn't have a rule book in front of him, but his instincts told him that utterly changing a society, almost certainly for the worse, was not the sort of behaviour to be expected from a well-mannered guest. He tried to think of –

Yes, but what would you run it on?

Good point. Excellent point. Yes, you've got me nailed to the floor on that one. So, let's forget all about it, shall we? (Actually, methane, or alcohol distilled from rubber leaves, or – No! Stop it!)

That's brilliant. They're going to be so excited when I tell them about it. Just think. No more stopping every five minutes to wind up the stupid rubber band.

Theo started to hum. He made no audible sound, of course, but he'd heard once that it was what the Maharishi used to do, to blot out all conscious thought. It worked up to a point. He could still hear her in his head, jabbering on about how wonderful his invention was and how it'd revolutionise travel between the Floats, maybe make it possible for them to build new ones; but at least he couldn't make out all of the words.

Eventually, after a dozen rubber-band-winding stops, they pulled up next to a long, low wooden hut, floating serenely under three enormous purple balloons. Getting off the raft proved easier than getting on, mostly because he wasn't quite so sure he cared whether he fell off or not. Inside, it looked pretty much the same as the girl's house had done, except that there were five chairs, and a pampered-looking rubber plant in a brass pot.

"That's the sacred rubber plant," she whispered. "That's why it's got a real metal pot."

"Ah."

A door opened, and a man came out. He smiled at the girl, then frowned. "I'm sorry," he said. "I don't think I know—"

"It's another one," the girl said excitedly. "He showed up on South 388H, and he's completely lost his memory, I've told him a bit about everything, and he's got this utterly amazing idea—"

"Um," Theo said loudly. "Are you the Duty Officer?"

The man looked shocked. "What, me? Do I look like the—?"

"He doesn't remember," the girl interrupted. "Anything. Except, he knew about laws. And he's thought of an incredibly clever way of making cars go without—"

"I'd like to see the Duty Officer, please," Theo said firmly.

"What, now?"

"If that's possible."

The man frowned. "I don't know about that. I'll have to ask him. Excuse me just a moment."

He withdrew, closing the door firmly behind him. The girl was looking at a piece of paper pinned up on the wall.

"The Duty Roster," she said. "It tells you who the Duty Officer is. Gosh."

"What?"

"Fancy that," she said.

"I can try, but you'll have to meet me halfway. What's so—?"

"You'll never guess who's on Duty today."

"No, almost certainly not. You could try telling me, though, if that wouldn't be seen as cheating."

She turned and beamed at him. "Him," she said. "The other one."

"Excuse me?"

"The other one like you," she said. "You know. The man who turned up and couldn't remember anything. Apparently, today's his turn."

Theo was just about to say something when the door opened again, and a different man came out. He froze in the doorway, stared for a moment, then clicked his tongue as loud as a pistol shot.

Theo, for crying out loud.

Theo couldn't do telepathy. Presumably it took time, and he'd only been there an hour or so. So he had to make do with words. "Hello, Max," he said.

Shut your face and get in here now.

The girl was gawping at the pair of them. "You know him?" she said.

"No," Max and Theo said simultaneously. "Go away," Max added. "Please. And you," he added, as the man came out to see what all the fuss was in aid of. "Vital affairs of state," he explained. "Essential meeting, total secrecy. Nobody must know. Got that?"

The man shrugged. The girl nodded eagerly. "Is this something to do with the exploding-gas car-propelling machine? Because I think it's really great."

Max grabbed him by the shoulder, shoved him through the door and slammed it shut behind them. "Theo," he said. "You total bastard."

Theo held up his hand. "Max."

"Yes?"

"Do I take it that you can do this telepathy thing they've got around here?"

"Yes, actually."

"Fine. Read my mind."

Didn't take long. Max's eyebrows shot up; then he said, "I see. I'm sorry you feel that way."

"I'm not."

"You'd really like to do that to me?"

"Yes."

"With a tablespoon?"

"Yes."

Max looked hurt. He was so very good at it. "Well, tough," he said, "because all the spoons in these parts are made of wood, and they'd snap. You'll just have to wait till we get home. Which won't," he added firmly, "be long now. Will it?"

Theo made an exasperated gesture. "Max, you arsehole," he said, "what are you doing here? You should be on the Disney planet."

"Which is exactly where I would be," Max replied angrily, "if it'd been up to you. And chances are, I'd have been Tigger-fodder by now, so it's just as well I used a bit of initiative and escaped, isn't it?"

"Max—"

"And why exactly are you trying to get these innocent, Arcadian people to abandon their sustainable, eco-friendly technology and start building gas engines? What harm did they ever do to you?"

"Max."

"What?"

"Shut up."

First time in their joint lives it actually worked. Even then, Max's reaction was to sulk. He folded his arms and sat down. "Max."

"Hm?"

"For pity's sake, how did you get off the Disney planet? You didn't have any of the kit. No YouSpace bottle, nothing."

Max did one of his insufferable smirks. "Oh, that," he said. "I just used my head, that's all."

"Makes sense. It's big enough, God knows. What did you do?"

"Oh, I was really brave," Max said. "You remember where you abandoned me, in that cave? Well, after a while I couldn't stand it any more, so one night I sneaked out, walked to the village, somehow managed to creep past the heavily armed guards without getting shot, broke into a bakery store and stole a doughnut. It was still pitch dark and I couldn't see my hand in front of my face, so I dragged myself all the way back to the cave. As soon as the sun rose, I looked though the hole in the doughnut, just like you told me to, and guess what happened? Nothing." He gave Theo a furious scowl, then went on, "Absolutely nothing at all."

"Max—"

"So I asked myself," Max went on, "is my dear brother playing funny games with me, or is it just he's so stupid he can't even—?"

"Doughnuts don't work like that," Theo said wretchedly. "It'd have worked for me, because the bottle was user-specific, but I'd have had to take you with me. And anyhow, the bottle's broken now, so it wouldn't work at all."

"Theo." Max blinked twice. "I know drivelling's what you do best, but there's a time and a place for everything, so please stop. Thanks," he went on, before Theo could explain his explanation, "but I'd sort of gathered the doughnuts weren't working. So I had to think of something else."

"What?"

Max's face suddenly changed. For Theo, who'd known him for so very long, it was quite an extraordinary moment; almost as if Max had cut himself, to reveal blinking coloured lights and circuitry under his skin. "I'm not sure, really," he said. "To be absolutely honest, it wasn't anything to do with me. I was sitting on the floor of the cave, wondering what I'd done to deserve being shafted and abandoned by my own brother—"

"Max."

"When suddenly," Max went on, "there was the most amazing bang, dust started coming down from the roof, and a huge great hole appeared in the floor. It must've caught me off balance, because the next thing I knew was, I'd fallen through the hole and landed on one of those ghastly see-through sidewalks they've got around here. And I've been here ever since," he concluded, "settling in and becoming really rather popular, though I say so myself. Mind you, wherever I go, people just seem to like me. It's a gift."

Theo opened his mouth, but no words seemed to want to come out and play.

"Oh, and there's one other thing," Max went on. "Doesn't actually seem to matter particularly much, but it's still as weird as a dozen ferrets in a blender. Take a look at this."

He took his left hand out of his pocket and extended it, fingers splayed. The centre of his palm was translucent.

At last, Theo found a word. It was, "Um."

"Theo?" Max narrowed his eyes. "I can tell from your face you're not quite as surprised as you ought to be. Does it mean something? What?"

Before Theo could find a way of not answering, the door flew open. Theo swung round and saw the man he'd first encountered when he arrived. He was scowling at them, either through barely controlled rage or because of the strain of holding a powerful-looking catapult at full draw.

"That's him," the man said. "Get him."

Half a dozen men in green smocks, also wielding catapults, pushed past him, grabbed Theo and shoved him up against the wall. The room was filling with people. Max tried to make a discreet exit, but they grabbed him too, although rather more politely. In the squash, Theo could just see the girl who'd found him. She looked furiously angry.

"It's him, isn't it?" someone said.

The crowd parted to let through a very old man, leaning on a stick. He tottered forward and examined Theo's face through a lens on a piece of string round his neck. Then he glanced down at the ancient scrap of paper he held in his left hand. It was a newspaper clipping.

"Yes," the old man said eventually, "that's him all right. That's Theo Bernstein."

There was a deafening roar of angry voices, abruptly cut short when the old man raised his hand. "Well?" the old man said.

Theo nodded. "Yes, I'm Theo Bernstein," he said. "But how did you—?"

The rest of the sentence was washed away by the surge of horrified gasps. "You admit it."

"Well, yes."

The girl burst into tears. Several catapults creaked ominously. "You're the Theo Bernstein who blew up the Very Very Large Hadron Collider?"

Sigh. "Yes, that's me."

"He admits it," someone yelled. "What're we waiting for? Chuck him off the edge, quick."

But the old man shook his head, and the crowd calmed down a little. Then someone said, "This can't be right, you know. All that stuff happened a thousand years ago. He doesn't look a thousand years old."

The old man gave the speaker a withering stare. "In fact, the explosion took place two hundred and seventy-three years ago."

"All right, he doesn't look three hundred. It can't have been him."

"Look at the picture," the old man said angrily, brandishing the clipping under the sceptic's nose. "It's him, it's the same man."

"And he's admitted it," someone else called out. "Quit fooling around and chuck the bastard, before he blows all of us up as well."

This suggestion met with considerable popular support, but the old man hadn't finished yet. "Just to make sure," he said, and turned to Theo once again. "You freely and sincerely admit that it was you who blew up the Very Very Large Hadron Collider?"

"Yes. Well, if you'd asked me that this time yesterday I'd have said yes, no question, but since then I have reason to believe that—" He looked round and decided not to try explaining about what Mrs Duchene-Wilamowicz had told him Pieter might've done. They didn't seem to be in the mood. "Yup," he said. "It was me."

This time the old man didn't have to impose silence. Everybody seemed too stunned to speak.

"You blew up the Very Very Large Hadron Collider," the old man repeated solemnly, "thereby causing the ecological catastrophe that made our world uninhabitable and forcing the survivors of our race to forsake the surface and adopt this wretched, primitive existence among the clouds."

"Yes – I mean, what? I didn't—"

A deafening chorus of booing and jeers, which the old man had some difficulty in damping down. In the end he had to stamp his little foot. "You didn't realise," the old man said scornfully. "Well, perhaps you didn't. I'm inclined to doubt that, though. After all, there's the evidence of the note."

"Note? What note?"

"The note you left," the old man said grimly, "on your desk at the Institute, written in your own distinctive, very untidy handwriting." From his pocket he produced another piece of yellow, crumbling paper. "Would you like me to read it to you? It says—" The old man cleared his throat. "I did it to rescue my brother Max. Mr Bernstein," the old man went on, folding the paper and putting it away. "That sounds very much like a confession to me."

Uproar. The girl, in floods of tears, was yelling, "Chuck him! Push him off the edge!" Then the man who'd been there when they arrived roared for quiet, and everybody stopped shouting.

"That other man," he said. "When they met, just now. That one called him Max."

Suddenly, every eye in the room shifted to the far corner, where Max was trying unsuccessfully to hide behind a very small chair. "That's what he said. He said, hello, Max. I heard him."

The old man's eyes were bulging out of his head. "Is it true?" he demanded breathlessly. "Is this Max?"

"Um."

"Well?"

Theo took a deep breath. "No," he said. "No, it isn't. I thought it was, but it's definitely not. I never saw this man before in my life."

The old man gripped his shirt front with both hands. "You're sure about that, are you?"

"Oh, absolutely. Don't know why I ever thought it was him. For a start, my brother Max was quite good looking."

Theo glanced at his brother, who was clearly torn between wanting to be good looking and fear of death. It was touch and go for a moment. Then Max said, "He's right. I never met him before. He's definitely not my brother."

The old man squinted at him. "How would you know?" he said quietly. "You've lost your memory."

That seemed to settle the issue. They hauled Max out of his corner and frogmarched him and Theo out of the hut on to the invisible walkway. They were chanting, "Horrible!

Horrible!" Theo had no idea how many of them there were, but it was considerably more than six.

They pushed them forward until their feet were right on the edge. The wind sawed at Theo's face, sharp as a blade.

Oh well, Max said inside his head. You tried.

He turned and looked at his brother. It was a little late to forgive him now, but –

Just not hard enough. Typical. You always were a useless bastard.

Then something nudged the small of his back, and he toppled and fell.

It occurred to Theo, as he fell and fell and fell and fell, that if he'd had his wits about him he'd have pointed out that, since he'd lost his memory too, nothing he'd said by way of admission or confession could be taken as reliable evidence, and all of it should therefore be disregarded. Or, if they were suddenly prepared to admit such evidence, at the very least they'd have to listen to Max when he told them he'd never met Theo before. It was, he felt, a pretty good point, and it was a real shame he couldn't go back up there and make it.

You wouldn't think you could get bored falling to your death, but it all depends on how far you have to go. Usually, it's just ten or twelve storeys, and you've only just got time to do the engulfed-with-terror thing and blurt out a quick blanket repentance of sins before you touch down and lose a dimension. But when it's a really, really long drop, there's a definite risk of ennui. Theo watched his past life flash in front of him, which took up maybe a second and was thoroughly depressing. He had his moment of regret about the unmade losing-his-memory argument. He turned his scientist's brain on to figuring out clever ways of surviving a drop from twenty thousand feet and came to the conclusion there weren't any. He hated Max – that used up a whole second and a third. And then he simply ran out of things to do. Not good enough, he felt. On a trip this long, the very least they could do was serve a simple meal and screen an in-fall movie.

It was only when he was very nearly there, and the wild blue sea was plainly visible below him, so close that he could see the white beard of froth on each tumultuous wave, that an idea struck him and made him gasp. Even while it was flashing through his brain like electric current across a sparkplug, he couldn't help howling with rage and fury at the inopportuneness of it all. Ten minutes earlier, and he'd have had the answers to everything, the whole bloody stupid mess, at his fingertips – in time, just possibly, to sort it out and get himself and his worthless brother to safety. As it was –

Theo sat up.

He'd got water in his eyes, his ears and up his nose. He coughed violently and spat out a mouthful of it. On all sides, the waves rippled and heaved.

He was in a bath.

And why not? It was, after all, water, and everything is just a matter of scale . . .

No! He shuddered with rage, slopping water over the side and on to the floor (carpeted in a sort of neutral beige). It's not fair, it's not right, I shouldn't be sitting in a warm tub engulfed in patchouli-scented suds, I should be dead –

He played that last phrase back and decided he was overdoing the moral indignation just a little bit. Even so, he was genuinely angry. He was a scientist, dammit. Inexplicable phenomena – magic, he glossed scornfully – just wasn't on, even if it saved him from a watery grave.

He lay back and stared at his little pink toes, which rose up out of the froth like ten bashful mermaids. I was falling. They shoved me off the edge, and I fell. I hit the water and here I am.

Which reminded him. He sat up, and caught sight of something on the white-wood-chipped wall. It was a framed embroidered sampler, which read –

You Are Here.

No map, just the words. Ah well.

He completed the survey, which revealed a heated towel rail, over which was draped a white towelling robe with a YS monogram on the pocket. He did a double-take, then, as the implications sank in, breathed a long sigh of relief. YS could only stand for YouSpace. In which case, this environment was something to do with the program (or, as he preferred to think of it, Pieter's fault) and he wasn't dead and in some sort of ghastly, logic-defying, scientifically impossible, Dawkins-baiting afterlife –

– And, now he came to think of it, he was safe, and well, and not in the slightest bit drowned, and Max was nowhere to be seen. He let out a long, long sigh of sheer joy and flopped backwards, shooting a tidal wave of suds over the bath rim and on to the floor. I'm alive, he realised. That's really quite nice, actually.

The joy didn't evaporate. It faded very slowly and gradually, roughly at the same rate as the bathwater cooled, from snugly warm to tepid to blood heat, until he decided it was time to (a) get on with the rest of his life, and (b) get out of the bath before he caught his death of cold. He put on the bathrobe, pushed open the door and found himself on a landing, opposite a door. He pushed that open too. He saw a small, nondescript room with two old, comfy-looking armchairs, a slightly out-of-shape sofa, a TV set and no windows. He shrugged and went in.

The TV set was on. It was broadcasting soft white noise and showing black and white lines, but when he walked in front of it, the noise stopped and the screen turned blue. Then text started to roll up it, *Star Wars* intro fashion, while an orchestral arrangement of 'Killing Me Softly' played in the background –

Muted congratulations!

If you're reading this, you've found the YouSpace Clubhouse. Welcome!

The YouSpace Clubhouse is a facility provided free of charge exclusively to YouSpace users. If you are not a registered YouSpace customer, please leave now through the door in the west wall. To make the door appear, say Door.

About The YouSpace Clubhouse. The YouSpace Clubhouse is available to all YouSpace users as a communal area, social networking arena and leisure and recreational facility. To access the Clubhouse, input Clubhouse into your personal interface module.

Why Muted Congratulations? We note that you didn't enter the YouSpace Clubhouse using your personal interface module. Therefore, you have accessed the YouSpace Clubhouse using the LastChance™ facility, an integral part of the YouSpace program.

About LastChance. LastChance™ is a function of FailSafe™ For YouSpace, the pre-installed YouSpace personal safety manager. If, during your YouSpace experience, you should encounter a situation inevitably resulting in certain death (such as, for example, getting killed) YouSpace will automatically transfer you to the YouSpace Clubhouse during the last fraction of a microsecond of your existence.

Since linear time does not pass inside YouSpace, you can now exist indefinitely within the YouSpace Clubhouse. While here, feel free to enjoy the wide range of leisure and educational facilities and gourmet cuisine provided for your comfort and wellbeing. Please note, however, that should you leave the YouSpace clubhouse (by walking through the door in the west wall accessible by saying Door; see above) you will immediately die. Please note that LastChance™ and FailSafe™ are registered trademarks of PVG Enterprises (Holdings) Inc.

Theo's mouth opened in a silent, wordless scream. He staggered, backed awkwardly until he bumped into one of the armchairs, and collapsed into it. For a long time, he could do nothing but sit, staring at the screen, trying to find a handhold that'd help him climb out of the well shaft of horror and despair he found himself in. Not alive after all, a voice kept saying in his head. True; and not dead, either. Instead, stuck in perpetual standby mode, in a small living room with light blue wallpaper and a slightly tatty beige carpet.

Finally, after a great deal of frantic scrabbling, slipping and falling back, he found the handhold, clung to it and hauled himself back up into the daylight of partial hope. True, he was as good as dead, trapped in a horrendous Sartre-esque nightmare of grotesque semi-existence, from which there was no way out other than total oblivion. But, he told himself fervently, it could have been so much worse, given the circumstances of his arrival. He might (he shivered from head to toe) have been trapped in this godawful place for ever and ever with Max –

"Theo?"

This time, the scream was neither silent nor wordless. True, the word was only "Nooooo!", but that was the best he could do by way of eloquence under the circumstances.

"Theo, pull yourself together and get a grip, for God's sake," Max said irritably. "Have you seen what it says on the TV?"

No words. Theo just nodded.

"It's awful. We can't just stay here. This place is a dump."

Nod. Manic grin.

"That's totally unreasonable. We can't be expected to hang around in this shithole for the rest of eternity. That's just stupid. I'd rather be dead."

"Door."

A patch of the opposite wall glowed blue, and the outline of a doorframe appeared, as though sketched in by a vast unseen Rolf Harris.

"I didn't mean it literally, you idiot," Max said irritably, and the door vanished. Theo whimpered and buried his head in his hands. "That's charming, by the way. Absolutely charming. You should be glad I wasn't killed outright."

"Why?"

Max ignored him. "Oh hell," he said. Then he dropped on to the sofa and put his feet up. "This is all your fault, by the way."

"My—?"

"Of course. If you hadn't blown up the VVLHC and trashed those poor people's planet, they would've have thrown us off the edge."

"But I didn't," Theo yelled. "I blew up our VVLHC in our universe. What happened back there was nothing to do with—"

Max shook his head sadly. "And you call yourself a physicist," he said. "Clearly, when the collider blew, it had quantum repercussions throughout the multiverse. All of which," he added helpfully, "are your fault too. I don't know, Theo, you always were such a careless bugger."

"Not my fault. Not!"

"Screaming and yelling won't make you right," Max said gently. "When you look at it calmly and dispassionately, it's obvious that when you blew up the VVLHC, you caused a fundamental rift in the fabric of, Theo, what are you doing with that cushion? Ouch. That hurt."

Theo threw the cushion on the floor, dropped back into the armchair and buried his head in his hands. He wanted to sulk, but sulking requires a fairly intensive level of concentration, and what Max had just said about the VVLHC kept coming back to him, like the taste of a frankfurter. A fundamental rift. Of course Max was using terms whose meaning he didn't really understand. He might have been Pieter's student for a while, but he'd never done any work; most of what he actually knew about quantum physics had most likely been gleaned from mid-afternoon reruns of *Star Trek*. Even so. A fundamental rift –

"It said something about gourmet cuisine," Max said after a while. "I'm hungry."

"What?"

"Gourmet cuisine," Max repeated. "You seen a kitchen anywhere?"

Theo looked up. "No. Maybe it's slipped down the back of the sofa."

Max mimed an exaggerated laugh. "If there's no kitchen," he said, "presumably there's some sort of room service."

"In hell?" Theo grinned wildly at him. "You think you can ring through to Reception and a demon with horns sticking out of his head'll come running with a toasted sandwich on the end of his pitchfork?"

Max frowned. "You're overstating it a bit there, aren't you? This isn't hell exactly."

"It is from where I'm sitting."

"I bet you," Max went on, "that around here somewhere – ah, here we go." He pounced like a swooping osprey and brandished a TV remote. "Now then." He pointed it at the TV set and methodically pressed all the buttons in turn. Eventually, a menu appeared on the screen.

"Guest Services," he said. "That'll be it. Right, let's see."

Theo looked at the screen, as Max scrolled down a list until he came to Food & Drink:

If you entered the Clubhouse via the LastChance facility, we regret that you are not permitted to access the Food & Drink facility. This is because you are a split second away from death and therefore do not need to eat or drink. Instead, why not enjoy the wide range of entertainment and leisure activities on offer in the Fun N Games locker, situated behind the sofa?

"Bastards," Max growled. "I'm starving."

Theo laughed out loud. Eternity, with nothing to eat, and Max. It just got better and better. "You're closest," he said. "Find this locker thing."

"I don't want entertainment and leisure activities," Max said furiously, "I want food."

"What you want," Theo started to say, then thought better of it. "The locker," he said. "Now."

Grumbling, Max slid off the sofa and investigated. "There's a shoebox," he said. "That's all."

"That must be it, then. What's inside?"

Pause. "This can't be it."

"Really? Why not?"

Max stood up, holding a small rectangular box. "All we've got in here are some kids' games," he said. "Pack of cards. Ludo. Snakes and fucking ladders. Happy Families."

"That's appropriate."

"That," Max said forcefully, "is not my idea of a wide range of entertainment and leisure activities."

Theo could see his point. "You sure there's nothing else?"

"Yes. No, I tell a lie. There's also a ball of wool and two knitting needles."

"Ah. That makes all the difference."

"It's junk," Max snarled, throwing the box on the sofa. "Sorry, but I refuse to spend eternity playing Ludo." He grabbed the remote and pressed some more buttons. "Surely there's at last something to watch. Yes, here we are. Options, that looks good. History Channel, boring. Home Improvement Channel. Well, it could do with it. Arts and Literature Channel, you must be kidding. Ah. Adult Channel, now you're talking. Oh."

To access any channel, first insert your credit card in the slot and key in your PIN.

"Don't look at me," Theo said. "They cancelled all my cards when I lost all my money."

"And I'm legally dead. Wonderful." Max dropped the remote on the floor and collapsed on to the sofa. "No TV, no entertainments, no food. This is a nightmare."

Theo breathed in deeply and counted to ten. It didn't work. It never had. "Max."

"What?"

"You know something?"

"What?"

Theo smiled sweetly. "You," he said, "are an arsehole."

It was as if he'd suddenly started speaking Portuguese. Max simply didn't get it. "Huh?"

"Arsehole," Theo repeated clearly. "You're horrible. You're the most pathetic excuse for a human being it's ever been my misfortune to meet. You're selfish, thoughtless, arrogant, inconsiderate, totally self-centred and quite unbearably annoying. You don't give a damn about how much trouble you cause for other people. You're feckless, shiftless and no damn good. And your feet smell."

"They do not."

"Your feet," Theo repeated sternly, "smell."

Max hesitated. "All right, maybe they do, a bit. But all that other stuff—"

"Perfectly true."

Long silence. "Really?"

"Yes."

"Am I really all those things you said?"

"Yes."

"Oh."

There was a moment of absolute stillness, such as hasn't ever happened since the beginning of the universe. Then Max said, "Really? You're not just saying it because you're pissed off?"

"No, Max. I meant every word. Every word was true."

"Oh."

Max was frowning. He looked rather like a scientist on the verge of making a revolutionary new discovery, something so original and out-of-the-box that the words to describe or define it don't exist yet. "I never realised," he said. "Nobody ever said anything before."

"Well, they wouldn't," Theo said kindly. "It's so obvious, they assumed you knew. It's like, when you go to Egypt, you don't grab the locals by the arm and point and go, 'Look! A pyramid!'"

"But people like me."

Theo nodded. "True," he said. "For a short while. Then they get to know you. Then the fact that you seemed pleasant enough at first glance only makes it worse."

"I'm popular."

"People were trying to kill you," Theo reminded him. "That's why you had to disappear."

"Yes, but only because I'd stolen their money."

"People can be so unreasonable."

"Not," Max said severely, "because I'm a basically unpleasant person. You do see the distinction."

"Don't wriggle, Max. You're a toad. Accept it. If we're going to have to stay cooped up in here for ever and ever and ever, it's vitally important that you acknowledge the fact that you're a shit."

"Would you go that far?"

"Actually, that's not far enough. You're a complete shit. You're what shit shits. Don't argue," Theo added firmly. "Just say, Yes, Theo. Can you do that?"

"Look—"

"Yes, Theo."

An agonised look spread over Max's face; somewhere between the torment of self-realisation and toothache. He opened and closed his mouth three times. Then he said, "Yes, Theo."

"What?"

"Yes, Theo."

"Sorry, didn't quite catch that. Say again?"

"Yes, Theo."

Theo smiled beautifully. "Thank you," he said. "You know what," he added, leaning back in his chair and resting his head on the headrest, "it's almost worth it, being stuck here and all, just to hear you say that."

Max looked at him. "Really?"

Theo nodded. "It means I don't have to hate you any more."

"Hate. Rather a strong word, isn't it?"

"In context, no."

"Ah. But you don't, any more."

"No."

The silence that followed combined the golden glow of peace and joy with the toe-curling embarrassment that always happens when men talk about their feelings. It lasted five seconds, which was plenty long enough. Then Max said, "How about playing snakes and ladders?"

"Love to."

"Fine. I'll be blue."

"No. I'll be blue."

Max opened his mouth, then stopped. "Sure," he said. "You be blue. You want to go first?"

"You can go first, Max."

"Thank you."

"No problem."

They played snakes and ladders. Then they played Ludo. They found that, if they cooperated instead of trying to win, they could stretch the game out for a very long time. Neither of them had a watch, there was no clock, and no window to indicate whether it was day or night outside (Theo had a shrewd idea there was no outside), but Theo eventually calculated, by counting seconds while feeling his own pulse, that the average game took nineteen hours, twelve minutes. When the score stood at 16 games to Theo, 16 games to Max and 378 games drawn (snakes and ladders), 29 games to Theo, 28 games to Max and 1,775 games drawn (Ludo), Theo said, "You know what?"

"What?"

"I'm bored with this. Let's do something else."

"What?"

"Let's escape."

Max looked at him. "The only way out of here is through the D-O-O-R in the wall," he said. "You know, the one that appears when you say the D word. I don't really think you want to go there."

Theo shook his head. "The only way out we've been told about," he said.

"Theo." Max made a noise like a tree being ripped out by its roots. "You're talking about sneaking out of death, right?"

"If you want to look at it in those terms, yes."

"Theo." Max leaned back in his chair and smiled. "Over the last few days—"

"Six years."

"Huh?"

"Six years. That's how long we've been here."

Max went very pale, but went on, "Over the six years we've been here, I've come to value the bond that's grown up between us, so the last thing I'd want to do is jeopardise our rapprochement by speaking out of turn."

"Same here, Max."

"Splendid. So, would it be all right if I just said something off the record and totally without prejudice?"

"Sure."

"And if you don't like it, you won't be offended or anything?"

"Of course not."

"You're an idiot, Theo. You're a complete moron."

Theo nodded slowly. "I'm not offended," he said.

"Good. Look, you may be a top-flight physicist and all that crap, but when it comes to sneaking out, compared to me, you're nothing. A novice. A sneaking-out virgin. I've snuck out of everywhere over the years – bedrooms, hotels without paying, countries ten minutes ahead of the cops. You name it, I've got out of it, in my underwear, by the skin of my teeth. If there was a Nobel prize for last-minute absconding, I'd be climbing out the bathroom window with it tucked under my arm. And I'm here to tell you—"

"Max."

"Death," Max said firmly, "is the one thing you can't sneak out of. There are no kitchens, there is no fire escape. This place here, it's not somewhere you can sneak out from, it's where you sneak out to. This is the walk-in closet in Death's bedroom, Theo. Now that we're here, we're here. Face it. There's no escape."

"Max."

Max gave him a furious glare. "What?"

"There's a door."

"There is now that you've said the D word. "

"No," Theo said quietly. "Another one. Look."

He pointed. Side by side in the wall were two doorways. One of them glowed blue. The other one was just a door; white, rectangular, panelled and fitted with a plain wooden doorknob.

"There," Theo said. "See?"

"That wasn't there before."

"Correct." Theo stood up, but didn't move towards the door-infested wall. "The other one only showed up when I said there's a—"

"Shh. Don't say that."

"Get a grip, Max, it's already here. It'll go away in a second. There," he added, as it faded away, leaving nothing behind except a blur on the retina and a faint scent of primroses. "But the new one's still there, look."

"Keep well away," Max said nervously. "We don't know anything about it."

"Don't be so feeble," Theo said. "It could be our way out of here." He studied it and frowned. "Or it could just be somewhere to put coats and stuff. We just don't know."

"We haven't got any coats. Or any stuff, come to that."

"It could be a pantry. You know, food."

That was a word that hadn't been spoken for quite some time. At the sound of it Max twitched slightly, like an old fish that's been hooked and thrown back half a dozen times, but still can't quite resist the implausibly dangling worm. "No reason to think it's that."

"No reason to think it isn't."

But Max only shook his head. "I'm not going through that," he said. "Not unless it's guaranteed a hundred per cent safe. Whoever designed this place has got a seriously warped mind."

Theo sighed. "Fine," he said. "I'll go."

"What, and leave me here on my own for the rest of eternity? Over my dead body."

"Actually, I'm not sure that's even possible in here. Look, if you're afraid of getting left, come with me."

"No. It's dangerous."

"Max, for crying out loud. It's a d—"

"Don't say it."

"Flat piece of wood with hinges and a handle. What is there to be afraid of?"

"Gosh," Max said, "let's see, now. There's death, and serious injury, and not-so-serious-but-still-nasty injury, and perpetual imprisonment, and the annihilation of the soul, everlasting damnation, let's not forget that—"

"Max. You haven't suddenly gone and got religion, have you?"

"It's an infinite multiverse," Max snapped. "Who knows what's out there? In an infinite multiverse, it's pretty much inevitable that somewhere there's a universe that was created in seven days by an old man with a long white beard and outmoded views on extramarital sex. If the stuff they made me read in school is anything to go by, I really don't want to end up there, thank you ever so much." He shrank back into the angle of the sofa, as if it was a snail's shell. "The more I think about it, the happier I am here. I mean, we've got light, heat, furniture, games. Each other," he added, just a fraction of a second too late. "What more could anybody ask, really?"

"Max."

"No. Forget it. I'm not going."

"Look."

The doorknob was turning. Max whimpered and grabbed a cushion. The door creaked, swung slowly forward, then abruptly vanished. In its place, sitting on the floor, was a jar of pickled walnuts.

"Oh," Theo said.

Max peered out over the top of the cushion. "Has it gone?"

"Yes."

"What's that?"

Theo peered. "Pickled walnuts."

"Food?"

"In a sense." Theo frowned. "No, stay there. I need to think."

"It's all right, I'll save you some." Max was on his feet, heading for the jar.

"Max."

"Theo, I'm hungry."

"Sit down. I think I know . . ." Theo tailed off. It sort of made sense, except that it was the kind of sense that had no trace of logic about it whatsoever. "Oh come on," he said suddenly. "It can't be. That's just silly."

Max stared at him in agony. "Theo, what are you talking about?"

"That." He waved towards the jar. "I mean, yes, it fits. But it's so childish. And it doesn't mean anything."

"What?"

Theo let go the deep breath he'd been holding in. "Think about it," he said wearily. "What's the oldest, feeblest joke in the world?"

Max frowned. "Why did the chicken cross the road?"

"The other one."

"When is a— Oh."

"Precisely. When is a door—" The wall started to glow blue. "Not a door."

"When it's a—"

"Jar, yes." Theo folded his arms and scowled. The blue door glowed and faded. "Thank you," Theo said. "Sorry, right. When it's a jar. Hey presto, a jar."

"Pickled walnuts."

"Probably just a random selection."

"I like pickled walnuts."

"Then it could be your subconscious mind affecting the otherwise random choice of contents, that's not the point. It's meaningless. It's a stupid, boring old joke, that's all. That's the point."

Max yawned. "In that case, maybe it's part of the entertainment and leisure facilities," he said. "Actually, that wouldn't surprise me in the least."

"It's got to mean something," Theo persisted. "Otherwise, what's it doing here?"

Max leaned forward. "If you're right," he said thoughtfully, "and if the pickled walnuts are just random contents, possibly influenced by my subconscious—"

"Yes?"

"Then it won't matter if I eat them, will it?"

Theo growled, then shook his head. "Go ahead," he said. "Be my guest."

"Thanks." Max vaulted over the end of the sofa, jumped across the room and grabbed the jar. "Oh," he said. "Shit."

"What?"

"They're out of date."

"Max."

"But you're not supposed to—"

"Think about it, will you? Where we are? Time has no meaning here."

Max turned the jar round slowly in his hand. "So you reckon they're probably OK?"

"Time has no meaning." Theo hadn't meant to shout, particularly not a phrase that made him sound like one of those strange men who preach on street corners. He lowered his voice a little. "So," he went on, "if we're in, effectively, a time-free zone, why is there a date on the label?"

"It's the law. Trading standards."

"The jar came from somewhere else." He rubbed his forehead with his hands as though he was trying to cold-start it. "Let's think about this," he said. "That stuff on the TV. You can get in here if you're a registered YouSpace user."

"Are there any?"

"Me. Or I was. Don't know if I still am since the bottle got broken. Pieter, I guess, but he's stuck on the Beach Boys planet." He scowled ferociously; he was missing something, something really quite obvious. When is a door . . .?

Blue flicker, again. He ignored it and sat bolt upright. "When it's a jar."

"What?"

"The joke. It's a clue."

Max drew a deep, sad sigh. "You know," he said, "I never could see the attraction in leaving cryptic clues. If it's important, you run a very real risk of nobody getting it. If it's not important, why the hell bother? Much safer just to say what you want to say; the treasure's up in the roof, George killed me, I didn't actually write this stuff—"

"Max."

"All right, it's a fucking clue. What does it mean?"

"I think—" Theo was staring at the wall where the door-that-wasn't had been. "It's – well, one of those things we don't talk about. But when it's not one of those things we don't talk about, it's a jar." Suddenly he sprang to his feet, crossed the room in three giant strides and snatched the jar out of Max's hands. "You know what this is?"

"Don't you start."

"I think," Theo said, "that this isn't a jar. It's a bottle."

Max frowned. "Nah. Neck's too wide."

"I think it's a YouSpace bottle," Theo said, in a high, brittle voice. "Because where does it actually say they've got to be bottles? They could be jars. Well, couldn't they?"

"You're doing it again, Theo. It's not kind, you know. Do please make an effort not to talk drivel."

Theo wasn't listening. "It's a glass container, open at one end. That's all it is."

"Full of walnuts," Max pointed out. "Does that make a difference?"

"The wine bottles were full of wine."

"So I should hope."

"So it shouldn't matter." Theo's fingers closed around the lid, but he couldn't seem to find the strength to twist it off. "Here," he said. "You do it."

"Me? Why me?"

"I don't know." Theo gazed at him blankly. "I guess it's the thought of maybe just possibly getting out of here, after six years. I can't actually bring myself to do it."

"You're scared."

"Yes, maybe I am. So are you."

"Ah," Max said sagely, "but in my case, fear is an essential function of my finely honed survival instinct. You're just chicken."

"I'm afraid it might not work."

Max looked at him for quite some time. "Here's the deal," he said. "If I open it, and it's not what you think it is, I get to eat all the walnuts. Agreed?"

"Agreed."

Slowly, Theo passed the jar over to Max, who snatched it, took a lingering look of pure desire at the walnuts, and tightened his hands around the lid like a finalist in the World Strangling Championships. "Doesn't want to budge," he muttered, "how about we just break it?"

"No!"

"Yes, but – hang on, I'm there." There was a faint pop as the seal broke, and Max lifted off the lid. "It's open."

"Good. Give it to me."

"No chance," Max said. "Not until I've—"

And then he vanished.

Theo sat for a while, staring at the place where his brother had been, now occupied by an empty jar.

Empty. The walnuts had vanished at the same moment as Max. Did that mean something?

Maybe. Maybe it meant that, wherever Max was now, he was just starting to feel the first pangs of indigestion that inevitably follow if you scoff a whole jar of pickles. Or maybe it was the crucial point which made all the –

Stop, he ordered himself. Think. Before we go any further, it's time for a Universal Theory of Everything. That's what a scientist would do. Besides, the easiest way of finding a path through a minefield is not necessarily the safest. Think.

He thought.

A tune he'd heard recently was playing in a loop in his head, over and over. If everybody had an ocean; that was as far as it went, nine notes. He shut it out and tried to assemble the data from which he was to draw his inferences.

Mrs Duchene-Wilamowicz – well, more about her later, but she'd said it was Pieter who'd blown up the VVLHC, just so as to test a component.

He'd been thinking about the maths; also, the eternal question, why me? The two were kind of linked:

– The maths didn't work; that was the little something about them that had been nagging away at him all along. He, Theo Bernstein, could make them work, but maybe that was the point.

He thought back to his days as Pieter's student, the set of problems he'd been given which had first caught Pieter's attention. According to Pieter, the way he'd set about solving them had been unique, revolutionary, totally original. It had also, of course, been wrong. The answers, as written down on a sheet of paper, had been incorrect. And yet Pieter had been astonished, riveted, captivated when he'd read them. Now, then. What exactly was it that Pieter had seen in those answers?

If everybody had an ocean

He ran a finger round the rim of the empty jar. What Pieter had seen – it came to him slowly and opaquely, as if viewed through frosted glass – was a different sort of mathematics; maths from another reality. One in which two plus two really does make six.

Pieter was looking for a way into other realities. Suddenly, in a routine dollop of homework, he recognises the mark of someone who's been there – like Columbus, roaming the streets of Madrid dreaming of a new world, bumping into a stranger wearing an I Love New York baseball cap.

But, Pieter reasoned, this man, this kid, can't have been there, because as yet no bridge exists.

But, Pieter reasoned, he must've been there, because he's wearing the baseball cap.

Therefore, Pieter reasoned, it's simply a matter of time. He will go there, he will acquire the baseball cap, and then he'll come back.

But, Pieter reasoned, travelling from the future to the past is impossible.

In, Pieter reasoned, this reality it's impossible. Not where he's been. Not where he got the cap. Where he's been, time must be different. Time must have no meaning.

At which point, Theo conjectured, a bright light would've lit up inside Pieter's head, and he'd have reasoned something like this –

There is a multiverse where everything is possible.

In some place in that multiverse, what I'm trying to do is

possible. Here, it's not possible. There, it is. Now, if only I could go to there, what I'm trying to do would be possible. My problem is, not that I can't get where I'm going, but I can't get there from here.

But, Pieter reasoned, if only –

Theo snatched his hand away from the rim of the jar as if it was red hot. If everybody had an ocean. Well, yes; the ocean is a reasonably convenient metaphor. It's an element that both separates and connects the land masses. Everybody, every reality, does indeed have an ocean, namely the barrier that keeps each different reality separate from the others. What everybody doesn't have, what everybody needs –

(He closed his eyes.)

– is a boat.

Put it another way. What do you do if you know what you want the answer to be, but you can't make the maths come out that way? You cheat.

And Pieter had cheated. But that sort of behaviour always comes with a price tag. The trick is, if you want to come out on top, to get someone else to pay.

Theo took the jar in his two equally visible hands.

Free access to the Clubhouse is available to all registered members. They can come, and they can go. They can also, if they feel so inclined, import pickled walnuts, to enjoy as a savoury snack between exits and entrances. What they do with the empty jar after they've finished with it is a matter between them and their ecological sensibilities. If they choose to leave their trash behind them, so be it.

Theo looked into the jar. He had an odd feeling that the jar was looking back at him, but that was probably just because he'd read Nietzsche and had a vivid imagination.

The operating system of YouSpace, he decided, is that it doesn't have one. You just say what you want. Of course, if nobody bothers to tell you that, or if they leave you a set of completely false and misleading instructions, you can get yourself into all sorts of bother. But if you know the truth, it's so very, very simple.

I want to go home.

But, to make it interesting, he went the long way round.

Also, he stopped at various points on the journey, to test his newly minted hypothesis and establish a few facts. He stopped, for example, at his parents' house, approximately a week after he'd been born. He paid a flying visit to Pieter van Goyen's rooms at the university, back when he'd been a student there. He dropped in on the Very Very Large Hadron Collider, half an hour before it blew up. Once he'd got the hang of it, it was a bit like being a bird flying over both time and space. Provided you kept your head, didn't lose your way and stayed well clear of falcons and cats, it was a piece of cake. It was fun.

One last circuit – from the Beginning to the End, in a low, lazy, circling sweep – and then he banked into the flow to slow down, selected a point on which to land, swooped, deliberately stalled and dropped (just like a bird landing on a twig) into the time and place of his choosing. It was all right, he thought, just before he got there. It's just like a faculty party. I don't have to stay here if I don't like it.

He knocked on the ancient oak door and waited. Pieter's voice called, "Come in."

Pieter, sitting in front of a roaring log fire with a glass of sherry in his hand, was much younger, of course. You don't notice so much how people age if you see them regularly; and then you happen to find an old photograph, and suddenly it's painfully obvious. In Pieter's case, the change wasn't so much downhill as sideways; the straggly hair over his ears was a sort of smoker's fingers tawny yellow. Also, the wrinkles he had yet to acquire had suited him, made him a bit more grave and wise looking, a bit less like an elephant seal in glasses.

"Hello, Pieter," Theo said. "Max."

Max just looked like Max. His hair was longer and he hadn't shaved in a while – sheer affectation, of course, because even when he'd been on the run from the bloodthirsty gamblers he'd owed money to, he hadn't exactly been sleeping in ditches, and would've had ample opportunities for shaving and combing his hair. But that was Max for you. If he's on the run, he has to look like a fugitive. Correction; he has to look like What The Well-Dressed Fugitive Is Wearing This Season.

"Theo," Pieter said, frowning slightly, "shouldn't you be in New York?"

"Should I?" Theo tried to remember. "Oh yes," he said, "of course I should. You sent me to some damnfool seminar on isotonic wave diffraction. I wondered why at the time. Now I know."

Max shifted uncomfortably in his seat. Theo beamed at him.

"You're looking well, Max," he said. "Death suits you."

Max glowered at him. "That's nice," he said. "I'd have thought you'd be pleased I'm still alive."

"I was," Theo said, "when I found out. Well, not pleased. That's not really the word. Torn between impossible hope and desperate reservations. It's all right," he added, as Max pulled a bemused face, "I've had time to get used to your continued existence. You don't know it, but we just spent six years banged up in a tiny apartment together, playing Ludo. Pieter," he went on, before Max could reply, "why on earth did you ever give your students sherry? You hate the stuff and nobody under the age of seventy drinks it any more. Is it just tradition, or is it written into the university's charter somewhere?"

Pieter raised both eyebrows. "Would you like a drink?" he said.

"Love one," Theo replied. "I haven't had a drink for six years."

Pieter shrugged and poured him a sherry, which Theo slung back in one frantic gulp. "Another?"

"Oh yes."

He made the next one last a whole second. "I expect you're wondering," he said, "what I'm doing here."

"Just a bit," Pieter said, "since you're supposed to be in New York. Did you miss the plane or something?"

Theo shook his head slowly. "No," he said. "I caught the plane, got there safely and on time, spent four days sitting through a whole bunch of very dull lectures and presentations, then came home when it was all over. And to this day I don't know what isotonic wave diffraction is. Not that it seems to have made much difference."

"You can't have spent four days," Max put in. "The seminar only started yesterday."

But Pieter was looking straight at him. "Shut up, Max," he said. "Theo—"

"Yes?"

"I can explain."

"Excellent. That means I won't feel the need to kick your head in." He smiled and put the empty glass down. "First, though, I need to ask you something. Who's Dolly Duchene-Wilamowicz?"

Pieter looked startled. "Dolly? She's my sister. Why? You've never met her, have you?"

"That's fine, Pieter. Good answer. Now, then." He sat

down and put his feet up on Pieter's Louis Quinze card table. Pieter winced but didn't say anything. "I'm going to tell you what you want to know, and then you're going to explain, and then I may just murder both of you. It'll depend on what sort of a mood I'm in when we get there."

"Theo—"

"I say murder," Theo went on, "but I don't imagine any jury would convict. Not homicide but pesticide, they'd say, and they'd be quite right. I'll have another sherry, Pieter, since you're offering. It tastes like stale diesel, but I'm getting to like it. Thank you." He looked down into the glass, thought about it for a moment, then shook his head. "Maybe not. All right, where shall I begin?"

– But that was such a good joke that he couldn't stop himself from laughing, which he did for quite some time, until Pieter said, "Theo!" quite sharply. That did the trick. Theo sat up straight, cleared his throat, and said, "At the beginning, I guess. Well, there was this enormous explosion. The Big Bang. With me so far?"

Max was giving him a scornful glare, but Pieter had gone very pale. "We can skip that, don't you think?" he said.

Theo frowned. "All right," he conceded, "but we'll come back to it later." That was another really good joke, but this time he kept a straight face. He looked down at his hands, as if to reassure himself of something, and went on, "Fast forward," he said. "What's today's date?"

Max looked at his watch. "18 August 2007. Why?"

"Just checking. A few other salient facts. Max, you've just been declared officially dead. Pieter, you've just proposed my name for the shortlist to run the proposed Very Very Large Hadron Collider project. Yes?"

Pieter nodded. "You're not supposed to know that," he said. "But, yes, I've recommended you. I think you deserve it."

Theo gave him a horrible look. "I'll pretend you never said that," he said. "Also, Pieter, you're looking for financial backers for a really weird, far-out new product that'll revolutionise the entertainment industry."

Pieter nodded slowly.

"Not that it matters a lot," Theo went on, "but your principal backers are your sister, who married a billionaire—"

"Otto Duchene-Wilamowicz," Pieter said. "He was ninety-one, she was twenty-seven. They warned him, marrying a girl that age might prove fatal. You know what he said? If she dies, she dies."

"Whatever. Also, someone called Bill, with a daughter called Matasuntha."

Pieter's eyebrows shot up. "How did you—?"

"Coming to that. The trouble is," he continued, snuggling into his chair as far back as he could go, "you've done all the maths, and realised it won't work. What you have in mind isn't possible."

Pieter hesitated, then nodded.

"And then you remembered me."

Pieter closed his eyes. "Yes."

Max was obviously dying of repressed curiosity, but, before he could say anything, Theo went on, "I can't be bothered to tell you a whole lot of stuff you already know, so here's the bottom line. It worked. I'm back. I did it." He paused for effect. "I created YouSpace."

"You what?"

"YouSpace. That's what it's called."

Pieter frowned, then shook his head. "Don't like it. We'll need a snappier name than that if we want it to really take off."

"Tough," Theo said firmly, "because that's what I've called it. I created the YouSpace device. Not you. Me."

Max said timidly. "What's YouSpace?"

"Ah." Theo smiled and turned to him. "Here's where you're just about to get involved. On 15 August '07, Pieter's only just got the germ of the idea. Suddenly, out of the blue, who should turn up on his doorstep but his prodigal pupil Max Bernstein. Help me, pleads Max, they're after me, I need a place to hide, you're the only one I can really trust. Odd you should say that, Pieter replies, because it so happens I've got a really ace hiding place, I just need someone to try it out for me. Oh, and some poor fool to take the blame, of course."

Pieter looked away. Max just looked terminally vague.

Theo held up his two visible hands. "YouSpace," he said. "Really good idea, shame it won't work. You know why? Because, in order to access all the possibilities of all the alternate realities in the multiverse, you'd have to go back to the one point in time when all those possibilities were still gathered up together in one place, in one primordial glob of protomatter, right at the Beginning, before the Big Bang. It'd be like going to the central bus station; from there, you can get a bus direct to anywhere. Well? Am I right?"

"Theo—"

"Not now, Pieter, I'm on a roll." Theo smiled joyfully, and reached across the table to pick up a newspaper. He flicked through and found the page he wanted. "Top Scientists Warn VVLHC Project Could End Universe," he read out. "Of course, there's bound to be scaremongers, flat-earthers, fruitcakes with sandwich boards saying the end is nigh. But there's always a tiny grain of truth in the pearl of tabloid lunacy. If the VVLHC did go wrong and blow up, in a certain very specific and improbable way, it could do really weird stuff. It could rip a hole right through the fabric of space and time. Couldn't it, Pieter?"

"I guess."

"And so it did." Theo dipped his head in a respectful

salute. "Really great bit of science, by the way, figuring out exactly how to sabotage it so it'd make a hole you could navigate through. But like I said, I'll come back to that in just a moment." He turned to Max. "Well, we all know what you've been up to. Want to hear about what I've been doing?"

Max shrugged. "Not particularly."

"What the hell. Here goes, anyway." This time, he drank the sherry. When the burning feeling had passed, he gave them a brief summary of his career, from the explosion at the VVLHC up to the point where he'd watched Max open the walnut jar and vanish—

"You're crazy," Max said. "Nuts."

Theo nodded slowly. "Look at my hands," he said. "You can see them? Both of them?"

"Of course."

"Of course you can. I guess," he went on, putting his hands behind his head, "I should've figured it out much earlier; when I landed in a succession of alternate realities that'd been hit by some sort of catastrophic disaster. The Disney planet, the Australian pope planet, the global warming planet, the Venice-in-the-sky place, all had something in common. Some clown had done some catastrophic thing, and pretty much trashed a huge chunk of the planet. At the very least I should've tumbled to it when the Venice-in-the-air people recognised me. What I should've realised was, in all of them the same thing had happened. The VVLHC had blown up. It's the one and only event that's common to all realities, every single reality in the multiverse. Or at least," he added, giving Pieter a good, solid stare, "it is now."

Long silence, then Pieter shrugged. "Good call," he said. "Just like you said. A hole I could navigate through."

"Which you made," Theo said, his voice suddenly cold, "deliberately, so you could move from one to the other. YouSpace. With a little help from me."

Pieter's head lifted, then dropped. The movements were linked, and deliberate.

"Thank you," Theo said solemnly. "I'll take that as a confession. And we'll come back to it in a minute. Before that, I'd just like you to confirm my hypothesis. After all, we're scientists, aren't we?"

Pieter drew a long breath. "When I sabotaged the Collider, you were still inside the building. You survived the blast only because you were projected into the rift I'd made in the fabric of the multiverse. Satisfied?"

"Go on."

"The moment I saw that amazing calculation you did in your first year I knew you'd already been to an alternate reality. The technology to do that didn't exist. Therefore, you'd travelled in time as well. There was a temporal paradox. You'd been there, but you hadn't been yet. But" – Pieter pulled out a huge white handkerchief and dabbed at his forehead – "that didn't seem to matter. The experience was somehow retrospective." He folded the handkerchief neatly and dropped it on the floor. "Like you being here now, I guess."

"You guess. Good guesser, aren't you?"

"You'd been there," Pieter said furiously, "it'd already happened. So, I knew, when I shot you into the rift, I knew you'd survive, and come back. And then—"

"In order to get back, I'd have to either discover or invent YouSpace."

Pieter lifted his head defiantly. "Which you've done," he said. "Obviously."

"You cheated!" All the anger came rushing out, like the crowd at the end of a big game. "You couldn't figure it out, so you cheated. You stole my work which I hadn't even done yet. Call yourself a scientist? You're a phoney."

"Let's call it a collaboration," Pieter said. "Naturally, it's more usual to tell your collaborator first, but I know you too well, you'd have got stroppy about—"

"About blasting an enormous hole in the structure of reality. Yes, just a tad."

Pieter looked at him. "But I didn't," he said. "Not really. You know that. I just—"

"We'll come back to that in a minute," Theo said icily.

"It's been well over a minute," Pieter replied. "But I don't need to say it, do I? You know."

"I don't," said Max.

"Shut up, Max," Theo and Pieter said simultaneously. Then they looked at each other. Theo nodded his head slowly. "You know what this means," he said. "You and me—"

"Yes," Pieter said. "Hell of a thing, but someone had to do it."

"We're God." Theo scowled horribly. "And, to be canonically correct, there really ought to be three of us, but I'm damned if I'm going to be part of a Trinity with him."

Pieter shrugged. "Holy Ghost," he said. "Well, he's legally dead. And besides," he went on, "isn't that what all scientists really want to do, deep down? Play God?"

But Theo shook his head. "I don't believe in God," he said. "Not in the ordinary run of things, and especially when he turns out to be me."

"Your choice," Pieter said. "I prefer to see it as a duck scenario."

"A—?"

"If it walks like a duck and quacks like a duck. After all," he said with a grin, "now you can be anywhere you like, any time you like, and to you all things are possible. As far as eternal life goes, there's this Clubhouse thing you mentioned. Seems to me there's only one divine attribute you're lacking, even if it is rather an important one."

"Really? What's that?"

Pieter grinned. "Forgiveness."

Theo thought about it for five seconds. "Nah," he said. "To forgive is divine, and I'm not. Sorry. Ask the Holy Ghost there, he'll forgive anybody anything for a handful of pickled walnuts."

"I don't know why you're both picking on me," Max said. "I haven't done anything."

After he'd stormed out of Pieter's room he walked for a while, just walking, going from rather than going to. Eventually, he found himself on a high bridge over a river. It was just starting to get dark, and the white and yellow lights of the city sparkled in the water. Theo stared at them balefully. No point in jumping, he'd just wind up in the Clubhouse again. He might just possibly have the courage to launch himself off a bridge – been there, after all, done that – but walking through the glowing blue door would be something else entirely. He'd never be able to do that.

"Wonderful," said a voice beside him, "you've finally stopped. What are you doing here?"

He looked round and saw Matasuntha. She looked exactly the same as when he'd seen her last. That was, of course, all wrong.

"You can't be here," he said. "You're fifteen."

"Fourteen and a bit, actually." She dabbed a stray strand of hair out of her face. "Right now, I'm probably at home, in my room, with my headphones on, listening to a Lizard-Headed Women CD. How about you?"

"New York," Theo replied. "Seminar. Or, more likely, in the bar. How did you get here?"

She smiled. "I got bored waiting," she said. "So I thought I'd come and find you."

"Untrue."

Shrug. "All right," she said. "I was waiting for you to come back, and suddenly Max appeared."

"Ah."

"With his mouth full of pickled walnuts."

"I was wondering where they'd got to. And?"

"And he said, Hi, babe, gave me a peck on the cheek, borrowed a thousand dollars and bolted. So then I thought I'd come and find you."

Theo nodded slowly. "How?" he said. "The bottle smashed, remember?"

"I'm not sure." She frowned. "I was down in the wine cellar, looking on the off chance that there'd be a bottle that'd take you to find your own true love—"

"Why? I thought you said you were looking for me."

"When suddenly," she went on, giving him a foul look, "there I was, standing in a draughty corridor in front of a big old oak door. And I could hear voices, and yours was one of them. Also," she added, "Max."

"You eavesdropped."

"Naturally. It helped that I was still holding the wineglass I'd brought in case I found a suitable bottle in the cellar." She looked at him. "I think I understand," she said.

"Good for you. Maybe you can explain it to me some time."

"But if I'm right," she went on, "then surely I don't exist."

Theo sighed. "What we need," he said, "is an all-night café and cake shop opposite the Candelaria in Rio."

She looked at him. "Can we—?"

"Oh yes."

There was just such a café, also selling cakes. The bay was empty, half the city was derelict and the sky glowed an ominous shade of green, but Theo was getting used to that sort of thing. They ordered coffee and sticky buns and sat down at a table in the far corner.

"And that's about it, basically," Theo concluded. "Nobody ever invented YouSpace, as such. I got shot into a universe where it already existed, found out how it worked, more by luck than judgement—"

"Hang on," she interrupted. "The powder compact . . . "

He shook his head. "Garbage," he said. "Smoke screen. The operating system is, there is no operating system. You just think what you want to happen, and it happens. In the reality I got booted into, Pieter neglected to tell me that. Instead, he left me a fake user's manual setting out a totally bogus operating system."

"Oh. Why?"

"So I'd make a point of finding him," Theo said with a grin. "Whereupon, he'd be able to take possession of a fully operational YouSpace; job done. Only," Theo went on, "he didn't know me as well as he thought he did."

She frowned. "I don't—"

"He assumed," Theo went on, "that as soon as I learned that this thing existed, all I'd want to do is get it working and play with it. My desire, conscious and subconscious, would program YouSpace to do just that; meanwhile, the fake OS in the powder compact would take me straight to Pieter."

"Ah. Well, no, actually, I still don't—"

"Instead," Theo went on, "what I really wanted – deep down, where even I couldn't see it – was, first, to know if my poor dead brother Max was still alive somewhere and if so, to find him; second, to find my mother, who abandoned us when we were kids; third, to fall in love and live happily ever after. Playing with some toy was way down the list. So, you see, it all screwed up."

She shook her head. "Your mother."

"Mrs Duchene-Wilamowicz."

"What? You're kidding."

Theo beamed at her. "Actually," he said, "it was her who put me on the right track, figuring it all out. Like, at one point she said she was staying at her daughter's house. When I got there, it proved to be my sister Janine's place."

"So she really is your—"

"She also said, about Pieter, he's really smart, my brother."

Her eyes were round as full moons. "So she's your mother and Pieter's sister? That's so—"

Theo was shaking his head. "Too much of a coincidence? Of course it is," he said, "in this reality. Wildly implausible. Real Darth-Vader-is-Luke's-dad stuff. But, in an infinite multiverse—"

"Ah."

"Somewhere," Theo went on, "there's a reality in which she is my mother; right there in front of my nose for me to find, at a point when finding her is my number two priority. Just what I asked for, in fact. And that," Theo said, "is when I started looking at my hands."

"Your—"

"Yes." He reached out with one of them and took a piece of sticky bun. "Enormous hint, which went right over my head like a GPS satellite. When did my hand vanish? When the VVLHC blew up. What really happened when the VVLHC blew up? I moved from my native universe into a different, highly speculative reality absolutely riddled with temporal paradoxes and causality loops. The invisible hand was Nature's way of telling me that the place I was in was all wrong, but I was too dumb to realise."

Matasuntha nodded slowly. "So Mrs Duchene—"

"Pieter's sister. But not my mother. I went back and checked. After she left my dad, my mother married the senior partner of a firm of actuaries in Canada somewhere. To the best of my knowledge, she's perfectly happy. In my native reality, of course. Here—" He looked out of the window at the green afterglow of the sunset. "God only knows. Actually, no He doesn't. Sorry, private joke."

Matasuntha looked like she was doing mental arithmetic. "So the version of reality you were in after the explosion," she said. "It's what you really wanted."

"Apparently." Theo shrugged. "Only goes to show. In spite of really intense competition for the job, I'm still my own worst enemy."

"The version of reality with me in it."

"Yes."

"Designed to carry out your third priority."

"Yes, but let's not go there."

"In which you fall in love with me, but I'm already in love with Max—"

"You see? Even when fulfilling my wildest fantasies, deep down I'm a realist."

She was trying not to laugh. "So really, you wanted to lose all your money. And your wife."

"I suppose I must've."

"And you wanted a job shovelling guts in a slaughterhouse? That's icky."

"I think that was just part of a package deal." He looked straight at her. "If you want to yell at me, that's fine. I deserve it."

"Probably. Why?"

"Why? I've been—" Pieter's phrase. "Playing God with your life. I dreamed up the reality you've got to live in. You, not the kid with the headphones on. The one you're stuck in."

"You so didn't. I was born there. I've always lived there. You didn't invent it, you just turned up one day. So don't go thinking you had anything to do with it. Who do you think you are, anyway?"

Theo smiled. It wasn't a happy smile, and the joke it proceeded from was pretty dark humour. "Actually," he said.

She was staring at him, and he couldn't help thinking, she's smart, she's getting there without my help. On the other hand, he really needed to tell someone; mostly because, if he'd got it all wrong and there was a glaring mistake in his logic, he desperately wanted to hear about it.

"What does that mean?" she said.

He took a deep breath. "Here goes," he said. "All right. Pieter van Goyen blew up the VVLHC."

"Yes."

"In order to make a hole – more than that, a tunnel. A wormhole. Yes, that's a good word. If ever there was a worm, it's Pieter."

"Yes."

"So far, so appalling. It gets worse." He paused, trying to structure what had to come next. "Have you ever wondered," he said, "about the Big Bang?"

"Well. Not often, I have to say."

"I have. When I was a kid, I used to lie awake at night thinking about it."

"You did? That's—"

"Yes. And what I asked myself was, if in the Beginning there was a big explosion that blew up a lot of stuff, where did the stuff that got blown up come from?"

"A fair question," she said charitably.

"And all I could come up with," Theo went on, "is that the multiverse must be a circle, not a straight line. If the multiverse is curved, not linear, and Time is a loop—"

"There's no beginning."

He shook his head. "That's one way of looking at it, but

not helpful. I preferred to think that any point on a circle can be the beginning. Or the end. Or both."

She shrugged. "I could do with another coffee. How about you?"

"Now," Theo went on. "Consider what conclusions we've arrived at about YouSpace."

"Sure," she said. "after I've ordered another coffee. Where's that waiter?"

"Shifting between realities only works," Theo said, "if you can go back to the source, the terminal, the bus station. The point at which all possibilities are still implicit. In other words, the moment before the Big Bang. That's when all the matter and all the energy is still cooped up in one single blob. A second later, and it's already starting to fly apart. Directions have been chosen, trajectories have been committed to. As soon as the Big Bang goes bang, there's no going back."

She'd forgotten all about coffee. "No," she said. "No way."

Theo shrugged. "If it's a circle, the beginning can be any point. Also the end. And the end of the universe is exactly what some people said would happen if the VVLHC ever blew up."

"Nutcases," she said. "Journalists."

"Maybe they were right. Maybe, when Pieter set off his fireworks, the multiverse ended. And began." He licked his lips, which had become very dry. "I was there. It was a pretty big bang."

"Oh my God."

"We'll come to that," Theo said drily, "in a moment. Let's think about what happened next. All across the multiverse, I came across realities that all had one thing in common. A disaster. I think it was the VVLHC. And what's the only thing every reality in the multiverse has in common? The beginning." He breathed out slowly. "I think that in the beginning were the words, and the words were, Pieter, what the hell do you think you're doing? Followed by an explosion. Followed by—" He shrugged. "Genesis."

Her eyes were as bright as stars. "Making him—"

"Him and me. But not Max. I'm sorry, but you've got to draw the line somewhere." He breathed in again. "And that's why YouSpace works. I imagine Pieter would say something about omelettes and eggs; knowing Pieter, immediately followed by, which came first, the omelette or the egg? To which the only answer has got to be, both." He looked at her. "Have I missed something? Please tell me I've missed something."

She looked him straight in the eye. "And on the seventh day, God made himself scarce, hotly pursued by the product liability lawyers. Sorry, I'm not a scientist. I'm not qualified to comment."

"Please?"

"What do you want me to say? It's not your fault? Earthquakes, wars, mortality, entropy, the perennial paradox of evil in a dualistic moral system? Sorry, I'm not sure I—"

"Please."

She nodded. "It's not your fault. There. Better?"

He smiled feebly. "I guess it'll have to do," he said.

"My pleasure," she said. "Actually, I do feel for you. I remember, when I was a kid, there was an old priest we knew, and I asked him that old chestnut about can God make a rock too heavy for Him to lift."

"Yes? What did he say?"

She grinned. "Yes and no. A good answer, I've always thought. One I've always tried to live by, at any rate." She leaned forward a little. "If you really are God," she whispered, "do you give out lottery numbers?"

"I can do. The wrong ones, naturally."

"Of course." She leaned forward slightly more; he leaned back. "So," she said. "What about Max? And Professor van Goyen?"

Theo signalled to a passing waiter. "I forgave them. Sort of." The waiter had reached the table. "I'd like six empty beer bottles, please."

"Senhor?"

"*Gostaria seis garrafas de cerveja vazias, por favor.*"

"*Vindo direto.*"

She scowled impatiently. "Max."

"What? Ah yes. I forgave them. For some reason, they seemed rather put out about it."

"Really?"

"Yes." Theo shrugged. "Though maybe that was because I told them they couldn't have YouSpace. Or at least, they couldn't have access to the operating system I'd designed to go with it. And there was no point in them trying to figure it out for themselves, because it's fiendishly complicated and riddled with the most diabolical booby traps."

She frowned. "I thought you said there wasn't a—"

"I lied." A thought struck him and he smiled. "Which must mean I'm not, well, Him, mustn't it? Needless to say," he went on, "I'll relent and forgive them properly in due course, after I've taken a few simple precautions so they won't be able to do any harm to anyone. Ah," he added, as the waiter came back with five green bottles and one tall brown one on a tray. "Thank you."

She looked at the bottles. "Let me guess."

"No need." He patted his pockets. "Got a pen?"

She took one from her bag. He reached for the bill and tore it into five equal pieces, on each of which he wrote the words terms & conditions apply. Then he put one slip of paper into each of the five green bottles.

"This one," he said, picking up the brown San Miguel bottle and slipping it into his jacket pocket, "is for me. No terms and conditions. Complete freedom. I reckon I've earned it, don't you?"

She was gazing at the five Michelob bottles. "What about . . . ?"

"One for you." He pushed a bottle across the table at her. She stared at it but didn't touch. "And one for Pieter, one for Max, one for your Uncle Bill, since he did put all that money into Pieter's damnfool project. And one," he concluded cheerfully, "for fun."

"Fun?"

"Yes, fun." He touched a fingertip to the neck of the bottle, which glowed blue and vanished. "Hey," he said, shaking his hand and putting the fingertip in his mouth, "did you see that? That was cool."

Her eyes were still fixed on her bottle. "And the one you've kept for yourself—"

"Well." He made a vague and-why-not gesture. "One empty San Miguel bottle to bring them all and in the darkness bind them. If necessary," he added. "But it won't be, I'm sure. After all, I've given the others to people of unimpeachable integrity, so what could possibly go wrong?"

"What about the sixth bottle?"

"Oh, that." Theo smiled. "A pound to a penny it'll end up at the bottom of the sea. In which case, it'll get eaten by a fish, which in turn will get caught by the seventh son of a seventh son. That's what usually happens, and we're all still here, aren't we?"

She'd shrunk back when the bottle started glowing blue. Now she leaned forward again. "And what about you?"

"Ah. I've been thinking about that."

"And?"

He hardly had to think; it just happened. They were standing on a mountainside, looking down on a lush green valley quilted with maize fields. Above them, a white-capped peak rose into a clear blue sky like a helpfully pointing finger.

"For pity's sake, Theo," she said. "You could've warned me. It's freezing."

"Not to worry." He turned his head and saw what he was looking for. "You're going back home in a moment or so. This way."

He headed up the steep slope until he reached the mouth of a cave. Inside, the embers of a fire were smouldering in the middle of the cave floor. At the back of the cave he could see a neatly folded blanket and a big stack of books. "Perfect," he said.

She stared at him. "What?"

"The life," he said, "of a simple hermit. A chance to catch my intellectual and spiritual breath. Oh, not for ever," he added reassuringly. "I'll probably be ready to come down again in, what, five years? Ten at the most."

"Ten years? In a cave?"

"Absolutely. When you've spent most of your life wallowing about in unearned money like a mud-wrestler, you need something like this just to get clean. Peace," he went on, sitting down on the floor and crossing his legs. "Quiet contemplation. And, of course, no material possessions except the absolutely basic necessities of life."

A solemn procession was winding slowly up the narrow track towards them. At its head, two old men in peasant garb each held one handle of a basket. Behind them, two more villagers and a second basket; behind them, a third. When they reached the cave they put the baskets down, bowed low three times and withdrew, walking backwards. Theo sat perfectly still until they were out of sight. Then he sprang to his feet and started to rummage.

"Ah," he said. "Not bad."

In the first basket there was crevice of tuna and scallops with caviar and fennel, crayfish ravioli with artichokes, sea bass braised in wild asparagus and cucumber, assiete of roast lamb, goats' cheese soufflé, rhubarb and strawberry crumble and a bottle of '77 Margaux. The second basket contained three designer suits, silk underwear and pyjamas and an inflatable water bed. The third basket was crammed with DVDs, games, the latest model X-Box, a laptop and a selection of upmarket lifestyle magazines. "I've always maintained," Theo said happily, "that the hallmark of a civilised society is how they look after the poor."

She helped him unpack and ate most of the ravioli. Then she looked at him. "It's nice of you to give Uncle Bill a bottle," she said.

He shrugged. "Terms and conditions apply."

"What terms and conditions?"

"Ah."

She frowned, then grinned. "Anyway," she said, "it was a nice thought."

"I dragged him into it," Theo replied. "You too. Just out of interest, though."

"Yes?"

"What the hell are you doing here?"

"You brought me here."

"Why would I have done that?"

She gave him a beautiful smile. "I told you," she said. "I realised Max wasn't for me. That made me ask myself where my true feelings lie. So, here I am."

He nodded slowly. "You honestly expect me to believe that."

"Of course. After all, you chose this version of reality. You wanted to find true love. Admittedly, it was only your third priority, which some people might find just a tad insulting. Still, there it is. Your wish is the multiverse's command." She edged a little closer. "What were you thinking of doing about it?"

Theo yawned. Far below in the valley, thin wisps of smoke

were rising from the hearths where the villagers were cooking his dinner. Presumably, if he went beyond the mountains, sooner or later he'd come to the radioactive wastelands left behind by the explosion of the VVLHC, but he couldn't work up the energy to feel guilty about that. And the morning and the evening were the eighth day. "Not sure," he said. "Like I said, I'm going to stay here and think about stuff for a while. Then I'll know."

"Oh, wonderful." She pulled a face. "So you expect me to hang around waiting for you while you do your hermit-on-a-mountaintop gig. That's so—"

"I don't recall asking you to wait for me."

"You implied it. Find true love, you said, and your subconscious press-ganged me. And now I've got to hang around for five years. Not meaning to be nasty or anything, but what part of the concept of free will are you having difficulty with?"

"Free will," Theo said, "is only meaningful in context."

"Huh? What context?"

" . . . 'With every personal injury claim over $995'. For a limited period only. Oh, and terms and conditions apply. They always do."

She sighed. "So you do expect me to go back home and wait patiently for you."

"Yes." He grinned. "YouSpace, remember? I'll be back about three seconds after you. You can wait that long, can't you?"

"I'm not sure. Don't push your luck."

He shrugged. She stuck her tongue out and vanished.

He sat for a while, watching the plumes of smoke and hoping they didn't mean that the simple peasants had overdone the tournedos Rossini. Then he got up, found the third basket and tipped it upside down. As he'd anticipated, there was something left at the very bottom which they'd overlooked earlier. A lump hammer and a cold chisel. And now for a Word from our sponsors.

He took them in his hands, sat down facing the rock and tried to think of something suitable.

extras

orbit

www.orbitbooks.net

about the author

Tom Holt was born in London in 1961. At Oxford he studied bar billiards, ancient Greek agriculture and the care and feeding of small, temperamental Japanese motorcycle engines, interests which led him, perhaps inevitably, to qualify as a solicitor and emigrate to Somerset, where he specialised in death and taxes for seven years before going straight in 1995. Now a full-time writer, he lives in Chard, Somerset, with his wife, one daughter and the unmistakable scent of blood, wafting in on the breeze from the local meat-packing plant.

For even more madness and TOMfoolery go to www.orbitbooks.net

Find out more about Tom Holt and other Orbit authors by registering for the free monthly newsletter at: www.orbitbooks.net

if you enjoyed
DOUGHNUT

look out for

THE ACCIDENTAL SORCERER

by

K. E. Mills

CHAPTER ONE

The entrance to Stuttley's Superior Staff factory, Ottosland's premier staff manufacturer, was guarded by a glass-fronted booth and blocked by a red and blue boom gate. Inside the booth slumped a dyspeptic-looking security guard, dressed in a rumpled green and orange Stuttley's uniform. It didn't suit him. An ash-tipped cigarette drooped from the corner of his mouth and the half-eaten sardine sandwich in his hand leaked tomato sauce onto the floor. He was reading a crumpled, food-stained copy of the previous day's *Ottosland Times*.

After several long moments of not being noticed, Gerald fished out his official identification and pressed it flat to the window, right in front of the guard's face.

"Gerald Dunwoody. Department of Thaumaturgy. I'm here for a snap inspection."

The guard didn't look up. "Izzat right? Nobody tole me."

"Well, no," said Gerald, after another moment. "That's why we call it a 'snap inspection'. On account of it being a surprise."

Reluctantly the guard lifted his rheumy gaze. "Ha ha. Sir."

Gerald smiled around gritted teeth. It's a job, it's a job, and I'm lucky to have it. "I understand Stuttley's production foreman is a Mister Harold Stuttley?"

"That's right," said the guard. His attention drifted back to the paper. "He's the owner's cousin. Mr Horace Stuttley's an old man now, don't hardly see him round here no more. Not since his little bit of trouble."

"Really? I'm sorry to hear it." The guard sniffed, inhaled on his cigarette and expelled the smoke in a disinterested cloud. Gerald resisted the urge to bang his head on the glass between them. "So where would I find Foreman Stuttley?"

"Search me," said the guard, shrugging. "On the factory floor, most like. They're doing a run of First Grade staffs today, if memory serves."

Gerald frowned. First Grade staffs were notoriously difficult to forge. Get the etheretic balances wrong in the split-second of alchemical transformation and what you were looking at afterwards, basically, was a huge smoking hole in the ground. And if this guard was any indication, standards at Stuttley's had slipped of late. He rapped his knuckles on the glass.

"I wish to see Harold Stuttley right now, please," he said, briskly official. "According to Department records this operation hasn't returned its signed and witnessed safety statements for two months. I'm afraid that's a clear breach of regulations. There'll be no First Grade staffs rolling off the production line today or any other day unless I'm fully satisfied that all proper precautions and procedures have been observed."

Sighing, the guard put down his soggy sandwich, stubbed out his cigarette, wiped his hands on his trousers and stood. "All right, sir. If you say so."

There was a battered black telephone on the wall of the security booth. The guard dialled a four-digit number, receiver pressed to his ear, and waited. Waited some more. Dragged his sleeve across his moist nose, still waiting, then hung up with an exclamation of disgust. "No answer. Nobody there to hear it, or the bloody thing's on the blink again. Take your pick."

"I'd rather see Harold Stuttley."

The guard heaved another lugubrious sigh. "Right you are, then. Follow me."

Gerald followed, starting to feel a little dyspeptic himself. Honestly, these people! What kind of a business were they running? Security phones that didn't work, essential paperwork that wasn't completed. Didn't they realise they were playing with fire? Even the plainest Third Grade staff was capable of inflicting damage if it wasn't handled carefully in the production phase. Complacency, that was the trouble. Clearly Harold Stuttley had let the prestige and success of his family's world-famous business go to his head. Just because every wizard who was any wizard and could afford the exorbitant price tag wouldn't be caught dead without his Stuttley Staff (patented, copyrighted and limited edition) as part of his sartorial ensemble was no excuse to let safety standards slide.

Bloody hell, he thought, mildly appalled. Somebody save me. I'm thinking like a civil servant . . .

The unenthusiastic security guard was leading him down a tree-lined driveway towards a distant high brick wall with a red door in it. The door's paint was cracked and peeling. Above and behind the wall could be seen the slate-grey factory roof, with its chimney stacks belching pale puce smoke. A flock of pigeons wheeling through the blue sky plunged into the coloured effluvium and abruptly turned bright green.

Damn. Obviously Stuttley's thaumaturgical filtering system was on the blink: code violation number two. The unharmed birds flapped away, fading back to white even as he watched, but that wasn't the point. All thaumaturgical by-products were subject to strict legislation. Temporary colour changes were one thing. But what if the next violation resulted in a temporal dislocation? Or a quantifiable matter redistribution? Or worse? There'd be hell to pay. People might get hurt. What was Stuttley's playing at?

Even as he wondered, he felt a shiver like the touch of a thousand spider feet skitter across his skin. The mellow morning was suddenly charged with menace, strobed with shadows.

"Did you feel that?" he asked the guard.

"They don't pay me to feel things, sir," the guard replied over his shoulder.

A sense of unease, like a tiny butterfly, fluttered in the pit of Gerald's stomach. He glanced up, but the sky was still blue and the sun was still shining and birds continued to warble in the trees.

"No. Of course they don't," he replied, and shook his head. It was nothing. Just his stupid over-active imagination getting out of hand again. If he could he'd have it surgically removed. It certainly hadn't done him any favours to date.

He glanced in passing at the nearest tree with its burden of trilling birds, but he couldn't see Reg amongst them. Of course he wouldn't, not if she didn't want to be seen. After yesterday morning's lively discussion about his apparent lack of ambition she'd taken herself off in a huff of ruffled feathers and a cloud of curses and he hadn't laid eyes on her since.

Not that he was worried. This wasn't the first hissy fit she'd thrown and it wouldn't be the last. She'd come back when it suited her. She always did. She just liked to make him squirm.

Well, he wasn't going to. Not this time. No, nor apologise either. For once in her ensorcelled life she was going to admit to being wrong, and that was that. He wasn't unambitious. He just knew his limitations.

Three paces ahead of him the guard stopped at the red door, unhooked a large brass key ring from his belt and fished through its assortment of keys. Finding the one he wanted he stuck it into the lock, jiggled, swore, kicked the door twice, and turned the handle.

"There you are, sir," he said, pushing the door wide then standing back. "I'll let you find your own way round if it's all the same to you. Can't leave my booth unattended for too long. Somebody important might turn up." He smiled, revealing tobacco-yellow teeth.

Gerald looked at him. "Indeed. I'll be sure to mention your enthusiasm in my official report."

The guard did a double take at that, his smile vanishing. With a surly grunt he hooked his bundle of keys back on his belt then folded his arms, radiating offended impatience.

Immediately, Gerald felt guilty. Oh lord. Now I'm acting like a civil servant!

Not that there was anything wrong, as such, with public employment. Many fine people were civil servants. Indeed, without them the world would be in a sorry state, he was sure. In fact, the civil service was an honourable institution and he was lucky to be part of it. Only ... it had never been his ambition to be a wizard who inspected the work of other wizards for Departmental regulation violations. His ambition was to be an inspectee, not an inspector. Once upon a time he'd thought that dream was reachable.

Now he was a probationary compliance officer in the Minor Infringement Bureau of the Department of Thaumaturgy ... and dreams were things you had at night after you turned out the lights.

He nodded at the waiting guard. "Thank you."

"Certainly, sir," the guard said sourly.

Well, his day was certainly getting off to a fine start. And we wonder why people don't like bureaucrats ...

With an apologetic smile at the guard he hefted his official briefcase, straightened his official tie, rearranged his expression into one of official rectitude and walked through the open doorway.

And only flinched a little bit as the guard locked the red door behind him.

It's a wizarding job, Gerald, and it's better than the alternative.

Hopefully, if he reminded himself often enough, he'd start to believe that soon.

The factory lay dead ahead, down the end of a short paved pathway. It was a tall, red brick building blinded by a lack of windows. Along its front wall were plastered a plethora of signs: *Danger! Thaumaturgical Emissions! Keep Out! No Admittance Without Permission! All Visitors Report To Security Before Proceeding!*

As he stood there, reading, one of the building's four doors opened and a young woman wearing a singed lab coat and an expression of mild alarm came out.

He approached her, waving. "Excuse me! Excuse me! Can I have a word?"

The young woman saw him, took in his briefcase and the

crossed staffs on his tie and moaned. "Oh, no. You're from the Department, aren't you?"

He tried to reassure her with a smile. "Yes, as a matter of fact. Gerald Dunwoody. And you are?"

Looking hunted, she shrank into herself. "Holly," she muttered. "Holly Devree."

He'd been with the Department for a shade under six months and in all that time had been allowed into the field only four times, but he'd worked out by the end of his first site inspection that when it came to the poor sods just following company orders, sympathy earned him far more co-operation than threats. He sagged at the knees, let his shoulders droop and slid his voice into a more intimate, confiding tone.

"Well, Miss Devree – Holly – I can see you're feeling nervous. Please don't. All I need is for you to point me in the direction of your boss, Mr Harold Stuttley."

She cast a dark glance over her shoulder at the factory. "He's in there. And before you see him I want it understood that it's not my fault. It's not Eric's fault, either. Or Bob's. Or Lucius's. It's not any of our faults. We worked hard to get our transmogrifer's licence, okay? And it's not like we're earning squillions, either. The pay's rotten, if you must know. But Stuttley's – they're the best, aren't they?" Without warning, her thin, pale face crumpled. "At least, they used to be the best. When old Mr Horace was in charge. But now . . ."

Fat tears trembled on the ends of her sandy-coloured eyelashes. Gerald fished a handkerchief out of his pocket and handed it over. "Yes? Now?"

Blotting her eyes she said, "Everything's different, isn't it? Mr Harold's gone and implemented all these 'cost-cutting' initiatives. Laid off half the Transmogrify team. But the workload hasn't halved, has it? Oh, no. And it's not just us he's laid off, either. He's sacked people in Etheretics, Design, Purchasing, Research and Development – there's not one team hasn't lost folk. Except Sales." Her snubby nose wrinkled in distaste. "Seven new sales reps he's taken on, and they're promising the world, and we're expected to deliver it – except we can't! We're working round the clock and we're still three weeks behind on orders and now Mr Harold's threatening to dock us if we don't catch up!"

"Oh my," he said, and patted her awkwardly on the shoulder. "I'm very sorry to hear this. But at least it explains why the last eight safety reports weren't completed."

"But they were," she whispered, busily strangling her borrowed handkerchief. "Lucius is the most senior technician we've got left, and I know he's been doing them. And handing them over to Mr Harold. I've seen it. But what *he's* doing with them I don't know."

Filing them in the nearest waste paper bin, more than likely. "I don't suppose your friend Lucius discussed the reports with you? Or showed them to you?"

Holly Devree's confiding manner shifted suddenly to a cagey caution. The handkerchief disappeared into her lab coat pocket. "Safety reports are confidential."

"Of course, of course," Gerald soothed. "I'm not implying any inappropriate behaviour. But Lucius didn't happen to leave one lying out on a table, did he, where any innocent passer-by might catch a glimpse?"

"I'm sorry," she said, edging away. "I'm on my tea break. We only get ten minutes. Mr Harold's inside if you want to see him. Please don't tell him we talked."

He watched her scuttle like a spooked rabbit, and sighed. Clearly there was more amiss at Stuttley's than a bit of overlooked paperwork. He should get back to the office and tell Mr Scunthorpe. As a probationary compliance officer his duties lay within very strict guidelines. There were other, more senior inspectors for this kind of trouble.

On the other hand, his supervisor was allergic to incomplete reports. Unconfirmed tales out of school from disgruntled employees and nebulous sensations of misgiving from probationary compliance officers bore no resemblance to cold, hard facts. And Mr Scunthorpe was as married to cold, hard facts as he was to Mrs Scunthorpe. More, if Mr Scunthorpe's marital mutterings were anything to go by.

Turning, Gerald stared at the blank-faced factory. He could still feel his inexplicable unease simmering away beneath the surface of his mind. Whatever it was trying to tell him, the news wasn't good. But that wasn't enough. He had to find out exactly what had tickled his instincts. And he did have a legitimate place to start, after all: the noncompletion of mandatory safety statements. The infraction was enough to get his foot across the factory threshold. After that, well, it was just a case of following his intuition.

He resolutely ignored the whisper in the back of his mind that said, *Remember what happened the last time you followed your intuition?*

"Oh, bugger off!" he told it, and marched into the fray.

Another pallid employee answered his brisk banging on the nearest door. "Good afternoon," he said, flashing his identification and not giving the lab-coated man a chance to speak. "Gerald Dunwoody, Department of Thaumaturgy, here to see Mr Harold Stuttley on a matter of noncompliance. I'm told he's inside? Excellent. Don't let me keep you from your duties. I'll find my own way around."

The employee gave ground, helpless in the ruthlessly cheerful face of officialdom, and Gerald sailed in. Immediately his nose was clogged with the stink of partially discharged thaumaturgic energy. The air beneath the high factory ceiling was alive with it, crawling and spitting and sparking. The carefully caged lights hummed and buzzed, crackling as firefly filaments of power drifted against their heated bulbs to ignite in a brief, sunlike flare.

A dozen more lab-coated technicians scurried up and down the factory floor, focused on the task at hand. Directly opposite, running the full length of the wall, stood a five-deep row of benches, each one equipped with specially crafted staff cradles. Twenty-five per bench times five benches meant that, if the security guard was right, Stuttley's had one hundred and twenty-five new First Grade staffs ready for completion. The technicians, looking tense and preoccupied, fiddled and twiddled and realigned each uncharged staff in its cradle, assessing every minute adjustment with a hand-held thaumic register. All the muted ticking made the room sound like the demonstration area of a clockmakers' convention. At either end of the benches towered the etheretic conductors, vast reservoirs of unprocessed thaumaturgic energy. Insulated cables connected them to each other and all the staff cradles, whose conductive surfaces waited patiently for the discharge of raw power that would transform one hundred and twenty-five gold-filigreed five-foot-long spindles of oak into the world's finest, most prestigious, expensive and potentially most dangerous First Grade staffs.

Despite his misgivings he heard himself whimper, just a little. Stuttley First Graders were works of art. Each wrapping of solid gold filigree was unique, its design template destroyed upon completion and never repeated. The rare wizards who could afford the extra astronomical cost had their filigrees designed specifically for them, taking into account personal strengths, family history and specific thaumaturgic signatures. Those staffs came with inbuilt security: it was immediate and spectacularly gruesome death for any wizard other than the rightful owner to attempt the use of them.

Once, a long long time ago, he'd dreamed of owning a First Grade staff. Even though he didn't come from a wizarding family. Even though he'd got his qualifications through a correspondence course. Wizardry cared nothing for family background or the name of the college where you were educated. Wizarding was of the blood and bone, indifferent to pedigrees and bank balances. Some of the world's finest wizards had come from humble origins.

Although . . . not lately. Lately, Ottosland's most powerful and influential wizards came from recognisable families whose names more often than not could also be heard whispered in the nation's corridors of power.

Still. *Technically*, anybody with sufficient aptitude and training could become a First Grade wizard. Social standing might influence your accent but it had nothing to do with raw power. *Technically*, even a tailor's son from Nether Wallop could earn the right to wield a First Grade staff.

Unbidden, his fingers touched his copper-ringed cherrywood Third Grade staff, tucked into its pocket on the inside of his overcoat. It was nothing to be ashamed of. He was the first wizard in the family for umpteen generations, after all. Plenty of people failed even to be awarded a Third Grade licence. For every ten hopefuls identified as potential wizards, only one or two actually survived the rigours of trial and training to receive their precious staff.

And even for Third Grades there was work to be had. Wasn't he living proof? Gerald Dunwoody, after a couple of totally understandable false starts, soon to be a fully qualified compliance officer with the internationally renowned Ottosland Department of Thaumaturgy? Yes, indeed. The sky was the limit. Provided there was a heavy cloud cover. And he was indoors. In a cellar, possibly.

Oh lord, he thought miserably, staring at all those magnificent First Grade staffs. It felt as though his official Departmental tie had tightened to throttling point. *There has to be more to wizarding than this.*

An irate shout rescued him from utter despair. "Oy! You!

Who are you and what are you doing in my factory?"

He turned. Marching belligerently towards him, scattering lab coats like so many white mice, was a small persnickety man of sleek middle years, clutching a clipboard and looking so offended even his tea-stained moustache was bristling.

"Ah. Good afternoon," he said, producing his official smile. "Mr Harold Stuttley, I presume?"

The angry little man halted abruptly in front of him, clipboard pressed to his chest like a shield. "And if I am? What of it? Who wants to know?"

Gerald put down his briefcase and took out his identification. Stuttley snatched it from his fingers, glared as though at a mortal insult, then shoved it back. "What's all this bollocks? And who let you in here? We're about to do a run of First Grades. Unauthorised personnel aren't allowed in here when we're running First Grades! How do I know you're not here for a spot of industrial espionage?"

"Because I'm employed by the DoT," he said, pocketing his badge. "And I'm afraid you won't be running anything, Mr Stuttley, until I'm satisfied it's safe to do so. You've not submitted your safety statements for some time now, sir. I'm afraid the Department takes a dim view of that. Now I realise it's probably just an oversight on your part, but even so . . ." He shrugged. "Rules are rules."

Harold Stuttley's pebble-bright eyes bulged. "Want to know what you can do with your rules? You march in here uninvited and then have the hide to tell me when I can and can't conduct my own business? I'll have your job for this!"

Gerald considered him. *Too much bluster. What's he trying to hide?* He let his gaze slide sideways, away from Harold Stuttley's unattractively temper-mottled face. The thaumic emission gauge on the nearest etheretic conductor was stuttering, jittery as an icicle in an earthquake. Flick, flick, flick went the needle, each jump edging closer and closer to the bright red zone marked Danger. In his nostrils, the clogging stink of overheated thaumic energy was suddenly stifling.

"Mr Stuttley," he said, "I think you should shut down production right now. There's something wrong here, I can feel it."

Harold Stuttley's eyes nearly popped right out of his head. "Shut down? Are you raving? You're looking at over a million quids' worth of merchandise! All those staffs are bought and paid for, you meddling twit! I'm not about to disappoint my customers for some wet-behind-the-ears stooge from the DoT! Your superiors wouldn't know a safe bit of equipment if it bit them on the arse – and neither would you! Stuttley's has been in business two hundred and forty years, you cretin! We've been making staffs since before your great-grandad was a randy thought in his pa's trousers!"

Gerald winced. By now the air inside the factory was so charged with energy it felt like sandpaper abrading his skin. "Look. I realise it's inconvenient but—"

Harold Stuttley's pointing finger stabbed him in the chest. "It's not happening, son, *that's* what it is. *Inconvenient* is the lawsuit I'll bring against you, your bosses and the whole bleeding Department of Thaumaturgy, you mark my words, if you don't leg it out of here on the double! Interfering with the lawful conduct of business? This is political, this is. Too many wizards buying Stuttley's instead of the cheap muck your precious Department churns out! Well I won't have it, you hear me? Now hop it! Off my premises! Or I'll give you a personal demonstration why Stuttley's staffs are the best in the world!"

Gerald stared. Was the man mad? He couldn't throw out an official Department inspector. He'd have his manufacturing licence revoked. Be brought up on charges. Get sent to prison and be forced to pay a hefty fine.

Little rivers of sweat were pouring down Harold Stuttley's

scarlet face and his hands were trembling with rage. Gerald looked more closely. No. Not rage. Terror. Harold Stuttley was beside himself with fear.

He turned and looked at the nearest etheretic conductor. It was sweating too, beads of dark blue moisture forming on its surface, dripping slowly down its sides. Even as he watched, one fat indigo drop of condensed thaumic energy plopped to the factory floor. There was a crack of light and sound. Two preoccupied technicians somersaulted through the air like circus performers, crashed into the wall opposite and collapsed in groaning heaps.

"*Stuttley!*" He grabbed Harold by his lapels and shook him. "Do you see that? Your etheretic containment field is leaking! You have to evacuate! Now!"

The rest of the lab coats were congregated about their fallen comrades, fussing and whispering and casting loathing looks in their employer's direction. The acrobatic technicians were both conscious, apparently unbroken, but seemed dazed. Harold Stuttley jumped backwards, tearing himself free of officialdom's grasp.

"Evacuate? Never! We've got a deadline to meet!" He rounded on his employees. "You lot! Back to work! Leave those malingerers where they are, they're all right, they're just winded! Be on their feet in no time – if they know what's good for them. Come on! You want to get paid this week or don't you?"

Aghast, Gerald stared at him. The man was mad. Even a mere Third Grade wizard like himself knew the dangers of improperly contained thaumic emissions. The entire first year of his correspondence course had dealt with the occupational hazards of wizarding. Some of the illustrations in his handbook had put him off minced meat for *weeks*.

He stepped closer to the factory foreman and lowered his voice. "Mr Stuttley, you're making a very big mistake. Falling behind in your safety statements is one thing. It's a minor infringement. Not worth so much as half a paragraph in *WizardWeekly*'s gossip column. But if you try to run this equipment when clearly it's not correctly calibrated, you could cause a scandal that will spread halfway round the world. You could ruin Stuttley's reputation for years. Maybe forever. Not to mention risk the lives of all your workers. Is that what you want?"

Harold Stuttley swiped his face with his sleeve. "What I want," he said hoarsely, "is for you to get out of here and let me do my job. There's nothing wrong with our equipment, I tell you, it—"

"Quick, everyone! Run for your lives! The conductors are about to invert!"

As the technician who'd shouted the warning led the stampede for the nearest door, Gerald spun on his heel and stared at the sweating etheretic conductors. The needles of each thaumic emission gauge were buried deep in the danger zone and the scattered drops of energy had coalesced into foaming indigo streams. They struck the factory floor like lances of fire, blowing holes, scattering splinters. The insulating cables linking the conductors to each other and the benches glowed virulent blue, shimmerings of power wafting off them like heat haze on a dangerous horizon.

Balanced in their cradles, the First Grade staffs began to dance.

"We have to turn off the conductors!" said Gerald. "Before all the staffs are charged at once or the conductors blow – or both! Where are the damper switches, Stuttley?"

But Harold Stuttley was halfway out of the door, his clipboard abandoned on the floor behind him.

Wonderful.

Now the etheretic conductors were humming, a rising song of warning. The air beneath the factory ceiling stirred. Thickened, like curdling cream, and took on a faintly blue cast. He felt every exposed hair on his body stand on end. His throat closed on a gasp as the etheretically burdened atmosphere turned almost unbreathable. Something warm was trickling from his nostrils.

He should run. Now. Without pausing to pick up his briefcase. Those conductors were going to invert any second now, and when they did—

"Bloody *hell*!" he shouted, and leapt for the nearest cable.

It wouldn't disengage. None of the cables would disengage. He ran up and down the benches, tugging and swearing, but the leaking power had fused the cables to the cradles and each other.

He'd have to get the staffs clear before they all got charged.

Stumbling, sweating, parched with terror, he started hauling the gold-filigreed oak spindles out of their cradles. Tossed them behind him like so much inferior firewood, even as the air continued to coalesce and the etheretic conductors juddered and sweated and discharged bolts of indiscriminate power.

In his pocket his modest little cherrywood staff began to glow. It got so hot he had to stop flinging the First Grade staffs around and drag off his coat, because it felt like his leg was burning. Moments after he threw the coat to the floor the wool burst into flames and disintegrated into charred flakes, revealing his smoking staff with its copper bands glowing bright as a furnace.

The First Grade staffs he'd released from confinement leapt about the floor like popcorn on a hotplate. Those still in their cradles began to buzz. On a sobbing breath he continued tearing them free of the benches.

Ten – twenty – thirty: oh lord, he'd never finish in time—

And then the staffs were simply too hot for flesh to touch. As he fell back, scorched and panting, the power's song became a scream. Both thaumic emission gauges exploded, the top of the conductors peeled open like soup cans . . . and a torrent of unprocessed, uncontrolled etheretic energy poured out of the reservoirs and into the remaining First Grade staffs.

The thaumic boom blasted him against the nearest wall so hard he thought for a moment he was dead, but seconds later his blackened vision cleared.

He wished it hadn't.

Terrible arcing lines of indigo power surged around and through the staffs he'd failed to pull free of their conductive cradles. The emptied conductors, ripped apart from the inside out, lay fallen on their sides. Two ragged gaping holes in the ceiling directly overhead spilled sunlight onto the dreadful aftermath of undisciplined thaumic energies. Through them spiralled two thin columns of unfiltered emissions: the leftover power not captured by the staffs escaping into the wider world beyond the factory.

Groaning, Gerald staggered to his feet. If he didn't shut down that self-perpetuating loop of energy pouring through the First Grade staffs it would continue to build and build until it exploded . . . most likely taking half the suburb of Stuttley with it. It wasn't a job for a lowly probationary compliance officer, or a Third Grade wizard who'd received his qualifications from a barely recognised correspondence course. He doubted it was even a job for a First Grade wizard . . . at least, not one working solo. A whole squadron might manage it, at a pinch. But that was wishful thinking. There wasn't time to contact Mr Scunthorpe and get him to send out a flying squad of Departmental troubleshooters. There was just him. Gerald Dunwoody, wizard Third Grade. Twenty-three years old and scared to death. *So long, life. I hardly lived you . . .*

Looming large before him, the howling, writhing mass of thaumaturgically linked First Grade staffs, bathed in unholy indigo fire. Abandoned on the floor at his feet, his pathetic little cherrywood staff, as useful now as a piece of straw.

And scattered around him, four of the First Grade staffs he'd managed to rescue before the massive conductor inversion. Rolling idly to and fro they glowed a gentle gold, their filigree activated. They must have been caught in the nimbus of exploding thaumic energy.

Everybody knew that Third Grade wizards didn't have the etheretic chops to handle a First Grade staff. Even using a Second Grader was to risk life, limb and sanity. Attempting to use one of those erratically charged First Graders was proof positive that sanity had left the building.

But he had no choice. This was an emergency and he was the only Department official in sight. Instincts shrieking, fear a gibbering demon on his back, he reached for the nearest activated First Grade staff. If it was one of the special orders, keyed to a specific wizard, then he really was about to breathe his last—

A shock of power slammed through his body. The world pulsed violet, then crimson, then bright and blinding blue, spinning wildly on its axis. Something deep inside his mind torqued. Twisted. Tore. His vision cleared, the mad giddiness stopped, and he was himself again. More or less. *Something* was different, but there was no time to worry or work out what.

Bucking and flailing like a live thing, the staff struggled to join its brethren in the heart of the magical maelstrom. Gerald got his other hand onto it, battling to contain the energy. It felt like standing inside the world's largest waterfall. The staff was channelling the excess energies from the atmosphere, attracting them like a magnet. Pummelled, battered, he wrestled with the flux and flow of power. Poured everything he had into taming the beast in his fists.

But the beast didn't want to be tamed.

Gasping, fighting against being pulled into the maelstrom, he opened his slitted eyes. The etheretic conductors were empty now, their spiralling columns of power collapsed. But the trapped staffs within the indigo firestorm continued to blaze, amplifying and distorting the energies they'd consumed. Only minutes remained, surely, before they exploded.

And he had no idea how to stop them.